PENGUIN BOOKS

Separate Beds

PRAISE FOR ELIZABETH BUCHAN

'Deliciously told, with characters you warm to at once,
and I loved every page' *Daily Mail*

'A thoughtful, clever examination of a marriage – and a life –
at the crossroads' *Sunday Mirror*

'Wise and sharp in equal proportion, and absolutely compelling reading'
Penny Vincenzi

'For women of all ages, a poignant, unforgettable novel' *You magazine*

'A finely written, highly intelligent romance' *Mail on Sunday*

'Buchan deftly juggles multiple characters and plots in a perceptive
analysis of contemporary life' *Independent on Sunday*

'Enthralling, sophisticated storytelling' *Woman & Home*

'Shafts of wit and wisdom that lift the novel above the commonplace'
Sunday Times

'An excellent story . . . strong imaginative power . . . wonderful
atmosphere' Joanna Trollope

'A wry, poignant look at love and grief' *Easy Living*

D1422204

Also by Elizabeth Buchan

Separate Beds

ELIZABETH BUCHAN

PENGUIN BOOKS

PENGUIN BOOKS

Published by the Penguin Group
Penguin Books Ltd, 80 Strand, London WC2R ORL, England
Penguin Group (USA) Inc., 375 Hudson Street, New York, New York 10014, USA
Penguin Group (Canada), 90 Eglinton Avenue East, Suite 700, Toronto, Ontario, Canada M4P 2Y3
(a division of Pearson Penguin Canada Inc.)
Penguin Ireland, 25 St Stephen's Green, Dublin 2, Ireland (a division of Penguin Books Ltd)
Penguin Group (Australia), 250 Camberwell Road, Camberwell, Victoria 3124, Australia
(a division of Pearson Australia Group Pty Ltd)
Penguin Books India Pvt Ltd, 11 Community Centre, Panchsheel Park, New Delhi – 110 017, India
Penguin Group (NZ), 67 Apollo Drive, Rosedale, North Shore 0632, New Zealand
(a division of Pearson New Zealand Ltd)
Penguin Books (South Africa) (Pty) Ltd, 24 Sturdee Avenue, Rosebank, Johannesburg 2196, South Africa

Penguin Books Ltd, Registered Offices: 80 Strand, London WC2R ORL, England

www.penguin.com

First published 2010

001

Copyright © Elizabeth Buchan, 2010

All rights reserved

The moral right of the author has been asserted

Set in Garamond MT Std 12.5/14.75pt by Palimpsest Book Production Limited,
Grangemouth, Stirlingshire
Printed in England by Clays Ltd, St Ives plc

ISBN: 978-1-405-91042-2

www.greenpenguin.co.uk

MIX
Paper from
responsible sources
FSC
www.fsc.org
FSC™ C018179

Penguin Books is committed to a sustainable
future for our business, our readers and our planet.
This book is made from Forest Stewardship
Council™ certified paper.

ALWAYS LEARNING   **PEARSON**

'This bed thy centre is, these walls, thy sphere'
John Donne

For Annabel

Chapter One

Zosia said to Annie, 'I'm glad you got home before I left.'

Annie dumped a whole lot of Christmas shopping on the table and ran her fingers through her hair. Bad-hair day. Very bad-hair day. 'So am I. Are you in a hurry? Would you like a glass of wine?'

There were just the two of them in the kitchen and the house was quiet and dark. Zosia always turned the lights off as she worked through the rooms. When Annie commented on this thrift, she had replied, 'We must not waste,' for the deprivations of Zosia's upbringing were lodged deep in her.

Annie retrieved a half-drunk bottle of excellent claret left over from the previous evening and gave her a glass.

Zosia took a mouthful and leaned back in the chair. 'Very nice, Annie.'

'Here, look . . .' Annie burrowed in a bag and shook out an expensive man's sweater. 'That's for Tom. Unimaginative, I know, but I haven't a clue what he wants these days. And here . . .' She produced a leather notebook. 'That's for Emily. I've still got to get Jake and Jocasta's. But look at these . . .' She waved a box of Christmas lights, plugged them in and, razzle-dazzle, hoop-la, a river of brilliance looped over the table.

'Beautiful, Annie.' Zosia closed her eyes. 'You always make everything so.'

Warm, sparkling clean, filled with things that made life easy and convenient . . . the house that had everything.

Not really, thought Annie, and the old feelings tore at her chest. This place will never be beautiful while we are as we are.

Remember . . .

The front door opened and closed. 'Mia . . .' She uttered the name she had called so many times since her daughter had left. Her voice quivered with pain and anticipation. 'Mia, is that you?'

'It's only me.' It was Tom and he refused to meet Annie's eye.

Mia had been gone for a couple of weeks and a silence had fallen over the family. Tom had promised to go up to Manchester to try to make contact at the university to which Mia had almost certainly returned as she had every intention of finishing her degree. But, by the look of him, he hadn't done any such thing. 'Sorry,' he confessed. 'Something came up at work.'

He was lying. What Tom should have said was: I didn't want to go and look for Mia because I feel so awful/ashamed/angry . . . you could take your pick as to the explanation. Actually, if Annie knew anything about her husband all of them applied.

'So, work came before your daughter.' Annie plucked at a lock of her hair and the anguish turned to aggression. 'As always, Tom.'

'Don't start.' He shrugged.

At that moment, Annie hated him more than she had ever hated anyone. It was a new emotion and its intensity

2

was akin to love. She also hated herself because this would never have happened if she and Tom had been cleverer and clearer about their marriage. 'If you won't go, I'll go.'

'She won't see you, Annie.'

'How do you know?'

He looked at her oddly. 'You accuse me of not knowing my children. But I do know Mia. She won't see you . . .'

Tom had been right. That had been then and Mia still had not come home, or phoned. She had written just once.

She had been gone for almost five years.

Come home. Please . . .

Annie draped the lights artistically over her handbag and smiled at Zosia. 'I'm not telling you what I've got for you.'

Zosia pointed to the diamond ring on Annie's finger. 'Do you want me to clean it before I go?'

Her mother's ring (and her grandmother's before that): hugely valuable but, more than that, part of Annie and irreplaceable. Zosia enjoyed handling it and she loved to please Annie, who slid it off her finger. 'Go on, then.'

Zosia buffed away and Annie watched her affectionately. 'Did I ever tell you Emily stole it? She must have been six or seven. There was such a fuss and everyone was pulling out drawers and upending the rubbish. I was so angry when she owned up. Poor little girl was shaking. But Tom talked to her. Tom was – is – always so good with her, and Emily confessed between sobs she thought I was going to give the ring to Mia.'

Zosia slid it back across the table. 'But it's true you can only give it to one of them.'

Annie said, 'We couldn't help laughing at Emily, which

3

was unfair on her and made her cross. At the time it was funny.' She stopped herself and Zosia laid a hand on hers. After a moment, Annie asked, 'So, have you booked the ticket?'

'Yes. I will be gone for Christmas and New Year, as you said I could.'

'Good.'

Zosia raised her eyes to Annie. 'You are very kind to pay for the ticket. I am grateful.'

The two women smiled at each other. They went way back – to the day Zosia had turned up on the doorstep in answer to Annie's advert for a cleaner and someone to help with the school runs – and were friends. It was a friendship springing out of a mutual empathy and a willingness to listen. 'Careful,' Tom had warned. 'You're Zosia's employer.'

'It's nothing,' said Annie, as the phone rang. 'I want you to know how much I owe you. We owe you. For one thing . . .' Annie sounded a touch wry '. . . I love talking to you.' She picked up the phone. 'Tom?' She listened. 'Oh, OK. Fine. See you.' She replaced the receiver.

She poured more wine for Zosia. 'That was Tom. Not coming home till late. Last-minute dinner with someone from the Foreign Office.' After a minute, she added, 'It's been ages since Tom and I had supper together.' A moment of further reflection 'It happens in the run-up to Christmas. That's the World Service for you . . . all the media, I imagine.'

'Of course,' said Zosia.

They exchanged a look.

Annie knew what Zosia would have liked to say: 'Tom spends more time than he should on his work and has done for years.' And it was true that, since Mia had stormed out, things had been bad, really bad. But not bad enough for them to fold entirely.

At seven o'clock, Zosia leaped to her feet and declared she must go. Annie knew she liked to be home in time to phone her mother in Warsaw. At the door, Annie kissed her cheek fondly and said, 'See you next week.'

The door clicked shut and the house was still. If only, Annie thought. If only . . . *if only* . . . So many things. If Tom hadn't taken Mia's room, I could sit in there for a bit and think about her. But Tom now occupied the room — usurper by default.

She wandered back into the kitchen, drank the rest of her wine and observed the Christmas lights still draped in a starry Milky Way over her handbag. After a while, she reached for the pile of post Zosia had placed on the table and slit open the top envelope.

A plain card stamped with the House of Commons insignia was from Sadie who had written 'love from Us' and underlined 'love'. A further note on the left-hand side of the card revealed penitence: 'Sorry about this.' And 'PS Yup, Christmas *is* designed to torture women. PPS Give Tom a kiss from me.'

'Wretch,' murmured Annie. How often did she and Sadie speak? Practically every day. Had they sworn not to send each other Christmas cards? Yes. But the (sweetly duplicitous) joke was that Annie had already posted hers to Sadie. 'Sorry about this,' she had written on the left-hand side of the card – and inserted a handwritten piece of paper: 'Dearest Sadie. You make me laugh so much. Try not to kill Andrew over the holiday.'

Each knew exactly what the other was driving at. It had been obvious from the moment they'd met a decade since when Sadie had turned up with Andrew on an MP's fact-finding hospital visit to St Brigid's. Having negotiated the arid patch between her second and third marriages, during which she had fled to England from the US, Sadie brimmed with thankfulness and relief. Annie was more or less coasting through her marriage and worried that her responses to life had become muted. Yet, they recognized each other as cut from the same cloth. True, if she and Tom had still been talking, really talking, really in tune with each other, and Sadie had been as settled as she was now, the quality and energy of their friendship might have been less intense. For a start, there would have been less necessity for the deep trawl of each other's thoughts and minds.

Annie worked through the rest of the cards, placing to one side those that could be pinned to a ribbon and hung in the sitting room and, on a separate pile, those that required a response.

'Give Tom a kiss from me.'

Annie frowned. She recollected a fleeting and careful meeting of their mouths on Tom's last birthday. Well meant. Dutiful even, but nothing more. ('I am drunk on you,' he had once said, after kissing her.) But since then?

She opened the final card, which was large and expensive-looking, and the angel from Leonardo da Vinci's *The Virgin of the Rocks* winged into the kitchen. Characteristically shadowed in the artist's unmistakable manner, typically mysterious, heavy-lidded, yearning, he was both messenger and guardian, carrying secrets he would never tell.

Something about him – a sadness, a darkness, loss –

spoke to Annie as she sat on in the empty house in which there was no Tom, no Jake or Emily. No Mia.

No one.

Traditionally, May weddings are unlucky but Tom and Annie didn't care about superstition and went ahead. Ignoring superstition was part and parcel of their supremely assured, unencumbered-by-the-past generation's behaviour. They told themselves that they were obliged to cut through the taboos of the past – so a May wedding it was. (Anyway, it turned out to be cheaper than one in June.)

In the early days, Tom might well have said on coming home: 'Tell me everything about your day.' In the early days, Annie almost certainly would have been agog to know what was going on in the World Service and why. As the young wife and then new mother, she remained utterly convinced of the importance of Tom's work. This belief did not waver even when he began to come home later and later – until she realized that she was not coping very well. 'I'm not a piece of elastic,' she warned him. 'Sooner or later I'll snap.'

Tom replied, 'I promise – I promise to do more.'

He had observed his vow as best he could. Battling with his schedules, he had pitched up at the Nativity play featuring the twins as Mary and Joseph, sat beside Annie, held her hand and almost wept with pride – which made Annie's knees go weak with love for him. 'Thank God I didn't miss seeing them, Annie.' He got to the interviews with the head teacher, who wanted to discuss why it might be that Emily had taken to hiding in the lavatories over break, and to the regular gritty exchanges with Jake's science and maths teachers and, praise be, kept his temper.

All noted and applauded. Yes. *Yes*. That was what Annie had asked of Tom and he had made heroic efforts to oblige: 'Of course I want to be there for the children.' All the same, as Tom rose in the hierarchy, she sensed the balance shifting and his withdrawal into a place where she and the children were unwelcome. Little by little. So imperceptible that, to begin with, Annie didn't spot it. 'You are my life, Annie.' 'And you are mine, Tom.' Poetry and the moonlight had to fade, was fading, did fade – 'How do I love thee, Annie? Let me count the ways.' But this was to open a door into a cold, barren place.

She took to observing herself critically in the mirror – were her eyes growing dull, and what had happened to her arms? – then gave up eating butter during the week. Wonderful, delicious butter – bad. Horrible, oily, non-transgressive substitute – good. Who was kidding whom? Even if (by some glorious witchery) her arms became as toned as Madonna's, she knew she was missing the point. The early accord struck at the beginning of their marriage was fading.

'What sort of life is this?' she had asked, when Tom took to going into the office on Saturday mornings after the twins had left primary school. On that occasion he had grabbed her around the waist and drew her close.

'Ours,' he had replied. 'What sort of question is that, silly?' His hand tightened. 'Annie, I can't afford not to be there. Can you see that? Do you understand?'

'I do. And I don't.'

'I love my job. Please, Annie, support me, and one day I'll do the same for you.'

'I want to you to be happy,' she told him, searching his face for the key to draw him back. 'I want you to succeed.' But he was looking through and beyond her, down the street and into the office where, for the time being, the greater part of him wished to be. He threw out a decoy: 'Annie, I love you. Truly.' Annie had no doubt that he meant what he said. But the nuances were shifting, for she understood instinctively that Tom didn't mean it in the way he used to.

The ironies were not lost on her. (Neither, to be fair, were they lost on Tom.) What she had first so admired in him – the consuming, passionate commitment to his work – had ended up stealing a march on them. It had been like travelling with the dearest and most trusted of companions who, having agreed on the pace, the distance and the final destination, had run on ahead. Without reaching out a hand. Without warning.

How does one mourn something that is not technically broken? She posed the question to herself over the years, searched for the answer and, at times, experienced a sinking sense of loss and panic – because there was a difference between being married and being together. She could not quite believe that the silence and the space opening up between them were happening. She could not quite believe that she and Tom might fail.

Then Tom missed Jake's big sixth-form match. 'How could you? How *could* you?' Annie raged at him. He was angry with himself and bluffed, 'I have to network. Everyone does.' By that stage Annie had her job at St Brigid's Hospital and longed to say, 'And I don't?' But it was too crude a response to their current predicament, a combination of raising children and working – and, working herself, she understood only too well the forces that pulled a parent this way and that. 'We have to do better,' she told Tom. 'Yes,' he agreed. 'We must.'

'I wish, Tom . . .'

It was yet another Saturday morning and Tom was heading for the door. 'You wish what?'

'That we – or the children at least – were as important as your work.' Thickly spreading a tuna-and-mayo (forbidden) mixture on ciabatta, tucking bottles of raspberry smoothie and water into the cool-bag to assemble a picnic. They were going to Thorpe Park to terrify themselves on roller-coasters ('Mum will wimp out'), eat candy floss and other dietetically unsound delights, and the children had been heading towards excited hysteria – until Tom had announced he couldn't make it after all. A silence fell, as thick as the tuna-and-mayo sludge slapped between the bread, and he felt it. Oh, yes, Tom felt it. He hovered in the doorway. 'Stop it, Annie. Stop making trouble for me.' She bit back the words *But aren't you making trouble for yourself?*

As it turned out, he had been.

In the still, dark, quiet house, Annie applied lipstick in the mirror and smoothed down her hair. It made her feel better. She ran her finger around the edge of her lip to tidy it up . . . and her hand froze. An excited, radiant face was reflected back. It was hers . . . but not hers, for it belonged to the past. In its grey eyes and yearning expression could be read an anticipation of life, a dreamy confidence that all would be well. This was the girl who had looked up from her book to watch Tom talking to his mother, or to snatch a glimpse of Tom reading, or to tease him with lascivious glances over a table while they ate the meal – shepherd's pie, stew, fishcakes – she had prepared. This was the girl who had in all innocence imagined that, with sufficient energy and good intentions, life could be manipulated for the good of everyone.

In that prelapsarian age, she and Tom had watched over the other with the careful attention of guardian angels, had listened to each other's heartbeat with a sense of astonishment – and sometimes panicked because a heart's beat was so fragile. Then the pulse had fluttered because existence was a wonderful, radiant thing – so much so that sometimes, when she thought about it, it made her cry.

In the sitting room, she pinned the angel card to the ribbon with the others, stepped back and waited for someone to come home.

Chapter Two

In February, Tom arrived home from work as a troubled national bank was finally taken into state ownership and, in tandem with the sepulchral-toned newsreader on the radio, announced, 'It's possible we're in for a recession.'

Annie switched off the radio. For some days now she had been listening to reports – US sub-prime problems, the January slump in the UK stock market etc., etc.: money traders were predicting a global downturn and a fall in interest rates. 'I wouldn't have known.'

'Very funny.'

He frowned and turned away. She frowned and turned away, but not before noticing that Tom had a pallor – almost unearthly – which had not been there when he had left that morning.

He asked, 'Supper when?'

'Fifteen minutes or so.'

He fidgeted with the evening paper. 'Good day?' He dredged the question out of a diminishing stockpile of good manners, and without enthusiasm.

'We've got through.'

'So you did.'

The radio pattered on with its story of economic up-heavals. Outside a car horn hooted rudely.

Tom searched in the wine rack and alighted on the bottle of red that Annie knew he had been saving for a celebration.

Immersed in thought and still worryingly pale, he poured out a measure, swirled it around the glass, took a mouthful and swallowed it. Then he recollected his wife. 'Sorry, would you like one?'

Annie accepted it, the glass chilly between her fingers. 'Actually, someone died today who shouldn't have,' she admitted. Now senior manager at St Brigid's, she encountered death most days. Of course, any unexpected death was awful and regretted, but this one would be a source of trouble.

Tom appeared to be struggling with a strong emotion, but he managed to say politely, 'I'm sorry.'

It was then Annie realized that something was wrong, really wrong. 'Tom, what's up?' She placed an experimental hand on his arm.

'*Nothing.*'

'OK. OK.' She stepped back and, after a moment, continued: 'There's bound to be lawyers in. Possibly a court case. The patient was admitted with pains in his stomach but was left on a gurney in the corridor in A and E and died between checks.' She felt the throb of anxiety and sorrow for the people who would be grieving. 'It's pretty dreadful.'

With an effort Tom said, 'I'm sorry . . . It will mean trouble for you all.'

Mollified by his attempt to sympathize, she said, 'Yes. It will.'

She hoicked the remains of a ready-made *coq au vin*, a packet of mange-tout and early Jersey Royals out of the fridge and set about making supper. No longer much of a cook, she had become adept at the on-line delivery system. 'Tom, he was only thirty-two. That's barely time to breathe.'

Imagine if it was Jake or Emily. Or . . . Mia. What would she do? In a way, she did know. Quite literally, she would not be able to live if something happened to them. That thought was inadmissible, too. She plucked a kitchen knife from the wooden block and reached for the packet of mange-tout.

She was expecting Tom to respond for he held strong views on the National Health Service and, occasionally, they had talked over the way it was going. Then she noticed he had refilled his glass pretty smartish. 'Tom, are you sure nothing's wrong?'

He refused to meet her gaze. 'Yes . . . no. It's fine. See you in a minute.' He gathered up glass, bottle and briefcase and headed into the hall.

She heard his heavy tread up the stairs and the snap of his bedroom door shutting. She picked up the mange-tout and slashed open the plastic covering.

. . . 'Dear Annie,' read the note that had arrived in her university pigeon-hole. 'Please don't come to Redpath's lecture on Thursday as I won't be able to concentrate. I am sick with longing for you and I have to get my essay written on whatever the old poseur is sounding off about otherwise they will chuck me out.' It was signed: 'An Admirer', and included the PS 'A clue . . . (reasonably) tall, dark and handsome.'

Of course she had hastened to the lecture hall, sat in the hushed and stuffy auditorium and listened without understanding a word to Redpath striving to communicate the mysteries of semiotics. Prickles ran up her neck and her skin felt on fire. At the finish, she swivelled around – and encountered a locked-on, intense blue gaze.

Tom was (1) tall – OK, reasonably tall, (2) dark, (3) not so much handsome as a rogue with raven's plumage, which was much, much better. Even if his appearance hadn't unearthed a mysterious need in her, of which until then she had been ignorant, she would have fallen for his energy. And his humour.

'You're so beautiful,' he told her, many times, and for those opening months in their relationship she was led to believe that she was a unique blend of Helen of Troy, Cleopatra and Marilyn Monroe. Her skin glowed, her waist shrank to a tiny circle and she lost all desire for food and possessions.

Prince Tom Charming shook her awake, proffered a key to an exciting life – and then kissed her. It was a fairytale, she confided to her older sister, Lydia. Without knowing, she had been waiting for Tom Charming.

Shortly after they graduated, Tom walked into a job at the BBC World Service. Shortly after that, he arrived at Annie's flat with a bunch of red roses, so dark they were almost black, and begged her to marry him.

'So, what did you say?' asked Lydia, when Annie rang her.

'What do you think . . . ?'

She and Tom ate the supermarket-confected *coq au vin* in silence. These days, eating in silence was not unusual. Neither was it hostile. Just neutral. Actually, Annie found it useful because, after a day of talking and organizing, it gave her time to think.

She speared a piece of chicken on her fork, slathered it in the wine sauce and placed in her mouth. Tuesday tomorrow . . . and she and the team would have to face the aftermath of the patient's death. Again the throb of anxiety and sorrow. Dead or alive, the search for a child could never cease. Never. You caught the back of their head in a crowd, their ghostly presence at the Christmas table, an echo of their voice in the garden. Deliberately, she concentrated on other things. The little toe on her right foot was sore. Shoes too small? She had been seduced by the linen sheets she had spotted in the boutique off Bond Street. The colour of Devon cream, they had the smoothest of weaves and a thread count off the register . . . Write a shopping list . . . What about the evening dance class she was toying with?

Her plate was almost empty but Tom had barely touched his. 'You eat so fast, Annie,' she could hear him say. These days it was a criticism, but once upon a time he might have added sweetly, lustfully, 'More time, then, for other things.' On that one, Sadie took Tom's side, saying, with that characteristic little shake of her blonde head, 'If you chew each mouthful fifty-two times you remain slim. It's simple.' What planet did these fifty-two-times chewers inhabit? Didn't they have jobs or small children? How was it possible to spend so much of the day masticating?

More time for other things . . . Like everything else, sex had its flowerings and nadirs. The long, delicious, subterranean episodes under duvets with Tom . . . or the wilder ones outside, when taking risks was easy, necessary even. The snatched, urgent, shuddery coming together while babies napped. Much later on, the perfunctory performances when Tom and she literally gasped for sleep, not orgasm, which always made them laugh. The gradual erosion of their emotional connection in favour of purely physical sensation . . . then the gradual erosion of desire for each other. Then, since Mia . . . nothing. Or, rather, nothing truthful or meaningful. Or comforting or sustaining.

'Sorry about the meal.' Annie put down her knife and fork. 'I didn't have the energy to make anything. Hope you don't mind.'

He didn't look up. 'I don't expect you to cook.'

'No, but I realize it's expensive buying ready-made.' She willed him to look up. 'Tom, that's one of the reasons I thought the kitchen needed a face-lift. It would prod me into action and I know you prefer homemade food.'

Impossible to place when exactly Annie had stopped enjoying being in the kitchen. Three children and a career had killed the urge to cook creatively (all that running around sourcing organic this and that). Then Mia had gone. Or was it that the overload in the media about cooking and cooks made her cross? Time was, she had immersed herself in the, frankly, almost pornographic prose of the best cookery writers, who described the texture of flaky pastry or the aroma of almond with precise and aching sensuality. She had read them, admired them but, when the going was tough, chucked them aside in favour of Mother's Little Helper: the ready-made meal.

Time gone.

Have you, Annie Nicholson, taken happiness, sexual satiation and partnership for granted? Guilty as charged. She had taken for granted that, provided one stuck to the rules more or less, *things would be all right*. When they hadn't been, the heart had gone out of her for cooking and such-like. Furthermore, she suspected Tom felt the same. She must ask him. She really must ask him. Some time.

Tom was struggling with a forkful. Too much wine, she thought. It always took his appetite away. He had got what he wanted – *the job* – and the material advantages with it, but it hadn't left him unscathed.

'Tom,' she said, out of the blue, 'has it all been worth it?'

His head reared up. 'Not now, Annie. Please.'

She speared a final flake of chicken on her fork and tried again: 'About the new kitchen. It's going to be nasty for a few days while they fit the units and I certainly won't be able to cook. But we can go out to eat. Or we can have a good lunch at our office canteens and just snack in the evening.'

Annie couldn't be sure, but had he winced?

In a few days' time (the schedule having been carefully worked out so that it would be ready by Easter, the pleasant, slightly ramshackle kitchen, with its large table and creaky sofa, was due for evisceration. Fashionable Shaker units in pale cream would be installed, plus an immensely expensive French range cooker. With the latter, the salesman had pointed out chattily, it was possible to cook for ten, twenty . . . No problem.

Cooking for twenty? Had she lost her wits lusting over its gleaming hob, its cast-iron trivets and two ovens? She had no desire to cook even for one. It was going to be, she had told Sadie a trifle hysterically, the equivalent of the most expensive hostess trolley ever.

Tom's glass was empty, and he helped himself to the last of the wine. 'Annie . . .'

She stiffened. He sounded choked, troubled.

'Phwoar! Am I wet!' Emily, their youngest, burst into the kitchen, dumped a couple of carrier bags and peeled off a sodden mac to reveal tight jeans worn with two expensive (as Annie happened to know) T-shirts and a bulky tweed scarf twisted around the neck. The look was writer's chic, or Emily's interpretation of it.

Unburdened, she swung around. 'Hi, parents.' A deposit of last year's impacted leaves and mud fell from her shoe on to the floor. 'Sorry, sorry . . .' She wiped it up with a piece of kitchen roll, leaving a muddy smudge on the tiles.

Annie kidnapped the soaking mac and hung it over the boiler. Emily had been babysitting for a neighbour attending a parents' evening. Tomorrow her daughter would board a school coach and help to supervise the fourth-form outing to a local swimming-pool. The day after that, she resumed babysitting duties with yet another neighbour. This was not a programme designed to inspire faith in Emily's future earnings.

Please think, Emily. Annie was deeply afraid that her daughter was condemning herself to a fretful, fractious existence. Then she scolded herself for lack of faith and vision and tried not to mind that, in the eighteen months since she had left university, the tally of Emily's completed work added up to a short story published in *Metaphor*, a magazine with large literary pretensions and small circulation (Annie and Tom had bought up at least twenty copies and distributed them discreetly to friends and relations), and a novel that a couple of literary agents could not *quite* see how they might handle. 'But it was a close-run thing,' wrote the kinder one.

'If it had been any good,' a white-faced Emily had admitted a few weeks ago, 'I'd be there by now. It means I'm no good.'

'Listen to me, Em,' Tom had intervened. 'My publishing contacts tell me it's nothing to do with you being good or bad. It's to do with luck. And positioning. And how many celebrities they're trying to buy that week. And who has had a good day or a bad day when they look at your stuff. Nothing more.'

This was Cynical Tom, who took a bow ever more frequently. The other side of him, Idealistic Tom, had every faith in his daughter and applauded her willingness to forgo a settled income and a career path. 'There's something heroic about it,' he told Annie, mentioning in the same breath that he planned to give Emily an allowance to help her through the initial stages.

Now, in the soon-to-be-upgraded kitchen, Annie observed her husband. The raven's plumage had dulled and she could no longer interpret the light in his eye – and there were reasons for that. They lived together, but not together. Thoughts of leaving Tom ran like an uneven seam under the everyday routines and, once or twice, had forced themselves to the surface. One of the worst crises had been after Mia left and an uncaring Annie had served up a rotten dinner to Tom's colleagues. Reason for divorce, Mrs Nicholson? Answer: a tough stew. Yes? No? Almost. But that would have been too simple. The main reasons were too painful . . . impossible to discuss. Buried. *Buried.*

She pictured Tom and herself in a boat, paddling furiously in opposite directions. But not for very long because the picture winded her. Instead she chose to think that she and Tom had worked out a *modus vivendi* and it did them fine, much as the serviceable knickers and vest her mother had insisted Annie wear as a child had done fine.

'How many pages?' Tom was asking Emily.

Emily shook out a fake-leopardskin jacket from a Topshop bag and draped it over her shoulders. 'How cool is this?'

'How many jackets do you need?' asked Annie, but secretly she was pleased that Emily had indulged in something so normal (and unnecessary) as shopping.

Emily settled herself beside her father. 'Pages, Dad? Three.'

Three. Annie did the maths. If this latest novel, embarked on this morning, was approximately four hundred pages long, it suggested that The End would not arrive for another 133 days. And that would be the first draft – Emily had taken care to brief her parents that a minimum of three drafts was always necessary.

Tom put his arm around his daughter. 'Title?' Tender and caring as ever with his favourite child.

Emily raised a pair of cloned blue eyes to her father. Intense, molten desire to succeed burned in their depths, and Annie shuddered for her. 'I'm working on it. *Time Regained*?'

'Time bloody lost, you mean,' Annie could hear Jake saying. She smothered a grin. 'Think that one has been taken.'

'Want some help, Em?' Despite whatever was troubling him, Tom was putting himself out.

Emily leaned against him. 'Thanks, Dad, but no.'

They were peas in a pod, those two, despite the adolescent storms and tantrums to which Emily had royally treated them. Emily had helped herself to a greater dollop of Tom's DNA than the twins had – the blue eyes, raven-black hair, set of the jaw, and the tiny characteristic gestures that mimicked her father's. Other markers, even to the most unobservant, were their bouts of loftiness and of hysterical laughter.

Annie couldn't help laughing. 'You two look so sweet together.'

The phone rang. Tom disentangled himself from Emily and got up to answer it. 'Jake . . . all well?' He didn't wait for an answer before he said, 'I'll hand you over to your mother. We'll speak some time.'

'Hi, Mum.' Jake was his usual cheerful self. 'I just wanted to report that Maisie's check-up was fine. She's absolutely spot-on average for a twelve-month-old.' Annie listened indulgently as Jake chatted on. He planned to invite them over for tea on Maisie's birthday – he and Jocasta had been talking about a holiday and he was *really* pleased with his current work-in-progress. He signed off, 'Big kiss, Mum.'

Jake always made Annie's heart feel lighter. In many ways he was like Tom used to be. Tom disagreed – 'We're chalk and cheese, Annie' – and had once admitted that he never felt quite at ease with his son. It was true: something had gone wrong – or, rather, had never developed – between them. Annie remembered well explaining to a small boy clutching a teddy bear that his father was not coming home because he had to talk to lots of people at work. 'But he never talks to me,' said Jake. Since Jake and Jocasta's marriage, and Maisie's arrival, father and son had not seen much of each other at all.

And Mia?

Annie's new-year resolution had been not to think of Mia. This was broken every day. Even the merest whisper in her mind of her daughter prodded the wound. How was it possible, she asked herself, for the hundredth, thousandth time, that the dancing, coppery child, who had desired nothing so much as to please her mother, had ended up turning her back on them all?

Heavens . . . it had been only yesterday she was taking the children to swim in the noisy, chlorinated swimming-pool. There, a scarf bound (oh, futile gesture) around her head to stop the waterlogged air whirling her curls into corkscrews, she had released them into another element. First, a cautious romp in the paddling-pool, but as time passed, she, the mother, was relegated to a wary guardian-ship at the shallow end where she watched them bob and dive like downy ducks. Then came the day when she stood at one end of the pool and the three of them swam towards her. Little sleek otter heads. Thin bird limbs. Water churn-ing in their haste to reach her. They were part of her, and again the thought scorched across her brain that if one of them was to die she would die too. Yet their new mastery of the water, the alien element, marked the beginning of a separation – which prefigured another kind of death. *For which, Mrs Nicholson, you had better be prepared.*

But not yet, she had prayed silently, as she knelt by the side of the pool to greet her excited, triumphant team with a big smile. *Not yet.*

That had been long ago and far away – a time when the family had still been whole. Annie got to her feet. 'I'll do the washing-up.'

Chapter Three

Annie ran hot water into the sink. She was not a slow learner. In fact, she was as smart as anyone who had successfully held down a senior management job in a major hospital, but it had taken her all of her forty-nine years to understand that people do not change. They tried to and they did their best, but the colour and shape of the building blocks could not be altered.

The boiler thumped while Emily rattled on, endeavouring to describe the difficulties of writing. 'It *is* lonely, Dad.' On the other hand, she was revelling in the idea of being an artist (albeit an unknown one): 'It gives one *meaning*.' Then, again, it put one in an impossible position: 'The project seems so big. Even deciding which word to use seems too difficult.' No doubt expecting the usual encouragement and soothing advice, which Tom dished out in spadefuls, she tucked her hand under her father's elbow.

Tom remained silent.

Annie scoured a saucepan and decided to stick a toe into already choppy water. 'Emily, I know your father feels differently, and I realize I'll be up there with the great dictators of the world, but there is a strong argument that you should get a job.' She paused and sent a sympathetic smile in the direction of her daughter. 'Think about it. You'd feel less strained, you'd have a chance to look at the world. And, er, you could spend your own money in Topshop.'

Emily ignored her – nothing unusual in that. But Tom succeeded in confounding them both: 'Your mother's right. Maybe you should give it a break – get a job and come back to writing later.'

Annie swung round and sent him an old-fashioned look. Whatever else could be said about him, he was never flighty with his opinions. *Something's happened*, she thought.

'Oh,' said Emily, and went very quiet.

Tom continued: 'One should never be afraid of changing one's mind. There's an argument that you need more time to grow into your writer's skin and to experience the world, rather than sitting at home.'

Annie knew Emily would have trouble digesting this.

Emily fiddled with a fingernail. 'Dad, what's going on here? Why didn't you say all this before?'

Tom avoided Annie's eyes. 'Things change.'

Emily directed a suspicious blue gaze at her father. 'First you support my attempts at the artistic life, now you don't.' Her eyes slid towards the shopping bags. 'I know I'm sponging off you and that's bad. But . . . but, OK, I take the point. I'll think again.' She grabbed the bags and said, with some dignity, 'If you could just give me a week or so . . .'

She shot out of the kitchen, and they listened to her rapid ascent of the stairs.

Annie said, 'It's usually my role to be negative.'

Tom ran his fingers through his hair and then, to Annie's alarm, dropped his face into his hands. 'Sit down, Annie.' His voice was muffled.

Annie sat down cautiously. 'I'm listening.' A drink problem? Lately, Tom had been hitting the bottle a bit. An affair? She had been expecting it for years. Sadie said (and she should know) they were always grumpy and unreasonable before they confessed. The guilt trip provoked them to provoke you so that they could accuse you of the bad temper and bad behaviour that had *forced* them to flee into the arms of the secretary/younger model/your best friend. (Again, Sadie should know.)

So it was divorce, the end of her and Tom's long, flat road . . . Her mind leaped ahead. Selling the house. A one-bedroom flat into which she would cram her life and entertain friends to lunch (dinners didn't happen with single divorcees), frantically opening windows to dilute the odours of living and cooking in cramped quarters. Lonely evenings. A fettered spirit.

Annie closed and opened her eyes. 'Go on.'

He raised his head. 'I don't know how to begin.'

She laid her hands flat on the table, ready to grip the edge and hold on hard to the pieces of her disintegrating world. 'Just say it, Tom.'

'I've lost my job.'

When he thought of how it had happened, a cold sensation crept into his hands and feet. It had been very polite, very low-key, downbeat even. Full of awkward silences like a disastrous radio interview.

I'm sorry, Tom . . .

He had smelt it in the air for some time. Since Christmas, at any rate. Any fool would have done. He had lost a bitter turf war over the plundering of the English-language programmes by the regional sections during which he had argued that, since the regional sections were using so much of his material, it made sense to give him a bigger budget. There was the strategy document that, curiously, had not found its way into his in-tray. A couple of his peers had avoided him. The chatter around the water-cooler had been peculiarly feverish. He rang James to arrange the weekly prop-up bar session at Les Boissons. 'Hi, usual time, usual place?'

'No can do, Tom. Another time.'

'Any particular reason?'

'Do I have to give a reason?' James was defensive. 'Penny's demanding I go home earlier. She says she never sees me.'

The second Tom put the phone down it rang. It was Neil Bostock, an old foe from Associated Newspapers. He did not waste time in preliminaries. 'Is it true there's a cleansing of the Augean stables and you're being replaced by Matt Piper?'

A mallet smacked into Tom's head and he saw stars. 'Couldn't be less true.'

Neil's cynical laugh incorporated the phlegmy wheeze of a committed smoker. 'Not what I've heard. Consider this a friendly warning.'

'Or you're truffling wildly for a scoop.'

'Same thing.' Neil sounded almost affectionate, and a touch regretful at life's turpitude. 'You read it here first.'

Tom put down the phone again. Occasionally he wasted energy on the wrong thing and he was aware he did so now. Instead of taking the bull by the horns, instead of demanding to see the Director General and sorting out what was going on, instead of confiding in Annie, he sat miserably in his office. (This he could never confess to her.) Never before in his life, not even with the Mia drama, had he felt *powerless* – gripped by a paralysis of his guts and motor nerves, leaving him unable to move or even think.

Before the axe fell officially he had sufficient wit to book a session with a well-known solicitor who specialized in clear-outs in banking and media. He was known to strike fear into his opponents, and within five minutes Tom understood why.

'If they're making you redundant,' he said, 'there has to be prior consultation. Has there been?' Tom related the conversations so far, and they were noted. 'It would be prudent if you record all your dealings so that we have them at our fingertips. If, on the other hand, they're sacking you, you must demand chapter and verse as to why. If you wish, you can call me while you're talking this through. I find it often clarifies things quite quickly.' He gave a complacent little smile. 'This is not just about money, although I'm not averse to wringing as much out of them as possible. This is about planning the architecture of your future and it's important we get it right.'

Tom forced himself not to flinch.

'We'll go for a confidentiality agreement, a mutually agreed statement as to why you left the organization and mutually agreed reference. OK?' The solicitor expertly assessed how much the shell-shocked Tom could absorb. 'That will do for starters.'

Even then he hadn't told Annie, which he should have done. Quite apart from the practical considerations, he was wrestling with humiliation, which was the heaviest cross to bear. Soon everyone would know that his reputation and achievements had been found wanting.

When, finally, Tom was summoned to the DG, he looked

bad and, furthermore, like a bad proposition. Dark-ringed eyes and a pasty complexion accosted him in the mirror and he was forced to conclude: this was a man carrying the loser's plague bacillus.

As he packed up his office with the help of Maddie, his tearful assistant, there was a knock on the door.

'Come in.' Tom turned to confront a troubled-looking James.

Tactfully, Maddie vanished and Tom turned back to the papers he was packing into a box. Of course, James could not be blamed for what had happened but, in the way of the workplace, it was a pretty sure thing that he had known.

'Tom,' James addressed his back, 'does Annie know?'

'Not sure why that should concern you.'

'*Have* you told her?'

'As it happens, not yet.' He was aware that this did not read well, which made him marginally more conciliatory and he looked round. 'You could, at least, have made the last drink.'

James looked mightily discomfited, which confirmed to Tom what he had suspected. Who was he kidding? Tom had known when it had happened to others. Witnessing the mini-slaughters over the years, he had often reflected on what made an office friendship. Now he knew for sure it had limits.

'Yes,' admitted James. 'Are we still friends?'

Tom shrugged. At this particular moment he couldn't bring himself to comment. He and James exchanged a glance, packed with memories of shared highs and lows, and the burden of looking after number one in a highly political workplace while remaining halfway decent.

James kicked a filled box on the floor. 'You would have done the same.' The box rocked, and he kicked it a second time. 'They've got their eye on someone younger who has an "in" with the government.'

'Matt Piper. The press very kindly told me.'

James looked truly distressed. 'Did you really want me to tell you before it happened? No, don't answer. I know how you loved this job and the organization. More than anyone.' He shuffled his feet in an embarrassed way. 'You were the inspiring one, Tom. Some of your programmes were brilliant. You were a fantastic director. We all feel that. Look, I'll keep an eye on the India and HIV one. I know it was your particular baby.' He held out a hand. 'Keep in touch. *Please.*'

'No,' said Tom, from the depth of his rage and anguish. 'Best not.'

Half an hour later, accompanied by Security, Tom walked out of the office for the final time, carrying a cardboard box. Only a few raised their eyes from their screens. There were one or two murmurs, 'Goodbye', to break the queasy hush but others shrank back as he passed their desks on the way to unemployment.

He had no one to turn to, and his stomach hurt like hell.

Telling Annie was every bit as bad as he had imagined. He watched her groping to understand. He winced as she looked at him in a completely different way. From the first he had relied on her support and approval. Not entirely, of course, but significantly. He had liked to cup his hand around her delicately shaped head, stare into her eyes and see in them a validation, her loving approval, their sense of shared purpose. 'I wish I knew what you were thinking,' he had once confessed, saddened and maddened because it was impossible.

Her lids had snapped shut, masking a wicked, teasing, delighted gleam. 'Try me, Tom.'

Time . . . proximity . . . work had dulled all that and he couldn't remember when he had last fitted his hand around the frail, stubborn skull and pinched a (despised) curl, as soft and glossy as a baby animal's. Sometimes, during restless nights, his longing for the past was as sharp as a butcher's knife. But even that passed.

Annie pulled back her hair so hard with both hands that her features appeared scraped clean of flesh. 'Tom, we'll have to think what to do . . .' His spirits plunged into blackness.

These days, twenty years in a job was good going. Thirty was exceptional. Twenty years was sufficient to become expert in surviving management putsches and strategic rethinks, to keep the head down and to trade through upheavals. Thirty saw one beating them at their own game. And when you'd managed that, somehow it seemed unthinkable that the unthinkable would happen.

Annie caught her breath. 'I'm so sorry, Tom.'

He directed a shattered countenance at her. 'Not as sorry as I am.'

The drinking . . . She knew she should have asked sooner. 'You've known about this . . .'

He looked as though he might deny it, but decided against it. 'I knew something was going on.'

'For how long?'

'A week or so.'

'Why didn't you say?'

'Is it important?'

She absorbed the rebuff. 'OK, tell me what happened.'

He sighed wearily. 'One is summoned. One is told. There's a package waiting in Human Resources. I'll get the lawyer to look over it.'

He looked beaten, badly beaten, and she told herself to get up and hold him close. But she didn't.

He was saying, 'I take it your job is OK?'

'As far as I know.'

'The sick are always with us.' He grimaced. 'Sorry. I mean, at least one of us will bring home the bacon.' Then he muttered, 'I never thought I'd end up relying on my wife.'

The words Tom was using were all wrong. So was the flicker of sexism, which tended to show up for duty in the least sexist of men (which Tom was) when the chips were down. 'Brandy, I think.' She went over to the cupboard, extracted it and found two glasses. She poured liberal fingers, then slid one over to him. 'But why?'

'"Economies and synergy".' He drank some brandy. 'What stupid words they are.'

'When do you go?'

'Now. You don't keep the head of a division hanging around if you've synergized him.'

'And what's happening to the job?'

'Well, now, that's where it gets interesting. They say it's to be melted down and dispersed around, but I have a hunch that's not quite right . . .'

'Oh.' Pity shot through Annie. It was all too clear: it wasn't the job that was redundant but Tom. She braced herself to stop up the holes in the dam and help him. 'Ridiculous. They can't do without you. The place will fall apart.'

'I gave them the best years of my life.'

But that's it, she thought. Tom had loved his job more than anything, having tended it, considered it, paid it homage, spent time with it. He revered what the World Service stood for: to communicate, and to communicate well. He believed in these things. And, as any impersonal organization inevitably did, it was repaying him with a lesson in dispensability.

She said gently, 'Now we know for sure that institutions don't do loyalty.'

'Right,' he said. 'Double right.'

'How do you feel?' she asked.

'Skinned.' He finished the brandy. 'Flayed.'

Annie thought of the practical implications and her insides lurched. Money. Mortgage. Bills. 'We'd better plan what to do.'

He looked at her wearily. 'Let's discuss it in the morning.'

Each of them stared into their separate glasses of brandy and was silent.

Chapter Four

The bedroom was Annie's sanctuary. This was contrary to all her expectations. It was supposed to be a *shared* well-spring from which Tom and she would draw strength . . . a place of comfort and safety where they could talk and find peace in each other's company. But not so long after Mia had left the family and the gulf was the widest it had ever been, Tom had opted to occupy his daughter's empty bedroom opposite. He maintained it was because he slept badly – which none of the family believed. Annie never contradicted him.

'What happens if she comes back?' she once asked.

'If she does, then I'll move back,' was Tom's reply.

Neither she nor Tom had meant to end up in separate beds and in their separate territories. Yet both had retreated into them as a relief. With each little additional touch that Annie made to the room they had shared – new curtains, hanging the painting of fourteenth-century Pienza, which she loved, the antique American quilt – it had become more hers.

Bits of Tom were still *in situ*. He kept some of his clothes in the wardrobe and things in drawers. From time to time, Annie was jerked awake by the sound of him rattling in the medicine cupboard in the en-suite bathroom or searching in a drawer. Half asleep, half awake, those were the moments when, at the sight of her shadowy, rummaging husband, she experienced their estrangement most sharply.

Still reeling from his news, she kicked off her shoes, padded to the window and drew the curtains. Their weave (and extra interlining) was satisfyingly heavy to handle, and their tea-rose ashy pink suggested peace, erotic sensuousness and goodness: all the positive and beautiful aspirations with which Annie currently had a tricky relationship.

The morning had been normal – the kind of morning when she operated on automatic. Before leaving for work, she had stripped the bed and stuffed the sheets into the laundry basket. She had made it with clean sheets, drawing the bottom one as tight as a drum, as she liked it. She had dressed in her customary uniform of skirt, blouse and jacket, selected a pair of shoes that gave a nod to frivolity without going over the top, and tutted over the state of her hair. All accomplished in the calm, reasonably well-organized manner that Annie had perfected.

But tonight the feminine order of her bedroom was totally at odds with the storm that had been unleashed. It also struck her as ridiculous that Tom was across the corridor, battling alone with his shock.

She knocked on his door and went in.

Tom sat on the bed with the empty brandy glass, apparently absorbed in the spectacle of his bare feet. He did not even turn his head at Annie's entrance.

She sat down beside him. 'Are you sure you don't want to talk about it?'

'There's nothing to say.'

Silence.

Talking was Tom's thing. He had talked his way into university, into Annie's heart and bed, and into the job he had just lost. Fluent, funny, opinionated, he was tolerated even when he went too far and, in the old days, they had argued passionately, joyously, with gusto. Talking was his breathing, and silence was his dying.

The space between them on the bed seemed indicative. 'We can make plans, Tom, budget . . . until you get a new job.'

'Nice idea. Why didn't I think of it?'

'That won't help.' She was soft, conciliatory, let's-take-this-gently.

'Actually,' he was at his most sarcastic, 'the lawyer is concerned about what he terms the "architecture of my future". Everyone's concerned for the architecture of my future, including the organization that's just dumped me. It's terribly, terribly nice of them.'

'Well, you do have a future.'

He turned his head and glared right through her. She prayed that he couldn't see her panic. 'Don't you get it? I probably won't find another job. A fifty-year-old radio executive ain't exactly hot goods at the best of times.'

He sounded surprised at his own analysis – although they both knew he was probably right and Annie also knew she was expected to refute it. 'And you're going to give up, are you? Despite knowing that's rubbish.'

'Say that again in six months' time. Have you been listening to what's going on in the money markets?'

'Stop it, Tom.'

'Don't pity me, Annie.'

She set her lips. 'I'm not.'

Side by side they sat, not touching. Annie searched for an object on which to anchor and lighted on the long mirror hanging from a dodgy nail on the wall – Mia had insisted on having it before she'd stopped caring about what she looked like.

Tom's tightened fist rested on his thigh. If she reached over and picked up that clenched hand – a simple gesture – the odds were she could smooth out the fingers and stroke them into quietude. But she could no longer gauge whether he wished to be touched. For all Annie knew, he would push her away and that would wound her. Then again, she was out of the habit of touching him, of *wanting* to touch him.

'Just get through the next few days . . .' she pitched expectations low '. . . and then you can think.'

On the floor above, Emily banged an object down on the floor and her bed creaked.

'Go to bed, Annie. I can't think straight, nor can you. You can crow over me tomorrow.'

'Tom!'

He jumped up. 'Just go.'

Annie did her best. 'Listen to me, Tom. I'm on your side.'

His expression was bleak, his hand cold as he pulled Annie to her feet and manhandled her towards the door. 'Tomorrow.' He pushed her out into the corridor.

My God, she thought, with a flicker of outrage. It's come to this. She stared at Tom . . . and her outrage was deflated by a hard, painful pity for the hurt and humiliation he had inadvertently revealed by his actions. 'Goodnight, Tom.'

Within seconds their doors had shut and the corridor between the two rooms was again dark.

Sadie and Annie met frequently. Sometimes, in order to escape the Westminster village, Sadie drove down to St Brigid's and (Sadie very often in ridiculous high heels) they walked in the park at lunchtime where they discussed everything under the sun.

A frequent topic was Sadie's homesickness for her native Georgia – 'I'll get over it,' she said bravely. 'Or I'll just go for a divorce hat-trick.' Even though she was married to Andrew, the MP, Sadie's straight talking remained unchecked. Her habit of voicing the things that, by and large, Annie only allowed herself to think was useful and wonderfully stimulating in a friend but possibly did not do Andrew's career many favours.

Sadie could be funny. She could be rude. She could be alarming. But if the chips were down she was pure gold. When Annie phoned to tell her Mia had gone she came at once, winging like an angel into number twenty-two to make tea and dispense comfort while Annie sat broken at the kitchen table. She darted around the kitchen – it was a measure of her distress that she had abandoned the high heels for flats – then said, 'Tell me everything.'

Annie stumbled over her narrative of events. Sadie clicked her teeth. 'It's bad,' she said, and Annie loved her for being truthful. 'I can't do anything much for you.'

Annie raised her head. 'Yes, you can. Come with me to try to find her. Tom can't, or won't, go.'

There was only a second of hesitation. 'Of course.'

Together, they boarded a train north and made their way to halls of residence where they were refused admission. Retreating to the university registry, Sadie held Annie's hand while an embarrassed member of staff informed Annie that her daughter had instructed them that no information whatsoever was to be given out and by law they must observe this edict.

There was no redress and nothing to be done. Sadie took Annie home, held her while she sobbed helplessly and coaxed her into bed. She knelt down beside it. 'You must be strong, Annie. You mustn't give in.'

How not to give in? In the days that followed Annie roamed the house like a wounded animal. Mia's waterproof still hung on the peg. A pair of black jeans was in the laundry pile. Her old school bag lay abandoned in a cupboard.

The doorbell rang. One of Tom's contacts had sent them a box of expensive chocolates as a thank-you for dinner. 'Such a lovely evening . . .' and so on and so forth. Nauseated, Annie glared at the luxurious confection of box and ribbon, clawed it open and tipped the contents into the bin. There, she thought. *There.*

She bore the violated box upstairs and placed in it (1) a pair of Mia's laundered socks, (2) a torn maths exercise book, (3) a copy of *Where the Wild Things Are* in which, long before, Mia had written 'Belongs to ME'. Later, when it came, she added the letter.

Sometimes Annie could trust herself only to take the box out of its hiding place and look at it. Sometimes she teased the lid open the merest fraction with a finger, terrified that Mia would escape entirely. These relics of a childhood breathed longing and sorrow, things broken and festering. They conjured, too, a time when Annie had been happy, and she caught her breath at the precariousness of it, and the waste that life could turn out to be.

Only half joking, she had once remarked to Sadie, 'If only I had known about having children.'

'You're not serious?'

Annie tugged at a curl. *'No.'*

39

All the same, they agreed that Annie producing three children in three years was not the most cunning game-plan ever devised. 'It kinda wrings a girl out. Neither body nor soul remains honeymoon fresh,' Sadie remarked, in the Scarlett O'Hara drawl that had so fascinated the teenage Mia and Emily.

At the time they were having dinner in the House of Commons where she and Sadie sometimes holed up. The dining room was agreeably warm, full and noisy. A television screen in the corner revealed an almost full debating chamber with the Members stacked on the benches. Tom was working and Andrew, having crammed in a first course, had returned to the chamber for a big vote on the use of CCTV cameras.

Sadie was right. Three toddlers under five was plain bad strategy (and two of the many consequences were an enlarged waistline and fatigued skin tone). 'Emily wasn't planned,' said Annie. 'The twins were quite enough. But . . .' Sadie raised her eyebrows and Annie said, 'But Tom and I got carried away by – I quote from the catalogue – "the never-to-be-repeated bottle of Château Lynch-Bages, Pauillac, 1996".' She smiled at Sadie. 'Our look-out, and I could never wish any of the children away.'

'Even if they try to kill you with exhaustion and boredom?'

'Especially if,' said Annie. 'But it's lucky I'm not Napoleon.' She was keeping half an eye on the celebrity count in the tea-room. 'I would have lost the battles of Borodino and Austerlitz in one fell swoop.'

'Come again?' said Sadie, unversed in European history.

'Deficient in forward planning. Look, isn't that the Chancellor?'

The division bell rang for the vote and the television screen in the corner went temporarily blank.

Sadie said severely, 'Pay attention to me, Annie, and don't rubber-neck.' She put down her cup, placed her elbows on the table and leaned forward. 'So, what do we want?'

. . . 'Crazy, crazy woman,' said Tom, on their honeymoon. They had had hardly a penny between them, he loved fresh air and she loved walking. So, he had bought them both a pair of hiking boots and carried her away to the mountains above Salzburg. Of course, she couldn't (and didn't) resist twirling round and round in a green alpine meadow and singing, 'The hills are alive . . .'

When she came to a stop, he was looking at her with his heart in his eyes. 'You're embarrassing. Do you know that?'

She had laughed. 'Very embarrassing?'

'Off the scale.'

Down the years she remembered the iced-water quality of the air rushing down into her heaving lungs, the sharp peaks and blue sky and that look in his eyes. Tom had taken hold of her. 'I love you beyond speech,' he had said, 'but I have to tell you that you're no good as Julie Andrews.'

There was then nothing more that Annie could have wished for.

Later on, as they had descended through the trees, and dusk was gathering, she heard the owl's call. It had stopped her in her tracks: she was willing a repetition of the strangely beautiful, unsettling sound. She pictured the bird's flurry of down and feathers, its iron hunter body and powerful, unblinking eyes.

Tom had stood beside her, his warmth and closeness as

41

vital to her as her own heartbeat. 'I'll never forget it,' she had told him. 'I'll always listen out for the owl . . .'

Annie swallowed, but the lump in her throat refused to budge. She reached for the water glass. Grieving for remembered happiness did not do any good. Tom and she were different, oh, so different, now. Life lesson, Annie: however often its frames were played and replayed in her mind, the past was not retrievable. It was only a facsimile of a time when she had yearned and burned, and every cell in her crackled with life.

'Yes, what is it we all want?' asked Andrew, materializing above their table. 'Good question.' He sat down and slid his arm around his wife. 'My favourite people,' he said, and reached for his abandoned wine. 'Vote over, thank God.'

Annie thought, Why isn't Tom here?

I wish.

She smiled at Sadie and Andrew. 'You know what? I'd love to go dancing.'

Annie lay in her bed, listened to the wind blowing rain against the window and considered the options.

They could sell the house. To begin with, they hadn't been keen on the south London area where streets of solid family homes had been constructed by speculative builders. But number twenty-two suited them. 'Where else would we find a house that can fit in all of us?' Annie had demanded of a reluctant Tom. 'It's cheapish, spacious, there's a corner shop on the street, and who cares if it's ugly Victorian, not desirable Georgian?'

True, like much of London's housing stock, its anchor on London's earth was precarious. Each season, new cracks sprouted on the walls and in the brickwork. Whether they were the result of winter rain and the clay swelling, or summer drought and the clay shrinking, seemed irrelevant to Annie, who was (irrationally, perhaps) terrified the house would collapse. Tom, though, demanded to know which fissure belonged to which category – 'Because, you stupid twit, if we know precisely what is wrong, we can do something about it.'

Most important was number twenty-two's capacity to shelter the family with breathing space to spare. Over the years, there had been much switching of rooms. Three cramped bedrooms, plus a tiny bathroom, on the top storey had been designated for the children. But Mia had refused to sleep up there and now, with Jake married, only Emily occupied it. Not so long ago, the top of the house had echoed to the sound of Jake's music, to the clump of his biker boots and the incessant buzz of Emily's hairdryer. These days, it was mostly silent, save for the clack of Emily's keyboard and her radio.

Clearing out Mia's bedroom ready for Tom, Annie had unearthed evidence of her secret life in the pile of pamphlets stuffed under the bed. *The A–Z of Communism*, *Attacking the Status Quo from Within*, *Socialism in Today's Capitalist World* – the last having been written by Mia's boyfriend, Pete, in heavy-handed, apocalyptic prose. (She did not add any of these to the box.)

The wind was intensifying and blew a cataract of water against the pane. How particularly cruel it was, she reflected, to lose a job in the bleak no man's land after Christmas when winter had dug in.

Could they sell the house they had bought with such faith

and optimism? Their house. Her *home*. Annie put the option under the heading 'Last Resort'. There were plenty of alternatives over which to fret, including the 'if onlys' and 'things-that-should-have-been done'. Why had they left the roof retiling and the replacement of the sash window in Emily's bedroom until now? If hers was the only income, there were bound to be difficulties with the (hefty) mortgage and she puzzled over how to tackle them. Could they use a percentage of their savings to top-slice it? Or some of Tom's pay-off – surely he would get a pay-off?

They would have to talk about money.

Mental note. First thing in the morning cancel family villa with large pool on Croatian coast for last week in July.

'Family villa with large pool' had been Annie's attempt to weld the components of the family back together. It was big enough to accommodate them all . . . plus the extra bedroom was there for Mia. Just in case. But now she would never know whether turquoise water, meals on a balcony overlooking the bay and daily tomato and feta salads would have produced the right glue.

Jocasta would have no regrets. She didn't like her in-laws much, never bothered to hide her feelings and regarded the family holiday as a chore. Yet an optimistic bit of Annie insisted on believing that the relationship between her and her beautiful daughter-in-law held potential.

Tom had teased her about it. 'You two are never going to be best friends, Annie.' Couldn't she spot a reluctant recruit to the Nicholsons? 'Look,' he had said gently, when he realized that Annie was cast down by this, 'she didn't even bother to turn up when Jake told us they were getting married.' True. Jocasta had been glaringly absent when Jake had dropped his bombshell. A pin-sharp memory. The litter of Sunday papers, Tom and she drinking coffee in the sitting room, Jake leaping to his feet.

'I've got something to say. Mum, Dad . . . Jocasta's pregnant, and I'm going to marry her.'

The announcement had slipped from him with the quasi-defiant, quasi-bravado of the twenty-five-year-old who had suddenly grasped that he had to act forty. Then he had beamed, and joy had danced across his features – and Annie was tipped back to when a tiny boy had begged at every opportunity to sit in her lap and be read a story. (If she closed her eyes, she could still summon up the lemony shampoo fragrance of his hair.)

'Jake, are you sure?' she asked, with an odd sensation in her stomach. *Marriage. Grandchildren.*

Jake sobered up. The vigilant mother in Annie clocked that he was thinner than ever. He was also pale and strained, yet happiness was written all over him. So that was OK, she told herself.

Are you sure? She addressed his back silently, as he stood waiting for Jocasta to arrive at the register office. When he turned to face his bride, sleek and svelte, despite pregnancy, in a tailored grey suit, his happiness had become almost palpable, solid, wrapping him like a piece of clothing.

Not that she and Tom saw much of Jake and Maisie. They retreated into the house in south London, secured by Jocasta's banking salary, and only rarely ventured back to number twenty-two. Annie had hoped Maisie's birth would shake them all together in an upsurge of family emotion. 'What's all the fuss?' was a phrase that often fell from

45

Jocasta's glossy lips and, in so saying, successfully stuck a pin into the excitement of Maisie's arrival.

Annie had expected to be called to arms over babycare. She had pictured herself dispensing advice and taking charge of a shawled baby, soothing it in a way no one else could. She and Zosia had discussed stockpiling baby equipment and food, and how best to make a colicky baby sleep. 'In my country, Annie, the grandmother is very important.' As it transpired, Jocasta was far too efficient to fall back on a grandparent and the call never came.

'Don't be silly,' said Tom, when Annie happened to mention it at one of their almost silent suppers. 'You have a full-time job. Jocasta isn't stupid.'

It didn't stop Annie hoping.

Chapter Five

He never liked to say to others that he was proud of a piece of work, but he thought it privately. And he was proud of this one, plus it was one of his best pieces – which did not necessarily go hand in hand.

Jake inserted the photograph of the dining-room table into the ring-folder and labelled it: 'English walnut. Seats 10'. Since he had started up Nicholson Furniture, some of his projects had proved tricky. But this one had come together in a single smooth, interlocking manoeuvre. The wood had been available, the timetable right, and the client had given Jake his complete trust – the sole instruction being that the table had to be in harmony with the Georgian carvers destined to sit at either end. It was the commission Jake craved, which left him free to indulge his visions unfettered. That was, he believed passionately, the only true way for the artist and craftsman.

Sometimes Jake had to stifle a smile as the businessmen, bankers and trustafarians leafed through his manual of furniture design and put together their dream table or chair with, say, Georgian legs, a Victorian top, finished off with a Carolean flourish. The jumble broke the rules and ran contrary to his instinctive urge to protect the integrity of a piece. But if that was what pleased a client, it had to be done, even if it hurt a little.

'No need to be precious, Jake,' remarked the ever-practical Jocasta, when he mentioned it to her. 'It pays.'

To give an extra little puff to his ego, he riffled through the pages . . . Surely Jocasta could see that the gallery of tables, chairs, book ends and stands possessed a value over and above money?

A sketch of a desk was slotted into the final pocket – and he drew a sharp breath. Mia's desk: sketched quickly and without hesitation. The design was a simple one with strong, contemporary lines that would please the eye and be as functional as possible – 'Do one for me, Jakey. Please. None of your respectful, backward-looking stuff. Make me something to live with now.'

Amused, teasing, concerned (always concerned – with the starving hordes, the otter population and the plight of bees), her voice echoed breathily in his memory. The small, copper-coloured head, which matched his (the product of their father's darkness and Annie's fairness), and thin hands frequently colonized his vision. He was made from her, and she from him, and Mia was part of him. Just as his legs were part of him: always there and not considered that much – unless they were cut off as Mia had cut herself off.

He shut the ring-folder and added it to the nine others on the shelf above the desk.

It was late afternoon and almost dark. Aside from the relatively clean and tidy desk area where he talked to the clients, the workshop celebrated the aromatic mess of the woodsman. Stacked at one end was a pile of carefully selected stock. Cherry, walnut and rosewood, woods that were fabled and beautiful. The workbench ran the length of the windows and harvested the daylight. Racks of shelving, containing his varnishes, smaller pieces of equipment and reference books, took up the opposite wall. In the bench drawer were his electrical appliances – wire, plugs, fuses – all neatly stacked and colour-coded. This was part of him too. Releasing the inner life of a piece of wood was as necessary to him as breathing, but he liked the idea of the potential power of electrical things and had learned how to deal with them. Plus he had figured out when he was quite small that if he found out about things like electricity he had a chance of impressing his father.

The lighting was subtle: Jake had insisted on that and, this evening, it played over the woods and the tools in a way that pleased him profoundly. Aesthetics were important to him – otherwise he would not have been in the business of crafting commissioned work: he would have gone into mass production and made a lot of money. So he quested continually for exactly the right wood, to understand how it would shape up, and how his skill could release its patina and resonance. This was a demanding process, necessitating time, judgement and faith, which, as Jocasta liked to remind him, did not produce enough money to keep a dog in biscuits.

'Just wait,' he promised her. 'You'll be surprised.'

'That's about the only certain thing,' she snapped back.

Jocasta saw herself heading up the New Deal – successful working mother and wife – but without the self-consciousness of the early feminists, and he was proud of her toughness and vigour. 'Just do it,' she always said. 'If clients want rubbish they want rubbish. Why agonize?'

Was she right about the dog-in-biscuits level of remuneration? He consulted the order book and a vague question mark turned into a certainty. The orders were drying up.

The ring-folder stowed, he made his way towards the stacked wood for the last check of the week, sniffing at the dry sweet smell of shavings, the sharper acetone varnishes and the richer aromas from the oils. He placed his hand on the adze lying on the bench, its heft and smoothness fitting into his palm like a good friend's greeting.

After flipping off the lights, he switched on the alarm, locked up and headed for Fulham and home.

The second he opened the front door of their pretty house, Maisie cried out from the kitchen. An already coated and booted Lin shot out from the kitchen into the hall. 'There you are.' She glanced pointedly at her watch.

He registered the annoyance. 'I'm not late.'

She looked a little mutinous. 'No, but I have a date. You can tell Jocasta that Maisie ate a good supper but she needs a bath.'

Jake would never get used to being instructed in his daughter's routines by the posse of clock-watching girls hired to look after her. Lin was the latest in the line and, although Jocasta never got home until late, insisted on debriefing her through Jake or by note. 'You can talk to me about Maisie,' he reminded Lin. 'Quite capable.'

'Sure,' she said. 'I'm off. See yer.' In a trice, she had disappeared out of the door.

When she saw her father, Maisie giggled and waited to be kissed and lifted up. Her head nestled against his shoulder like a baby bird's and he blew gently into her ear, which made her shriek with pleasure. Bringing up a baby was bound to be hard . . . but he, Jake, had resolved to do it right. He would come home every day in good time. He would read her stories. He would listen to her. He would say, *You are wonderful. You are pretty. Don't you mind what anyone says about you.* He would never allow Maisie to become a stranger. He would never allow her to be frightened of him. He would do things with her.

'Let's build a crib together for Mia's dolls,' Tom had suggested to nine-year-old Jake. Jake remembered each word for it had been an interlude of pure happiness. 'I'll get the wood. We can do this together, Jake. Just you and me.' It was begun in a rush of father-son fellowship – but never finished.

Jake carried Maisie into the sitting room and balanced her on his knee. 'This is the way the farmer rides . . .' He bounced her up and down. 'And this is the way the lady rides . . . clip-clop, clip-clop.'

How miraculous she was. How on earth had Maisie acquired her smudged nose, hair like blonde candy floss, a tiny rodent front tooth and huge blue eyes? How was she the result of a night at a hotel in Positano with Jocasta when babies had been the last thing on their minds?

He glanced round the room. The previous nanny had been obsessively tidy but unloving. Lin was more affectionate but less tidy. A pile of toys had been left under the plasma screen. That evidence of carelessness would annoy Jocasta, who liked to come home to a house from which all traces of baby had been exorcized. In addition, there was the tell-tale discard of an empty DVD case – *High Noon* at a glance – plucked from Jake's cherished stack, which meant Lin had been watching it, which she had been asked not to do.

He hauled Maisie on to his lap and tucked her up close. 'And what have you seen, I wonder? Nothing disturbing, I hope.' The marker shot up his worry index and Jake frowned. Until Maisie had activated it in a number of baffling ways, he had been innocent of the worry index. Now it was his daily companion and the innocence of his previous life had vanished. For instance: (a) how to gauge what a twelve-month-old baby could take in from *High Noon*? (b) If it disturbed her, what effect might it have, now and later?

He looked up: Jocasta was watching them from the doorway. 'Hi. I didn't hear you come in.'

'You were occupied.' She continued to observe her husband and daughter with that shrewd look of hers. Apparently satisfied, she unwound a pale green pashmina from around her neck, took off her power-cut jacket and sat down beside him. After a moment, she reached over and took one of Maisie's hands. 'Hi, baby.' Then she leaned back against the cushions and shut her eyes.

'Bad day?'

'You could say that.'

'You're looking lovely,' Jake said, with the uplift her beauty constantly brought him.

Jocasta treated her looks briskly and matter-of-factly. She neither fussed over nor dismissed them, accepting them as part of the package she had been dealt, along with her brains and ambition. She inclined her head. 'Why's Maisie still up? She should be in the bath.'

'I wanted to spend some time with her. I thought you would too.'

'Maybe.' Jocasta plucked Maisie off Jake's lap and kissed

her cheek. Maisie grinned. 'Oh, my God.' Jocasta thrust her back at Jake. 'She needs that bath. I'll do supper.'

So it was with some surprise that Jake, having bathed, dressed and played Maisie a selection of lullaby mobiles, which finally persuaded her to tuck herself into the side of the cot and close her eyes, returned downstairs to find that Jocasta was still in the sitting room and had made no attempt at supper. Instead, she had poured herself some whisky and was consuming it by the window.

'Gone off duty?'

'Maybe.'

'I'm hungry. Get a move on,' he said affectionately.

But Jocasta was disinclined to move. Eventually she set the heavy crystal glass down on the table. 'I want to talk to you.'

'Can't we talk while we eat? Or can't we manage both?'

The corners of her big red mouth turned down. 'You're no good at sarcasm, Jake.' She squared up to him, and a frisson of alarm whispered through him. 'But we have to talk.' She seemed nervy and extra impatient as she paced the room.

'Jocasta, whatever it is, it can't be that bad.' He held up his hands. 'OK. I admit. I forgot to put the washing on.'

She swivelled around. 'I'm leaving you, Jake.'

He grabbed the back of the sofa. 'Have you drunk too much of that stuff?'

'I wish.'

'Not funny, Jocasta.'

'You're right, it's not funny, but it's the truth.'

The sofa offered some sort of support but not much.

'For some time now, Jake . . . I . . .' The normally fluent Jocasta fumbled for the words. 'You know I was never sure about having children . . . and when Maisie was on the way you persuaded me.'

'That's all in the past,' he said flatly. 'Now you've got her, it's quite different.'

'Sorry, but it isn't. Only sentimentalists, of which you are one, Jake, think . . .' She hesitated. 'I know it's conventional wisdom and all that, but you must understand that, sometimes, the right things don't happen.'

Jake unwrapped his fingers from the sofa. 'Stop it.'

But Jocasta's words kept coming. 'I know that you wanted things to work out. And, for your sake, I wanted it too. But you can't pretend what you don't feel.' She was twisting her hands together in a parody of penitence. Jocasta was never penitent. 'I'm sorry. It's my fault for allowing you to persuade me to marry you when I got pregnant.'

Jake groped his way around the sofa and sank down into it. 'Let me get this straight. Because you don't feel like a mother, you propose to leave me and Maisie?'

'Actually, that's not quite it.'

He looked up. 'Get me some of the whisky, please.' Jocasta obliged and Jake cradled the glass between nerveless fingers. 'Go on.'

She had the grace to look away. 'I've met someone . . .' She cut off any response from Jake and rushed on: 'Listen to me, Jake. I don't suit you. I know that and, if you're truthful, you do too. I've met someone who does, and it will be better for everyone in the long run.'

The bromide slipped off her tongue. Easy.

'Who?'

'Another banker.'

'But *who*?' He ran through the possibilities. It couldn't be the heavy-breathing Nick Fison – could it? Or that woman Lucy's husband. He was Mr Big at Goldman's. Wait a minute, there was no time for adultery if you worked for Goldman's . . . and, anyway, many banks and bankers were going down the pan and there were no more jobs . . .

'You wouldn't know him, Jake.' Jocasta read his thoughts, as she sometimes did with uncanny precision. 'He's American and I'm going to live with him in New York. He and I have talked it over. We'll live in the New York flat until his wife moves to LA with the children, and then we'll move into the house in Chatham.'

He watched the beautiful lips articulate his fate.

'Everything's arranged. Noah understands your position and is more than happy to allow me to be generous.'

Jake felt that he had been subjected to a trial without his knowledge and declared guilty and deficient. Then, with a panic he had never before experienced, he thought: Maisie. What about her? 'And have you worked out what's going to happen to Maisie?'

She drew up a chair – one of his, a delicate, pretty thing he had built for her in polished cherry wood. She sat down opposite him. 'Let's talk turkey.'

'What else?'

Jocasta's knuckles whitened. 'I'll move into the spare room. OK?'

'Do what you like.'

She leaned forward and, despite everything, Jake fixed proprietorially on her breasts under her blouse. He knew every inch of that body . . . the white skin that sheened with sweat when they made love, the slightly too long waist and the mole in the fold of her knee. What didn't he know?

He was familiar with the hard light that sprang into her eye when a deal was mooted. He knew, too, that she was greedy and driven – all of which, perversely, drew him to her.

'Jake, listen. You know we only got married because I was pregnant. I'm not proud of it. I'm not proud of anything, and I shouldn't have been sweet-talked into it. I shall go away to New York and leave you in peace. I won't ask anything of you or Maisie. I'll speak to the lawyer and tell him he's to transfer the mortgage to you, and I'll make sure the divorce is fair.'

'Let me get this straight. You're prepared to leave your baby daughter?'

Jocasta flushed violently. 'Yes.'

'My God,' said Jake, each word dropping like a stone. 'It must have been very, very bad for you to do this. You must have hated every minute of being with me.'

Jocasta did not reply. Skirt hitched sexily up her thighs, she regarded Jake with pity and slight contempt – which was far worse than anything else.

'I went shopping twice this week,' Emily confessed to Katya, as they roamed the aisles in Topshop.

'Did you feel bad? You did feel bad. You knew you'd feel bad.'

'OK. OK.'

Katya pulled the Therapist's Face. 'You're resolving your role in your family and the confusion is infecting your work.'

Emily's Therapist's Face was more convincing than Katya's. 'And you're conflicted between the need for constant hot showers and the masochist's urge to suffer.'

'Right.'

'Right.'

She and Katya were pedi-conferencing – an activity stolen from *The West Wing*. On the show, it involved highly significant ambulatory exchanges, preferably in a long corridor with offices opening off it. In real life a department store substituted just fine.

This morning it was thronged and swift progress was impossible. Crowds of fifteen to twenty-somethings (sizes 6–10) exclaimed over the merchandise on the racks, circled at a distance by wistful forty- and fifty-somethings (sizes 14–18), who didn't have a prayer of squeezing into any of the stuff.

Katya halted to examine a rack of T-shirts in oranges and yellows. 'I thought we had a pact that we'd ring each other up if the temptation got too great.'

Katya was a struggling artist, who waitressed at weekends to pay the rent for a room in a concrete block of flats on the edge of Hoxton. There was nowhere to paint in it and no heating. On her more hopeful days, she argued that bodily discomfort was a useful stimulus to creativity. On the not so good days, she confessed to the utter misery of being cold and cramped.

Emily said, 'We should concentrate on some positive imaging. I've worked out that I shop when my confidence is low.'

'Plus the shops are heated.'

Emily felt additionally guilty that she didn't have to fight the bodily discomfort problem. 'Kats, when did you *know* what you wanted to do?'

Katya looked smug. 'I was given paper and crayons when Mum potty-trained me. I just knew.'

They went past Swimwear and Emily felt more inadequate than ever. Her Damascene moment, which had commanded her to write, had arrived only recently. She had been finishing an English paper during finals. It had been hot in the hall, her pen was sticky and the paper was smudged and damp. 'Unlike her sister, Charlotte, who burned for fame and recognition, Emily Brontë rejected the "world without",' she wrote. 'Her rebellion was internal, a battle of the "savage heart" which was "heedless alike of Wealth and Power".' At that moment, she felt very close to her namesake – her own heart in turmoil and rebellious – and the thought flashed into her head: I can be a writer too. By that, she did not mean she could begin to approach anything as good as Emily Brontë's work – the audacity! – but she could inhabit the writer's undercover role with a huge sense of relief.

If the command had been late in arriving, it was, at least, clear. However, exactly what sort of writing was not clear and Emily spent a long time thinking it over. Biography, for example, was very respectable, particularly with men, who maintained it was the only thing they read. Fiction? As far as she could judge, men regarded fiction, especially popular fiction, as a substratum of pulp, the exception being crime. For some reason, violence and death on the page achieved an intellectual credibility that love and hope did not.

But fiction it had to be. At first her choice had been liberating and joyous and she was surprised she hadn't considered it before. It wasn't until she cast back over her childhood and recollected the notebooks filled with stories, which she had kept hidden under the mattress away from the twins, that she realized the foundations of the novelist had been laid.

The thrill of discovering her vocation lasted through the period of intense negotiation with her parents and her retreat to her bedroom/study under the eaves of number twenty-two, where everything was made as comfortable and pleasant for her as she could wish. All of this was before she had plodded painfully to page thirty of the first novel and shuddered to a halt. It was at this point that the silence in the room got to Emily. The air was stifling, the working day endless and her writing stupid. Apart from her mother, everyone was very tactful and kind about it. So much so that Emily ended up feeling like a charity case, *which of course she was.* In a second flash of understanding, she grasped that if her parents had forbidden her to write, she might have done a lot better.

Still, Emily gritted her teeth and got on with it, which was the only honourable thing to do. However, since the news of her father losing his job, it had occurred to her that, maybe, there were changes ahead.

'What about this?' Katya skidded to a halt in front of a rack of skirts and held up one the size of a curtain pelmet.

It was mid-morning and the noise level was rising. Emily felt a slight ache flowering in the back of her head, which she preferred to think was a result of creative tension but was probably more to do with the extra glass of wine the previous evening.

After queuing for twenty minutes to get into a changing room heaving with half-naked bodies, Katya tried on the pelmet and an acid-yellow top. 'Why am I doing this? I can't afford it.'

'That's lucky – neither suits you.'

They fought their way out of the changing room past

the saturnalia of discarded clothes and down the escalator. The pedi-conference recommenced in the basement. 'I went shopping,' Emily confessed, in a low voice, 'because I'm no good.'

Katya switched back to therapist-speak. 'That may or may not be true, Miss Nicholson. I have no way of knowing because you've produced nothing so far . . .'

'Hey . . .'

'But say it is true, how would you expect to get better?'

Emily clashed the hangers on a rack of short-sleeved sweaters. 'By keeping going. Practice. Thought.'

'None of which applies to shopping.'

The hangers made a satisfactory sound. 'You're wrong there, Kats. Completely wrong. Shopping requires both.'

She kissed Katya goodbye at the entrance to the Tube and watched her clatter down the steps. At the bottom, Katya glanced back over her shoulder and sent Emily a little smile. *Courage*.

That was Katya. How she had survived the hell of her warring divorced parents and the gruelling lack of money, Emily didn't know. It had left Katya sweet, flexible, happy to please, but with a certain hardness at the core which ensured that (to Emily's envy) she cruised easily through university, where Emily had met her.

'You're just like a sister,' Emily had told her, the first time she had taken her home and watched her mother fuss over the guest and feed her up with steak and chocolate mousse. Adding silently: *Far more than Mia ever was*.

At that Katya had kissed Emily, her bony fingers digging hard into Emily's back. 'Thank you.' Suddenly Emily realized that, far from relishing her freedom, Katya yearned for a fixed centre and the spider's web of relations and demands that Emily took for granted.

Not surprisingly, her room at home was as she had left it. Apart from Zosia, nobody entered it except herself. 'Wouldn't dare sully the place of creation,' joked Jake.

Her chair was tucked under her desk. Jake had knocked it up in an afternoon with some plywood and MDF and slotted it into a cramped space. It was not one of his better efforts but it would do.

Originally the bed had had a floral headboard (her mother had the worst taste) but she had tacked an alternative in plain blue over it. It was neatly made up and the edges of the quilt hung in the way she preferred. All traces of her previous shopping had been tidied away, the bags stowed in the recycling bin.

Her books on the shelves were colour-coded – 'Ridiculous,' said Jake – her makeup and brushes laid out in the formation she had evolved over the years, and her clothes were bagged or swathed in tissue.

But, to be honest, as a retreat the room sometimes felt barren and infertile. She also felt that she did not entirely belong in it.

The window had been left open a crack and she went to shut it. A streak of dust marred the sill and she wiped it with a tissue. Outside, it was growing dark and, yet again, it had rained. A light from the house opposite shone fretfully into the garden, picking out a clump of leaves and the slick of water on the patio. A wet robin fluffed out damp feathers on the shed, and the local top-cat, a black-and-white bully, stalked towards it.

'"Life wears away – I shall soon be thirty – and I have

done nothing yet,'" she found herself murmuring and gripped the window-sill. That was one of Charlotte Brontë's laments. Emily B had not been so prone to more obvious female neuroses and, in some respects, was more robust. 'And lust of Fame was but a dream/That vanished with the morn . . .' was the (far more laudable) line she had chosen to adopt.

Puzzlingly, the transition from undergraduate to adult had been less easy that she had imagined. It should have been as simple as climbing from one step to another but real life was proving to be . . . well . . . rather real. It was about the cost of bus tickets and National Insurance contributions and wrestling with pensions for forty years hence. Hardest of all, perhaps, was the realization that, in truth, nothing more was expected of Emily than to launch herself on to the same road as millions of others and to negotiate taxes, retirement and bus tickets. If she permitted it, Emily's life would be exactly the same as everyone else's: like a tiny, winking point among the millions of short-lived winking points in the night sky. Then you were gone in an instant – a shadow quickly forgotten. It was precisely the struggle to pin down existence that was where the slippery, exciting, exacting business of writing came in – and, with a burst of renewed passion, she vowed to rededicate herself to it.

There was a knock on the door. Her father poked his head around it. 'Can I come in?'

'Sure.'

As he advanced slowly into the room, Emily regarded him with some anxiety and a great deal of painful love. He looked thinner and had shed the vitality that had been so much part of him.

'Can I sit down?'

Emily pointed to the bed. Tom hitched up his cords and sat on the extreme edge. 'Sorry to be so formal but I want a little word.' He pushed a hand awkwardly through his hair. 'I'll come to the point.' He paused. 'Money. I'm afraid we're going to have to make changes.' She studied his downturned face. 'I hate this, Ems. I wanted very much to give you a chance . . . I believed it was important. Still do. But it's not going to be possible.'

Emily sat down in her chair and folded her hands in a manner she hoped hid *her* savage heart and any incipient rebellion and conveyed maturity. 'You want to stop my allowance.'

'Don't want to, Emily. Have to.'

Rising to an occasion was always exhilarating – the source of a serotonin lift and a moral tick. 'I was going to suggest it, Dad.' This was untrue but her father was not to know that. 'It's only right and you're not to worry about it.'

She went and sat beside him, gazing lovingly into the blue eyes. He was down and beaten, and she couldn't bear it and ached to protect him. 'I'm so sorry, Dad, that this has happened. You don't deserve it.'

'Little Mouse,' he said, using the old name, and leaned against her. At that moment, Emily understood that the transition between the all-powerful parent to the one who needed your protection could happen in the blink of an eye – and when it was least expected.

Her father sighed. 'It was a nice experiment, Emily. I'm pleased you got a bit of time . . . Most people don't. Incidentally, those who are jealous are the nastiest critics but never pay any attention to them.' He leaped up to the window and stared out at the jiggery-pokery, greenery-yallery jumble of pots, gnomes and trellis in the neighbour's garden, which Emily knew so well. 'Of course, you can live here, that goes without saying, but I'm afraid your mother and I will have to ask for a contribution to the bills.'

Emily had the curious sensation that she was moving in slow motion. She bent to retrieve a minute piece of fluff from the carpet and dropped it into the bin. She was tasting the bitterness of a lost opportunity – which she had taken for granted and was now to be snatched away.

'Just one other thing . . .' Her father turned round to face her. 'Keep an eye on your mother, will you? She's been used to a certain . . . standard of living. It might be difficult . . . you know.' He smiled uncertainly at Emily, and his eyes creased at the corners. 'She misses your sister. I know this is unlikely . . . but if you ever *did* hear from her, you would tell us? You wouldn't keep it secret?'

Always Mia, thought Emily. Old/young, male/female, Mia had only to fix those eyes on a listener and describe how she had rescued a tortoise – 'such a darling torty' – from cruel youths who had dropped it into the canal. Or she was starting a campaign to save the poor pigs/chickens from the wicked conditions in which they were kept. Or babies in Africa were dying from malaria and all for the want of a mosquito net . . . and everyone fell in love with her and reached for their chequebooks.

'Of course I'd tell you.'

Chapter Six

Sadie was right. Be strong. If at this particular juncture it seemed a bit ambitious it was, at the very least, a useful ambition on which to attach an anchor. *Think robust. Think survival.*

The morning after Tom had told her his news, she had been up very early. Down in the kitchen, she discovered a half-drunk mug of tea and a slice of toast with only one bite out of it, but Tom was nowhere to be seen. After a search, she tracked him down in the cellar.

According to local lore, an ancient rivulet ran under the street. As a consequence, the cellar smelt damp, musty and – as Annie always fancied – shrouded in time and decay. Whitewash peeled off the walls, the beaten-earth floor was cold and unforgiving, and the space was stuffed with empty bottles, rubbish, abandoned packing cases and racks of Tom's wine.

Looking cold and exhausted, Tom was stacking boxes in a corner.

'Tom, what are you doing down here?'

He did not look round. 'I need to make space for my office stuff that's being sent over.'

'There isn't room. Anyway, won't it spoil? You know, get mouldy?'

He turned round and knocked a couple of empty Kilner jars poised precariously on a makeshift shelf. Grabbing at them, he said, 'You won't want it in the house. You'd hate it.' He shoved the jars back on the shelf. 'Whatever else is going to happen, I wanted to spare you that.'

'Tom.' She stuffed her hands into her jeans pockets. 'It isn't your fault.'

'Isn't it?' His voice warned her not to trespass too far on his feelings. 'It's me they're getting rid of. Oh, I know they dressed it up about splitting the job. But it's true.' He looked away. 'I can read them.'

'Even so.'

He heaved the final box on to the top of the stack. 'Nice to know you don't blame me for that as well as everything else.' The dirt trapped between the boxes made a grinding sound. 'Nice to think you don't plan to crow over me.'

She flushed. 'That was uncalled-for.'

'Was it?'

'Stop it.' Annie knew he was lashing out because he was in anguish. All the same. 'We have to talk properly. About what to do. You know . . .'

'So you can make a list? Let me see . . . at the top. "Re-assure Tom that he's not a failure" . . . Or "Remember to take the old boy to the knackers' yard".'

'Tom, that doesn't help.' Impatient with her own verbal inadequacies, she shrugged helplessly. 'It's claustrophobic down here.'

Tom wiped his dirty fingers on a handkerchief. 'Yes, yes. Talk we must. But I can't think straight at the moment.'

'OK. OK.' She had to give him space. She was *willing* to give him space.

'You don't understand, the job was my life.' His admission

was shocking and she knew it had only been forced from him by desperation.

'I know,' Annie said. *I know.* 'And I do understand. I promise I do.'

He tapped his head. 'You do there,' he said. 'But here?' He tapped his chest.

She responded passionately: 'Tom, don't.' He glanced up at her through narrowed lids. 'I know that look. It means you don't want anyone to know how deep . . . how deep it goes.' She reached over and touched one of the unstable Kilner jars with a fingertip. 'But it's permissible to feel like that.'

He swung away from her. 'Am I so transparent? Yes, yes, of course I am. But, Annie . . .' Over his shoulder he sent her the ghost of a grin. 'But, yes . . . I *am* hurt. Hurting. I feel like . . . like someone has taken a knife to my guts.' Again he turned away. 'I want to kill them.'

She stared at the jars masked in their grime. *Did I really once make raspberry jam? Did Tom once have his job?* 'Tom, let's put your things somewhere else. This is not the place.'

He was bitter, very bitter. 'Why not here, Annie? Bury 'em. Like I'm buried.'

His misery was like a cloud of stinging insects whirling through the rank, confined cellar and it made Annie feel breathless. 'Come upstairs. I'll make the coffee.'

'You go. I'll finish stacking.'

Annie paused at the top of the steps and called down, 'You will get another job. Wait and see.'

He didn't answer.

In the days that followed, Annie left for St Brigid's at the usual time, abandoning Tom to work through his address book and sound out his contacts. In the evenings, he reported that, so far, there was nothing doing.

That week had turned into the next and dwindled to the weekend.

Saturday morning. After an uneasy night, Annie emerged from her bedroom and almost collided with Tom. On impulse, she pulled him into the privacy of her room and shut the door.

'What on earth . . . ?'

Tentatively, she touched his cheek – a gesture that felt odd and out of practice. 'You must talk to me, Tom. I mean . . . if you need to?'

'I'm doing my best.'

'We're not good at talking.'

'Why tell me that?'

'You must say what you feel. I'll listen.' She fixed her gaze on him. 'Tom, you might like to. You might *need* to.'

He looked amazed. 'No, I might not.'

OK. She was wasting her breath and took refuge in pulling back the curtains. The rings clanked and rattled on the rod and daylight flooded in. 'But I wanted to say that I am here.'

Tom acted as if he hadn't heard anything she'd said and inspected a photograph on Annie's dressing-table. It showed Jake and Jocasta wrapped up in outdoor things with Maisie, bundled up like a tiny fat dormouse, between them. 'Didn't know you had this.'

'Taken at Christmas.'

'Jocasta doesn't look that happy.'

'What do you mean?' Annie peered over his shoulder.

'What I said. Jocasta looks unhappy.'

'You mean, she isn't grinning like a maniac?'

Tom replaced the photograph and moved towards the door. 'It doesn't matter.'

'Tom . . .'

But he had vanished and she had no option but to follow him downstairs.

As she entered the kitchen, he held up a sheet of paper. 'What's this?'

'Shopping list.'

'"Micro-economic management",' Tom read out, 'divided into two sections. "Family economies" and "Me".' He looked up. 'That's honest, at least. What comes under the first?'

'Easier to say what doesn't. Organic steak, blueberries and quilted loo paper, that's what. It's Raspo from now on.'

'And "Me"?'

'Me' was more problematic. Of course she could find economies on a list that included hair, facials, waxing and manicures, but not without a pang. Clothes were not so vexed, for Annie had retreated into her blouses, black office skirts and trousers some time ago.

She cut a slice off the loaf and dropped it into the toaster. 'Your mother always said you have to make do with what Mother Nature saw fit to allocate. So, it looks like I'll be giving Mother Nature a go.'

The toaster emitted a clicking noise, which didn't bode well for its general health. 'Should we talk about money?' Her lips were suddenly dry. 'Go over the figures again? We haven't got very far.'

'Yup. We'd better.' Tom poured cereal into a bowl.

'Did you talk to Emily?' Annie asked eventually.

'Yes.' Tom was even more clipped.

'And?'

'As you might expect, Emily understood. She's a good girl.'

She placed the toast in front of Tom. 'You must eat.' She watched him play with the cereal. 'What are you going to do today?'

'Unpack the stuff from the office.' Pause. 'Actually, I thought the shed might be better. I might tackle clearing it out. It hasn't been touched for years.' He roused himself visibly to ask. 'And you?'

'Oh, shopping as usual,' she said, through gritted teeth.

Instead of saying, 'I'll give you a hand,' which would have been really very helpful, Tom said, 'OK, I'll be here when you get back.'

A little later, Annie threw the shopping bags into the back seat of the car and drove off. The radio crackled with predictions of financial Armageddon. Annie listened and thought, *It'll be over soon, surely*. Then she changed her mind: *Perhaps it won't*. A banking expert came on to talk about what happened when a bank went bust, and she found herself shivering because it all seemed too close to home.

Outgoings versus income? There was not going to be much competition as to which was greater. Maynard Keynes advocated spending your way out of recession but most of the Nicholson reserves of wealth (which had never been that great) had been expended before the axes of redundancy and economic uncertainties had fallen.

Think of Christmas only a few weeks back. Blush pink roses ('flown in' – so the upmarket supermarket label had read – 'from Kenya') for the table decoration. Expertly picked, they had looked magical with tiny white lights woven around ivy at the base of the vase – Annie's homage to the old masters. There had been almonds from Jordan, ginger from Indonesia and chocolates from Belgium. The bronze-fleshed turkey had been hand-reared and exuded (in theory anyway) a fragrance of the wild herbs that had been mixed into its feed. The Christmas cake had been made with bitter black cherries, doused with vintage brandy and hand-painted with holly and ivy motifs. Et cetera. Et cetera.

Tom had said, 'You're so good at detail, Annie.' But she was pretty sure it had not been a compliment.

Annie checked the rear-view mirror before turning left into the supermarket car park.

'Micro-economic management' went her notes.

(1) *No ready-made meals.*

The aisles groaned with French cheeses, fine wines, expensive meat and vegetables. List in hand, Annie cruised up and down, searching out the unfamiliar nooks and aisles that housed the store-brand and economy products. She even hunted in the reduced-price section, which she usually avoided because it was wrong to snaffle up things for which you could afford to pay full price when others couldn't.

As her hand hovered over a bottle of half-price bleach, Annie had the odd notion that her brain was changing. Make do and mend . . . The message shot down the neural pathways. She snatched up the bleach and slotted it into her basket.

(2) *Have list and do not deviate from it.*

Wrapped in a pale pink pashmina, the woman in front of her was executing the Supermarket Manoeuvre. Arm out, sweep products smoothly into trolley, move on. Arm out . . . It was a highly trained performance and had taken years of practice.

Yet another ultra-thin woman halted in front of the With-out section and netted gluten-free bread, lactose-free biscuits and dairy-free cheese. Not losing a beat, she moved on.

Sadie was a great believer in mental reprogramming. She was always rabbiting on about it. OK, Sadie, she thought, a trifle grimly. This previously careless (meaning, without care) happy shopper must undergo metamorphosis into a careful, prudent one.

(3) *Buy store brands.*

Annie applied a stiff dose of internal abrasive. The years of plenty had taken their hold and, she had to confess, the spirit was not entirely willing. Halting in front of the dish-washer section, she was faced by the ecologically OK brand she normally purchased, which was more expensive than the brands considered harmful to the environment. She hovered, fretted, considered and finally plumped for a cheaper one.

(4) *Pay with cash.*

'Excuse me.' It was the woman in the pink pashmina. 'Do you know if they have lobster here?'

Later, unpacking in the kitchen on her return, Annie was surprised to see that the total haul was still as bulky – and the bill had not been much reduced. She sat down to check it.

While she was thus occupied Emily, resembling nothing so much as a blind mole, shuffled into the kitchen and dropped a pile of laundry on the floor.

Annie glanced at her watch: mid-morning. Not so unusual. 'What sort of time is this?' She cupped her chin in her hands. 'Were you writing last night?' Emily shrugged. 'Did it go well?'

Emily stuffed a couple of bras, a pair of yellow and grey striped socks (the wasps), knickers in all shades, including a thong that resembled garden twine, into the washing-machine. 'It's OK, Mum, you needn't feel obliged to be interested.'

'But I am.'

Emily threw her a look. She slammed the machine door shut and twiddled the dial. 'I was up late looking for a job. The novel will have to wait.'

Annie twisted the bill between her fingers. 'Will you believe me when I say I'm sorry?'

Emily now made for the kettle. 'Let's not talk about it. OK. You want me to get a job. I'll try to get a job. End of.'

That scraped the raw place in Annie's heart. Emily was out to emphasize their differences in a manner that hurt. Of course children were different and separate from their parents, she told herself. Of course she mustn't waste time thinking it could be any other way.

Emily had never confided, would probably never confide, in Annie about The Writing – those confidences were reserved for Tom. But neither did they talk much about other things, which Annie longed to do.

What do you think, she might have expected to ask Emily, *of your boyfriend, or current politics, the latest novel . . . ?* Or, if she ever got married, would Emily want a white wedding dress?

Annie watched Emily slap the lid on the kettle, and an old sorrow drilled away like a maddened woodpecker. With a rush, she asked, 'You haven't heard anything from Mia, have you?'

'Nope.' Emily filled the kettle. 'And, frankly, I'd rather not.'

Emily had never spoken so plainly before, and Annie was taken aback. 'Emily, that's an awful thing to say.'

Emily dropped a teabag into a mug. 'The way I feel at the moment.'

'Ah,' said Annie. 'Goodbye to writing is hard.' She laid the back of her hand fleetingly against Emily's cheek. 'I'm so sorry.'

'Yes, I'm officially joining the grown-ups.' She softened. 'Sorry, Mum. That was awful of me. Early-morning grouch. But since we're on the subject . . . it's just . . . When Mia lived here everything she did was right, and everything I did was wrong.' She poured boiling water into the mug.

'That's not true.'

Emily lifted her eyes briefly from the task in hand. 'If you say so.' Her tone was final. She jabbed at the teabag. 'But she was your favourite . . .'

'Not true either.'

Emily barely took a breath. 'It's always puzzled me, Mum, that you of all people gave up looking for her.'

'I did try, you know that. But the university wouldn't help.' Annie's stomach contracted at the memory. 'They weren't allowed to tell me where she had moved to. Otherwise I would have gone there.' She pushed the milk jug over to Emily. 'It's much easier than I imagined to go missing if you're really determined. I went to see someone about it and they told me it's surprisingly common. Children do fall out with their parents. A lot. And irrevocably. Mia was over

74

twenty-one and she had made her mind up. Then . . . then she sent me a letter. After that . . .' She shrugged and turned away so that Emily couldn't see her distress.

Emily bent down to check the washing-machine. 'Would you have come after me, Mum?'

'You know I would.'

'And you wouldn't have given up?'

Annie turned back to her. 'How do you know I've given up?'

'But you have.'

'No, I haven't. I think about her . . . one day . . . Emily, I *haven't* given up.'

Emily was sceptical. 'OK, Mum. OK.' She grabbed a banana from the fruit bowl. 'Where's Dad?'

'No idea.'

Emily swallowed a mouthful of tea, hooked her ankle around a chair leg, sank down on the seat and made an obvious effort to throw herself into this woman-to-woman chat. 'Have you and Dad talked over things yet?'

'Not really.'

All of a sudden she looked severe and very adult. 'Mum. Dad's lost his job, for God's sake. You *should* be talking it through.'

Emily was right. Annie shifted uncomfortably. 'It's not so easy,' she said.

Mummified in the duvet, Tom dreamed the dream that had tormented him most nights since his sacking. No, no, not sacking . . . *redundancy*.

Once again, he strides into his office in central London, its cluttered and frequently dusty aspect a testament to how

75

hard he concentrates on the important issues. There are books piled with abandon on the desks and floors, potted plants, unclaimed coffee mugs, unexplained sheets of plastic, a pair of scissors cast aside on a desk top. He stops to survey it and to listen to the hum that sounds underneath the general clatter – the hum of connection to the world he so richly enjoys. This place is a nexus, a hub, and is known the world over, and he, Tom, plays his part in it.

Maddie is already at work, tapping away on her keyboard, and the agendas for three meetings scheduled for the day are laid out on his desk. He seizes the first. 'Outreach Strategy for the Upcoming Year'. His name figures a satisfying second on the circulation list, below that of the chief executive's.

Then he is transported to the meeting room, cunningly constructed with the minimum of light and fresh air to cause narcolepsy within fifteen minutes. Never mind: Tom is in his element, dominating the meeting, enjoying the attention of the chief executive.

In the office, the urgent phone calls are backing up. Maddie hands him the list of 'must do' for that day, and he sits back in the chair with a sensation of invincibility. It has taken years and hard graft for Tom and his peers to get where they are and they enjoy to the hilt playing Lords of the Universe.

'It was,' he tells Annie, who mysteriously materializes in the dream, 'about passion, commitment and the excitement of communicating. It was about not giving up.'

He woke shaking. He hadn't eaten the previous night and, come to think about it, he hadn't bothered with lunch either. His stomach growled.

It was over. It was all over – that life. It had ended as he walked out with the P45 and a cardboard box containing the few contact details he had managed to secrete, rubber bands, a half-finished tube of cough sweets, a stapler . . . and the rest of the useless stuff.

It was not yet dawn and the chill of a winter Monday morning was cradled in the unheated house. He knew he had to get out. Still stupefied with sleep and dreams, he got dressed in his corduroy office suit by mistake. No matter. Stopping only to grab his overcoat and scarf, he let himself out of the sleeping house and walked rapidly down the streets.

He hadn't thought what he was doing – but his feet of their own accord took a route he knew as well as the lines on his hand. Short walk. Bus. Another short walk past newsagents, the Inns of Court, the area where pigeons congregated and the latest coffee shop to arrive in the area.

Viewed from the pavement, his old office looked just the same – a smallish window among several dozen in a magisterial block. It had a sill that required maintenance and offered a convenient hotel for the summer pigeon that found its way there each year, only to disappear in winter. Office bets were that it *was* the same pigeon.

He shaded his eyes and gazed for a long time up at the building in which he had spent a considerable part of his life. It was extraordinary, *unthinkable*, that he had nothing more to do with it, or it with him.

It was fashionable to say that work should not dominate an individual's life. But Tom rejected that as dogma. If you loved something, believed in it, sacrificed for it, then it was going to dominate. Stupid to deny it.

He paced up and down for a little while, keeping the square block in his sights. Then he grew jumpy, and a blush of embarrassment and humiliation suffused him. What if any of his former colleagues saw him – a superannuated, ghostly figure haunting his former glories?

He fled towards the narrow strip of the embankment that opened up into gardens. Here, in the semi-dark, he sat on a park bench and contemplated the river in which was reflected the city lights. On the bench opposite a tramp slept, wrapped in newspaper, cider bottles littered by his feet. The faintest of mists hung over a sluggish river. The scene had its beauty, a little unearthly, a little tacky.

Dropping his head into his hands, Tom's tears soaked his fingers. There was no logical reason to feel ashamed, yet he did. And guilty . . . He carried a sufficiency of that already. He was letting the family down. *Thank God no one could see him here.* How would they cope financially? Who would employ him? Why him? What would he tell people? *Thank God he had held his head high when he left.* What would his friends and colleagues think? Used to the Tom with the top, interesting job, how would they view the Tom with no job?

Combing methodically through his memory, he tried to unearth the reasons why *he* had been chosen to go.

A second tramp shuffled by, a plastic bag stuffed into his coat pocket.

Tom fingered the cuff of his redundant suit. The cold crept around his feet, his stomach lurched and his loneliness settled like ice around him.

Welcome to the world of the outcast and the sad.

He wished he could talk to someone. *Annie, Annie, why have we forsaken each other? Will you understand, or is it too late? Is there nothing I can do to put it right?*

The chimes of Big Ben rang eight o'clock. Decided, stentorian sounds that summoned workers to their jobs. But not him.

Cold and stiff, Tom returned home for breakfast. Neither Annie nor Emily asked any questions but watched him devour his toast and coffee with a tactful sympathy that set his teeth on edge.

Afterwards he grabbed Annie as she was putting on her coat. 'Got five minutes?'

She glanced at her watch and said, 'If we're quick', a reminder – as if he needed it – that she had a meeting. Tom ushered her upstairs, booted up the computer and pointed to various columns on the screen. 'Just so you have an idea. This is the money we have in the bank. This is my pay-off. This is your income. And these,' he pointed to the fattest and fullest column, 'are the outgoings.'

Annie examined the screen. 'Seems doable.' Carefully neutral, she added, and he knew she was trying to spare his feelings, 'For the time being.'

'For the time being?'

'Until you get a job.'

Tom pointed to a figure in a column. 'Do you still think we can manage on that?'

'We'll have to.' Annie was searching in her handbag. She produced a hair tie, pulled back her hair and anchored it. 'If we can't we'll have to plunder your pay-off.'

'I've been meaning to talk to you about that,' said Tom. 'I've been advised to put most of it into a pension. It helps the tax position.'

Annie peered at the screen. 'Is that wise? Aren't the markets a bit queasy out there?'

'The adviser reckons it's only a hiccup,' he said. 'By the autumn things will be on the rise again.'

'That leaves us with practically no capital.' Annie looked round. 'Tom, you didn't tell me you were going to see someone about the money.'

'No.'

'I see.' She stuck her hands into her coat pockets. 'You didn't think I should be there?' There was a glimmer of hurt and sadness – which hurt Tom too.

In the circumstances, it was a reasonable question – but he didn't know how to answer it. Not least because he felt a fool and a failure. Not least because he felt he couldn't communicate with his wife. *Tom, the great communicator.* Instead, he reeled off a list of financial arrangements that was made up of pension down-payments and locked-in savings-account deposits. 'But I can't expect much from any of it at the moment. Interest rates, et cetera.' He appealed directly to her: 'It's too early for me to take the company pension without incurring a huge penalty. Are you OK with that?'

'So your pay-off is more or less used up?'

He glanced at the screen. 'That's right.'

'You should have consulted me, Tom.'

'Yes.'

The bedroom was far too warm. Tom got up to turn the radiator off and open the window. 'We'll have to ration the heating.'

'So you *are* relying on my salary.'

Tom thought of his early life and beliefs. Then – and Annie had often heard him do so – he had denounced the power of money as corrupting. 'Be careful what you wish for . . .' ran the old Chinese maxim. 'Correct.'

Head to one side, she considered this new configuration in the family finances, one that, to a degree, tipped the balance of power in her favour. 'Right,' she said, and Tom could have sworn she was not displeased – and he hated that.

Remember when the twins were born? Before their arrival, she had staggered around in a daze, a mass of aches, pains and alarms, finally grounded at thirty-two weeks by the weight of two babies pressing down into her pelvis. He had ferried the groaning, incontinent, nervous, thick-witted (by her own admission) Annie into the hospital and sat impatiently beside her, primed to provide steady, reassuring, consoling back-up. But, as the machinery of birth swung into action, he had been pushed aside. Instead he had observed from the wings a centre-stage Annie taking triumphant charge as her – their – babies debuted in the world.

Very much as she was taking charge now.

A shoal of fish with brightly coloured fins and tails swam across the screen, which then went blank. Tom pressed a button, and a graph of the UK stock market flashed up, detailing a jagged, uncertain path – like a drunkard's.

'Tom,' said Annie, from behind him, 'I do think that if you're relying on me financially, if only for short time, you should have taken me with you to see the financial consultant.' He looked round. She was buttoning her coat in an unnecessarily exaggerated manner. 'I won't go on about it because I know it's difficult for you. But . . .'

His face burned. 'Won't you be late for work?'

At the weekend, Tom announced he was off to see his mother to break the news. Annie offered to accompany him but he knew he had to deal with this alone. She thrust a bundle of magazines into his hands. 'Take her these.'

'Shall I give her your love?

Annie hesitated. 'Yes, do. Of course.'

Traffic was bad around Streatham, which meant that the car was in danger of overheating, a habit it had recently developed. *Oh, God, would they need a new car?* He wound down the window, and a cocktail of fumes and cold air slapped him in the face, reminding him how he hated the interminable tundra between Christmas and spring. How he longed for sunshine, buds on trees and inconvenient café overspill on pavements.

Reflecting on what he was going to say to his mother, he acknowledged that he should have brought Annie along. Hermione might not be Annie's favourite person, but his wife's mediation skills would have helped to negotiate this tricky visit in a civilized manner. Annie was all too aware that he could flare up at his mother's (frequent) criticisms and, all too easily, end up saying something unforgivable.

Remember?

. . . Annie informing him she was catching the train to Manchester in order to find Mia. 'You must come too,' she had told him, in the new, cold way she had adopted since that awful night. He owed his daughter that, she said. *After what he had said.*

But he hadn't gone. Annie had, but she had returned empty-handed . . .

The queue of traffic edged past the street market, which was in full swing. Exotic fruits were piled high on the stalls – mangoes, papayas, guavas and plantain were being dished out with amazing speed and a rat-tat-tat of repartee. On the fish stall, red mullet, sea bass and gurnard stuck their heads out of crushed ice, and cheap leather belts hung like ancient biltong on an adjacent stall. It struck Tom that it had been a long time since he had been out and about during the week in a non-working capacity, triggering a fresh surge of misery.

The questions ground on in his head.

How long had everyone known at the office? Had he been secretly marked with failure? Had it sat grinning on his shoulder for everyone to stare at except him? Had he failed the test-he-hadn't-known-he-was-sitting long ago and the bosses played him out until it suited them?

What he needed was a *Rough Guide* to the parallel world of the unemployed to instruct him on unemployed behaviour and what to do next.

Don't you worry. Their loss. Plenty more jobs . . . What if the kindly intentioned friends and relations who had phoned or spoken up knew nothing? What if the financial cataclysm outside was so bad that men – correction, *people* – like him had seen the back of their final job? And what could you do about age?

Cursing, he opened the window and breathed deeply.

Half an hour of grinding traffic further on, he arrived at the Manor House Home and, since the tally of visitors was always below zero, slotted into the car park in one automatic manoeuvre. Switching off the engine, Tom nerved himself.

Mother, I've lost my job. Or, *Oh, by the way, I don't work for the BBC any more.*

He got out of the car and almost slipped on a leaf-slick from the enormous sycamore shielding the home from the car park. Here, the air was sweeter and gentler, and the garden surrounding the house presented an attractive vista of greens and browns. It was all pleasing enough but, in his view, it could not in any way surpass the allure of London's dirty, clogged streets and its shriek of traffic. Furthermore, this was the last place he wished to be.

His finger hovered over the speed dial on his mobile. James would have something bracing and acerbic to say about the feminization of feelings. *We all have to bloody wail, these days.* Then he remembered James was no longer part of his life.

He couldn't confide to James that he wanted his job back, with a deep, visceral longing. Or that its loss had destabilized him almost to the point of breakdown – which he feared. He wouldn't be the first or the last to lose his wits over a job which had been taken away.

Approaching the house, Tom almost collided with a tall, unsteady figure clinging to a low wall. He hastened forward. 'Hallo, Colonel. Are you having trouble?'

Colonel Anscombe looked up with a pair of cataract-clouded eyes. 'Can't quite think where I am.'

'Near the front door. Is that where you want to be?' Tom hooked his arm gently through the colonel's – the old gentleman was wearing one lace-up shoe and one dilapidated slipper.

'Where I want to be?' The colonel seemed startled by the question. 'I want to go home and to bed with my wife.'

Tom swallowed. Colonel Anscombe's wife had died some ten years previously and his yearning for her neither wavered nor diminished. It was one of the constants of the Manor House Home.

'Take me home.'

The appeal was piteous and, faced with such distress

about which nothing could be done, Tom's own concerns receded. He glanced at the front porch where Esther, one of the care workers, was remonstrating with Mr Gilchrist who was carrying an old-fashioned, and very battered, attaché case. This was quite normal. From time to time, Mr Gilchrist's memory developed a snag and he believed that he was sailing on HMS *Windrush* from Jamaica to the UK and was required to guard his luggage.

'OK, Colonel, shall we get you inside and see if we can find a matching shoe? The slipper looks a bit treacherous.'

Having delivered him safely into the care of Esther, Tom skirted around the main wing. The plate-glass windows allowed the inhabitants – he had to stop himself referring to them as 'inmates' – a view of the garden. They also permitted you to see in.

As usual, the television was switched on in the lounge. In the chairs clustered around it, Mrs Taylor was staring hard at the screen, but her companions were mostly asleep.

His mother was playing bridge in the conservatory and bullying her partner. 'Do keep up, dear,' Tom overheard her say, in chilling tones, to the misfortunate paired with her.

Tom had inherited her dark colouring but, at eighty-two, her hair was now white, and the only suggestion of that mitochondrial link remained in her dark-grey eyebrows. Through the glass, she appeared more diminished than he remembered from the last visit. When he was small, she had always been whippet thin, but *strong*, and a Turkish cigarette would have been in evidence when she played cards (smoked fastidiously down to the stub).

Her decision to sell her house and move into the home had come as a shock. Tom had argued long and hard against it. He didn't know about care homes and what happened in them, but he felt instinctively they went against the grain. Think communal eating and sheets you could never be quite sure belonged to you.

'You don't know,' Hermione had countered. 'You don't know how dark it is when you're alone.'

'But you like living on your own.' Tom had been genuinely astonished.

'Only while I liked it,' she replied. 'Now I don't.' She had looked away. 'My body aches, Tom. It's not going to hold out for ever.'

As he watched, Hermione manipulated a card between increasingly swollen fingers, laid it on the baize and snaffled the trick. Her opponents – three of her cronies dressed in the uniform of elastic-waisted skirts, Viyella blouses and long cardigans – looked fed up.

It seemed to the grieving, shattered Tom that the scene possessed a ghostly quality. Life continued helter-skelter outside that picture window but it no longer involved those behind it. His mother turned her head and the once strong profile was presented to her son. 'Work is the great thing,' she was fond of reiterating, and had brought up her son to regard it as his first priority. She was equally fond of the truism 'Girls are different', but would never specify exactly how different.

He imagined his mother's reaction to his news. A slight narrowing of the eyes. A hint of chill stealing into the precise tones. A flicker of alarm and contempt. 'In my youth,' she was also fond of saying, 'men earned and women worked.'

Tom turned on his heel and fled.

Fool. Coward.
Jobless.

Emily had overslept again – whenever did she not? Hurrying out to a meeting in the City, Annie stopped to talk to her as she mooched over a late breakfast of yoghurt and tea. 'The writing . . .' she reiterated. 'You can take it up later.'

Emily winced. 'Stop right there, Mum.' Her tone was intended to banish Annie into the Arctic regions inhabited by tactless mothers. 'I don't expect you to understand, so there's no point in discussing it.' She dipped her spoon into the bowl. 'Dad's given me my marching orders and I'm ready to sell my soul. I *know* I've been indulged. OK?'

Annie ploughed on: 'Writing is always better when you're a bit older.'

Emily clattered her spoon dismissively. 'You're not to worry about *me*, OK?'

Annie knew that Emily's subtext was, *Not while you've got Mia to worry about.*

Time flowed backwards through the kitchen, pulling Annie through its hoops. She heard the echoes of three young children, heard herself scolding the seven-year-old Emily while a detached ten-year-old Mia observed.

She was unprepared for Emily's next remark. 'Mia was easier to deal with, wasn't she?'

Startled, she stumbled over the answer: 'I thought we'd been over all this . . . She wasn't my favourite. She wasn't easier . . .'

'Oh, yes, she was. Plus she did everything better. I've always been the difficult one. Or, rather, that's how you see

87

me.' Emily smiled grimly. 'It's OK, I'm used to it.' She added, 'Dad understands.'

Annie tried not to mind that, beside Tom, she was found wanting. 'Aren't we past all that, Em?'

Emily returned to the yoghurt. 'Sorry. You're right. I worry what *you* think, and you don't know what *I'm* thinking and none of us knows what Mia feels. It's a mess.'

The words were harshly uttered for Emily had not been endowed with an easy manner. While Mia had only to smile and raise a finger and people ran in all directions to do her bidding, Emily scrapped and fought to survive at school, and slunk home more than once with knees patchworked with grazes from playground encounters. Annie had endured many a sleepless night.

Annie braced herself. 'Can we discuss it another time? I'm a bit pushed.'

'Not a subject you wish to tackle? Sure. Point taken.' Emily jumped up and shoved her bowl into the dishwasher. After a moment, she turned round and said quietly, 'You know what today is, don't you?'

'Yes.'

'Five years today since she went.'

'Yes.'

'And you can think of nothing else.'

It was a statement, not a question. 'Yes.'

'Me too.'

A sharp prod of surprise under Annie's ribs. 'I didn't think you'd remember.'

Emily sighed ostentatiously. 'What do you expect, Mum? The family feeds off my sister's absence.' Annie's hand flew to her hair and Emily's blue eyes narrowed. 'Calm down,

Mum. Calm. OK?' There was a pause while all manner of history sifted past, and then she continued, 'You're right. We must concentrate on Dad.'

'Actually, I did want to discuss him, Em. Can I? I'm a bit worried about him. Will you keep an eye on him? He's going to need a lot of TLC . . .' She visualized the wounded Tom roaming the house. 'Yes, TLC.'

Emily's eyes danced with amusement. 'I love it.'

'Share the joke?'

'Just something Dad said. I hesitate to say this, Mum, but isn't propping up Dad *your* job?'

'It's everyone's job. And don't look like that. We're a family.'

'Now she tells me.'

Annie ignored her. 'He'll have to adjust massively. I've seen it often. Once someone leaves an office, that's it. It's a sort of death. Everyone remembers you, hopefully with affection, but you're no longer vital to it.' She paused. 'You're spoken of in the past tense.'

'Poor Dad.'

'I don't think he's sleeping very well.'

'How would you know, Mum?' Emily inquired, with a tinge of embarrassment.

'Do you expect me to answer that?' Annie gathered up her bag and briefcase. 'So, you will look out for him?'

'I always look out for Dad.'

'Yes, you do.' Annie paused. 'You do.'

Passing the recycling bin on her way out, Annie knocked it askew. She bent to push it back into place and spotted a Christmas card trapped behind it.

It was the one with the detail from the da Vinci painting,

The Virgin of the Rocks, showing the mysterious, yearning angel.

That previous, plenteous, lushly provisioned Christmas, which the angel had been sent to celebrate, had been Annie's creation. All that time and trouble with the décor and details – the shopping lists, the research as to where to buy the best nuts and flowers, the tasting of Christmas cakes, the lavish wrapping of presents. It had consumed and exhausted her, leaving her with no energy to think about anything else.

At Christmas lunch, Tom and she had largely avoided each other's eyes, Jocasta and Hermione had exchanged frosty words over Maisie's feeding habits, and Emily had looked as if she would rather be anywhere than in her own home. Picking her way through the stuffing and thyme-roasted potatoes, Annie had waited for the moment she dreaded.

Tom gave the toast: 'Absent friends . . .'

There it was. The difficult, heart-stopping moment.

You never got over a child's absence. It was the darkness, perpetually encroaching on the living present.

Tom rounded off the offices with 'Happy Christmas,' and held up a glass brimming with excellent claret. 'And, of course, we must toast the cook.' At that, he did look at Annie directly, and her breath was trapped deep in her lungs as it was when she climbed uphill.

Once upon a time her life had contained plenitudes – dance, music, deep, passionate emotions, and a quiverful of children. It still did, of course, but the quiver was a third empty.

Partly her fault.

Pinning the card to the noticeboard beside the fridge that evening, Annie murmured, 'Watch over us.'

Chapter Seven

'Mr Nicholson . . . Tom . . . thank you so much for coming in to see us. We enjoyed talking to you and we discussed your application very seriously.' The chief executive of the magazine company was verging on elderly, perma-tanned and (Tom would swear) Botoxed.

'Delighted,' said Tom, with a sinking feeling. After several interviews such as this one, he was plugged into the vibes.

'But we think that your experience has been a bit limited.' The rictus, a.k.a. smile, stretching the CE's lips would have looked more in place on a piranha. 'The BBC, admirable though it may be, is a cushioned organization. We need someone who understands the marketplace rough-and-tumble at first hand.'

Tom bit the inside of his cheek. *Why the hell had the headhunter set him up for this? Why the hell had he allowed himself to be put forward? Why the hell had they seen him?* He glanced around at the plate-glass-windowed executive office – it was day thirty-six-without-a-job and he was astounded that his life and his work had arrived at this point. He got to his feet.

'Naturally I'm sorry, but it was good to meet you.'

'What's this?'

Tom had returned home from the unsuccessful job interview, which had left him twitchy and humiliated, and was arrested in his tracks by the sight of a new, alarmingly expensive range cooker preening itself in the kitchen.

He dumped his briefcase on the table with a bang. 'Annie, have you gone mad?'

Annie half rose from the table where, if he knew anything, she had been waiting for the storm to break. 'I think I might have.'

'I thought we agreed . . . All the plans for the new kitchen were to be cancelled. You said you'd done it.'

'We did. I did.'

'Well, that didn't arrive here because it just felt like it.'

'They wouldn't take the cancellation for the cooker. It was either that or forfeit the deposit.'

Tom glared at the cooker, which appeared to stare back, an assured arrangement of hobs, ovens and warming trivets. 'You had plenty of time to tell me. Yes? More than enough time to beard me, the unthinking, uncaring dragon, in my den. The *unemployed* dragon. For God's sake, you must have taken time off work.'

'Yes. But I also took the decision not to waste our deposit.'

'Are you sure? Wasn't it that you wanted the cooker?' Tom kept his tone even.

'I wanted it, did I?' A dangerous look flew into Annie's eyes.

She was clearly taken aback by the accusation and he went in for the kill. 'How much?'

She named the sum, and the breath whistled out between his teeth.

He bent down to examine a couple of scratches that had occurred during installation on the cupboards flanking it.

'It was a lot of money to throw away,' Annie had also

modified her tone, 'at any time . . . but especially if you haven't got a job.'

'Throw that in my face, too.' He straightened up. 'Go on.' He moved over to the sink and ran himself a glass of water. 'This should have been a joint decision.'

'I suppose so,' she said indifferently, twisting her mother's diamond ring around her finger. It was an old habit she indulged when she was tired – or at bay. 'But I know you've got a lot on your plate.'

He pointed to the ring. 'Bad night?'

She held his gaze, and the unhappiness in her grey eyes had never been so marked. 'As it happens, yes.'

'Oven on your conscience?'

Annie spread her hands flat on the table. The ring glittered and she seemed totally absorbed in its beauty. 'And who didn't warn me that you were frightened of losing your job? Who went to see the financial consultant without me?'

'OK. OK. I was out of order.'

He inspected the cooker more thoroughly, and fiddled with a couple of the knobs. 'You know, they never paint on the markings with long-lasting paint. It'll wear off.'

'Is that so?'

He turned on one of the hobs and a hollow popping noise filled the hush. 'I haven't told you things because you were unapproachable,' he confessed. 'I didn't want to worry you. You were so busy with the hospital.'

'I'm sorry you thought like that . . .' she was growing angrier '. . . but what do you imagine I've had to put up with all these years while you set up camp in the BBC and proceeded to rule the world? You could barely be bothered to come home after the children got bigger.'

When Annie was angry the tip of her nose coloured. Normally the sight amused him. Not this time. 'No more than your bid to succour the huddled masses. And how well did you look after your family? And, by the way, your nose has turned red.'

Annie looked furious. She hated being reminded of her nose. 'Who are you to talk? The great communicator who can't talk to his family properly. You should hear . . . Jake . . . on the subject.' She folded her hands across her chest. 'I did *not* neglect my children or the family.'

'This bloody cooker.' He opened and banged shut the door of the larger oven.

At moments like these Tom deployed the antidote of good memories – sweet ones, funny ones. Anything.

. . . Spotting Annie walking along the university cause-way outside the library building carrying a heavy canvas satchel of books. The sun had been in her eyes, which made her blink. Her hair was piled high on her head, revealing the swoop of tender, unblemished flesh from neck to back, which he loved to touch. When she saw that he was waiting for her, she broke into a smile of such joy and pleasure that he'd thought his heart would crack . . .

Now he felt a sigh throttle up through him, from a deep, sad place.

Annie dancing. She had loved to dance. *The honeymoon dance.* Ridiculous. Sweet. How often had they made fools of themselves? Being silly, deep into being young . . . He had told himself he had a duty to dance until dawn, whether he wanted to or not, because his youth would pass.

Youth would pass.

He had been right. Why didn't she dance now? Why didn't he?

Annie looked shattered. 'You see, we're at it again.' She turned her head away. 'We shouldn't be. Not now. We should be facing the facts . . .'

She's going to tell me it's all over. The thought went through Tom, bringing in its wake a physical anguish so biting it winded him. Finish to a marriage that had started out so bravely and jauntily? The subject had been aired between them. When had that been? Ah, yes, when they had quarrelled so bitterly over a ready-made stew Annie had served up at dinner party for Tom's colleagues. It had not been a good meal, and he had been embarrassed by what he took to mean as her non-caring. He had accused her of not bothering and she had flashed back at him, 'Do you know the hours I work?' Added, 'What happened to the man I married who wouldn't have cared about the meal?'

Now, he was the one to hit out: 'What facts? There are no facts, except you've bought a cooker we can't afford and somehow neglected to tell me about it.'

. . . 'We should leave each other,' Annie had told him, as they had faced each other over the empty foil cartons of that disastrous ready-made meal. 'And each take our bitterness elsewhere . . .'

'Tom, I just want to help you sort things out. That's all. Not quarrel over a cooker.'

. . . 'Sorry, sorry', she'd apologized, when things had calmed down, as she had tamped the cartons into the bin and out of sight . . .

'Tom?' She pulled a strand of her hair straight. 'Answer me.'

'Not now, Annie.' He felt too weary and beaten to respond. 'Not while I'm like this.'

She bit her lip. 'No. No, of course not.'

She had been wrong not to tell Tom about the cooker, of course she had, and it piqued her that she had been so high-handed.

'I shouldn't have been angry,' she confided to Sadie on the phone. 'He needs help. I must be kind. And there are the children to think about.'

'Here we go,' said Sadie. The childless Sadie, who had scolded her on more than one occasion for being all things to the family.

'It's instinctive,' Annie endeavoured to explain, 'and you don't mind, really. Putting yourself out for good reason has a purpose. It means a lot.' However, as the children had become adults Annie, who had frequently sacrificed her own comfort for them, felt less sacrificial and a great deal tougher. Something to do with the thinning of her female hormones, which, she gathered, happened as you approached the fifty-straight before hammering down the highway to crotchety and demanding old age like Hermione's.

But it was no excuse for taking advantage of Tom's misery.

Sadie was on the case. 'I expect you'll be very British and tell me that you'd never kick a man when he's down and it's up to you to keep the show on the road.'

'I don't want to end not liking myself.'

'What sort of reason is that?'

'An important one.'

Annie climbed into bed, arranged the sheet and duvet comfortably around her and picked up a book from the bedside table. She was halfway through a history of the plague, which had excited her interest when she'd spotted it in a bookshop. She laid it on her knees. Once upon a time Tom had read poetry to her last thing at night. She would drowse as he read a Shakespeare sonnet, a sharp and funny Wendy Cope, or a tough, highly wrought piece of Auden or Eliot. The sound of his voice, the occasional flash of his pyjamas between her closed lids, his closeness – *their* closeness – had made her feel safe, and her love for him was almost a physical hurt. Sometimes he laid a hand on her cheek as he read. Sometimes she was curled up against him – and for ever after she associated the poems with Tom's feel and smell.

She couldn't remember precisely when it had come to an end. Probably around the time Tom was promoted to section chief – the beginning of his career climb and the gradual erosion of the intense, full-on accord of their early marriage, which had left Annie to bear the brunt of childcare.

Nostalgia for that discarded intimacy was painful. Without it, life seemed bleak and troubling. Without it, the plans she used to make for Tom, herself and the family were empty exercises. She laid the plague book aside, padded over to the door and propped it open. The light from Tom's room shone under the door and she observed it thoughtfully.

Leaving the door open, she went back to bed, switched off the light and settled down.

Chapter Eight

It was mid-morning and the house was quiet but, Emily fancied, it had become a watchful place. It was as if the spirits of its occupants gathered behind their respective closed doors and listened out for each other.

She clopped downstairs from her room in clogs. Every step was familiar. Having lived here all of her life, Emily knew every grain of the floorboards, every ruck in the carpet. She found it difficult to imagine ever living anywhere else.

In the weeks since her father had been at home, there had been subtle, almost unnoticeable changes, but changes nevertheless. Now there were two of them ensconced at their laptops scouring the net for jobs. Spring was coming and it was growing marginally warmer and, occasionally, when Emily opened her window, where there had been silence she could hear the urgent click-clack of his keyboard directly below hers.

Tapping on her father's door, she poked her head around it. 'Hi.'

Tom was at the makeshift desk, which he had contrived with a bit of hammering and a sheet of MDF when he had moved into the room. Unsurprisingly, it was ugly and not very convenient. Piles of books and papers fanned around his feet. The window was open and, when Emily pushed the door wide, the papers threatened lift-off and he grabbed at them.

'How are you doing, Em?' He did not look round.

'Seven applications in . . .'

Her father swivelled. 'Who to?'

Emily reeled off a publishing house, a magazine company and a theatrical agency. Plus, the joker in the pack, Condor Oil, who were advertising for an in-house copywriter.

The last had caused her to wake, sweating, in the early hours. What if the near-impossible happened, the arrow hit the target and she found herself at an interview dressed up in office garb?

'Condor Oil is offering a good salary and benefits.' The remark was addressed more to herself than to her father.

'Perhaps I should apply.' He turned back to the screen. 'And what are you doing?'

'Oh, this and that. I've been checking up on your grand-mother's investments,' he said, which surprised Emily for her father rarely discussed the family's finances with her or Jake. 'We rely on them to pay for the care home . . .'

She observed his back and was made aware again that the balance between parent and child was shifting in an alarming manner. The loss of his job had hit him hard, and he seemed so sad and shrunken in spirit. It wasn't just her imagination that his sweater hung more loosely on him. Until recently, she had considered him pretty much invin-cible – the father who sat at the head of the table, who whistled in the garden and humped heavy objects around, whose job gave him a moral authority and glamour.

Putting what she hoped was a comforting hand on his shoulder, she bent over to look at the graph displayed on his screen. 'And what's this?'

When it came the answer was suspiciously nonchalant. 'A bit of spread-betting on the banks. Nothing serious.'

'Banks! You always say you want nothing to do with them.'

Her father's voice sounded strange. 'Might as well get some mileage out of the situation. Get one's own back on the system.'

'OK. Explain.'

Tom dropped his hands into his lap. 'It's a sort of informed guessing game. I agree to bet five pounds a point, say, on the share price of Barclays going up or down. I have to choose.'

'And?'

'In Barclays' case, I reckon it's going up. In February when things were not so good it was four pounds. Just now, there seems to be a bit of a rally in the market and it's climbing. When it reaches four pounds fifty I'll have made two hundred and fifty pounds. More if it climbs further.'

Emily's relationship with fiscal prudence, indeed with money, was enduringly frosty but she knew enough to recognize a suicidal venture. 'Dad, please don't do this. It's mad even for professionals.' She gripped his shoulder hard. 'It's gambling. And it causes trouble. I'm sure Tod's father got into trouble this way.' She thought of the muttering in the press and media and wished she had paid more attention. 'Are you *sure* the market's rallying? You could *lose* a lot of money.'

'Don't worry, I've got it under control. It's not very much money, a couple of hundred pounds.' He looked away and she knew it hurt him to say, 'I've got the time.'

For a wild second or two, she wondered if her father had had a breakdown. This was not him, gambling with graphs and banks. Maybe boredom had driven him to the edge of the cliff. Then, with a slightly sick feeling, she realized he had struck some crazy deal with reason. If he couldn't hold his job, at least he could do this, was probably what he was telling himself, and she was so fearful she could barely speak. Her grip was tight enough to force him to turn and face her. With all the urgency she could muster, she said: 'Dad. Please. Think about it. Not a good plan. It's a very, very bad plan. What happens if you lose?'

'I've set up a stop-loss limit. And I close each night. It's a couple of hundred pounds. Nothing big.'

That was her father all over. Determined. Emily knew it of old and had reason to fear it. It was responsible for many sins – insisting they walk to school at least twice a week and absolutely no Sky television. Oh, and the other fun one, signing the whole family up for skating lessons at the local ice rink on Saturday mornings – to which he had not turned up.

'Does Mum know about this?'

'No. And you mustn't tell her. This is private. I want to surprise her. I'm doing all right at the moment.' He grinned boyishly. 'It feels good, too.'

'Dad . . .' she chose her words carefully '. . . are you doing this because you're not earning any money and as the man you feel you should be?'

He hesitated. 'Good question, if a bit obvious, but no.'

But she knew she had hit on something. To her surprise, Emily heard herself utter, 'You can't *do* this to Mum.'

Now the blue eyes were stormy and suspicious. 'Do I have your word, Emily?'

Mum? Dad? Emily wasn't used to managing secrets at this level. And, although she always maintained she was on her father's side, when it came to a choice she was torn. 'OK,' she said. 'I won't say anything. But how long have you been doing this?'

His eyebrows shot up. *Excuse me.* 'A couple of weeks.'

'And have you made or lost money?' She sounded just like the appalling Miss Burte on Economic Application in Minor Germanic States, for Heaven's sake. When he failed to answer, she continued, 'Dad. This has got to stop. Promise me.'

Still he said nothing, sitting with his hands folded in his lap. Emily gazed down at the crown of the dark head, now flecked with grey. Never before had she engaged with her father on this level, and putting a brake on him was a hurtful process that pulled up those old demarcations by the roots.

The bareness of his/Mia's room almost broke her heart. Save for the narrow single bed, the terrible desk, old-fashioned wardrobe and his corduroy jacket draped over the chair, there was not much evidence that he occupied it in any profound way. It was as if he was only perching there before moving.

The idea made her feel sick.

'Sorry, Dad.' In anguish at his loss of face, she put her arms around him and hugged him. She would have given much to be dealing with the old, overbearing *paterfamilias* again. 'I shouldn't interfere.'

Tom switched off the screen. 'Actually, your mother hasn't gone to work this morning. She's – she's sacking Zosia. I don't want to go downstairs to witness the carnage.'

'Sacking Zosia?'

''Fraid so.'

As they spoke, the front door closed quietly, finally. Tom looked at Emily. Emily looked at Tom.

'It will kill your mother,' he said, and his self-hatred shocked her.

'What will it do to Zosia?'

Together they descended to the kitchen where, her back to the door, a dressed-for-the-office Annie was stowing saucepans in a cupboard.

'Mum?'

Annie stopped what she was doing but did not look round. 'It was awful, if you must know,' she said, in a choked voice. 'Zosia cried. I know it isn't anyone's fault, but I feel we've let her down.' As she turned Emily saw her cheeks were wet. 'Zosia's a friend.'

'I'm sorry,' said Tom.

Emily looked from one to the other. 'Whose decision?'

'Does it matter?' Her mother's cheeks stained a faint pink. She flicked a look at Tom. 'It was a joint one.' She brushed back the lock of hair that tended to tangle over her forehead when she was agitated. 'I gave her a month's money and Pat Hillaby's number. She might get work there.'

'A month,' said Tom.

Annie glared at him.

Emily had clocked the gesture, the very tangled hair and, at the same time, something else. 'Mum, where's your ring?'

Her grandmother's diamond ring. Huge. A five-stone beauty of considerable value on which Emily's eyes had frequently lingered. *Riches I hold in light esteem . . .* Of course she held riches in light esteem, but the ring was something else.

Annie had gone silent.

'You haven't *lost* it, Mum?'

Her mother flapped a hand, another familiar gesture. In the past, Emily had interpreted that as *don't bother me* but, with maturity, she had come to regard it as a sign of acute distress.

'Annie?' inquired Tom, with an edge to his voice.

'Yes.' Another nervous stroke of the hair. 'My ring?' She sent an agonized gaze in Emily's direction. 'I've sold it.'

'What?' He sounded as if a cattle prod had been applied to him.

'To pay for the cooker.' To Emily's horror, tears ran down her mother's cheeks. 'I don't know what Mum would say.' She wiped her face on a sleeve.

Tom grabbed Annie's wrist. The shrunken figure of upstairs had vanished. 'You can't have.' He examined the now naked right hand with its strip of extra white skin on the fourth finger. 'You didn't have to do anything so drastic.'

'Yes, I did. It's my fault we have the cooker.' She cast it a virulent look. 'I had to do something.'

'Oh, Annie,' said Tom. 'I can't bear it.' He turned away. 'I can't bear it.'

Emily's feelings of bereavement for the ring were not entirely straightforward for she had hoped she might inherit it. The shameful thought popped fully formed into her mind: *but neither would Mia.*

Her father was saying, 'You should have asked me. We could have done *something.*'

Her mother sounded resigned. 'I didn't do it to make you feel bad, if that's what you're thinking. I could have done, but that isn't the point. I did it to get us out of a hole.'

'You should have *told* me.'

'Tom, the cooker is paid for. We don't have to worry about it any longer.'

'Mum, Dad,' said Emily. 'There's no point.'

As one, they swung round and faced Emily.

'Don't interfere, Em,' said her mother.

'Emily, I don't think this is your business.'

At first, Emily was inclined to take enormous offence. It was her business: it was everyone's business in this house. They would all have to live with the fallout. Then her parents turning on her in this united fashion when, for once, she was entirely blameless, struck her as funny. She suppressed a grin.

Almost without a beat, her father returned to the fray. 'And will you enjoy a cooker that's cost more than the national debt?'

'You know I won't. So there's no need to rub it in.'

Emily reckoned she was eavesdropping on a private conversation and edged towards the door.

'What on earth made you choose it in the first place?' demanded her father.

Her mother shrugged tiredly. 'Trying to make it all work. Trying to whip up enthusiasm.'

Glancing back, Emily caught a snapshot of her father opening and shutting the new cooker's oven doors, and her mother's bent head as she stuffed a sheaf of notes into her briefcase and snapped it shut.

Oh, my God, she thought. What else could happen to this family?

Jocasta had been sleeping in the spare room and at night after work she packed her belongings, sweeping clothes out of wardrobes, books off shelves, and arranging for her share of the furniture to be taken away.

They argued once or twice over who should have what but mostly not. In a rare show of guilt, Jocasta stuck to her original declaration and insisted that Jake must have the house. As a gesture of goodwill, she would continue to pay her share of the mortgage until the legal side was sorted out.

It took several weeks, and the pretty house was increasingly denuded, but no more so than Jake felt.

As she was finally leaving Jocasta tossed at him, 'Jake, you mustn't blame yourself.'

Her cool, patronizing nerve left him gasping. *Beat a dog when it's down.* Since Jocasta had stuck her knife into his ribs, Jake had barely functioned. He woke up feeling as if the lenses had been wrenched from his eyes and checked more than once in the mirror to verify that the man he could see reflected was still him, Jake Ian Nicholson, who breathed, ate and partially slept. Despite all this, he had not thought to blame himself entirely. It was the one thing to which he clung. 'Get lost,' he said.

'I intend to.' She looked round the sitting room with its comfortable furniture and fashionable lighting, and her gaze rested fleetingly on a pink-dungaree-clad Maisie parked in her chair. 'Don't worry.'

At that he caught her arm and searched her face. 'Honestly, were you never happy with me?'

Yes, she had been. He knew she had been. At times. At first. Before Maisie.

She wouldn't look at him. 'Jake, don't.'

'Tell me.'

'No, not really.'

'Liar.' He was desperate to wring some kind of concession from her.

'As I said, not really.'

Her indifference lashed him like a whip. 'And you really think you'll be happy with this man?'

'With Noah?' She seemed a little startled at the notion. 'Probably. Possibly not. How do we ever know? But I'm taking the risk.'

This was not the response of a woman gagging to throw everything over for a lover, and Jake derived a primitive satisfaction from her lacklustre tone. With a bit of luck, Noah would fare no better than he had. With a bit of luck, Jocasta would make him as miserable as she was making Jake.

He watched and asked sourly, 'And what makes you think you can stay in the US?'

'The bank has arranged everything. I've been promised a transfer. In fact, it suits them, and they're used to dealing with visas et cetera.'

Jocasta shrugged herself into her black cashmere coat. It was cut to fall sharply from the neckline and emphasized what Jake considered her Parisian fragility – a beautifully shaped head set on delicate, bony shoulders.

He snatched Maisie up from her chair and held her out. 'OK. You don't want me. But what about your daughter?'

Jocasta's hand froze. 'I don't want to leave Maisie exactly, but that's the way it's turned out.' She touched Maisie's cheek with a finger and whispered, 'I'm not a natural mother, baby. I know I'm not.' She turned her gaze on Jake. 'It's something I've had to face up to.'

'What I can't get you to understand is that it's not all about you but about Maisie and her needs. How's she going to manage without a mother? I don't believe you don't care about her and what matters to her.'

He carried Maisie over to the window and the pair of

them looked out at a couple of plastic bags being whipped along the street by the breeze. Her mother would be a constant absence in Maisie's little life – and he could have killed Jocasta for it.

The coat fastened, Jocasta picked up her bag and brief-case. 'Can I kiss you goodbye, Jake?'

He ignored her. 'Look, sweetie-pie, there's a big dog over there.'

'Jake . . .'

'Say "dog", Maisie.'

'Jake!'

He swung round so swiftly that he jerked Maisie's head and, instinctively, cradled it against his chest. The agony of the past weeks rose to the surface. 'Go away,' he said. 'Hurry away.'

Jocasta went pale. 'There's no need to sound so . . . dangerous.'

'How lucky you are that everything bounces off you.'

She licked her lips. 'If you mean I refuse to see things in the sentimental way you do, Jake, then I suppose that's true. But I've faced facts, made a decision and, one day, you'll thank me.' She rattled the chain on her key-ring. 'I just thought it would be good to say goodbye in a civilized way.'

The minute quaver in her voice told Jake that Jocasta was not quite as cut and shut about the matter as she would have him believe – and new, alarmingly atavistic, emotions boiled in his chest. 'You've decided to break up this family, Jocasta, and if you imagine I'm going to let you kiss me goodbye, you're mad.'

Jocasta recovered herself and shrugged. 'Then I'll go. Our lawyers will keep us in touch and I'll come over and see Maisie as often as I can.'

Chapter Nine

A few days later, Tom rang Annie at work. 'I'd like to talk to you. Can we meet in the Magpie?'

Tom taking her for a drink was a rare occurrence these days and, more than a little curious, Annie turned up only to discover him moodily flipping a beer mat over and over. Heart sinking, she ordered them a glass of wine each and a packet of salt and vinegar crisps to share. The Magpie was a defiantly unreconstructed old-fashioned pub – none of your glass and chrome but plenty of dark-wood furniture and dimly lit nooks. Seated on banquettes that had seen better times, they faced each other across a table that bore the imprint of many glasses.

'Just like we used to . . .' she said. 'Do you remember?' Before the children, they had met frequently in a pub after Tom finished work to drink beer, eat crisps and play cards or darts.

'Yup.'

She caught the echo of real distress. 'Tom, why couldn't you talk to me at home?'

He looked away. 'Emily's there. But I might as well get to the point.'

'Which is?'

'My mother.' He reached over and laid his hand on Annie's. It was a considered gesture, not genuine, not really meant for her, and she felt the first whisper of alarm. 'You know Hermione relies on her investments to pay the bill for the home?'

'Of course I do.' Now she knew what was coming.

'They are not doing so well at the moment . . . I can't quite figure out why. Too much of the portfolio invested overseas? Cut in US interest rates? An underlying unease? Also, I think we sold a chunk at just the wrong time. Normally, I would pay any shortfall and hope for the best . . .' Tom gripped her hand hard. 'Annie, it looks as though we can't afford to keep her in the home at the moment. I'm going to have to ask you to let her come and live with us.'

'No! Not your mother.' She whipped her hand out from under his. 'That you should even *ask*.' She rubbed her bare finger. 'To live with us? For how long?'

'Till I've sorted it out.'

The anger erupting in Annie shocked her. It was so raw, so unmanageable, so *murderous* – and its surprise was the greater because she had trained herself to live with unmanageable emotions. 'I hate you for even considering it,' she said – and that shocked her too. Her tooth bit hard into her bottom lip – and the discomfort added to her outrage. 'On top of everything else.'

Tom turned white. 'Annie . . . Annie . . . listen to me.'

'Apart from Mia, Hermione has never shown the slightest trace of affection for the children or me. But that doesn't matter, I suppose, unless she comes to live with us. Then it would. Haven't we got enough to cope with?' She knew perfectly well that she was being ungenerous. 'And would you do your share?'

He looked sick. 'For God's sake, I know I haven't done my best in the past. This would be different.'

'How often did you promise to help?' Words were Tom's business. *Had been* his business. She thought of the evenings when she had been left to cope with three small children and then, as night followed day, of the subject that festered between them. 'You never even made time to look for your own daughter. You said you would but you never did.'

'Annie . . .'

'Think how Hermione will feel. What will it do to her?'

'I've got the message.' Tom got to his feet. 'We're getting nowhere.' A stubborn, bitter look closed down his face. 'I'm leaving.'

'Don't you bottle out now, Tom.'

With Annie at his heels, Tom pushed his way through the pub's other punters and out into the car park. The air was chilly and damp, and there was a hint of impending rain. Threading their way through the cars, Tom came to an abrupt stop and Annie banged into him. He executed a smart turn-about and caught her by the shoulders. 'Your answer is no?'

Annie flinched and stepped back from him, and his hands fell away from her. Life had been difficult, but *possible*. The job, Sadie and other friends, plans . . . good books, films . . . 'Yes,' she hissed. 'No.' She turned away. The chill air slapped at her face and the damp was making her hair curl – which added to her despair.

'Annie . . .'

At first she couldn't find the car and searched frantically, spotted it – only to realize on reaching it that Tom had the keys. Sighing with misery, she leaned against the damp metal and dropped her head on to her arm. *I am bloody going to leave you*, she thought, *no ifs and buts*, and the idea was so final that a lump sprang into her throat.

From behind her, Tom said, 'Annie, can't we pull together?'

Silence.

'Annie, *please*.'

Tom had not forgotten about the ring.

They were in the car on the way to break the news to Hermione. Annie was fretting because they hadn't consulted the children but Tom had argued that it would be better to tell them when things had been settled.

At Streatham, the traffic ground to a customary snail's pace. The weather had abandoned its spring promise and reverted to chilly bluster, interspersed with intense showers. Even the nascent buds on the city trees looked cold.

Annie was searching for her notebook, which had disappeared into the recesses of her handbag. She piled makeup bag, hairbrush, wallet, an assortment of glasses' cases and address book into her lap.

Tom was asking, 'Did you feel awful when you sold the ring?'

'Surprisingly detached.' Annie touched her unoccupied finger. 'I thought I wouldn't be, but when push came to shove . . .'

It was a lie. Giving up the ring had hurt more than she'd thought possible for an inanimate object. Letting go of it was to say goodbye to her mother all over again but the hurt was private. Annie put the stuff back into her bag. Her mother had never rated pride. Her opinion had been that it got you into trouble. Annie disagreed. It seemed to her that pride carried you over quite a few hurdles and situations, but she agreed on one thing. When pride took a knock you couldn't think of much else.

Tom kept his eye on the road. 'Once the nobility has worn off, you'll really miss it.' For a moment he sounded like the old, teasing Tom. 'I'll give it a couple of weeks.'

A laugh escaped from Annie. 'I'll remind you to check with me.'

'But, Annie, I think you were wonderful to sell it.'

Her eyes flew to his face. *Remember the first time she saw Tom, and the lurch of her heart?* 'Really?'

'Really.'

They were approaching the care home, and Annie concentrated on what lay ahead. She looked out of the window at a parade of bungalows and stockbroker Tudor houses flanked by laurels and monkey-puzzle trees. Tom was twisting in the wind, miserable, at bay, the worst she had ever seen him. And it wasn't any use thinking that things would be all right because, almost certainly, they wouldn't be.

. . . To her surprise, Tom had appeared in Annie's bedroom the previous night. He began, stopped, stuttered, tried again: 'I need you with me, Annie.'

'Need me?'

'As it happens.'

No, no, she thought. *How dare he?* Yet his muttered request had crept under her defences . . .

They drew into the Manor House Home and parked. Annie clutched the notebook on her lap. 'Have we really thought this through?'

'There's no other option.' He sounded very, very bleak.

'Shouldn't we discuss it a bit longer?'

He turned to her, and she recoiled from his misery. 'To what end? We need a hefty sum each month to keep my mother here. There's no longer a hefty sum available . . . I no longer have a job to supply any shortfall. What part of it don't you understand?'

She said quietly, 'You're asking a lot of me.'

'I know. But I'm also asking a lot of myself.' Pause. 'As I should.'

'But *will* you be there? Will you do your bit?'

He jerked the keys out of the ignition. 'Of course.'

Hermione was waiting for them in her room, which was suspiciously tidy and fiercely heated. 'They always muck me out when they know you're coming,' she maintained. 'Otherwise they don't bother. I'm paying to be kept like a pig in a sty.'

Hermione's complaints had flowed pretty well non-stop since she had taken up residence in Manor House a couple of years back. Naturally, Tom and Annie had done their best to investigate them. But they had quickly realized that solving any trifling problems was not really the point. Hermione liked to stir the pot. Boredom? Malice? Whatever the explanation, her skill at sowing suspicion was considerable and, mindful of the horror stories in the media, Annie always followed up any complaint.

Tom bent over and kissed his mother on the cheek and she submitted, more or less graciously. To Annie she extended a hand, a gesture the children were convinced she had copied from a photograph of Queen Victoria entertaining her imperial subjects that used to hang in Rose Cottage.

'Annie, so nice that you could fit me into your busy timetable.'

'Mother.' Tom was sharp.

Hermione was never less than well turned out, usually in a tweed skirt and a cashmere sweater. These she bought in quantities, wherever and whenever. Annie had a vivid memory of Hermione's stockpiling activities (which would not have disgraced a professional retailer) on a family holiday in the Scottish borders when she was supposed to be helping out with the children, who were eight and five at the time. 'I know you're cross about this,' she had said, as she buzzed off in the family car to the nearest wool mill, 'but you'll do the same one day, and a good thing too.'

'I'll kill her,' Annie had hissed furiously to Tom in the privacy of their bedroom, which they were being forced to share with Emily.

'It's her holiday too,' he said.

Tired and played out, Annie had ended that holiday – which had undoubtedly tested the relationship – mistrusting her mother-in-law and had mistrusted her ever since.

Tom sat down opposite his mother, and Annie busied herself tidying the pot plants on the window-sill.

'Say what you've come to say,' said Hermione.

Tom wasted no more time. He explained that he had lost his job – and that was one problem. 'I see,' said Hermione, who clearly didn't. The second problem, Tom continued, was equally serious. He leaned forward and said earnestly, 'Hermione, I'm afraid your finances have taken a battering recently. The thing is . . . your income isn't sufficient for you to stay here.'

Hermione looked thunderstruck.

At the window, Annie ripped away savagely at the decaying leaves of an African violet.

'Please look at this.' Tom held out a spreadsheet crammed with figures.

Hermione barely glanced at it. 'I leave all that to you. You're the man of the family.'

'OK.' Tom smoothed the spreadsheet over his knee. 'It shows that, at the present rate, your money will run out in approximately six months' time.'

Hermione possessed a repertoire of laughs, and she favoured this audience with one of the harsher ones. 'So?'

'It means –' began Tom.

Hermione shot a glance at Annie. 'It means you will have to look after me.'

Crushing a fistful of dead leaves between her fingers, Annie said, 'Given the financial circumstances, yes, we're suggesting that you come and live with us.'

This time, Hermione's laugh was appreciably strained. 'That must hurt you to say.'

'We'll try to make you as comfortable as we can.'

'And that, too. Heroic.'

'Tom,' Annie said quietly, 'do you think you could ask your mother . . .'

'Hermione,' Tom warned, 'this is not the time.'

Hermione caved in. 'Forgive me, dear. It's the shock.'

Annie dropped the detritus into the bin by the door. A sweet, spicy scent clung to her hands. 'As I said, we'll do our best to make you welcome.'

Hermione's hooded lids drooped over her eyes. 'I expect you will.'

Thrown by this unexpected shift, Annie crouched beside her mother-in-law's chair. 'I promise we will.'

All of a sudden, Hermione appeared shrunken and very frail. 'I've got used to it here,' she confessed, in a low voice, 'and now you say I have to leave.'

'I thought you hated it.' Tom was as surprised as Annie.

'I know its ways.' She glanced at Annie as if for support.

'The routines, you know. I didn't like them at first, and I was angry with myself for . . . being here but I've made myself fit in.'

Annie strove not to sound reluctant. 'You can have a routine with us.'

Hermione cast around for a problem, and found one. 'I have coffee with Sheila every day. I wouldn't have her to talk to.'

'We'll bring you to visit her.' The quicksands were folding over life as it had been at number twenty-two and there was nothing Annie could do about it.

'I see.' Hermione looked away and out of the window. 'Maybe I could have a cat.'

Annie moved fast to head that one off at the pass. 'We'll think about it later.'

Hermione was not stupid, and could read the runes as well as anyone. She abandoned that tack. She folded her hands in her lap. 'It's awful being old.'

Annie regarded the stricken figure with increasing apprehension. She raised her face to Tom's and, with the leap of empathy that had bound them so securely together in the past, perceived that he did too.

Late that night, when they were getting ready for bed, she and Tom happened to collide in the corridor between the two bedrooms.

'Sorry, I was cross earlier.'

'That's all right.'

'I can't thank you enough.' A dressing-gown-clad Tom touched her arm. 'I want you to know that.'

She searched his face. 'You'd better wait and see what happens before you thank me.'

'I promise you I'll take the lion's share.'

Annie shivered. 'I hope we can make her happy.'

'There's nothing else we can do.' He gestured to his bedroom. 'I'll move upstairs to Jake's room.'

A moment of silence.

'Yes.' She smoothed back her hair. 'Of course.'

With Tom only a step or two away across the corridor, the fiction was maintained that their lives were still cobbled together. If his door was ajar, she liked to catch sight of him moving around in the faded tartan pyjamas that were long past their sell-by date. Occasionally, they shouted to each other across the neutral corridor and the times when she had bad dreams she left her door open deliberately.

'That seems sensible. I'll work out what needs to be done.'

Upstairs, an astonished Emily was conducting a difficult phone call with Jake. 'I can't believe you haven't said anything to us,' she said, bewildered that he should have kept such momentous news to himself. 'Why didn't you? You must be feeling . . .' The writer searched for the best word but could only come up with '. . . dreadful.'

'I couldn't . . .' said Jake, at his end of the line '. . . I couldn't believe that Jocasta meant what she said. Then it took time for her to make arrangements to actually go.' He paused. 'I just wanted to lie low. You understand? Like an animal.'

'Does anyone know?'

'No.'

Shameful as it was, Emily felt satisfaction that Jake had come to her first. 'How's Maisie?'

'She's been a bit difficult, which is not surprising. Babies sense upheaval.'

'I suppose Lin can help.'

There was a silence. 'That's another thing. Lin is going.'

'Why?'

'I'm having to let her go.'

'Jake – then what? It sounds bad.'

'It is. Money.'

'Business bad?'

She heard him sigh. 'Might be.'

She collected her wits. An unfamiliar, complicated scene was opening up and even she – the writer in the garret with her head (metaphorically speaking) wrapped in a towel – understood that childcare would be vital to allow the pieces of Jake's life to fall into place. 'Jake, don't make decisions before you've thought them through. OK? Look, I can come over and we'll talk.'

'Thanks.'

She could tell he was grateful for the support and discretion. Again, the feeling of warm satisfaction. Instead of being the ignored non-twin, she was contributing. She pressed on: 'But, you know, you can't keep this quiet for much longer.'

'No. I need a bit more time.'

'You can trust me.'

'I know I can.'

Emily smiled. Then, in view of the gravity of Jake's news, she wiped it from her face.

Jake and Mia. Mia and Jake. Throughout her growing up, they had been indisputably glamorous, their unity impenetrable and exclusive. Their faces turned away from their younger sister.

How you saw your childhood was important. Correction: how you *perceived* your childhood was important. She had been ever hopeful that the twins would include her. *Let's ask Emily*, she willed them to say. *She'll know what to do.* But they never did. Instead, dreaming of the day when she would feel less puny and inadequate, she was left with her nose pressed to the pane. Hence she had learned that she could never compete with Jake's effortless cool and the Mia who made people laugh and their spirits rise at the sight of her. However magical and powerful Emily might wish to be, a triumvirate would never happen.

There was no option left but to go her own way and that was when she discovered the sustenance to be found in books – every book she could lay hands on whether she made sense of it or not. It was thus she stumbled across Martin Heidegger, the philosopher, whose writings were well-nigh impenetrable to Emily, except in one crucial aspect. He had written of his lonely, neglected childhood and Emily shuddered with empathy. He was the 'boy who plunged himself into dusty old books'. She was the girl who was doing the same. He 'felt himself to be king among the many books he didn't understand, but each one of which he knew and reverently loved'. And it was true of her.

Emily Brontë had also written: 'I'll walk where my own nature might be leading.' This Emily also understood – and although she could not consider her habitual hikes to the library the stuff of a truly subversive secret life, the fact that she felt she had one gave her a sense of purpose.

When Emily was eighteen, Mia had taken herself out of the picture, which was terrible. Then again – if Emily was truthful – perhaps it hadn't been so terrible for her. At the time, Emily had been horrified and fascinated by the family scenes.

. . . 'Em, I'm going. For good.' Throwing things into a bag. Jeans, boots, hairbrush . . .

Still shaking from witnessing the row between Mia and the parents, Emily sat down with a clunk on Mia's bed: 'You can't.'

'Watch me.'

'But why?'

'Because Dad is such a hypocrite. And Mum is the same. Anyway, this is a horrible family. All mucked up. . .'

'But you don't abandon a family because they aren't perfect.'

'I do,' said Mia . . .

If it hadn't been before, and instinct informed Emily that it wasn't that mucked up but just averagely and depressingly dysfunctional, the family certainly was after Mia had left. Jake acted as though a stake had been driven through his chest . . . Her mother . . . her mother had wept unceasingly and her father had disappeared into the office and not emerged for weeks. It was the non-unity of her parents that brought her up short, and a chilly realization spiked her comfortable assumptions. When had that happened? When had they become so distant from each other? But that, she concluded, was the trouble with childhood and adolescence. The ongoing struggle to grow up had been so all-consuming that she had nothing left for anyone else.

'Remember the nice moments,' she wrote in her notebook. The *rare* nice moments. 'In the car on the way to Scotland. Three over-excited, high-decibel-emitting children. The mother driven to threaten, "You know, children,

I can do quiet and menacing very, very well." At the wheel, the father laughing so hard he was forced to stop the car. "You crack me up," he told her. "Quiet and menacing!" He swivelled round to face the enthralled audience on the back seat. "Children, which is the biggest whopper?" Afterwards he kissed the mother: "Never change.'"

Why would Mia wish to abandon what had made her? 'It's because I'm different,' she had declared, with tears running angrily down her cheeks. 'I don't want to think like you all. I don't want to be what you are' . . .

Tomorrow Emily had a second interview with Condor Oil, the first having been a preliminary sort-out. Preparing methodically as usual, she laid out her clothes and checked over the portfolio. The tasks were quiet ones, requiring little effort, soothing in their everydayness. As she patted and folded, she prepared herself to step out of one role into another. The mundane. Was it friend or enemy to the writer? All too often the mixing up of dreams with real life resulted in conflict and thwarted desire – which was the stuff of fiction.

She stopped herself. That kind of speculation was now redundant.

Drifting into sleep, a series of highly coloured imaginings of Jocasta and Noah-the-top-American-banker invaded her mind. Of course, what her sister-in-law had done was not unknown, but its impact would upset the Nicholsons. Not least, it shattered the picture of the successful, principled, *happy* Jake. The Jake who pronounced (helped, it must be said, by having a high-earning wife) that he didn't care much about money, and people ought to *make* more things. The Jake who said it was rubbish that children and work could not be balanced.

That Jake was the person who had reassured Emily that he had never hated anyone in his life, that people were essentially good and principled, and who loved passionately and successfully. She had breathed in the clear, positive message: *no hatred.*

The image despoiled, she mourned it.

She turned over and faced the window. Keeping Jake's secret from her parents would require deception, which was new to her. Intriguing? Yes.

Deception. Does it rot the soul? Or introduce a thrilling element into the everyday?

Stop it, she scolded herself.

As her body gradually softened and relaxed, she pictured a dark blue sky fretted with pulsating stars. As she watched with her mind's eye, a world haloed by a rose-pink light mounted into that blue velvet. It was a fresh and beautiful sight and, gazing on it, Emily was gripped by a yearning for passion, for deep-seated, committed love – and for the story of her life to begin.

'OK,' he practised aloud. 'It's like this.'

My wife so despised me and thought so little of her daughter that she's fled to the other end of the earth.

No, that wasn't right.

Jocasta has left me for another man and another continent. Thank God, she has also left me with our daughter and, not so good, the mortgage.

No.

It was a sensible, mature, mutual decision between consenting adults . . .

Better.

Jake needed to get the story straight before he unleashed

his news on the parents. Maisie in his arms, he roamed the house while he worked on it. (A story that, thus far, had culminated with Jake phoning Jocasta as she was about to board the plane to New York and informing her that she was both wicked and wrong.)

Fact: Jocasta had gone, it was late on Saturday afternoon and the house felt as empty as a nuclear wasteland. He slotted Maisie into her bouncy chair in the kitchen and sat down with paper and pencil.

While Maisie cooed and batted her arms about like a tiny nestling, Jake made lists of figures, added and subtracted.

Mortgage? He had not recognized the Jocasta who admitted: 'I don't deserve the house, Jake. But you'll have to take on the mortgage eventually.'

Childcare? Living expenses? Projected income? All the practical considerations that did not come easily to him.

How come a baby who ate practically nothing managed to use so many nappies? Why did the manufacturers of baby food make the pots either too large or too small? These considerations had existed previously and, of course, he had dealt with them. But they had not impinged on him in this leaden, despairing manner. Now they would – continuously. He checked off the next couple of weeks in the workshop's order book. Not good. A ripple of panic went through him.

The bell startled him.

Wrapped in a capacious, belted macintosh, Emily stood on the doorstep. 'I thought I'd better come over.'

For a magic moment, Jake imagined it was Mia who somehow, miraculously, had intuited that he was in trouble – and felt ashamed that he minded it was only Emily. 'You look like a spy or a flasher.'

Emily put her arms around him and held him tight. 'I would have come at once if you'd told me. You must feel awful.' Suddenly, his disappointment vanished, and he felt so grateful for Emily's support. He buried his head in his sister's shoulder and closed his eyes. The scents of camomile shampoo and clean hair took him back to a more innocent time.

He ushered her into the kitchen. She threw off the flasher's mac, revealing a tiny skirt and thick black tights, and swooped down on Maisie. 'Hallo, Birdie.' She made the silly face that adults did with babies. She looked up at Jake. 'Is she doing all right?'

Jake filled kettle. 'A bit restive and grizzly at night. She's looking for Jocasta.'

Emily's voice wavered. 'It's not *fair* on Maisie. Have you really got rid of Lin?'

'I had to,' he said.

Emily asked the obvious: 'How do you work?'

'That's another thing.'

'Oh, God,' said Emily.

Jake felt his grimmest yet. He slapped the lid on to the kettle, switched it on and began, half-heartedly, to tackle the backlog of washing-up. Every nerve and bone in his body seemed to hurt and a ravening sensation opened in his stomach, as if he hadn't eaten for days. At the same time, the idea of food was repugnant.

Emily continued to coo at Maisie. A delighted Maisie shrieked back. Jake slotted a washed plate into the rack.

'You didn't say anything to the parents?'

'Jake, you've got to tell them some time.'

'I know,' he said irritably. 'I *know*.' Then he heard himself say something pretty stupid: 'It's partly the parents' fault.'

She sent him a reflective look. 'I don't think you mean that.'

'If I hadn't got so used to their lacklustre marriage, where they hang together by the skin of their teeth for no good reason other than inertia, I might . . . Oh, I don't know. Forget I said it . . . It's my fault I didn't recognize the signs.'

Emily demanded, 'Tell me. What signs?'

'Don't go using me as material for a novel. OK?'

'Unfair.'

'Not as unfair as being left by your wife.'

She had the grace to look away. 'Actually, I'm job-hunting. The novel will have to wait.' She extracted Maisie from the bouncy chair and settled her on her lap. 'Apart from anything else, you're in a panic. And that I do recognize from Mum and Dad who've been panicking massively. Did you know Mum sold her ring to pay for the new cooker?'

'No, I didn't.' Jake chucked teabags into two mugs and poured hot water over them. 'I'm sorry. And I'm sorry about the writing.'

She shrugged and ran a hand through her hair – reminding him of their father. 'Needs must.' Her smile was a trifle grim. 'But we have to stick together, don't we?' She re-inserted Maisie's foot into her sock, which had fallen off. 'God, this is grubby. When did you last do the laundry?'

Faint stirrings of hysteria threatened to back up in Jake. Get a grip, he instructed himself. 'I have no idea.'

Emily got to her feet and handed Maisie to him. 'OK. Time for a bit of organization.'

Jake was grateful, very grateful, to Emily, who should not have felt she had to give up her Saturday evening to run around after him. She should have been out on the town with Tod – although the way in which she referred to the nice but fey Tod did not indicate that she considered it a sacrifice. She was also very practical and a considerable amount of cleaning and tidying was accomplished in a astonishingly short time. In addition, after rummaging in various cupboards she produced spaghetti with tomato sauce.

At the moment, his responses were pretty dulled and selfish but he could not have failed to be struck by her obvious wish to help or by the slight aura of sadness and anxiety that hung over her.

He roused himself sufficiently to ask, 'Everything all right with you?'

She grimaced. 'It's a bit difficult at home. You know Dad. Really, really gutted.'

When she left he kissed her and swore to himself he would remember that she had come to his rescue. Then he forgot about Emily, and fell into a sleeping-waking pattern during which Jocasta came and went.

You've no money, a voice said in his sleeping ear. *But you do have a baby and a mortgage.* And again: *You'll get into debt.*

'We will stick together,' Emily had promised.

At least she understood what human beings should do for each other, and what they needed.

Guiltily he remembered the texture of the dry soil and thick laurel leaves in Battersea Park where he and Mia had grubbed out dens designed to keep Emily out. Guiltily he remembered her cries of distress, their relentless policy of exclusion, and the lengths to which they had gone to upset her, which was easy for she had been small and slow to grow. 'That child was starved in the womb,' his father used to joke, which distressed his mother and angered Jake. How dare his father be so unfeeling and tactless and hurtful when Mum

127

did so much for everyone? Unlike Tom, who was never much around. After one of their stupid wrangles over Jake's refusal to take politics at A level, he accused his father, 'Bet you're nicer to the people in the office than you are to us.'

He wasn't sure if his father had ever forgiven him for that.

The clamour in Jake's head faded. He fell back into sleep and found himself labouring on a vast bookcase, which demanded ever-more precise measurements and a plenitude of finials, architraves and recessed beading.

Then he woke up again. Dozed. Woke.

Sewn into the wake-sleep periods, the apparitions came and went.

In the early hours, he woke properly. Maisie was crying. Head buzzing, mouth dry, he fumbled out of bed and tried to remember if he had decanted water into her bottle.

He hadn't, and her cries intensified as he fumbled around the kitchen and climbed back upstairs. A drenched pair of cornflower blue eyes accosted him as he lifted her on to his knee. 'You really shouldn't need a drink in the night.'

The sobs abated. Maisie relaxed against him. One arm banged the bottle, the other was tucked peacefully against Jake's torso.

While she drank, Jake considered the vows he had taken during his life. *I take you to be my wedded wife* – that was null and void. The other was to protect Maisie and to give her the chance of a good life. He remembered the night she was born, its white-gold dawn aftermath and the accompanying aftertaste in his mouth of flat champagne and bad hospital coffee. He had been changed, utterly changed.

Save for Maisie's snuffles, the silence was crushing.

When she had finished, he sat her up and rubbed her

back. Already he was beginning to understand her body language better – and satisfaction trickled through him.

He waited for a rude and gusty spasm of air to be released through her rosebud mouth before lifting her into the cot and tiptoeing away.

Downstairs, he poured himself a slug of whisky, which did dreadful things to his head and stomach, and eyed the phone. Eventually he put a hand around the receiver. It was cold – not as cold as stone but as cold as plastic material in an unheated house. He dialled.

'Jocasta . . .'

'Jake?' She was startled.

'The man you married. The very one. Having trouble remembering?'

'What do you want?'

'You have to come back. You can't walk out on us.'

'You're drunk.'

'Possibly.'

'Listen, Jake. We've been through this –'

'You've been through this,' he interrupted. 'Not me.'

'*I*'ve been through this. It's decided. I've gone away because what we had didn't suit me, and I would have made you and Maisie unhappy. What can I do to make you believe me?'

Hope finally died. He had loved Jocasta – oh, he had loved her – and he had believed that his love would be sufficient for them both. But it hadn't been, and it wasn't.

In those final moments before hatred and disgust took over (which Jake knew they surely would) he bade goodbye to that love.

He put down the phone. Now it was post-Jocasta. Post-marriage. Post . . . what?

Chapter Ten

One of the consequences of Tom losing his job was to make Annie view hers in a different light. And it wasn't just the spectacle of an unshaven Tom looking up from the breakfast table and saying brightly and heroically, 'Have a good day.' It was a shift from regarding a good job with sufficient intrinsic interest and remuneration as a guarantee to self-respect – almost a luxury – to a position where the anxieties of being the sole breadwinner had never been so acute.

Annie's mother had loved a good cliché and had plenty of them for most occasions. 'Don't knock 'em, Annie.' She had been chopping carrots like the Demon Barber at the time. 'They're a fall-back when the going gets tough . . .' Coming to terms with the new situation, Annie found herself – *thanks, Mum* – repeating to herself, *A change is as good as a rest*. In the circumstances, it was useful as she grappled with Tom's new situation. And what about her own? If she had ever felt dissatisfied with parts of her work, the loneliness of being the family's sole breadwinner swiftly ironed out any pockets of resistance.

What would happen if she lost *her* job?

Electrifying patients and staff in a pair of red high heels with lipstick to match, Sadie swept down to St Brigid's and took her out for a backbone-stiffening lunch. Annie found herself airing these fears.

Sadie looked astonished. 'Sakes, you can always find

another one.' She reached over the table and patted Annie's hand. 'You Brits don't understand about get-up-and-go.'

'Fine. So the *Mayflower* didn't sail from these shores and we didn't have an . . . admittedly embarrassing . . . empire on which the sun never set?'

'Well, here's the thing.' Sadie twinkled sardonically over her spelt and pumpkin salad. 'All you did was to create Little England in the jungle. That's not the same thing as thinking out of the box.'

'Remind me, Sadie, why are we friends?'

'Because.' Sadie grew serious. 'Annie, how is Tom?'

'Going for job interviews and coming home looking like death. It's really tough. The economy and all that.' She entertained an all-too-vivid picture of Tom aimlessly wandering around the house. 'I feel agonized for him. He's been cut off at the knees.'

'For God's sake, Annie. Are you ill? No. Are you alive and well? Yes. Have you a roof over your head? Yes. What's there to be cut off at the knees about?' She added, 'Send him over to me. OK?'

'Never. You're an official man-eater.'

Like Cleopatra's, Sadie's smile reflected infinite variety and wisdom. 'Just because I've had three husbands doesn't mean I want yours. I love my Andrew. ' She poured out the last of the wine. 'Drink up, this is on me.' She peered at Annie. 'Do I detect an expression that suggests I'd be welcome to Tom?'

Annie grinned. 'That's quite another topic.'

The Middleton Wing was the hospital's administration block where the meeting had assembled to discuss the case of Samuel Smith who had died earlier in February in A and

E. (Tom had been right that it would cause trouble.) The company included two consultants, union representatives, a lawyer, plus the usual suspects from Annie's department and the press officer.

Her boss, Charles Thompsett, got to his feet. Ten years younger than Annie, he was fast-tracking up the NHS bureaucracy, liked to be known as Chuck, and cultivated an impatience that was sometimes justified. 'Ladies and gentlemen . . .' He was as oily smooth as only a fast-tracker could bring themselves to be. 'I'm sure you're all aware that Samuel Smith's parents are suing the hospital for negligence.' He glanced around the faces at the table. 'This is a most unfortunate case. Of course, our thoughts are with Mr Smith's family but . . .' he barely checked himself '. . . but apart from anything else the press are on to it. I've already talked to a couple of editors and they tell me they think there are grounds for representing it as gross negligence in a failing hospital.'

There was a sharp collective intake of breath.

Chuck consulted his notes. 'You all have a copy of the internal report. Please turn to page one.'

Samuel Smith had arrived in A and E at 1.32 p.m. in considerable distress from abdominal pain. There had also been a major traffic incident with multiple injured and, as a result, he had not been triaged for half an hour.

This last fact alone was troubling. If it had been one of my children, thought Annie, I would be shouting it from the rooftops.

At 2 p.m. Samuel Smith had been heard to call out from the gurney where he had been placed in the corridor. No one was free to respond.

Annie could not bear to think of how Samuel Smith must have felt as he lay dying on that unforgiving gurney.

There were murmurs and rustles in the warm, coffee-scented room. One of the consultants got up, poured himself a cup and helped himself to a Jammie Dodger and a custard cream from the plate.

At 2.30 p.m. Samuel Smith was heard to call out a second time. Again, no one was available to respond.

Chuck looked up from the notes. He was grim. 'Did anyone have contact with Samuel Smith at this point?'

Annie did not need to check her reports – much of what they said was burned into her memory. 'No. But Nurse Flynn heard him calling out for his mother.'

The press officer coughed and the lawyer wrote a note at high speed.

'You should all note that timings concerning Samuel Smith's admission fell within the target times. This is important and forms part of the defence,' said Chuck.

Annie glanced around. The consultants exchanged a look and one union representative wore a belligerent expression. The majority at the table would be thinking the same thought: target times are irrelevant if you're dying and requiring help. No one, including herself, was going to spell it out.

'. . . absolutely sure of the facts before . . .' Chuck was saying. He continued in this vein for a while longer and finished, 'I'm going to hand over to Annie Nicholson.'

She was used to this. Even so, her heartbeat quickened. 'You will all have been briefed on this case. The timetable is likely to be this . . .' She outlined the legal and administrative procedures and indicated how they would affect the parties present around the table. She ended, 'No one is to discuss this case outside the proper channels and certainly not with the media.'

When she sat down, Chuck raised an eyebrow a millimetre. You did fine, it said. 'Questions?' he asked. He took care not to focus on anyone in particular.

The biscuit-eating consultant raised a hand. A crumb of custard cream clung to his cuff and he brushed it away fastidiously. 'As the representative of A and E, I will be reviewing the procedures but I'm convinced that doctors are not to blame.' He paused. 'This unfortunate death is the result of too many targets and too much paperwork, which we have talked about many times. In my view, it could have been avoided.'

One of the union representatives, smart, dapper and razor-sharp, cut in: 'We would like to make clear that we feel strongly that our nurses are not accountable. If there is blame to be apportioned, and there will be, we would insist that a close look is taken at managerial practices.'

The medics at the table had retreated into their bunker. In a long, trying war, hostilities had again opened up between them, the managers and administrators. Into the gap between the opposing factions, thought Annie, despairingly, would fall Samuel Smith and his too-brief life. What are we missing that we cannot work together? she wanted to demand. Why do the sick get sidelined? Why do we, the managers, get it wrong?

'We must be careful,' she closed proceedings, 'not to indulge in internal disputes. This case is, first of all, about whether we failed a patient or not, and second about the hospital and its reputation.'

Afterwards, Annie found herself peering at herself in the

female washroom. The mirrors needed cleaning and she appeared blurred around the edges. Snatching up a tissue, she leaned forward and rubbed away until her image emerged sharper and clearer. Battle was for the young – only they could stand its physical ordeals and psychological terrors – and going into battle also depended on a degree of coercion.

Samuel Smith had been only thirty-two. Not so very much older than her own children. That made her think of Tom, whom she had left stuffing clothes into the washing-machine, and her mood darkened.

She tucked back an unruly lock of hair and regarded the result.

'Are you all right?' Sarah, her assistant and friend, poked her head around the door and broke into her reverie.

Annie whipped around. 'Fine. Just hating the hair.'

Sarah looked a tad sceptical. 'And . . .'

Annie regarded the curls that, over the years, had given her so much grief. 'Only good when I'm pregnant . . . How sad is that?'

. . . Arriving back from hospital, bearing the tight-wrapped forms of the twins, her hair manageable and glossy from pregnancy hormones, skin glowing with post-partum exhilaration. Tom ushering her up into the bedroom and her gasping on the threshold for he had filled it with roses – dusty pink, pearly white, beige – and the double bed made up with clean sheets. It had been a room scented with flowers, with excitement – and with love . . .

Sarah said, 'When you're done having the bad-hair moment you're wanted by Him.'

When the twentieth-century architect had tacked Middleton Wing on to the main Victorian building, he had abandoned the notion of putting in windows that opened, and during warmer weather, the stuffy atmosphere often made her feel light-headed. The Admin offices honeycombed a corridor along which patients were wheeled on the way down to Theatre Five. Occasionally, and guiltily, Annie glanced up from her desk to witness a nurse's struggles to manoeuvre a patient, but an unwritten rule kept Admin behind their doors.

Chuck had the largest office at the end of the corridor. Jabbing a finger at a chair, he indicated that Annie should be seated while he finished a call. But the call couldn't be finished quickly and Annie BlackBerryed a message to Sarah. Surgeons refusing to use cheaper gloves ordered by Procurement. Message is: don't care how f***ing expensive Biogel gloves are, and what savings the cheaper brands will make, that's what they want. Also say that if Admin can't get their fat heads around their needs then they should go home. You to sort?

Actually, it wasn't *so* funny. Procurement should know better than to allow trenches to be dug. Sorting out the rubber-glove skirmish meant hours of extra negotiation, plus the upshot was not in any doubt. The surgeons would get their Biogel gloves – bought specifically for their use.

Chuck put down the phone. 'Well done, Annie. We've made a start.'

She pushed a curl behind her ear. 'There's a meeting with the lawyers next week. It's been put into your diary.'

'There's one other thing.'

She anticipated what it was likely to be – which wasn't difficult. Chuck's ambitions dictated his actions but, to be fair to him, his ambitions were not exclusively directed to his own advancement. He was genuine about wishing the hospital to be a good one. They all were.

'Superbugs?'

'Got it. We've had a tip-off that the DoH is about to issue new guidelines. They'll be sending in the superbug squad and it would be good if they found we had it in hand.'

Samuel Smith's death was already retreating into a background of problems, statistics, meetings and political agendas. The day looked set to be a long one and she returned to her office to draft her strategy.

Late afternoon found Annie, with Sarah striding beside her, walking the hospital corridors. They were making for Day Surgery, which, with its high turnover, offered as good a starting point as any.

Nursing staff always affected not to pay attention to Admin whenever the latter came into sight. All the same, Annie knew perfectly well that their antennae switched on to full alert. *We are the medics. We have the knowledge. You do your best to make it difficult for us. You take away our powers of decision.* It wasn't always, or necessarily, hostility but it did not take much for their suspicions to tip over into it.

She said to Sarah, 'Go check the cleaning and cleaners.'

The sun struggled through the resolutely sealed window in Reception, lighting a pile of tatty magazines. Clipboard on knee, Annie sat down and noted her observations.

(1) One patient used the handwash at ward entrance. Rest ignored it.
(2) Nurse dealing with discharged patient went to keyboard without washing hands.

The nurses at the station chatted to each other. One wore shoes that needed repairing. The other was too thin. She noted the facts and filed them. Tom always said that observation was an art, and it required to be worked on. At the thought of Tom, her stomach tightened.

Before she left Day Surgery, Annie interviewed one of the theatre sisters, a beautiful dark-haired woman.

'You want the real story?' She was hesitant, but the urge to speak out was too strong. 'It's the budgets that are responsible for the superbugs. Aiming for too high a patient turnover, economizing on air changes in theatres, and no time or money for barrier nursing. What more do you need? You can spend weeks, years, doing all the research in the world, but the solution to the problems is, in one word, money.'

More battle lines.

The day seemed interminable, and she returned home feeling like a limp rag. Emily was upstairs and, the clocks having gone forward three or so weeks back and the evenings being lighter, Tom had eventually set about putting his plan into action for sorting out the shed.

She was contemplating making herself some tea – only contemplating, mind, because it required effort – when the doorbell rang.

To say that she was astonished to see Jake on the doorstep with Maisie, plus several suitcases, was an understatement.

'Hallo, Mum,' he said. 'I'm afraid I'm in trouble and I've got to come home.'

She experienced a blinding sense of *déjà vu* – a throwback to the time when she could not spread her arms wide enough to accommodate everyone, when the twins needed X, Emily Y, and her husband Z. 'Of course,' she said, holding them out now to take Maisie, who settled into them with a contented sigh. 'You'd better tell me.'

The handle of the garden fork had split with age and Tom heaved it out to take to the dump. The not unpleasing smell in the shed was of dry, aged soil, chalky garden feeder and a whiff of urban fox. Cobwebs spread over the roof, adorned with mummified spiders' corpses, which hung down like macabre earrings. Sweeping out the worst webs, Tom was confronted by the clutter of decades. Rusting sieves, discarded seed packets, jars containing murky sediments. A shelf tilted precariously, and the heaped garden implements reflected their neglect. Tom picked up the rust-eaten, useless sieve and chucked it outside. Then he culled about two dozen plastic flowerpots in varying sizes, seed packets so old they were rigid, plus a couple of empty fertilizer packets.

As he worked, he recollected the times when, as a small boy, he had taken refuge in his father's shed, a resolutely masculine retreat where his father had smoked his pipes. 'Dad, what's electricity?'

'Shush, Tom.' His father had pointed to the sign above the door: NO TALKING. His old tweed jacket, the odour, sweet and penetrating, of the tobacco he preferred. Peace that, as a boy, Tom hadn't appreciated.

It was years since Tom had tackled this task, and it could not be said that he particularly enjoyed it. It smacked of the last resort, the sort of activity occupational therapists dreamed up to give the day a point. A couple of months ago he had occupied an office from which he looked out as ruler on his subjects – although he would never have admitted to that. A couple of months ago he was busily preoccupied with programming, international politics, budgets and lobbying. Sorting flowerpots didn't really cut it.

So went his thoughts – particles flitting randomly here and there. If he didn't get a job soon, he would have to discuss with Annie selling the house and various other stratagems. Yesterday his credit-card statement had arrived with a couple of expensive items racked up on it from his previous life, including a club membership he would have to cancel. Like many in his position, worrying about money made him miserable but it had to be done.

He parcelled up what he could in black plastic bags, and stacked up the rest. His gaze fell on the fork, which, now he thought about it, he had inherited from his mother when she had cleared out her cottage. He picked it up. *Smooth with age. Pleasing. Trustworthy.* He held it for a little longer and it occurred to him that his father might have used it. He reached for a piece of sacking and scrubbed at the tines until the steel began to shine through. Was he echoing the habits of his father? It was then Tom knew he couldn't possibly bin the fork. With a bit of ingenuity, he could tape around the split handle and it would be perfectly serviceable. Or he might ask Jake to do it. He stowed it back inside the partly eviscerated shed.

He came back into the house to find a whirlwind had spun through the kitchen.

'Hi, Dad.' Wearing one of Annie's frivolous frilly aprons, Jake was stirring the contents of a saucepan on a previously gleaming stove.

Annie was seated in front of Maisie's high chair, spooning green pulp into her mouth. 'There you are, Tom.'

A small *tsunami* of plastic bags, laundry and soft toys had washed through the hitherto orderly kitchen.

'What on earth . . .?'

'Open your mouth, Maisie,' Annie coaxed. She pressed the spoon to Maisie's pursed mouth. 'Open.'

'Jake, why are you here?'

Annie made an aircraft sound and swooped the spoon up and down. Maisie giggled and opened her mouth wide enough for Annie to insert it. Much of the green pulp landed on the baby's face. Tom noted this with a touch of bewilderment.

'Lovely broccoli, Maisie,' said Jake, whisking about with the saucepan. 'And now delicious rice pudding.'

'Ugh. Poor Maisie.' Wearing the clogs that all the family hated, Emily clattered into the kitchen and slapped sluttishly over the tiles. 'In a hurry, Jake. Need to get at the stove.' She seized a second saucepan and broke a fistful of spaghetti into it. 'Oh, hi, Mum. Didn't clock you. Good day?' She peered into the fridge. 'Got to eat before I go. Do we have any pesto from the deli? We usually do.'

'That deli is expensive,' said Annie.

'Jake, don't take this the wrong way, but why are you here?' Tom asked again. 'Are we babysitting?'

Emily hauled a tin of tomatoes out of the cupboard. 'Good pesto isn't that expensive, Mum, and goes a long way. Buying a cheap and nasty variant is false economy.'

Annie deftly steered rice pudding into Maisie, and white gloop now mixed with the green. 'False or not, we can't afford the deli.'

'I'll buy my own,' said Emily, crossly.

'Hey,' said Jake. 'Did you hear that? Emily offered to buy something.' He pranced about in the apron.

Emily wrestled with the tin. 'Do you know? I don't think we've sat down and eaten a meal together for ages.' She pointed to Leonardo's angel, which Annie had pinned up on the noticeboard. 'Mum saved you from the recycling, now do your bit for peace and harmony in this family.'

No one paid any attention.

Tom regarded his dirt-streaked hands. One of his fingers sported a minor graze and a muscle in his back twitched from unaccustomed use – reminders of the long, lonely, unproductive day. 'Do you have to?' he asked Jake.

'Do I have to what?'

'Wear that wretched apron.'

Jake gave a little laugh but his easiness vanished, leaving in its stead a pale and haunted figure. Tom was irritated by his son's overreaction. 'For God's sake, Jake, I haven't issued a world-war warning.'

Annie wiped Maisie's mouth and hands and dropped the cloth into the sink. 'Tom,' she said. 'Let Jake explain.'

Tom looked from one to another. 'What am I missing?'

Jake outlined the situation and Tom was brought up short. Jake did not deserve this. He remembered the boy: 'Dad, I'm off to find the Wild Wood,' and the resolute little chap clutching a teddy bear setting off down the garden.

Emily ate her pasta.

'The business is failing . . . for the moment,' Jake continued. 'I'm letting the house and I have to come home for a few months, just until I'm straight again, if that's all right.'

'Of course it is,' said Annie. She bent over and kissed Maisie. 'You are a disgusting little bird.'

'Dad?'

'Just a moment while I wash my hands,' said Tom.

In the downstairs lavatory, he allowed the water to run for a long time before soaping up. He peered at his reflection in the small mirror. The truth was, he had no idea how to handle his son now that he was in trouble, and the knowledge threw him – even more than he was already thrown.

On his return to the fray, the apron had been cast over a chair. Jake was talking intently with Annie and he caught him saying, 'He doesn't want me here.'

Emily raised her head from the bowl of pasta. 'Jake . . .'

Tom sat down. 'If you mean I don't want you here, that's rubbish, Jake.'

Jake placed both hands on the table and leaned towards him. 'I know what you're thinking.'

'I barely know myself what I'm thinking.'

Annie tensed at his tone, and Emily groaned. 'You're at it again, you two.'

Jake lost it. 'Why fudge the issue, Dad? I'm the son who doesn't match up. Despite all the talk, the left-wing values, what Dad really wants is a son who brings home readies by the barrowload. Sorry, Dad, you didn't get him. And now I'm home again.'

Jake was wrong – but he was also sufficiently right – and Tom knew perfectly well that Jake wouldn't have said any of it unless he was devastated. But it didn't stop him losing his temper, and the chair screeched as he levered himself to his feet. 'If that's what you think . . .'

'I *know* that's what you think. You don't like what I do – you never have.'

'It's not a question of whether I like what you do or not. It's a question of whether you're earning a living.'

'And you have a job at the moment?' The words slipped out of Jake, so quick and so cunning that they took time to sink in.

There was an appalled silence.

Tom heard another child saying much the same thing: 'You don't like what I am, Dad. Tough. Human beings are different. Families are different. If you don't understand that, you don't understand anything . . .'

Annie hissed, 'Tom, Jake has just been left by Jocasta. This is not the time to get into the job argument.'

Jake glanced at his mother. Tom was aware Jake frequently took a bearing from his mother – and that annoyed him too. He wanted to say: *Consult me sometimes, Jake.*

Even though I don't deserve it.

'Sorry, Dad,' Jake said stiffly.

He had provoked his sweet, kindly son into lashing out at him – precisely because Tom wasn't sweet and kindly.

Jake added, 'But, Dad, you must let people be.'

Tom knew, he just knew, that he was in danger of repeating the biggest mistake of his life. But Maisie saved him. The angry adult voices were frightening her: she threw her arms up and wailed.

Looking down, Tom encountered a bewildered little face and his anger evaporated in the urge to put things right. 'It's all right, Maisie. Here . . .' He bent down and picked her up. Her baby hair was like so many butterfly legs against his cheek, and her baby smell held the scent of innocence and promise, the qualities that, long ago, he had vowed to keep intact for his own children. He held her close. 'Grandpa's here.' He looked up. 'I'm sorry, Jake. That was unfair of me.' He paused. 'Will you forgive me?'

'Of course we have the room.'

She and Tom had retreated to her bedroom. Tom prowled around it, picking things up, throwing them down, mostly in the wrong place.

'We don't,' he said.

Annie's hairbrush was chucked on to the bed. Long ago, Annie had trained herself not to be exasperated by Tom's refusal to observe where her things lived. It was called marital strategy – and still required years of work.

'We all used to live here once.' She ticked off on her fingers. 'Jake and Maisie can use the rooms up top with Emily. We know that Emily sleeps like the dead and probably won't be disturbed by the baby.'

'And?'

'And what? Your mother? As agreed, in your room.'

In the silence that ensued, they digested the implications.

'Tom . . .'

'Annie . . .'

Their words collided.

Annie sank down on the bed and smoothed her skirt. *Boiled wool. Grey. Boring?*

Tom's dark head was bent over the photo of Jake and the cross-looking Jocasta. Funny . . . Annie scrutinized the bent head. The hair on the back of his neck grew in the same way as it always had. Once she had delighted to look at it. Still did, really.

Annie found herself fixated by the displaced hairbrush. It was a black Mason Pearson, ancient but still operational and a favourite. She reached over and touched the bristles. Somehow she had to find her way through the thicket of the present and make sense of the situation.

'Listen, Annie.' He sat down beside her. 'Jake should be able to cope on his own.'

'Like you are?'

'I am coping.'

'No, you're not.'

'You always defend him.'

She said, as reasonably as she could, 'And you never do.'

From down below, Emily shouted up, 'Are you two OK?'

Tom shot to his feet and said wearily, 'For God's sake, we can't even have an argument in peace. I'm going out for some fresh air.'

'Wait.' Annie grabbed at Tom's arm. 'I'm coming with you. We have to discuss this together.'

'Leave it, Annie.'

She tightened her grip. 'I *am* coming with you and we *will* discuss it.'

'Go away.'

She had seen that shuttered expression before. Oh, hundreds of times. 'Ah, that's it. You want to be allowed to wallow in solitude.' She poked a finger into his chest. 'Don't deny it.'

Miraculously, the weariness dropped away, and he grinned down at her. 'I'd forgotten how obstinate you can be.'

'No, I just know you better than anybody.'

He held her gaze a few seconds longer. 'So you do.' He reached out a hand. 'Come on, then.'

She searched his face. Old times? 'Fine.'

They ended up catching a bus at the end of the road. Annie could count on the fingers of one hand the number of times she had been on one with Tom since they were married. It was full, and they were forced to stand close, heads and bodies pressed together. She murmured into his ear, 'You have to support Jake.'

He did not reply, but his grip on her waist tightened.

They decanted at Vauxhall Bridge and made for the path along the river embankment. The day had been warm and overcast but the evening sun had broken through the cloud layer and the atmosphere was brightening.

Inhaling river air, Annie felt better at once. This was a favourite London walk, and she headed towards Waterloo Bridge. As usual she set a fast pace and Tom strode just a fraction behind her, a bobbing presence registered at the corner of her eye.

Passing the Houses of Parliament on the north bank, which glinted under the sun, Annie stole a look at Tom and the changes she perceived in him were dismaying. He seemed stooped, and the loss of his optimism and attack was marked. 'Why not set up a consultancy?' She was going carefully, tactfully.

He was silent for half a minute or so, then replied that since it seemed likely that the economic outlook was no longer so rosy it would be difficult. Plus there were, oh, approximately a million consultants all chasing one assignment.

'I know you've been trying, but you mustn't give up. Yet.'

He came to a dead stop. 'I had a job,' he said, and a world of regret was reflected in his eyes. 'I did have a job.'

The tourist season was not yet in full spate, and only a smallish queue had formed by Embarkation at the London Eye. Hopeful ticket touts patrolled up and down and cameras flashed.

Tom poked her arm. 'How about it?'

She glanced at him, and nodded.

In a very short time, Annie and Tom were ensconced on the seating area in a pod and inching towards the zenith. The pod was only half full. A trio of girls in high-heeled boots and tight jeans whispered to each other. A solitary man with earphones hunched over on the bench and trained binoculars on the Houses of Parliament. A pair of toddlers careered from side to side calling to their fond and – clearly – indulgent parents.

Tom and Annie exchanged glances – and she knew he was thinking: *We were like that once.*

She placed her mouth against his ear. 'Did we let ours get away with murder?'

'I hope not.'

That time had gone, and their children were no longer an extension of herself. Blink, and they had grown up. How had that happened?

The pod crept upward and London's panorama shrank. Annie shivered.

'You OK?' asked Tom.

'Actually . . .' Annie was surprised by the onset of her fear and dislike of being suspended in a pod above the Thames. 'I'm not so sure about this. It's a strange feeling. Sort of abandoned in space.'

'That's the point.' Tom dragged her up from the bench and over to the viewing rail. 'Look. It's great. You can see things from a different perspective.'

She clung to the rail. To ground herself, she regarded her feet. *Size 39. Slight suggestion of bunion on right foot.*

'Sissy,' he whispered.

River, roads and buildings retreated, and the horizon now curved very slightly. *Think macaroni cheese. Think contents of laundry basket. Shirts, socks . . . Good.* She was beginning to feel a little nauseous.

She returned to the bench, and he made no move to stop her. Her panic more or less neutralized, Annie took stock. Tom was keenly observing Canary Wharf's skyscrapers, his jaw set in a familiar way. She was fairly sure that he was mulling over the new words that were creeping into the language – *credit swaps, derivatives, greedy bankers* – which brought her up short. What was going on in the wider world was, at this moment, of so little importance to her that she was deeply ashamed. That was the trouble with Trouble: it had made her turn inwards, seeking the selfish survival instincts.

As they inched over the zenith, the nausea retreated and she felt more in control. Gratified that her knees had returned to load-bearing duty, she rejoined Tom and made an effort to consider the larger perspective. She pointed to the glittering towers of the City. 'You say the future is no longer so rosy but isn't it a good thing? Turbo-capitalism getting rid of its fat?'

'Do you know what? At this precise moment I don't care.'

Silence.

'Shouldn't you?'

He turned on her. 'Yes. There's a whole raft of issues to worry about.' A tinge of colour trickled into his cheeks. 'But I can't get past how angry I feel about what's happened to me.' His fingers dug into Annie's forearm and it was not a loving gesture.

She peeled them off. 'And you're angry with me, too, I

think.' He didn't confirm or deny it. 'You can be angry with me, Tom, if it makes you feel better.'

He ran his fingers through his hair. 'Did I take it all too seriously? I think perhaps I did. If I hadn't cared so much about what we did and achieved, then being banished would be easier.'

She looked directly into his wounded eyes. 'Tom, you don't believe that.'

'No, I don't,' he admitted, after a moment. 'You're right. I couldn't have done it any other way.'

'Nor should you.'

He was silent, but she could tell that her words had helped.

Tom had once said: 'Someone listening to the service might feel there was solidarity between humans that has nothing to do with race, nationality or religion but with what was right and loving . . .'

That had made her love him all the more.

'"The baroque frontiers, the surrealist police . . ."' Annie had plundered Auden to quote back at him. 'And broadcasting wriggles past them.' Tom's eyes had lit up because her response signalled that the connections between them were alive and strong . . .

Those new-married, private exchanges had been as stirring, and as binding, as any that had taken place between them physically.

During their long discussions, Sadie and she had nibbled away at the subject of marriage. Why do it? What's in it? How many times was Sadie going to try it before she was satisfied? The last had made them laugh. Equally, a rough tally of the millions Sadie had abandoned with her first two mega-rich husbands had had them crying into their tequila.

After they'd seen *Four Weddings and a Funeral* together –
accompanied by a large tub of popcorn – they had emerged
and begun to argue over it. Sadie considered the film sentimental. 'No,' said Annie, 'it recognizes that we're eternal
romantics and long for the ideal . . .'

'That's because you're sad,' Sadie had pointed out, with
the expertise of been-there-and-got-the-T-shirt. 'Tom is
never at home. From what you say, your marriage is not
what it was. And you haven't decided what to do about it.'

The feel-good delight from the film had faded. Annie's
stomach had heaved with too much popcorn. 'Cheer me
up, do.'

Sadie shot her a look. 'One day, you and Tom will have
to sort it out.'

'Yes and no,' said Annie. 'Tom's gone off-piste. I've gone
off-piste. The children take up every spare moment. It's
that stage of our lives.'

After Mia had left and the situation between Tom and
Annie was very different, Sadie again tackled Annie. 'Why
do you carry on with the charade?' she asked.

'Because,' the broken Annie had replied, 'there is no
reason not to. There is every reason to stick to things
precisely because they are rock bottom.'

'Do you love him?' Sadie demanded.

'Yes. No. Not at the moment. Not for the foreseeable
future.'

Sadie had grown angry and berated Annie for cynicism
and fatalism. 'You deserve better for yourself. If your
marriage sucks, you should get out of it, like I did.'

'OK, OK,' Annie had said. 'But I don't have the energy
just now.'

But, deep in her heart, she had been thinking, *What if Mia came back and found that Tom and I were no longer together?*

Annie turned to look towards the west. An imminent sunset was sending fingers of pink light across the horizon and a hush fell inside the pod. Beyond the city and the confines of a small island, another lush, uncolonized world where all was well appeared to rise above the horizon and present itself to her dazzled gaze. For a second or two, she even imagined that Leonardo's angel was winging through the darkening sky, bringing . . . what?

Tom was observing her closely and Annie shuddered with exhaustion. All was not well with their world.

On the way home, they resumed the discussion about Jake.

'Jake and Maisie will have to find somewhere else.' Tom was less vehement than previously. A good sign? 'Otherwise it'll be a nightmare. The house is only so big, and the money is tight, although that's not the main reason.'

'Jake is your son, Tom, and he's in trouble. He needs support and help with the baby. Give him a few weeks and he'll get on his feet.'

'We've got my mother to look after.'

They were at the bus stop. A woman and her small son, alongside them in the queue, grinned as their argument became audible to the onlookers.

'Listen to me.' Tom pulled Annie aside. 'You've got enough on your plate. It'll be too much. Won't it?'

Exasperated, she searched his face, but dropped her voice, 'Tell the truth, Tom. It's nothing to do with my comfort, it's more that you don't want Jake back home.'

Tom's eyes turned icy. 'Not true. He's a grown man and

he can't just pitch up on the doorstep and demand to be taken in.'

'But that's precisely what family is for.' She paused to rally her forces. 'We've been here, Tom, and I'm not going to let you do it again. Whatever you may feel about Jake, he's still entitled to our support and it's our absolute duty to give it.'

'I'm not proposing to abandon him.'

'Refuse to step up when he's at a crossroads and he'll believe that's precisely what you've done.'

'Thank you for the lesson.'

She tried again: 'Tom, remember, if you hadn't –'

'If I hadn't *what*?'

'You know very well. Once you've told a child to go, they go. They don't come back.'

Dangerous territory.

'Shut up, Annie.'

Out of the corner of her eye, Annie spotted a 77 draw in to the stop. The doors opened, disgorged, and the waiting passengers filed on to it. Without further ado, she nipped on to the platform and pushed her way into the centre of the bus, up the stairs and commandeered a seat on the top deck.

The bus moved off. Annie looked down to see Tom running alongside it, mouthing something at her. *You fool*, she thought. Then, at the sight of his ridiculous stick figure, she laughed.

The route was a familiar one. As the bus nosed its way along the Wandsworth Road, Annie asked herself, *Was it as much my fault?* It was an old question, one she had grown weary of asking – and of never answering.

At the Junction, she disembarked and, like an addict in search of a fix, hurried up the Falcon Road and turned right. Here, the houses had as yet to be gentrified and displayed varying degrees of neglect and indifference on the part of their owners. A dispirited lime tree struggled for existence and, in the front gardens, many of the rubbish bins were overflowing.

Annie halted in front of a house with an iron gate hanging by one hinge. She wasn't proud of herself, and knew perfectly well that she was being ridiculous. She didn't know if Mia lived here or not. But not knowing opened a margin for hope.

Greedily, she scanned the ground-floor window and the one above, both of which sported pairs of tatty curtains, for any changes that might offer a clue. Signs of occupation? Check. Anything different? Check.

She played over a piece of fantasy theatre of which she never tired. *Mum, what are you doing here? I've come to see you. I am so glad you have . . .* And she would say: *I have searched for you everywhere, my daughter. I glimpsed your face in the crowd. I heard your voice in the street . . .*

A voice said in her ear: 'Annie?'

She whipped around. 'Tom.'

He was half laughing, half frowning, out of breath and grabbing at her hands. At his touch, Annie's tears threatened.

'You abandoned me . . . Annie, what are you *doing* here?'

He looked at the end of his tether, and so anxious that she told him. 'Ages ago, I phoned Mia's friend, Kate Sinclair – you remember her? – to try and get some information. She didn't know any more than we did except she thought Mia and Pete might have rented a house in this street. So I come here sometimes.' She bit her lip. 'Just in case . . . I might see her.'

'And you never said.'

'No.'

He looked away. 'You were so determined that it was my fault.'

'Yes. No . . .' Annie swallowed. 'Let's get one thing straight. You don't want Jake to come home because it means you'll have to share a bedroom with me.'

'It's been a long time.'

'But you don't want to?'

'*You* don't want to. It was you who said that.'

She was bewildered. 'I said it?'

'After Mia left, you said you never wanted me anywhere near you again. And the idea of me in your bed sickened you.'

'That was then. I was furious with you. But I can't remember *actually* saying that.'

Tom's eyebrows shot up. 'People remember things differently.'

'You never came back. You made it plain you didn't wish to.'

He shrugged. 'Appearances aren't always . . .'

Sometimes she dreamed of change between them. Reconciliation even.

'If Jake comes to live with us, will you have me back in your room?'

Annie looked this way and that. So long. So much water and so many bridges under which it had flowed. 'Yes,' she said.

Chapter Eleven

It had turned out to be a late night, a Friday-night special in fact. Far later, and far in excess of the quiet drink Emily had planned. After such a night, it was achingly early to be up.

Preparing for it the previous evening, Emily had inserted herself into her skin-tight Topshop jeans and frivolous Primark jacket – bought at a particularly intense pedi-conference with Katya. She had planned an evening programme characterized by common sense and restraint.

The mirror reflected coolness and fashion savvy. So positive was the image that, as she folded and tidied everything else away, she conducted a debate with herself. Was it possible to be a serious writer (admittedly on hold) and yet so interested in fashion? Applying the eyelash curler, she was reassured (as was often the case) by Oscar Wilde: 'It is only shallow people who do not judge by appearances. The true mystery of the world is the visible, not the invisible.'

A further coating of (visible) mascara completed the evening's sentimental education and out Emily went.

'Only one' drink with Tod, the more-or-less boyfriend and striving poet, turned into two or three. The gastropub had been warmly lit and cosy and she was happy enough sitting across the table from him, sipping cold white wine and talking about nothing much. Anything they might wrangle over was not sufficiently contentious to be dangerous or so bland as to be boring (but skated perilously close on occasions).

This gently flirtatious state of affairs was possible because they had never really been passionate about each other – merely mildly intrigued. Once the affair slithered to a halt, which Emily sensed it would, friendship would be possible.

Then she had told him about the interviews, and what had resulted, and things got a bit sticky.

'I don't believe it,' he said, and an odd look crept into his eyes and remained there for the rest of what had turned into a not-so-satisfactory evening.

Hence the need to down an extra glass or two of the Pinot Grigio.

Head throbbing, she made her way downstairs. The backs of her clogs clunked against the stair treads – 'They have to go,' said Jake.

Jake, usually so good-natured, was being prickly about a lot of things, including the clogs. But, for reasons that were not entirely selfless, Emily was prepared to throw him plenty of rope and ignore the tide of his and Maisie's things that threatened to submerge the top floor.

Reputedly, every writer harboured a sliver of ice in their hearts and Emily could not make up her mind whether to admire or condemn herself for her willingness to use her brother as copy.

'Jocasta has gone. Abandoned me . . .' She had overheard him talking on the phone, she wasn't sure to whom. 'But I'm having trouble believing it . . .' There was a pause. 'Her lawyer's been in touch. Yes, very expensive and I know I must deal with it . . .'

How would Jake's abandonment read on the page?

Which precise word or phrase fitted the mould? 'Bitterness' . . . 'Humiliation' . . . 'Profound sadness'? No. 'Grief' was a better choice. Embedded in 'grief' was an august sadness, and it suggested a sweeping overview of the terrible things human beings inflicted on each other. Consider Phaedra, who loved her stepson and drove him to his death, before hanging herself. Actually, given that particular analogy, Emily did not feel that 'throwing Jake plenty of rope' was appropriate.

Deep, deep grief. Profound grief?

The words clinked in her head, like stones under the sea. This was the school for words, the inner workshop, and what she liked to think of as the creative process. Later, she planned to write them down and to scrutinize how they appeared on the paper for she had learned that what sounded well frequently did not work within the structure of a sentence or a paragraph.

Jake appeared on the stairs above her. 'War is declared on all clogs.'

'Bugger off,' she said, seized by a longing to be living in her own place, on her own terms.

Emily steadied herself. Admittedly she was a little uneasy on account of the wine, but her sleep had been fractured by a teething Maisie's night calls and fatigue scratched at her eyeballs, so goodness knew how Jake was feeling.

Her own news vying for attention, she loped down to the first-floor landing and prepared to negotiate the boxes that had sprouted outside her father's/Mia's bedroom.

Its door was ajar and Emily glanced through. Invariably and infuriatingly early risers, her parents were clearing it out in preparation for her grandmother's arrival. Her mother was laying out the contents of a drawer in order on the bed, while her father – typically – swept brushes and combs into a bin liner.

'Hey.' Emily hovered.

Her mother waved a hand, but her father looked round. 'Emily.'

She leaned against the door. Despite the muddle of objects and bed linen – or, rather, because of them – the room had a forlorn aspect. 'Hard work,' she offered.

'How would you know?' Her mother was at her driest.

Emily flushed. 'No need to be like that, Mum.'

Tom pushed past Emily with the bulging bin liner and dumped it in the bedroom opposite. Scratching his head, he surveyed the room he was about to move back into with the air of a traveller arriving on alien territory.

He's nervous, thought Emily, with a rush of empathy, and judging by the tense set of her mother's body, she was too. Emily's fists balled. *Please don't let this be a disaster*, she willed, as ever Tom's protector.

. . . 'Mum blames Dad for your going,' Emily had informed Mia, who had rung her once, and only once, after she'd stormed out and before the iron curtain finally clanged down. 'She told me she'd never forgive him.' Mia, who'd sounded hoarse from weeping and strain, had replied, 'It's not my business. They're not my parents any longer.'

'Mia, grow up.'

'You grow up, Emily. Take a look at the world as it really is . . . It's not an advert for happy families.'

Emily felt Mia's vengeance settle over her. 'You'll regret it.'

'Never,' said Mia, buoyed up by martyrdom and self-

righteousness. 'You don't understand. You can't understand . . .'

Emily never told anyone about that phone call. What
was the point?

'Do you want to hear my news?' she asked.

Her mother looked up from a pile of her father's shirts
on the bed and directed a searching stare at her. Ill? Pregnant? Emily knew exactly what was running through her
mind and she enjoyed waiting for a couple of seconds
longer before she dropped it into their laps: 'I've got a job.'

Clattering down the stairs to the kitchen, Emily filed
away their astonished faces into the writer's cache. *Speech-
less . . . Bone-deep surprise.*

Jake had been up for hours scuttling as noiselessly as possible between his and Maisie's bedroom on the top floor.
Since Jocasta's departure, Maisie had rarely slept past the
five-thirty mark and she was not picky as to which day of
the week it was. He had tried everything he could think
of – putting her to bed a little later, giving her an extra
bottle in the evening – but the ploys didn't fool his daughter. In the past – that far-away country of his marriage – he
used to stuff his fingers into ears and sit it out. Yet if he
had learned only one thing during the last painful weeks, it
was never to leave his daughter grizzling in the early hours
when she was likely to wake a whole household.

'She's OK, isn't she?' asked Jocasta, when she had rung
the previous night for an update and he told her about the
early waking.

Jake struggled to keep his temper. 'She's missing you,'
he said. 'What do you expect?'

'She'll probably get over it.'

Music played in the background and someone was moving around the room from which she was phoning. Probably Noah. He closed his eyes. Coming up against the realities of Jocasta and her new life was unbearably painful. 'Is there anything else you want?'

'Yes. I'm afraid I was a bit hasty in saying I would sign over the house. My lawyer has advised me against it.'

'I've been meaning to tell you I've let it,' he said. 'I couldn't afford my half of the mortgage. Don't worry, they're good tenants. As soon as I'm sorted, I go back in.'

'Oh.' At her end, Jocasta went quiet. 'No doubt the lawyers will talk to each other on that one. Send me the details of yours. Are things bad with the business?'

'There's a recession on, Jocasta.'

'Not for the very rich, thank goodness.'

Again, he sought relief by closing his eyes and blocking out the daylight. That way, life seemed possible. 'You know perfectly well I haven't got that sort of client base. But I'm managing.'

'Only managing?'

'For God's sake, is this an inquisition?' He added stiffly: 'How's the job . . .' and, with indescribable self-hatred, heard himself say '. . . in the US of A?' which made him sound puerile.

'Let's say I'm making headway.' She didn't sound that convinced. Aha, he thought, with a vindictiveness that made him feel much better, not that easy, then? 'Jake, I'll be in touch. If we set our minds to it, this divorce can be dealt with easily and quickly.'

The air at five thirty that morning had been sharp, but

the sky had been washed by pink tints and suggested warmth to come. Jake's burgeoning relationship with nature was an unexpected consequence of hands-on childcare. As Maisie sucked away at a bottle, he was free to stare out of the window and, each day, his acquaintance with London bird life deepened.

It was never a good idea to think about Jocasta. For starters, his heartbeat ratcheted up at least three notches. He wondered if she had turned New-York-glossy – and whether she walked to work in her suit and trainers, like high-flyer women were reported to do.

But here was the puzzle. How was it possible for that which had begun in an upwelling of excitement and positive, tender love (which surely she must have shared in a little?) to turn into such bitter disaster? How could he have read her so wrongly, and how could he have put himself into a position that had left him so scourged and suffering?

He picked up Maisie and carried her down to the first floor, glancing into his mother's room as he passed. Both parents were sitting on the bed with slightly dazed expressions.

'Everything all right? You both look poleaxed.'

'We are,' said his father, with a grin.

'What's happened?'

'Emily will tell you.'

Jake continued downstairs. Just before the final step, his foot slipped and he pitched forward. In the split second before he regained his balance, his head seemed to explode with pain and despair. He was disintegrating – he was a failure – he –

Thinking this was a great joke, Maisie gurgled, and Jake was brought up short. 'Oh, my God, Maisie,' he whispered, pulled himself upright and deposited Maisie on the hall floor. Shaking a little, he leaned against the newel post.

The wooden ball that topped it was polished by handling, and inviting. Jake had grasped it thousands of times but this was when he became *aware* of its whorls and striations for the first time in a significant way. And he, the woodsman! How remarkably sane an object it was, as wholesome and as beautifully shaped as he would wish his life to be.

Parked at his feet, Maisie protested. Jake looked down. A trusting, hungry little face encountered his, and he smiled. Whatever had he been thinking? Despair and breakdown had to be off the menu. His daughter's needs were more pressing than his – for the wound in her life made by her mother's departure was far more dangerous than any he might have suffered.

However, on picking her up, he was dealt a sharp reminder of the realities. Intimations of the larger perspective, or of the obligation to be unselfish, vanished. Maisie smelt. Growling, he climbed back up the stairs to the room under the eaves where the nappies were kept.

Eventually, making it to the kitchen bearing the clean, more-or-less sweet-smelling package that was his daughter, he discovered Emily contemplating a bowl of porridge in a hopeless fashion.

The kitchen seemed only half awake and functioning: whiffs of the previous night's stew floated in the corners, butter and jams littered the table, and a swathe of crumbs indicated that his parents had breakfasted but not cleared up. The dismembered newspaper had been cast aside. Its headline read: 'Forecast: Unemployment Will Go Up'.

Emily propped her head in her hand.

'Early teetotal night, I take it.' Jake lifted Maisie into her chair.

Emily stuck a spoon into the porridge. 'Has anyone told you you're a waste of space?'

Jake was ultra-dry. 'Someone mentioned it.'

'Oh, God.' Emily's head jerked up. 'Sorry, Jake.' She got up and deposited the porridge in the sink, wandered over to the dresser and leaned back against it. Her mother's precious blue-and-white plates rattled a warning. 'You know how it is. Nice bar. Wine the colour of a prize canary. French fries. Tod being nice and asking about the writing . . .' She stopped and a look of consternation swept over her features. 'Actually, he wasn't so nice.'

Jake paid absolutely no attention. Emily's on/off relationship with Tod had long ceased to interest any of them – much as the bowl of tepid porridge had failed to engage her.

'Tod's very good at understanding the struggle to write,' she said at last.

'Oh, yes, that struggle.' Jake attached a plastic bib around Maisie's neck. 'The struggle not to mind that you're not, like hundreds of others, struggling into work. Tricky, that one.'

'Double negative,' Emily pointed out acidly.

Jake had gone too far but he didn't care. 'For God's sake.'

'Don't we like each other any more?'

Emily was hurt, but Jake didn't care about that either. That was what emotional adversity had done to him – turned him hard and unresponsive – and he tried to mind. He brushed back Maisie's hair, licked a finger and smoothed her eyebrows. He had always hoped he would be the sort of person who rated empathy and worked to achieve it.

That seemed to him to be the most profound moral duty in life but, just now, the will to act on it had vanished.

'Here.' Emily handed him a pot of baby food. 'Lovely apple purée and additives. Shouldn't you be making her food, not feeding her this stuff?'

'Shut up.' But he took the pot with a grateful smile. Emily bent over and kissed her niece, who gurgled politely.

'Did she keep you awake? I do try to cut her off before she goes full throttle.'

Emily straightened up. 'You must be tired.'

'I am. By the way, what's up with the parents?'

'You wanna know?' Now he was paying proper attention he saw she was brimming with a secret and anxious to tell him. *Just like Mia used to do.*

'Jake.' Emily's seriousness was almost touching. 'I've got a job.'

This *was* unexpected, and Jake felt a flicker of chagrin. He busied himself with Maisie and did not look at Emily. 'A job? That's – that's wonderful.'

'You could make more effort to sound enthusiastic.'

'I am. I am.'

'This is a proper job. Salary. Benefits. Pension, the lot.'

He switched on the wholehearted smile. 'You must be the only person in the country to have pulled off such a coup right now.'

Emily ducked her head, which meant she was pleased. 'Thanks.'

In every family, Jake supposed, there was a hierarchy of both expectation and contempt. If his father despised Jake's occupation, then Jake had taken (shameful) comfort from Emily's pennilessness.

His hand shook as he wrestled the bib away from a replete Maisie. One chair. One coffee-table, small. Those were the sum total of orders in Nicholson Furniture's book. Whichever way he looked at his current position, it appeared more excruciating than anything else. Plus, and there was no merit at all in this reflection, there would no longer be the luxury of regarding Emily as an even weaker link than he was.

'Do you understand?' Emily heaved Maisie up and began to pace up and down, the baby pinned to her breast like a brooch. 'I'd like you to understand, Jake. Tod doesn't. He thinks I've sold out. I know I sound like the worst sort of indulged kid, but I don't want to do this job at all. With things as they are, though . . . I don't expect much sympathy, but a bit would be nice.'

The truth was Jake had no sympathy to spare.

Upstairs something thumped on the floor, and there were sounds of a tense exchange.

Emily shrugged and pointed to the ceiling. 'Don't go there. But aren't you going to ask about the job?'

'Consider yourself asked.'

'Condor Oil. Writing press releases and speeches and things. One of a big in-house team.'

'Good God.'

'Had three interviews.' She looked so pleased and eager. 'But I got through.'

This was worse than anything, for Jake now realized the extent of Emily's sacrifice. Never . . . never would he have imagined that his shy, dreamy sister would fetch up working for an oil company. The quality and depth of that sacrifice dealt him a sharp knock.

*

Annie noted the time on her watch, then rechecked – the automatic gesture of a long-time working mother. Technically, this was a normal Saturday morning: the weekly shopping (no pesto, beef, French cheese or blueberries); her newly instituted weekly cooking session (fish pie, spaghetti Bolognese, and chicken breasts in some sort of sauce, to be decided); an exhausted perusal of the papers; a couple of loose ends to tie up on work projects.

But this was not going to be exactly a normal weekend and she and Tom were going to shop together to get the stuff required for what was now called Hermione's room. List in hand, she made the final inspection. Post-Mia, post-Tom, it had been emptied, neutralized and fumigated of its previous inhabitants. She inspected the window catches, peered into the cupboard and punched the mattress on the single bed – the bed Tom had occupied for so long. Squinting at the curtains, her lips twitched. Tom always said she had a nasty habit of checking up on his handiwork. It was, he teased, a feature of obsessive-compulsives. And which category, she countered, did his habit of checking up on her come into? Tom protested loud and long that he did nothing of the sort. 'Well, then,' she had said, 'I'll suggest to the *OED* they rewrite their definition of "control freak".'

Not for the first time she wondered about the power of one's own nature to direct behaviour, even if one knew it was unproductive behaviour, and how little one could control it.

Unearthing a cache of single socks, a pair of rogue pants and a rolled-up shirt in a bottom drawer, she felt warmly smug. Having been boiled once too often in the washing-machine, the socks were past it. Annie chucked them, plus the pants and shirt, into the bin liner.

A screw had worked loose on the cupboard hinge. She fetched a screwdriver and wrestled to re-anchor it. Tom reappeared. 'You're not doing it right. Here, let me.'

'Go away, Tom. I can manage.'

'Annie, you're putting it in at the wrong angle.'

She swirled around. 'Go away, or I'll drive it through your head.'

Left alone, she continued with her work. The radio played Schubert's String Quintet, which always made Annie ache, yearn and mourn but for what she had never quite managed to locate. Finding it too disturbing, she fiddled with the dial and a voice filled the room, explaining the HIV rates in India. 'Tom!' She whisked out of the room and leaned over the banisters. 'Tom, the India programme – they've put it on Radio 4.'

She went back into the room and sat down on the bed to give it her full attention. It was a good, thoughtful programme – no doubt about that – and Tom would have spent energy and passion on ensuring it got made. As the credits were listed, she glanced around and spotted him hovering by the door.

'Any good?' He seemed nervous and more than a little sad.

She smiled up at him. 'Excellent. The best.'

He nodded. 'Well, that's something. At least I did something,' he said, before disappearing back downstairs.

A final search of the cupboard. She scooped up a single cufflink, which had rolled into the back, a simple green knot from which much of the colour had leached. Minus its partner, it seemed forlorn in the palm of her hand.

Ages ago on holiday in the South of France, when the children were still young and the Nicholson economy was booming, she had bought the cufflinks for Tom. Then they had seemed interestingly non-conformist and she had enjoyed seeing him wear them.

She had lived so intensely that summer, rejoicing in an unburdened mind, a captive to sensation. There was sun. Scratchy sand burning the soles of her bare feet. Swanky yachts painted in dazzling whites, and windmill sails in reds and blues. The turquoise slap of the sea. The violet and granite hues of the *maquis* rising behind the bay. Tom holding her as they watched a sunrise. Tom buying fruit in the market, tousled and satiated with food and sex.

Definitely, some memories were there to act as life-belts, to be thrown over waters of extreme distress and sadness and clung to.

Cufflink in hand, Annie descended to the kitchen.

Here, the table was still littered with breakfast things, the pile of crockery in the sink had mounted, and the occupants seemed to be scratchily at odds with one another.

A piece of buttered toast dangled from Emily's limp hand. Jake was eating a plate of congealed porridge by the window. Tom was drinking coffee and making faces at Maisie, a spatter of slop trailing across the draining-board indicating his flight path.

Maisie lolled in the high chair and blinked rapidly, which was a sure sign she was sleepy and needed her nap. Annie almost said something to Jake but bit it back. She had resolved that Jake was in charge of his daughter, and intended to keep it that way.

None of them indicated that they had registered Annie's

presence. She was used to being wallpaper. And at this point, with her kitchen taken over by a noisy, fractious army, being wallpaper was absolutely fine. *Remember?*

. . . The kitchen had been ringing with the shouts of three small children and two adults at bay and, in the background, the radio rumbled on regardless.

'Sit,' Tom had commanded the seven-year-old twins. 'Down.' Then he turned on Emily who (no doubt to impress the twins) was zooming around the kitchen on her scooter. 'If you don't stop that . . .'

The table groaned under a pile of sausages, mash, ketchup, buttered peas, a white loaf (they hated brown), orange juice, token sticks of celery and an apple crumble.

Hands on hips, Annie sidestepped Emily and laughed at the chaos. 'If you don't all sit down, you won't get supper.'

And Mia, coppery hair tied on top of her head, darted out of range with elfin cunning. 'Can't catch me.' She executed a couple of pirouettes, dancing out of the kitchen into the hall and, with hindsight, it seemed to Annie even then that Mia was taking herself away.

The neighbours must have heard Tom's half-enraged, half-amused bellow: 'Come here!' . . .

The light shifted off the coppery tints in Jake's and, just discernible, Maisie's hair. Before Tom, Annie had gone for men with looks that were basically Saxon and chimed with hers. The surprise (among many surprises) of being overwhelmed by a dark smoulderer had always intrigued her. Still did, if she was truthful.

The twins looked indisputably English – autumn tints, freckles and hazel eyes. Mia berated her parents for her division of the genetic spoils. 'I so long to be pretty,' she told her mother, before she had become serious and ignored issues like beauty. 'But no chance if you look like a milk-maid.' Emily – 'lucky, horrible Emily' (Mia's terminology) – had inherited the allure of the mysterious Celt, all white skin, blazing blue eyes, dark hair and a tendency to uneasy introspection that had made for a rocky adolescence.

Jake had been born with inner poise and had set sail through childhood and adolescence on a fair wind. Annie had marvelled at his seemingly effortless progress. He was a craftsman and tinkerer. 'I like to know how things work, Mum.' Kettles, machines and, of course, searching for pieces of wood to store in his room. 'Don't get him,' said Tom, more than once, who wanted Jake to study politics or, at the very least, economics – the subjects he felt were of use in the modern world. 'You don't know him,' she responded. 'You must try to understand him.' To his credit, Tom had tried and, when Jake was still quite small, they had fiddled around with carpentry together. The results still roosted in the attic. A half-finished doll's cradle, intended for Mia, and a box for treasures that had never got its lid, if Annie remembered correctly.

Mia's going had thrown the family but, for obvious reasons, it had affected Jake from the roots up. He was never angry or obviously down but Annie knew, she just knew, that an element had gone missing. 'It's like eating food without salt,' he confessed, when she'd tackled him on the subject. Then Jocasta had come on the scene and Jake was diverted. It wasn't an obvious coupling but, concluded the ever-watchful Annie, it was likely that the restless and raven-ing Jocasta was attracted by Jake's unruffled good spirits as much as his rangy good looks.

Her lips tightened. If Jocasta was ever arraigned before a court of human justice, Annie would be on her feet to condemn her for extinguishing the glow and sweetness in her son.

Abandoning the porridge, Jake cut himself a piece of bread and shoved it into the toaster. 'Maisie needs a sleep. I'll put her down in a minute,' he said tiredly.

Tom trod carefully: 'Are you going to the workshop at all? If you like I'll look after her, but not for too long as your mum and I have to shop and paint your grandmother's room later.'

Good Lord, thought Annie. That must be a first.

It was an olive branch. Of sorts.

Jake considered. Annie held her breath.

'Thanks, Dad. That just might suit.' Jake balanced the toast in one hand and spread raspberry jam over it with other.

Annie let her breath out. 'Don't any of you do anything as revolutionary as eat your meal at the table?' she asked, by way of diversion.

Emily threw her a look implying that her mother had only recently emerged from Noah's ark. From over his shoulder, Jake said, 'Haven't noticed you sitting down, Mum.'

She dropped the cufflink into Tom's lap. 'Recognize it?'

He frowned. 'Should I?'

'Oh, never mind,' she said.

Jake finished the toast and put on his denim jacket. If possible he had lost weight and it hung more loosely on him. 'I'll be off.' He bent over and kissed his daughter. 'Tweet, tweet, Birdie.' He flicked a look at Tom. 'Thanks again, Dad.' Then he was gone.

Emily stacked her used crockery in the dishwasher and wiped the table. She seemed grave and preoccupied, and Annie said, 'It's brilliant news, Emily.'

'Do you think, Mum?' She sent Annie an apprehensive smile. 'Yup. It's OK.' But she seemed disinclined to discuss it further.

Then she, too, was gone.

Tom was muttering nonsense to Maisie. He undid the safety strap, extracted her and cuddled her into his shoulder. 'Bed for the Bird, I think.'

He nodded at Annie – and for a terrible moment she had the feeling that he was acknowledging an acquaintance he had met in the street.

Then he said, 'Got to get used to this.'

Yes, they would have to, thought Annie, left to herself in the kitchen. She didn't know whether to laugh because most of her family had come home, or to cry because Jake was badly hurt and her routines and peace were well and truly shattered.

Dirty saucepans tottered on the sideboard. 'Bloody family,' she muttered aloud, as she ran hot water into the sink and began to make inroads into them. She glanced across to the noticeboard where she had pinned up the angel. 'I'm glad I rescued you,' she said, and hoped nobody had heard her.

What a mess everything is, she thought. And: *How muddled*. This conclusion, combined with her sorrow for Jake, made her cry and the tears ran down to vanish into the suds in the sink.

Chapter Twelve

It had been a long time – almost half a decade – but it seemed much longer since she and Tom had shared a bedroom. And Annie was at a loss as to whether to undress in front of him or to take refuge in the adjoining bathroom.

Already the latter's white-towelled femininity had been diluted. While Annie had held sway, she had enjoyed garnishing it with soaps, expensive bath oils and a selection of white ceramic dishes. Tom's shaving kit, his battered brown washbag and dark green towels were an intrusion on her careful *mise-en-scène*.

Tom was putting more stuff into a drawer, and she hovered uncertainly in the doorway. Usually, as she got ready for bed, she hung up her clothes as she removed them and laid out the next day's. This was a sequence designed to minimize effort the following morning – such were the habits evolved to suit the working mother. It was not very exciting but it was life-saving, and the truth was she had grown used to considering herself a *useful, sensible* person.

'Try to disguise it,' was Sadie's tart advice. She was right, of course. How would Tom react when he was confronted by her fuller waistline close up? What would she feel about his? The plain and ridiculous fact of the matter was that she was anxious about revealing her body to the man with whom she had lived for all these years.

Maturity was the ability to accept one's lot. Much had

been written in that vein and – Annie glanced down at her midriff – it was a great deal more palatable on a page. She observed Tom's bent back. Goodbye, then, the flash and brilliance of youthful shooting stars, the yearning to ride on wilder shores, and a supple body.

Tom groaned. 'Done.' He pressed a fist into his spine and straightened up.

Oh, my God, which side of the bed should she make for? In the old days, she had occupied the left but, during the years of solitude, had found herself migrating to the right.

Annie knotted and reknotted her dressing-gown cord.

A pair of black lace-up shoes in his hand, Tom turned round. 'I think I'll chuck these out.'

'Charity shop?'

'Sure.' He turned back to the job in hand.

Annie retreated into the bathroom and slumped against the closed door. She and Tom were not close, and hadn't been for years, and here she was as nervous as a bride. The logic was . . . Well, there was no logic.

Undressing rapidly, she put on her nightdress, brushed the obstinate tangles in her hair and creamed her face. The mirror did not spare her the truth. Nevertheless, the image in it reflected, against all reason, the mad optimism and the obstinate spirit that had got people through a long, punishing war.

She ran a finger along her stuff on the shelf, and picked up the bottle of La Perla scent. Cool and ultra-smooth between her fingers, it invited the useful woman Sadie had warned her she must not be the chance to experience the erotic and the sensuous. A quick squirt, and mist drifted over her shoulders.

Annie was ready.

Hopping around on a pale leg, Tom peeled off his sock. A lock of hair flopped over an eye and, despite the ridiculous pose, he suddenly appeared much younger.

Annie avoided the white legs (had they always been that white?), slid into the right-hand side of the bed, arranged herself and pulled out a report on hospital cleaning practices that she needed to read before the morning. Her intentions were firm but her attention was anything but and her gaze was drawn inexorably to Tom.

First off, he pushed aside her hairbrush and slotted his own beside it on the dressing-table. It fitted its new niche. Annie reapplied herself to the paper on her lap.

It was quickly clear that the beautiful theatre sister had been correct. Budgets lay at the root of the superbug problem. Annie endeavoured to tick off the salient points.

(1) *It didn't matter where her hairbrush was.*

She sighed and tried again.

(2) Old-fashioned, effective methods of scrub and disinfect require more man hours. Therefore more expensive.
(3) *How far would the usurpation of her things and spaces go?*
(4) Superbug infection rates rise from 0 to 0.69 per 69 cases per 1000 days or approx. 100,000 cases per year.
(5) *Grow up!*

Tom inserted a wedge of shirts into a drawer that had been occupied by her sweaters.

Budgets. She returned to the report and tried not to think of the unhappily compacted shirts she had ironed. Tom kicked the drawer shut and padded into the bathroom.

Much splashing.

A crash of china and an oath.

He emerged from the bathroom, cradling two pieces of a white ceramic soap dish. 'I'm very sorry, Annie.'

'Oh,' Annie said. 'Oh.'

The dish had been purchased – French, expensive – on a trawl through one of those shops done up in taupe and white that only stocked objects in taupe and white. When it had been whole and functional, she had enjoyed it a lot.

'I'd like to say I could mend it but it's past repair, I'm afraid,' said a rueful Tom. 'I'll get you a new one.'

She thought of the luxuries that were no longer admissible. 'Don't worry.' Throwing back the duvet, she seized the wastepaper basket and held it out. 'It belonged to the days of wine and roses.'

'Sure?'

'Yes.' The pieces slid into the basket and Annie bade them farewell.

Back in bed, she gave up on the report, settled down and pulled the duvet around her. She closed her eyes and welcomed the darkness, only to be jerked almost upright as Tom whipped back the duvet and plonked heavily down beside her.

'Oh . . .' The cool air hit her shrinking body.

Tom busied himself arranging the pillows. Suffering from hay fever, he had imported his hypo-allergenic ones, which jostled beside Annie's goose-down. They smelt, and felt, alien.

Annie resettled herself.

The newspaper rustled very close to her ear. Her eyes flew open. Tom was wedged back against the headboard and was deep in the leader page. She closed them tight. A sliver of light inserted itself between her clamped eyelids but she willed herself into sleep.

Fifteen minutes or so later, Tom asked loudly, 'Am I keeping you awake?'

'Don't even think about it,' she murmured.

Some time during the night, Annie realized she was cold. Wallowing in the shallows of a deep sleep from which she had been dragged, she did not at first understand why. She touched a shoulder. Bare. She felt her midriff. Startled, she rolled over and encountered Tom's unconscious form shrouded in the entire duvet.

Annie's lips twitched. She simply could not think of any comment to direct into the chilly air.

Tom was in his element.

Energy coursed through him. He felt fit, well and ready to go.

The section and regional heads were dribbling into the building and taking the lifts up to the meeting room. Soon, he would join them and take his place at the head of the table and faces would turn towards him.

He punched a number into the office phone and James answered almost at once. 'Tom?'

'You OK with the report?'

'Sure,' said James, but there was a touch of uncertainty.

'Do you want to come down here and we'll go over it?'

While he waited for James, he put in a quick call to his contact at the Foreign Office. Battle was about to commence. The Foreign Office wanted to cut the budgets to the service. Absolutely nothing new about that. The BBC World Service, which spoke 'unto nations', would fight any threat and Tom would be there on the front line. Nothing was more important than keeping this channel of communication open and flowing. Nothing was more important than ensuring that debate and ideas and campaigns could be heard across the world – and if he had to work night and day (as he sometimes had done) to make sure it happened he would do so.

The FO contact was bland enough and, listening to him, Tom doodled on his pad. By the end of the conversation, and expert in decoding Whitehall-speak, he had gained sufficient information to form the opinion that, if they were clever enough with the figures and lip service, they would be left to their own devices.

James had come into the office and was spreading sheets of paper in front of Tom on the desk. He was elaborately casual, which went only halfway to disguising his nerves.

'It's not as bad as all that.' Tom flashed him a smile. Having joined the service on the same day, he and James were old companions.

James grimaced. 'Almost.'

As friends, they had shared much during their years with the BBC. The World Service was probably staffed with more brilliant people than most institutions and James was one of them. But, like James, the majority of these clever, committed people had the habit of modesty and not many relished being in the spotlight. But Tom did. He didn't mind it at all.

Today James was on show and having a bit of a wobble. Tom checked over a paragraph of the paper. 'This is good,' he said. 'Really good.'

James whistled through pursed lips and knocked a fist on the desk. 'Thanks.'

Tom leaped to his feet. 'Off we go, then.'

'How're Annie and the children?' James gathered up his papers.

'Annie? Oh, she's fine.' Tom reached for his jacket. 'I think the children are fine too. Don't see much of them, really.'

'Oh,' said James, and Tom thought he detected a hint of smugness. Of reproof, even. 'Ours infest the house. Penny complains she doesn't have any time to herself.'

Tom frowned, and hunted for the meeting's agenda. 'Onwards,' he said, clapped his hand on James's shoulder and ushered him out of the office. 'Listen, I've got some ideas that I think could go down well. Can I lob them at you while we walk?'

'Of course,' said James. He was silent for a beat. 'Do you ever stop, Tom?' His tone combined admiration and exasperation.

A wakeful Tom replayed the scene, one of many from his working past, pausing over every detail, each a reminder of what he had been and how he used to be. It wasn't a useful thing to do but he couldn't stop himself. Yet. Maybe in the future he would be able to push himself onwards.

On the floor above, Maisie was emitting a series of sparrow calls that increased in intensity and plaintiveness. Tom hated hearing her cry – far more so than when it had been his own child, which was not too good a reflection on his parenting record. Annie had occasionally accused him of never hearing the children at night. *Either you're flat out, or there's a pillow stuffed over your head.* But Maisie's distress aroused a visceral feeling of distress in him and he couldn't cope with it.

He listened for a footstep up above. None.

He squinted at the dark shape that was his wife and realized . . . what? Lack of sleep must have tried her sorely when the kids were little, particularly Jake, who had slept badly for several years. With hindsight – oh, hindsight! – he realized he should have thought about it more, but in those days her job had not been so senior. 'Your need is greater,' Annie had always maintained, or something like it, often (now that he looked back) tired out of her mind. But then he had never thought to question it.

Maisie's cries geared up to a full-frontal assault on the eardrums. Still no sign of Jake and, unable to bear it any longer, Tom slid out of bed, padded upstairs and scooped up the baby.

Sobbing, angry and sopping wet, she banged her head against his shoulder. Tom held her close and, for a moment, imagined he also held the ghosts of his own three babies in his arms. 'Hush, Maisie.' He reached over for the bottle of water by the cot, sat down and gave it to her.

Maisie attacked it with the reproach of a thirsty and neglected infant. After a moment, she quietened and settled against him.

Like an old pro, Tom congratulated himself, as quiet fell and the dawn prepared itself in the sky outside. *I'm her bulwark*. The notion pleased and warmed him.

The room was cluttered with baby equipment – changing mat, Johnson's lotion, assorted clothes, a basket in one corner, cotton-wool balls and plastic disposal bags. The elderly curtains were frayed at the edges and the carpet needed replacing. The room was stuck in a time warp of twenty years ago and it was bloody freezing. Yet, curiously, he felt happier here, holding Maisie, than he had for weeks.

He was changing Maisie's nappy (rather well, he reckoned) when Jake stumbled into the room in a T-shirt and boxer shorts, his hair in cockatoo barnet. 'Good God, Dad,

I had no idea it was you.' He cast a glance over the nappy-changing operation. 'Or that you claimed babycare as one of your skills.'

'She'd been crying for a while, and I was awake.' He snapped the nappy shut, bent over and gave Maisie his finger to hold. 'All right now. Grandpa did the trick while your daddy snored.'

Jake's elbowed him aside. 'Don't you believe a word of it, my Bird. Your grandfather is currying favour.' Curious and slightly sceptical, he gave Tom the once-over. 'I thought you never did this sort of thing, Dad.'

Tom flinched. A world of misunderstanding was wrapped up in the statement, plus a history that contained its fair share of bad moments and missed chances.

. . . Jake eating ice cream when forbidden. Jake being monumentally sick through the long night before a crucial meeting between Tom and the section heads. Annie trailing up and down stairs with clean sheets and disinfectant. 'He's calling for you,' she had told him.

'I can't,' said Tom, anchored to the bed. 'I just can't.'

'Why didn't you come, Daddy?' asked a white-faced little boy, the following morning. 'I wanted you.'

Technically, it was only a small failure . . .

'It was always Mum . . .' Jake picked up his daughter. 'But actually, Dad, now that I'm having to do everything, I don't blame you. I see why it was so difficult.'

'But your mum managed,' said Tom.

Jake smiled sweetly. 'But Mum is Mum.'

The strangeness of the night – its silence and suspended life – enfolded father and son in a peace not possible during the day, loosening the tensions between them.

'I didn't get up very often,' Tom found himself admitting. 'I should have done more.' In the dim reaches of this particular night, the everyday seemed far away. 'Jake . . .' The old sins gathered in a battalion to haunt him. 'Jake, *was* I such a bad father?'

Jake smiled. 'I have to say you were on my back a lot. You weren't there very much.'

That hurt. 'I set out to be such a good one.' Tom flinched from contemplating his failures – but it was necessary. 'Didn't we do things together? Didn't we do carpentry? Didn't we make a crib for Mia? Stuff like that?'

'Yes, but . . .' Jake began to say something, thought better of it and shrugged. 'Water under the bridge. OK? Listen, thanks for getting up.'

Outside, a bird tried out the first song of the day. 'Jake . . .' Tom would have liked to continue the conversation.

'Dad, go to bed.' Jake placed a now sleepy Maisie back in her cot and tucked her up. He stroked the small cheek. 'Do your old dad a favour and go back to sleep.'

All long, lean legs and tousled hair, Jake was anything but 'old dad': he was a showy, sexy package of energy and youth. In contrast, in his pyjamas and dressing-gown, Tom was Father Time.

Jake repeated, 'Go to bed, Dad.' He checked that the blanket over Maisie was drawn tight. 'Just one thing . . . I know you have reason, but you've been pretty short with Mum. The Black Dog is sitting on your shoulder but . . .'

'Have I?'

'Yup.'

A tarpaulin appeared to drop over Tom. 'Point taken.' *Point taken.* 'You've lost a wife and I've lost a job.'

'Thanks again, Dad.' Jake's whisper followed Tom out of the room.

He made his way downstairs and climbed stiffly into bed, lay on his back and stared up into the darkness. He knew that he should look forward to the rest of his life. He knew that, compared to many, he was lucky. Yet he was racked by loss and longing for the job he no longer had. It was there, sharp and unequivocal – the thorn driven into his heart.

He put up a hand to shield his eyes against the darkness and grief, and Annie moved and sighed in her sleep. He could not be sure but he thought her hand brushed lightly against his thigh.

Just after dawn, Annie woke up seriously freezing. Yet again, the duvet had migrated to Tom. Gritting her teeth, she got out of bed and went to fetch a spare one from the linen cupboard on the landing. It was an old one, which had done faithful service at sleepovers, and bore the stains of spilled drinks and midnight feasts.

It was also a single one. This meant a gully opened up between her and Tom, along which chilly air circulated with malevolent gusto. She tried lying flat, which she hated doing, gave up and turned on to her side.

Sleepless.

If it hadn't been closer to breakfast than dinner she might have got up, gone downstairs and searched out the brandy. From time to time, she had resorted to it and found it settled her. Anyway, she remembered now that they had run out and brandy had gone on the luxuries-not-to-be-replaced list.

No brandy, then.

Her brain busied itself with questions of money and debt, which she was worried they might, along with hundreds of others, slip into. 'Mum, you're a doomster,' Mia used to tease her. But thinking the worst was only sensible because, when it arrived, one had almost become friendly with it. Debt was a killer. It changed people in unexpected ways, drove them to extremes, and she was nervous about confronting the challenge if the economy got worse and Tom never worked again. A description she had read of Elizabeth I came to mind: 'She was afraid but never lost her head.' (Whence had she dredged that one up?) The great Queen had wrestled with possible national bankruptcy and bad teeth. She had also had to give up sex to preserve the nation.

Annie turned over towards Tom. Sprawled on his side, his shoulders hunched, he seemed as unreachable as ever.

As she watched, he rolled over, and Annie was vouch-safed a flash of belly, lightly dusted with dark hair. Curiously, her current anxieties made her think about sex more than she had done for some time. What would it feel like after so long? When was the last time? Four months? Longer? Yes, longer.

Whenever, it had been pretty joyless. Pretty mechanical.

She resettled herself and squinted at towards the window. The early light outside was, as yet, dim and unsure of itself. It had a quality peculiar to the moment of transition just before summer arrives, a perfect papery foil for the season's pastel colours.

Was Sadie right? Would it have been better, a more honest way of behaving, to leave Tom?

'Annie.' His voice sounded in her ear. 'Go to sleep.'

She turned her head but, in an instant, he had fallen back into unconsciousness.

Annie could negotiate pay rises with the best of them. Her budgets were neat and decisive. She had a working knowledge of insurance, pensions and the other tedious necessities of modern life. She relied on herself, and had grown used to doing so. But what lay ahead, and the weight of carrying a wounded Tom, made her realize how much she still depended on him.

Please, she thought. *Don't go under, Tom.*

The gully of air between them seemed colder and deeper and she tucked the midnight-feast-stained duvet around her torso and tried not to think of the orange drinks, chocolate biscuits and God knew what else contained in its depth.

Actually, Annie did not like being on the right-hand side of the bed after all. She preferred the left.

Chapter Thirteen

'The Nicholsons stumble on,' Annie informed Sadie, when they met for a catch-up in a wine bar.

Sadie had just had her hair done and it gleamed soft and perfect in a way that Annie could only envy helplessly. 'And mother-in-law?'

'Moving in at the weekend. What with one thing and another, the arrangements took longer than we thought. Finances and stuff, and she wanted to take her time and we couldn't deny her that.'

'You know,' said Sadie, unexpectedly, 'it might not be so bad.'

Annie aimed a kick at Sadie's foot, clad in a thigh-length leather boot. 'Take my place?' Then, with a rush, she said, 'Thanks, Sadie, for listening to everything. I don't know what I'd do without you.'

'I don't mind homage,' said Sadie. 'In fact, I was born for it.' She adopted the wise look Annie knew so well. 'Have you and Tom decided what you're going to do?'

Annie gave a tiny shrug. 'Working on it.'

'You know what?' said Sadie. 'At risk of repeating myself, if you live with someone, you might as well get to understand what's going on in their head.'

Annie couldn't resist. She grinned naughtily. 'Easy when you change them so often.'

'I never said I was perfect.'

Annie kissed Sadie on her scented cheek. 'You're a witch. Please don't change.'

But witchy Sadie had a point.

Soon after breakfast on the designated Sunday, Tom and Jake departed in the hired van and family car to collect Hermione. Emily and Annie stayed behind, Emily to babysit and Annie to fuss over last-minute arrangements. She got busy with dusters and polish.

'Mum, there's no need to clean the house from top to toe.' Emily edged past Annie, hard at work on the landing.

Zosia had gone to work for Pat Hillaby. Naturally, her mourned departure had had consequences for the good order of the house. The idea was – and Annie had issued the edict – that the occupants of number twenty-two should be responsible for and clean their own territories. The results were, to shine the best light on them, variable.

Annie pointed to a streak of dirt on the skirting-board. Emily put her head knowingly to one side and said, 'Oh, I get it. It's a mother-in-law-daughter-in-law thing.'

Seizing a breathing space, Annie sat down at the kitchen table to catch up with the accounts, which now featured prominently in her routines. However, despite the rigour and expertise she had at her fingertips for work budgets, her control over the domestic one was less sure. The figures would dodge here and there. With a life of their own, they chased after Annie and wrestled her to the ground. Aha, they seemed to say, we control you.

Every so often, she glanced up and eyed the cooker. That, too, was the enemy: the malevolent beast crouching in its corner, readying itself to unleash its torments. Like malign besiegers materializing out of nowhere, the cooker, defective vacuum cleaner and piles of laundry silently encircled Annie and, oh, how her horizons had shrunk. The winds of change were whirling across the world and here she was tallying up her enemies in the shape of dusters and tricky accounts.

The hands on the kitchen clock moved far too quickly.

Technically, there was no more time to worry. No more time for conjecture. No more space to ask, is Hermione going to make life impossible? But Annie had a feeling that she had (a) opened Pandora's Box, (b) set herself up for a life of constant sniping, and (c) not sufficiently understood that strangers, who arrived wired up with their quirks and dislikes like a computer mother board, don't necessarily merge quietly into a household.

Clutching Maisie, Emily puffed downstairs and into the kitchen. 'Wow, she's getting heavy.'

Annie held out her arms. 'Give her to me.' She accepted the solid package of her granddaughter as a relief from her apprehensions. She stroked the downy head. 'Hallo, Birdie. Did you have a nice nap?'

Maisie sported one bright red cheek, and the little mouth was pursed with some grievance or other, almost certainly hunger, and Annie got to her feet.

Emily ran the tap for a glass of water. 'Hey, look at that. There's a for-sale notice in the window of the Fergusons' four-by-four.'

They peered through the window.

'More space in the street, then.' Emily drained her glass.

'The Hillabys are selling theirs too.'

'So there is a God.'

'I must remind you that, before Dad lost his job, we weren't so very different.'

Emily's sigh was a gusty one. 'Big changes, Mum. Will we cope?'

She was obviously thinking as much about the job as anything else. Annie's maternal watchdog leaped out of its basket. 'Are you feeling all right? Not sickening or anything?'

'No . . . but . . .'

'But?'

'The house seems changed, not quite itself.'

This was true. So far they were tiptoeing around the new arrangements. Hermione was not only going to occupy Tom/Mia's room but she would also annex for her exclusive use the tiny second bathroom on that floor, which, since Jake and Maisie's arrival, Emily had been using on the grounds that the equally small top-floor bathroom couldn't accommodate them all. Emily had not been *that* ungrudging about it, especially in view of her new status as a wage earner.

Emily went cryptic. 'We'll change shape.'

'Don't know what you mean.' Unsure of what Emily was getting at – though no doubt it had some literary application – Annie took refuge in the practical. 'Rusk *hors d'oeuvre*, Maisie?' She handed it over and a tiny fist clamped over it. She glanced at the clock and looked away again.

The ever-watchful Emily was on it. 'Are you worried, Mum?'

The question disarmed her and Annie was checked in the process of warming up Maisie's goo in the microwave. 'Not really. A bit of an adjustment, that's all.' She slammed the door and decided it was better to be honest. 'Oh, all right, yes, I am worried.'

Emily's blue eyes sparked up. (Taking notes, Annie concluded.) 'You can be honest, Mum. I bet you're furious at having to accommodate Gran.' She extracted Maisie's bib and spoon from the drawer and handed them to her mother. 'I would understand if you're furious and feeling trapped.' She sent Annie a sympathetic smile. 'It's not everyone who agrees to look after their mother-in-law.'

Recklessly, Annie surrendered the spoon to Maisie. 'No choice. Your grandmother's income has dropped to practically nothing and your father can't help until he's got a new job.'

'If . . .' said Emily.

'When,' countered Annie.

'Is he trying?'

'Oh, yes, he's trying. Making lots of applications, some unsuitable. Can't see your father as a sports-centre administrator.' ('Of course I'd take it,' he'd said, when he informed Annie he had applied. 'If offered.')

'No,' Emily reflected. 'I hear him sometimes on the phone to the old office. They're not happy conversations and I can see it upsets him.'

'I wish I could sort it for him.' Annie twisted her finger where the ring used to be.

Emily's gaze lingered on the bare finger. 'He has to sort it for himself, Mum.'

'When did you get so wise?'

'And, for the record, I think you've been brilliant.'

Wresting the spoon back from Maisie, Annie's eyes misted. A compliment from Emily was a precious thing.

'Again, purely for the record,' Emily continued, 'Maisie's got gunk all over her hair.'

A little later, a doused and spruced Maisie was settled into the playpen that now colonized a corner of the kitchen. Annie returned to the accounts. As feared, the replacement guttering at the front of the house had been eye-wateringly expensive. 'You know,' she said, crossing out 'Hair' on the to-do list, 'I'll probably have to give up going to Shandon's and find a cheaper hairdresser.'

'Piece of advice,' said Emily. 'Don't.'

Startled, Annie looked up, encountered her daughter's eye, which contained a tart admonition, and burst out laughing.

'False economy. Giving up the good haircut is in the same category as buying cheap pesto. We've talked about it.'

'We did,' Annie conceded, adding, 'It's so nice to have a daughter.' Too late, she slid into the trap. '*Daughters*, I mean.' She swept up the bills and stacked them in the folder. 'Have you . . . have you by any chance . . . ?'

At a beat, the atmosphere changed.

'Been in touch with my stupid, obstinate sister? No.' Emily stuck her hands on the edge of the table and bent over. 'Don't you think I would have told you?'

'Emily, don't look like that. Please. But have you *any* news from anyone?'

'No.' Emily was wary.

The goodwill between them had vanished. Emily marched over to the phone, snatched it up and shoved it in front of Annie. 'Why don't you try and find her yourself? Isn't it about time? We all spend so much time tiptoeing around the problem, agonizing over where she is, or just feeling guilty . . . so, just do it.'

Annie did not move. 'Guilty?'

'*Of course* Jake and I feel guilty. We're her siblings.' *Guilty*, thought Annie. 'Go on, Mum.' She seized the phone, dialled, listened and shoved it against Annie's ear. 'Go on, ask Directory Enquiries. See if they can trace her name.'

Annie snapped off the connection. 'Directory Enquiries don't do that.' She poked at the phone, which transcribed a half-twirl on the flat table surface. 'Are you sure she hasn't been in touch with Jake?'

'Why don't you ask him?' snapped Emily.

There was a short, unhappy pause. 'Emily, there's no need for *you* to feel guilty.'

'What do you know, Mum?' Emily shrugged and the closed look came down. 'Forget it.'

Annie glanced down at the phone. 'I long for reconciliation. Especially now.' She looked up at her daughter. 'The family *is* important.'

Emily's expression was unreadable. 'Mum, it's none of my business, really, but the-family-is-important shtick would go down better if you and Dad . . .' She paused. 'You were happy once.'

Yes, we were, Annie thought. Very.

She could duck the issue. Or she could acknowledge it. She could confess to her daughter that her parents' good intentions and ambitions, and their capacity for happiness, had stumbled at the hurdles. And if this was true of marriage, it was true of everything else in life. At what point, for instance, had she realized that struggling with hospital bureaucracy was pretty much hopeless and that, tarred and feathered by her defeats, she took greater pleasure these days from drinking a cup of coffee and reading the paper in peace than fighting the battles? At what point had Tom decided it was easier to stay late at the office than to come home and read to his son *whom he did not quite understand?*

'So?' Emily busied herself brushing crumbs off the table.

'I heard you,' admitted Annie at last.

Emily said, in the new mature way she was developing, 'OK.'

Annie got up and replaced the phone in its cradle. 'Mia can't be happy without her family.'

'Of course she can and probably is,' Emily said flatly. 'But I'll tell you something, I don't think she and Pete will still be together.'

Annie caught her breath. 'What makes you think that?'

Outside, there were sounds of arrival and whatever Emily had been going to reply remained unsaid. The two women braced themselves.

'I don't want it there.' Hermione pointed to the old-fashioned television that Tom and Jake had positioned as discreetly as possible in the corner by the window.

Despite continual airing, the smell of paint lingered in the room, the freshly washed windows glittered eerily and all traces of its previous occupants had been banished. It was a virgin place, urgent to be refilled and replenished.

Tom wiped a sweating brow. 'Where do you want it?'

From her perch in the armchair under the window, Hermione pointed to the opposite corner. Tom and Jake took up position and flexed their knees, ready to lift the

TV. Restraining Maisie, who, seemingly overnight, had developed the ability and desire to walk, Emily hovered in the doorway.

'Stop.' Annie consulted the room-to-scale plan on graph paper over which she and Tom had laboured. 'If you do that, you won't get the chest of drawers and the bed in.'

'Nonsense,' said Hermione.

Annie hunkered down beside her and explained the diagram. 'Believe me, we've measured it out carefully.'

Hermione gave Annie one of her I'm-looking-at-a-witless-person stares. 'Tom, dear,' she cut across Annie. 'Do give it a go. I'm sure it'll work.'

Annie whipped upright and walked out of the room. She wasn't proud of doing so, but it helped to divert her desire to strangle her mother-in-law.

The old black battle lines instantly re-established themselves. 'You don't think a mother should be at home looking after her children?' Or: 'Believe me, Annie, I do know my son.' Or, on the lighter side: 'Good Heavens! You've never made a soufflé?'

The newly wed Annie had put down her difficulties with Hermione to the self-consciousness of a new bride. Traditional stuff, she concluded in what, she now saw, was a faintly patronizing way – until she overheard Hermione on the phone describing her to a friend as 'unsatisfactory'. That gave Annie food for thought. For God's sake, she might have been a piece of shoddy clothing or a toaster with a permanent glitch. After a sleepless night, she decided to tackle Hermione and ask what precisely *would* make her satisfactory.

'Annie,' answered Hermione, not in the least discomposed

and, as always, impeccably made-up, coiffed and cashmered, 'I have no idea what you're talking about.'

Neither did Annie. It was impossible to put a finger on it and say: *That is what I mean.* For Hermione had been – was – both clever and subtle in the manner in which she fought to keep a hold over her son. Behind her waywardness was marshalled a thwarted intelligence, which had had too little on which to feed. 'She should have had a job,' Annie informed Tom. 'She would have made a fine industrial baron.'

Tom, being Tom, never got it. His reaction used to make Annie laugh. 'Her bark is worse than her bite,' was all he could manage.

Pace her own mother: clichés had their uses when dealing with tricky subjects and she forgave him. 'All I ask, then, is that you always listen to me as carefully as you listen to her.'

'Done,' he said.

Thus she had borne the lash of the older woman. It was the cross she accepted in exchange for her passionate love and her happiness.

Had been.

She recovered a little of her composure and called out from the stairs, 'I'll make some tea.'

Actually, Annie felt sorry for Hermione, and very sorry for the manner in which this move had peeled away her privacy. The process had been a weary counting out of a life in black plastic bags and stacks of coat hangers. There were suitcases filled with no longer pristine sweaters, a rack of dresses in man-made fibres, for it was only the latter that could survive the slash-and-burn laundry tactics of a care home, and a supermarket carrier bag filled with bars of soap. 'People keep giving me soap,' Hermione complained. 'I'm like a public washroom.' Having sorted through them, Annie had some sympathy. Hermione might yearn with all her might for the sensual perfumes of youth, yet once society's inherent ageism had kicked in, she was relegated to dull lemon and lavender.

There was a crash from above and Tom hurtled downstairs into the kitchen. 'Jake's knocked a picture to the floor. The telly doesn't fit.'

Annie fetched the dustpan and followed him back upstairs.

Over his shoulder, he said, 'Am I missing something? I haven't heard, "I told you so."'

'Consider it said.'

The spectre of Hermione with an infected foot was not a happy one and Annie spent considerable time checking the carpet for glass splinters, which held up the moving in.

An impatient Tom stood over her. 'Here, let me.' He knelt down beside her and brushed over the pile. 'Ouch.' He examined his hand. 'Splinter.'

'Give it here, Dad.' Jake applied pressure, Tom yelped and his son teased, 'Hardly a war wound.'

Tom cried out: 'Stop.'

Annie took pity. 'Come with me.'

She led Tom to their bathroom and searched for tweezers and antiseptic. Tom sat on the edge of bath and watched her.

'Hold out your hand.' Annie dabbed the site with TCP and, tweezers at the ready, bent over.

Moving noises continued to emanate from across the

corridor but in the bathroom it was quiet while Annie probed. Embedded at an angle by the base of his thumb, the splinter was going to take a bit of finessing.

'Am I hurting?'

'Yes.'

'Badly?'

'Incredibly.'

Her eyes flew to his. His were wry, hers must have been registering alarm. His lips twitched, hers twitched.

'Keep going. I'll live.'

'Hang on.' Annie rooted in the bathroom cabinet for a safety pin, the tip of which she dipped into the antiseptic. 'I'll have to cut it open a bit.'

She peeled back a tiny flap of flesh and dug around. The wound flowered scarlet, and she dabbed at it. Then again.

Tom's flesh . . . Tom's DNA . . . Tom's blood . . . which he had shared with her to create the children. Then it had seemed extraordinary, and now even more so . . .

'You all right, Annie?'

The point of the pin hovered over his thumb. It was the well-remembered moment of tension: that second suspended between desire and its fulfilment, which they'd used to enjoy.

She blinked. 'I'm fine.'

Triumphantly, she prised out the splinter and dropped it on to the cotton wool. Both of them peered at it.

'Not bad.' Tom laid his unwounded hand on her thigh.

Disconcerted, Annie stuck a plaster on to his thumb, and began to clear up. 'We'd better go and see what's happening.' She bent over to drop the debris into the bin.

Tom stood up, towering above her. 'Have I thanked you properly?' Straightening, she almost hit him on the chin and he laughed and steadied her. 'I do thank you, you know.'

He meant Hermione and all that was to come with her, and she divined his apprehension correctly. 'Listen to me,' she said. 'We're looking after her and she's not at the mercy of the state.'

'Yet,' he said. An eyebrow flew up. 'I'll remind you of this in a couple of months' time.'

Annie searched his face. Dark shadows under the eyes, the still mainly dark plumage, the old swagger lurking there somewhere but buried for the moment. 'You do that.'

She turned to stow the tweezers in the cabinet and Tom reached out to stay her hand. 'OK?'

At his touch, Annie felt the faintest stirring of excitement. 'Emily said a strange thing to me today. She said you and I were happy once.'

'Well, we were,' he said. 'Weren't we?'

'Yes, we were. Very.' She put away the tweezers and closed the cabinet.

'Are you coming?' Jake called. 'I need a hand.'

Reassigned to the position it was originally allocated, the television dominated the room, which, after her possessions had been shoehorned in, had shrunk to one considerably less spacious than Hermione had occupied in the care home. Squeezed in elsewhere were Hermione's chest of drawers, a small bedside table, the bed and a pair of cherished Chippendale chairs, which she never permitted out of her sight. On paper, this accumulation of objects had looked fine. In practice, it did not.

'This really won't do,' Hermione was saying, but there was a desperate note in her voice.

'It'll have to, Hermione,' said Tom. 'It's the best we can manage.'

Annie knew he was hating the exchange and hated not having managed his mother's affairs better for her. 'It looks fine,' she said brightly.

Jake knocked a picture hook into the wall and hung up the portrait of Hermione as a young woman – a good painting and one that frequently took an observer by surprise for it depicted a slender, dreaming woman in a yellow frock.

Annie began to place a selection of novels and biographies in the bookshelf. 'Hermione, shall I arrange them alphabetically?'

'Do what you like.'

Annie glanced around. Her mother-in-law's shoulders looked particularly vulnerable, and the set of them seemed to beg for care and kindness. To Annie's shame, she would have to brace herself but it would be done. She returned to the task in hand. Biographies of Mary, Queen of Scots, Churchill and Margaret Thatcher were predictable enough, but a well-thumbed copy of Ian McEwan's *Atonement* was not. She riffled through the pages and a photo slipped to the floor. Annie glanced at Hermione, who was busy informing Jake that he should have hung the painting a little lower, and picked it up. It was old – taken in the late forties or fifties – sepia-coloured, and the features of the young man in uniform it showed were indistinct. But it was possible to see that he was smiling as he leaned against an army vehicle on the edge of what appeared to be a tropical jungle, smoking a cigarette. Except that it had been taken abroad, it did not give much away. Yet it was clear from the intense creasing around the edges that it had been handled often. On the back was written, 'Max, 1952'.

It caught Annie up short. Of course, Hermione had her own past about which she, and very probably Tom, knew nothing. Of course she did, and it was to display carelessness and arrogance to forget. She slipped the photo back inside the book and placed it on the shelf.

Hermione paused between berating Jake and her son to direct a question at her daughter-in-law. 'What about that tea?'

The house was full. Every room was occupied, and the cries of a young baby were mixed with the competing voices of young and old adults. Annie paused on the stairs up which she was sneaking to grab a moment of solitude.

Where could she go to think? Where, in this busy honeycomb of a house, could anyone find privacy? Where would Tom work?

In the bedroom, she sat on the bed and switched on her laptop. The world's economies were still giving cause for alarm and a footballer had committed adultery. She clicked into her email and sent the following to Sadie:

Day one of full house. Mood resigned. Roots at risk.

Chapter Fourteen

Tom was woken by a screwdriver boring into his head. Someone was sobbing. Under the duvet, his hands balled into fists. If that was Maisie, what was Jake doing? Then, to his horror, the sounds cohered and became comprehensible.

'Help, help,' was issuing from Hermione's room. 'Someone help me.'

His heartbeat notching from zero to sixty in two seconds, Tom was out of bed in a trice, leaving a recumbent Annie. Various scenarios flashed through his mind. His mother had fallen out of bed. She had banged into the furniture in the overcrowded room. Why hadn't he put his foot down and insisted that the worshipped Chippendales went elsewhere?

He discovered Hermione in an enveloping, lace-edged nightdress and plaited hair, sitting bolt upright in bed, terror written all over her face.

'Hermione, are you OK?'

Her head jerked in his direction. 'Why are *you* here?'

'You're living with us now, Hermione. Remember?'

She shook her head in a confused way. 'I didn't know where I was. I couldn't work it out.' She pressed the ball of her thumb to her cheek. '*Where* am I?'

Tom hadn't seen his mother in her nightclothes for years, and it was an intimacy that made him uncomfortable. 'You're living with Annie and me now. In London. You're bound to be a bit confused to begin with, but it will pass.'

'I see.' But Tom's words had hop-skipped over a membrane and Hermione didn't see. 'I should be in my room.'

'Why don't I make some tea?'

It helped to do something practical and he ran downstairs and boiled the kettle, returning with a mug of Lapsang Souchong, which she accepted. The tea settled her a little and, while she drank it, Tom explained yet again where she was living and why.

Hermione fussed around, searching for a buffer on which to put the hot mug down on her pretty bedside table. 'I thought husbands and sons made sure they provided for their women.'

Only just masking a snort of semi-hysterical laughter, Tom explained, 'Things have changed a little.'

'You *think* they have, Tom.'

She looked past Tom to the clock on the shelf, and he was reminded of how hard it had been as a child to elicit any show of give from his mother. He never doubted that she loved him, but it was a love that burned from a distance, encased in a glass lantern. When he had been a tiny, clinging boy, she had peeled him off her like sticky tape, or refused to come when he cried. 'We mustn't spoil Tom.' He had learned not to take it personally.

In the quiet, the clock's tick magnified. 'Are you sleepy? Shall I try and make you more comfortable?'

She shifted fretfully, and Tom read her thoughts. *She was a prisoner . . . she ached to take flight . . . she ached to be young . . .* 'I don't know what I want.'

To his relief, Annie appeared at the door. 'Is everything OK?'

'Hermione wasn't sure where she was,' Tom explained.

In the low light of the bedside lamp, hair tumbling over her shoulders, Annie was mussed, yearningly soft and sweetly tousled. Under her open dressing-gown she wore a sprigged cotton nightdress, washed so often that it held more than a hint of transparency. As she moved towards Hermione and him, he caught the painterly flash of flesh tones, and was reminded of the hidden surprises of her body, the goose-down give of it under him . . .

Annie tied her dressing-gown cord around her middle and assessed the situation. 'Hermione, you don't look comfortable. If you get out of bed – can you do that? – I'll remake it.'

Tom lowered his mother into the chair, and Annie set about the bed with much stretching of undersheets and patting of pillows. An initiate in the temple of bedmaking, Tom watched.

'There.' Annie straightened up.

She helped Hermione back into bed, then leaned across her to tuck in the sheets and he was presented with a vignette of the entwined figures of his still supple wife and his stiff, lined mother. Annie moved and her hair fell down, obscuring both their faces from Tom's view. It was – what was it? – a living sculpture composed of two women and every woman, absorbed in a simple task, and it most definitely excluded him.

Most people suffered from feelings of isolation: it was a condition of being human, for God's sake. Annie used to understand and responded to Tom's confessions. Silly ones – *the feedback wasn't that great, the bastards.* The big ones – *what are we all trying to do?* In return, she had dropped her own secrets and fears into his willing ear. Messages had flowed back and forth between them, like those racing down optic fibres, binding them ever closer, giving colour and depth to their life together – and he missed them.

The final tuck made, Annie straightened. What would he, could he, confide to her now? Miserably aware that others were judging him – *he failed, kicked out* – he suspected she was judging him, too. What would she confide in return? He didn't know, for he had no clue as to her thoughts these days.

Hermione murmured something and Annie answered in an undertone.

All long ago. His memories of having young children were patchy but those he retained were sharp enough. The family on a cool, darkening English beach, the children's cries to each other echoing in the dusk. Annie crouched over the picnic basket. Four faces outlined in the white flicker of a driftwood fire. The taste of imperfectly cooked spare ribs. He and Annie had never reprised those times much either. Those particular experiences had come – and they had gone.

'There.' Annie looked at him. 'All done.' Hermione was peacefully settled.

Back in bed, under their separate duvets and occupying their separate sides, Tom and Annie whispered to each other.

She brushed her hair off her face. 'I never imagined we would be back to broken nights.'

He rolled over to face her. 'Sorry, Annie. I'm sure once she's settled, it'll be fine. The home didn't say anything to you about night waking?'

'No.'

'Nor me.'

It was Annie's turn to ask a question: 'Do you think her mind is still a hundred per cent?'

He was startled. 'Why?'

'Sometimes I get a feeling she isn't quite here. She is, obviously, but she isn't.'

'Rubbish.'

Annie turned on to her side, but not uncompanionably. It was more a shifting of bodies into comfortable alignment. 'OK, rubbish.'

He fingered a strand of her hair spilling on to the pillow. 'You'll be tired tomorrow.'

'I know,' she murmured, with the little snuffle he remembered she gave when falling asleep.

He imagined the line of her limbs under the nightdress and the slope of her breasts. 'Sorry about that, too.'

The snuffle again. 'So am I. Big meeting.'

Touching her hair gave him a pang and he thought of the times when they had been happy and free with each other – when he had had job, a healthy bank account, a firm purpose and commitment. Now they were not happy and free with each other, and Annie had had to sell her ring because his bank account could no longer rise to the challenge. He hated being a witness to her distress, and her new habit of rubbing her empty finger. But he hoped to sort that with the spread-betting and buy her a new ring out of the proceeds. And, of course, contribute to the bills. *Note to himself* : whenever he thought about his ventures on-line, which were frequent, his spirits lifted. It was a good feeling.

Additional note: at five thirty the previous evening the

market had steadied and his position on recovery had been several points in his favour.

Tom breathed a sigh of relief into the dark and, again, Annie stirred.

'Tom, do you mind very much being at home?'

The cold air rushed to colonize the trench between the duvets. 'Yes, I do.'

'I'm sorry, truly sorry.'

'Home isn't *so* bad,' he admitted, with reluctance. 'But I hate . . . I hate feeling so powerless.'

In the morning, Emily ran downstairs, dropping a sour remark through the open door of her parents' bedroom as she went. 'You made enough noise last night.'

'Remind me. Was it you who got up to help out?' said her father.

'Uncalled-for, Dad.' She dropped down a couple more stairs and shouted over her shoulder, 'Some of us have to work. Some of us have been at our new job for a week and need the beauty sleep.'

Silence.

Oh, God, why did she have to say *that*? How could she?

Breakfast was eaten at a lick before she flung herself out of the door, clutching a large handbag that contained a spare toothbrush and paste. Too much coffee in the office gave one coffee breath.

As she strap-hung on the crowded bus, Emily ran over her finances for the nth time. If she put aside that much each week, dropped Topshop – well, cut down the visits – absolutely no cappuccinos, then, yes, the new job meant she could afford to move out of home. Early days and probably too risky to do anything definite – but it was on the agenda.

The bus driver was one of nature's jokers who lived to challenge his passengers' powers of balance and endurance. Emily was obliged to forget other considerations and concentrate on keeping upright. Passenger ebb and flow pushed her up the centre of the aisle and back again, each time passing the man in a window seat, dressed in jeans and a shabby jacket, with a rucksack on his knee. He gazed serenely out at the passing parade of streets and shops. Obviously he was not on his way to work. Or not in the sense that she was.

She felt a spasm of homesickness for her bedroom eyrie, followed by resentment, which, she reminded herself briskly, was unjustified. Resentment was self-indulgent. Totally. Nerves always upset her equilibrium – and, as a new recruit of one week, she was still at the nervy stage of the job.

Condor Oil was housed in an office block in a style that could only be described as 'extreme brutalism'. It was daunting, ugly and made no concession to the joys of architecture. In fact, concluded Emily, as she hastened towards the gloomy lifts, the architect could not have been aware there were any joys to be found in life, let alone in his creations. Yet there was something in his dour vision. You got what you saw with Condor Oil. Pausing at the entrance to the office, she inhaled, held her breath and steadied herself, knowing that she had a lot to learn about office demeanour, whose rules she still had to investigate.

Don't be too exuberant first thing. If you're late, disguise it. If you want to get on, observe the hierarchies.

That was a start.

Very soon, she was clacking away on her keyboard, composing a press release on the latest oil-price hike, which had to be tactfully conveyed to the public. Her face was a pale reflection on the screen and she grimaced. No longer did she have the luxury of dickering over a word's *resonance*; *description* was of no use. Neither was a highly charged sensuous *atmosphere* – although it could be said that a degree of psychological *insight* was obligatory. Goodbye To All That. Eyes closed for a second. Summon the image of a kitchen sink in which swirled hundreds of thousands of words. Squeeze eyes tighter shut, pull the plug and they were gone.

Positioned by the keyboard, her mobile jumped as a text message came in. 'Pedi at Zara?' Emily did a double-take. For a second, she read the signature as 'Mia' not 'Kat'.

Go away, she addressed Mia silently. *Go.*

Would she ever get the measure of the situation? Her feelings for Mia scuttled about like mice and never settled. The good Mia crusading for the world and the insufferable Mia who ensured that the family spotlight was always trained on her. Hate her, love her. It would be easier to settle if Emily was just plain indifferent. Twins and their mysterious connection she understood, and Mia and Jake would always commune even if they didn't meet. But why should she bother with the sister who had walked out on them with her boyfriend, Pete – a blazing, spitting firebrand who hated the family, 'and that includes you, Emily' – who could 'tolerate no longer the smugness, the insensitivity, *the lifestyle*', and never wished to see them again?

She tried to imagine the tiny, fastidious Mia in bed with big, shaggy Pete, and failed. Easier to remember was the car-crash of Mia's accent after Pete's Yorkshire vowels had been grafted on to her southern intonation. 'Isn't that affectation?' Emily had inquired of her sister. 'You can't avoid being who you are.'

It was a mystery why Mia, that shiny, sunny sprite, should have undergone such a metamorphosis into the grim, the humourless and, furthermore, one who hated so much so vehemently . . . Finding Mia asleep over a Marxist tome in the big armchair in the sitting room, one thin hand tucked into her neck, the other, a pale, frail thing, in her lap. Sleep had relaxed the coppery head and her outrageously long lashes were on display. (At one stage Emily had longed to pull them out.) At Emily's approach, Mia had woken and looked up expectantly, thinking perhaps it was Pete or Jake. When she had realized who it was, she had scowled. 'Oh, *you*,' she said.

Emily had looked down at her sister and thought, *Mia will never love me but I can cope without that love . . .*

A ray of sun struck Condor Oil's upmarket pot plant, positioned by the water-cooler, which made it look healthier than it was.

'Are you with us?' Mike, her immediate boss, was hanging over her.

Emily gave a tiny start. 'Of course.' She pointed to the screen. 'I was about to wing this over to you.'

'Sure.' Mike was very attractive in a metrosexual way and Emily was sure he knew it. But he seemed good-humoured enough. 'We thought you might like to join the team for lunch.'

Reposing in Emily's bag beside the toothbrush and paste was a seeded spelt bread tomato and bean-sprout sandwich.

No butter. No mayonnaise. It was exactly the sensible, economical and worthy lunch she intended to eat most days. As she and her mother had discussed: (1) spending money on lunch was wasteful; (2) she could do a little work on the novel; (3) needs must, she didn't know anyone.

'That would be very nice.' Emily looked up at him. 'What time?'

The chosen restaurant had been written up recently in a Sunday colour supplement. The floor was polished oak, the décor minimalist and the lighting state-of-the-art. One wall glittered with a long mirror, and an aluminium bar ran the length of the room, the waiters dodging expertly around it.

They were a party of eight, which had meant two taxis (Emily had worried about her share of the fare), and some more than passable Sauvignon Blanc had been rushed to the table. It was all very pleasant.

Mike had sat himself down beside her, and his manners turned out to be good. What a difference it made to be asked questions about oneself. So many of the men, in particular bankers and lawyers, she sat next to at dinner parties just talked about themselves.

'So,' Mike was saying, as he tackled his grilled half-lobster, 'have you given up your ambitions to write or are they merely on hold?'

This was tricky. Emily regarded the modest omelette and tomato salad adorning her plate. She did not wish to suggest that she was not wholehearted about the job. On the other hand, she was not about to do a St Peter and deny the thing she loved. Mike poured a garlic-butter puddle over the lobster. Noting the way the yellow gloss settled over the white flesh, she replied, 'I've come to the conclusion that it takes time to become a writer and I see it as something for the future.' Mike raised an eyebrow. 'And I'm committed to this work.' *Press releases, for Heaven's sake.* 'Writing, er, needs patience.'

Go on, she thought. *Dig yourself into a big hole.*

'Does it?' He was indeed laughing at her, but with some sympathy. 'As a member of Generation Impermanence, I think it's a good thing to consider something is with you for the duration.'

'Good,' she murmured, still fascinated by the yellow-red combination of lobster shell and butter.

'Emily, would you like a piece of lobster?' Without waiting for an answer, he speared a chunk and placed it on her side plate. 'You should have ordered some.'

'It's a little too extravagant.' All the same, she took the lobster and wolfed it.

'You have butter on your chin.' He offered her the corner of his napkin. 'That's better.' He smiled. 'You don't have to worry, this is on expenses.'

'Really?'

'Yes.' His smile broadened and, with that, Mike proceeded to initiate Emily into the office politics. These were, by his account, pitiless and intricate – and also, to her surprise, fascinating. So, too, was the group discussion on the geo-political fortunes of Condor Oil.

All the while they continued to drink the good wine and to eat the excellent food. Emily abandoned some of her nervousness, laughed frequently, contributed her mite to the conversation, promised to tell Mike more about the (temporarily) abandoned novel and, once back in the office, found herself cruising through the afternoon's work on an agreeable plateau.

Once upon a time, long ago, he and Mia had lain out on the lawn in the back garden and stared up into the sky. Mia wiled away the time by describing the clouds. 'Flirty', 'bad-tempered' or 'languorous'. Not so good at words, he had been hard pressed to match her verbal dexterity – and, at this miserable point in his life, with his feelings locked in frozen storage and inaccessible, he was even less eloquent and tongue-tied.

Mia had the knack of pushing Jake to take a closer look at his surroundings: to take notice of people, issues, objects in a way his parents failed to. Nothing new in that, he supposed, as a new recruit into parent rank. To be ignored must be one of the eternal sorrows of the parent – and those, he was aware, lay ahead.

Today, as he picked his way over the cobbles to the workshop, the clouds were definitely languorous and, with the air warming for summer, the adjacent canal was beginning to smell. Tucked into Victorian railway arches, the other businesses – a motorcycle-repair outfit, a second-hand music shop stuffed with old records and DVDs, and a second-hand bookshop – were up and running.

'Hi,' he called out to Dave, who was stacking boxes of books inside his cramped interior.

Dave looked up. 'Jake, hi. Can you build me a bigger shop?'

Unlocking the door, the familiar scent of wood, resin and varnish washed over Jake. He hovered in the doorway, fighting off the inertia and despair that threatened to dissolve whatever resolution he still retained.

Here's the thing, Jake. One minute at a time.

Unlocking the filing cabinet, he extracted his order and account books. It took a cursory glance to confirm that he had logged in only one commission for a small display cabinet, despatched the previous week.

The order book was now empty.

Jake sat down at the bench. How to resurrect an almost-dead business? Advertising – required funds. Internet marketing – he would investigate. Personal contacts – limited but worth a try. Business plan – would ring accountant. Credit – try bank.

He could hear Jocasta's voice: 'For God's sake, Jake, if you're running a business you have to be practical and hard-headed.' She was always pressing him to set up systems, apply for grants and make friends with his clients.

He had laughed, buried his face in her hair, and whispered, 'But that's not the point. I want to be free to design without fuss.'

And Jocasta's exasperated 'You won't have a business, then.'

Perhaps she had had a point.

Jake hit the phone and embarked on an extensive ringing round of clients and contacts to see if there was any business to be had. The exercise took up half the morning, and the results were patchy. It was increasingly clear that things had changed. In times of plenty, it was hail-to-the-craftsman-king. In times of economic uncertainty, the craftsman was dispensable.

'No dice for me either,' said his friend Bob, who specialized in historic wood restoration, when Jake rang him. 'The fountain has dried up and thirsty we will be.'

'Thanks, Bob.'

'Any time.'

Jake also rang the letting agency to check that the rent was coming in from the house and was relieved to be told that all was in order. In the back of his mind, there was the hope that he and Maisie would be able to move home in the not-so-distant future.

'Have you got a plan?' Tom had asked him, only the previous evening.

'As much of a plan as you, Dad.'

Tom gestured to a pile of white envelopes on the table waiting for stamps and said curtly, 'Job applications, actually.'

His mother had been ironing the Interview Shirt for his father and the cluck of the steam iron punctuated their exchange. 'Dad,' said Jake, as polite as he could muster, 'don't you think you should be doing that?'

He had caught his father on the hop, if not the raw. Annie propped up the iron, which hissed in a friendly manner. Tom's brows snapped together. There was a second or two of impending storm before he joined Annie at the ironing board. 'Should I be doing this, Annie?'

'*Dad* . . . you shouldn't have to ask.'

'Sweet of you, Tom.'

Tom moved Annie away from the ironing board. 'Isn't it?'

Later on, his mother had drawn him aside and taken his hand. 'Jake, darling. You look exhausted.'

'I am,' he said and, seduced by her tender concern, permitted her to see some of his turmoil. 'It's not just looking after Maisie, it's more I can't see where I'm going now. I can't see what's best.'

She stroked his fingers, pressing down slightly on the joints in an effort to massage away the tension. It was as if she was saying, I helped to give you life, but only you can run with it.

Jake looked up from his desk and eyed the stack of wood at one end of the workshop. Walnut, cherry, pine – an inventory sounding sweetly on his inner ear – that provided the vocabulary by which he lived. As he mused over it, it occurred to him that, since the wood was valuable, he should put an extra lock on the door. Jocasta had always said he should.

And where was she? Tucked up in a big soft American bed with Noah ... Jake raked his wounds. *Stop. Don't think about a naked Jocasta.* Neither would he reflect on the narrow single bed to which circumstances had banished *him*.

The phone still depressingly silent, he paced around. Assembled in neat rows, his woodwork tools were as he had left them, now so little used that a layer of astral dust had sifted over them. He touched one or two, to allow himself to feel their familiar shapes. Finally he threw out a couple of empty tins just to feel he'd done something.

Someone knocked at the door and pushed it open a trifle. 'Hi – anyone there?'

Annoyed at the interruption, Jake swung round. 'Yes?'

The door opened properly and a girl appeared. 'Are you the repair shop?'

'No.'

Dressed in high-waisted trousers and a gingham blouse, she was tall with plenty of curves, fresh-faced and rather lovely. 'Oh. Is there anywhere I could get a heater fixed?' She hovered on her Doc Martens. 'It's my lifeline.'

He noted the weary inflexion. 'Wouldn't it be cheaper to buy another one?'

A pair of rather fierce eyes were directed on him with a look to curdle milk. 'No,' she responded flatly. 'That would be a waste.'

Right, he thought. Got the picture. Earth maiden. Greener than chlorophyll. Dolphin-friendly nets. Retread-tyre shoes. Depressing light bulbs . . .

She cast a look around the workshop. 'Could *you* help?'

'Sorry.'

'Oh.' She raised a hand to brush back her hair from her ears and he spotted a livid bruise on the wrist. 'OK. Sorry I asked.'

He worried about the bruise. 'Perhaps I could take a look.'

The restorative effect of his words was nothing short of miraculous. 'Wonderful.' She disappeared only to reappear, dragging a cumbersome electric heater with her good hand.

Jake was appalled. 'Is that how you got that bruise? How far have you had to carry it?'

She gestured out of the window to the block of flats that towered grimly in the distance. 'Not too far.' She glanced at the pile of Jake's ledgers and the leather satchel he used to carry papers, and a smile glimmered at the corners of her mouth. 'But a little different from here, shall we say?'

He noticed that she winced when she nursed her wrist. 'OK. Let me look.' He bent over to diagnose the heater's ills.

While he did so, the girl roamed the studio. 'How long have you been here?'

'Three years.' He teased a wire out of the plug. 'But not for much longer. Business has more or less collapsed.'

'And you're giving up.' It was a statement but, to his surprise, he detected criticism. She ran a finger over a plank of English walnut and inspected the shelves of tools. 'You're very orderly.' She leaned forward and sniffed. 'Nice.'

The fault was easy to spot. 'Loose wire,' said Jake. 'It needs replacing. If you hang on a minute, I think I can do it for you.' He hoicked open a drawer, which contained his graded coils of wire.

She said politely and seriously, 'You *are* tidy.'

Because he was so rattled, the observation grated on Jake. 'You have to be.' He selected the wire and banged shut the drawer. 'Otherwise you get distracted. If everything's in place, you're free to think about the important things.'

'Such as?'

He looked up. She was leaning against the workbench, eyes half closed, drowsing almost and obviously exhausted, and he knew that she was not interested in his answer.

Leaving her to her reverie, he worked in silence. The repair was simple and took no time. He reached down and plugged the heater into the socket. Almost immediately, a smell of burning dust filled the workshop.

The girl's eyes flicked open. 'You do know how things work.'

'I've tinkered a bit. I like to get to the heart of an object. The chicken-and-egg sequences of gadgets.'

'So,' she murmured, 'unlike the little boy pulling wings off flies, you dismembered kettles and dreamed of steam engines.'

Despite himself Jake laughed – and felt better. 'You've

got it. Finding the shape that lies in the wood or the block of marble – or, believe it or not, a heater.'

She sent him a slightly sceptical look. 'Brilliant,' she said at last, and a proper smile lit up her beautiful features. 'Thank you. You've no idea what a difference . . .' She dug around in her trouser pocket and produced a ticky-tacky purse of a sort often found in catalogues that sold products from the Third World. 'How much do I owe you?'

'Nothing.'

A hint of obstinacy. 'I insist.'

'Insist away, but it's on the house.'

She was the first to look down. 'Then thank you again.'

Jake helped her to carry the heater to the door. As she lifted it up, she asked, 'What's your name?'

'Jake. And yours?'

'Ruth.'

In the afternoon she was back. This time with a toaster tucked under her arm. 'I'm being a bad penny, I'm afraid.'

He grinned. 'Surely not.'

'I've been telling my old ladies about you.' She proffered the toaster on two hands, treating Jake to a full view of the bruise. 'It belongs to my next-door neighbour. Mary's pretty elderly and she's really missing her toast. Could you?'

Jake had already run through a toaster's components in his head. Fuse, element, et cetera.

'She wants to pay.'

He gave the toaster a preliminary once-over. Crumbs rained on to the bench and he brushed them into the bin. 'If it's the element, I'll have to send off for a replacement. That's easy enough.'

'Will this do?' She proffered a note.

'Sure.'

Ruth stuffed her hands into the pocket of the pea-jacket she now wore over the gingham blouse – a jaunty version of the Marseille sailor. 'There's plenty more where that's come from.' She gestured to the stack of wood. 'I need a bookshelf and a work station. Maybe . . . if the business . . .' She reached over and touched the edge of the bench. 'It's good to meet someone who can actually make things and mend them.' She seemed to be perfectly at ease. 'You see – I mean, now that everybody's up against it, things will have to be mended because people won't be able to afford new things.'

Jake had sussed the problem. He tapped the side of the toaster. 'I'm pretty sure it's the element. It'll take a week, but it'll be quite safe if you leave it here. It could do with a clean-out too.' He checked his watch. 'I'll have to go. My father's looking after my daughter and I promised I wouldn't be late.'

'How old is she?'

'Maisie? Year and a bit.' Then Jake found himself telling Ruth, 'Rather surprisingly, my father has taken to baby-sitting. I think it's because she can't talk back and gives him unquestioning adoration.' He placed the toaster on the shelf. 'Do you have children?'

'No.'

It was clearly a subject she didn't wish to pursue and he changed tack. 'What do you do?'

'I have a dressmaking business, Betty Grable. Fifties clothes.' She gestured to her outfit. 'I collect old patterns and make them up. The business is OK-ish. I'm working on a website and it's building slowly.' Again her smile lit up her features. 'It's good.'

For a second or two, a dazzled Jake imagined that a fresh-faced angel was hovering in his earthbound workshop. 'Sounds good.'

Ruth vanished and Jake sat down at the bench, startled by how far the encounter had prodded the numb, cold bits of him into activity. Pretty girl. *Beautiful* girl. But, then, beauty wasn't everything. He bit his lip. But it wasn't nothing either and he was weary of the now-familiar ache of unhappiness and humiliation.

He scrutinized the toaster with a fresh eye. Ruth was right. Lamps, toasters, vacuum cleaners were everywhere and, sooner or later, they went wrong. And now that money was getting tighter their owners would be disposed to mend rather than discard them. How clever of her to see it. How gallant that she had pointed it out.

He reached over for his notebook and wrote, 'Repairs done?'

Chapter Fifteen

No longer able to work in his bedroom, Tom set up his computer, plus Anglepoise light, in the sitting room – a move that had caused Annie anguish.

'But where else?' Tom decided he must fight for some space in the house or he would suffocate.

'What about the shed?'

'I can't work in the shed.'

'Sheds are good, Tom. Men and sheds have a bond. Yes?' She was only half joking. Annie was at her most cajoling but he knew she knew she was beaten. 'I worked so hard to make this room nice.'

True. Once soothing and unobtrusively elegant, the room would be downgraded if Tom made it into his office. But since Zosia's departure it had been a more or less permanent mess because it got left off the skimpy cleaning rota. Since it retained only a flavour of its previous existence, it had dwindled into a no man's land. The family came and went, leaving behind papers, an empty coffee cup, a dented cushion. A stack of elderly magazines had partially toppled to the floor. The wastepaper baskets needed emptying, the window-ledges dusting, and the curtains only infrequently got looped back into their ties.

Tom applied himself to the data on the screen – the portal through which he was sucked into his silent, exciting world.

Barclays shares had reached five pounds. Compare this to the early part of the previous year when Barclays shares traded at seven.

The process – tracing the coloured graph lines, analysing the figures, stabbing a finger on the button – was akin to the best malt whisky burning down his gullet or the first hit of a Havana on the back of the throat. Contemplating what might be possible triggered the adrenalin rush.

Having studied the data, he knew there were success stories as a result of men (it was usually men) acting boldly. *Hypothesis*: recovery would happen. *Action*: double exposure. He decided to go in *additionally* to bet on the other banks on top of what he had already bet. The still, chilled voice of reason informed him that if he only held his nerve then the ship would sail into port.

He pressed the button.

Tom swept up his wallet and keys, and stuffed them into his pockets.

Annie and Emily were at work, Hermione had ordered a taxi and taken herself off to the nearest library – 'Bit extravagant, dear, but needs must as no one is here to take me in the car' – and Jake was busy persuading Maisie to have her mid-morning nap.

Maisie was making her protests felt. Tom ran halfway up the stairs and called out, 'I'm off.' Another squawk from Maisie. 'Jake, if she wants to stay up, let her.'

Jake appeared with Maisie in his arms. At the sight of her grandfather, her mutinous little face weathercocked into sunny delight.

'You know,' said Tom, 'she might be getting too old for the mid-morning nap.'

'Hell,' said Jake, whose mood had not been good since he had returned from the workshop. 'That's all I need.'

'Just a thought.' Tom clattered down the stairs. 'See you later.'

Having flung out a careless succession of warm days, the weather had decided to send out a wake-up call, and it was both windy and cool. As good a moment as any, reflected Tom, as he emerged from the Underground half an hour later, to venture back into the arena.

The offices had not changed. They were eternal and, despite the lectures to himself, he regarded them with trepidation. James had offered to meet him for their lunch in the Bombay Bicycle a couple of streets away, but Tom had felt that part of his rehabilitation should be to face where he had once flourished.

Even so, while the wind blew up dust and litter, he procrastinated for a good five minutes.

'Nice to see you.' Sam, the doorman, handed Tom his visitor's pass and the greeting cheered him up.

The open-plan vista of desks and office clutter was as it had always been but there was a subtle change. Tom no longer held any power over it. The office now functioned without him.

He walked past Alice's desk.

Alice started. 'Goodness, Tom. How are you?'

The question did not require an answer. Alice would not wish to know, and it was impossible for Tom to explain: *Actually, I feel like an amputee.* Or: *I miss the companionship.* Or how he missed, for God's sake, feeling overburdened and overworked.

'Fine.' He made the bland, unselfish reply.

Typus interruptus, she nodded and said, 'Good,' while her fingers twitched over the keyboard.

Tom continued on his way. Sealed behind the glass walls of his office, James was talking on the phone. He looked up, registered Tom and a wary expression sprang into his eyes. He held up two fingers, hunched over and swung his chair around so that his back was to Tom.

Tom forced himself to stand at ease. One hand in pocket, easy expression, slightly bent knee. Out of the corner of his eye, he watched a figure sloping furtively through the corridor between the desks.

It was Ken, with whom he had worked for many years . . . the Ken who had clapped Tom on the shoulder and wished him the best with tears in his eyes . . . the Ken who now edged out of sight without a word of acknowledgement.

These people had been his colleagues, if not his friends. Their dealings together had been straightforward(ish) and comprehensible – survivors and adapters who understood each other.

But failure stank, and redundancy was felt to be contagious. Of all people, Tom knew that perfectly well.

Five minutes or so dragged past. James was talking ever more urgently into the phone. Again Tom tapped on the glass. James swung round and directed a what-the-hell? look in his direction. Tom mouthed, 'I'll wait in the restaurant.'

He left without a backward glance. As the lift doors closed behind him, he could have sworn there was a collective exhalation of breath.

I will not let it get to me, he swore to himself. *I will not.*

On returning home, he walked into the sitting room at

number twenty-two to discover Jake had commandeered the computer and was taking a call on Skype. A little window superimposed on the PC screen revealed the bronzed and skinny Jocasta.

Jake was hunched over the keyboard and their conversation was jarringly stiff. 'Thirty degrees. That's hot.'

'It's summer here, Jake.'

At Tom's entrance, he looked up. 'Sorry, Dad. Didn't know you'd be back so soon.' He addressed the screen. 'Sorry, Jocasta, I have to go. Next time I'll show you Maisie.'

'Hold on – I need to know a bit more about my daughter.'

'She's having her afternoon nap.'

There was a short pause. 'I miss her.' Jocasta's red mouth opened and shut.

Fully aware that he had had too much to drink during the gut-shrivelling, pointless lunch with James (which Tom had cut short), Tom threw his jacket on to the chair, pushed Jake to one side and commandeered the screen. 'Jocasta, if you want to know about your daughter, you shouldn't have left her. I'm not sure how you imagine that an odd question or two from your sunny spot will begin to tackle your daughter's needs, but let me tell you something. They don't. And they won't.'

Compared to what Tom would have liked to spell out – betrayal and dereliction were mild variants – the words failed to scale even the nursery slopes of what he felt.

'Dad . . .'

Jocasta blinked in astonishment. 'Tom, this is none of your business. I was having a conversation with Jake.'

'Not my business? If you think that, you're stupider than

I thought, Jocasta. By abandoning her, you've made it everyone's business.' Tom was warming up nicely. Maisie was blood of his blood and bone of his bone, and he *would* defend her. 'Tell me, do you lie awake at night and listen to her crying for her mother?'

There was a pause. 'If I were you, Tom, I'd hesitate before giving me lectures on childcare.'

'Precisely. I know what can happen. All manner of evils. And if you are referring to Mia, which I take it you are . . .'

Jake reached over, severed the link and Jocasta vanished. He was tight-lipped and furious. 'What the hell do you think you're doing, Dad?'

'Saying what someone should say.'

When Jake lost his temper, which was rare, he did it thoroughly. 'And? Your point?'

Tom's response reflected his own hurt and humiliation. 'Maisie needs to be spoken up for. Jocasta has behaved abominably and she should be informed of that. If she can't live with you, then she should at least live near her daughter.'

'You should hear yourself, Dad.' Jake's jaw unclenched a little. 'This is my business, Dad. Mine and Jocasta's, not yours.'

'I'm her grandfather.'

Jake didn't bother to answer that one. 'Contrary to what you might believe, I've given my dealings with Maisie's mother some thought. I'm trying to preserve some kind of relationship with my faithless wife in order to help Maisie and you've just done your best to scupper it.'

Tom recollected Maisie's desolate night cries. 'Jocasta needed to be told.'

Jake was icy. 'Don't you understand it's not your business?'

OK, conceded Tom. He knew perfectly well that parents have no impact whatsoever and the parental voice is the equivalent of a gnat's whine at a football match and just as irritating.

'. . . and not that we ever listened to you. And what makes you think you were such a great father?' added the angry Jake.

His son's words hurt him in a way Tom wouldn't have believed possible, and goaded him to even deeper fury – and the argument took flight, snaffling up all the unresolved issues between the two from down the years. 'At least . . .' his voice swelled into a roar '. . . I supported my family!'

Jake turned a disconcerting shade of white. 'I don't believe you said that.'

Actually, Tom didn't either and would have done anything to take the words back.

Jake stood up from the computer. He looked a trifle shaky but the icy tone was used to deadly effect. 'First off, Jocasta and I are not your business. Second, you have got to accept a fact of life that your children are different from you. In my case, I did not wish to spend my life in an office under the laughable delusion that I made a difference.'

Tom winced. 'Stop now, Jake. We've said enough.'

But Jake was on a roll. 'Or that people respected me. Because nobody respects anyone. They mock you and they put up with you because they have no choice.' He continued in a tone that Tom was startled to recognize as one he had frequently extracted from his arsenal of voices when the children were younger. 'I've always thought your attitude to the office was naïve, Dad, fondly imagining, as you did, that a Utopian partnership existed between boss and worker. It didn't and it won't.' He shook his head. 'Why you spent so much time there, I can't begin to imagine.'

Tom held up his hand. 'We're done, Jake.'

'No, Dad. You're going to listen to me.' Jake knitted together threads of his case. 'I wanted to make something different of my life . . . to make good, useful objects that were also beautiful and desirable. I'm having trouble achieving those aims and I would have thought you'd sympathize.'

Good, useful, beautiful, desirable. Jake was telling him in so many words that the corruptions of a settled salary, final pension scheme and expenses had so insidiously infiltrated his thinking that he had forgotten his early idealism.

The argument was threatening to veer way over the safety line and Jake was still mid-flow. 'You preach one thing and demand another from your children.'

Did all his children think this? 'So I'm entirely to blame?' Jake shrugged.

A stunned Tom reminded himself that, however sharp their differences, Jake was his son. He made a huge effort. 'Jake, I'm on your side. It may not sound it but I am.'

Jake pushed his hands deep into his pockets and studied the floor. He was clearly making a decision about which way to go. Then he looked up at Tom. 'Thanks, Dad.'

A voice from the doorway interrupted them: 'For goodness' sake! The whole street can hear you.'

Both men swung around.

'Hermione!'

'Gran!'

'I thought you two were killing each other.' She observed

them both with an indulgence she never displayed to the women in the family. 'You do get carried away.'

Hermione was dressed in a blue-green light wool skirt and matching cardigan with gold buttons, and her hair was pulled back into its customary chignon.

'Hermione . . .'

'All it takes is a little restraint,' she was saying. 'I couldn't believe my ears. You should both know better. Are you going to tell me what's going on?'

The two men glanced at each other. 'Of course,' said Tom. 'But why don't I make you some tea and bring it up?'

Jake edged past his father. 'Come on, Gran. I'll help you upstairs.'

Tom heard their slow ascent and overheard Jake say, 'Gran, your brooch isn't fastened properly. Would you like me to do it?'

'Oh dear . . .'

'I'll deal with it.' Jake was both gentle and consoling, neither of which had he been with Tom.

'Would you, Jake? How helpful you are.'

Tom abandoned the idea of tea, let himself out into the street and headed for the pub. It was full of punters – who, no doubt, all had jobs. Pushing his way through them, he ordered a pint and made rapid inroads into it. There was a band tightening around his head and a sour, bitter taste in his mouth.

Channels of communication? Debates, ideas and campaigns? A duty to others? The precepts by which he had previously lived had lost their clear-cut certainty. And so had he. Instead of the enlightenment, the mode of good living, the salary and the status he had fondly imagined he had achieved during his career, he realized that he had been merely a fish gasping for air.

Maisie was crying again . . .

Annie shuddered mutinously up from a deep sleep and her wilder dreams and forced herself to concentrate. No, it wasn't the baby. It was Hermione.

Beside her, Tom slumbered peacefully. One half of her protested: *I have a job, for goodness' sake.* The other, the better trained, polite and sentient half, belonged to the generous Annie (which she tried to be), who knew that Tom was exhausted from having got up to see to Hermione for several nights running and who would be grateful if she was to take up some slack.

The night light, which Hermione insisted should be in her room, cast a muted glow. The rest of the room was in shadow. Apparently asleep, Hermione lay on her back, the bedclothes trailing on the floor. One hand, with a snake vein crawling over the wrist, was out-flung. She was restless and, every so often, she muttered a word or two.

Just visible above the bed was the painting of Hermione the young woman. In a light and frivolous yellow frock, she was seated on a bench beside open french windows, surrounded by a garden, which the painter suggested ached with scent and colour. The picture always managed to shock Annie – the contrast between the dreaming girl then and the Hermione of now could not have been crueller. That transition was happening in her, too. In all of them. Perhaps one needed to be reminded of how young and feeling one once had been or the future appeared too fearful. In order to counteract the indignities and inconveniences of physical decay, the spirit supped greedily on memories of a time when the senses were wild and full of desire.

As unobtrusively as possible, she rearranged the bedclothes over the older woman and bent to tuck them in.

Hermione's eyes snapped open. 'Is that you, darling Max?'

Tom's father had been William, known as Bill, and had died when Tom was nineteen. 'Hermione,' she whispered, 'it's Annie.'

The other woman fixed her eyes on her. 'But Max should be here. He promised, and I've been waiting for a long time.'

'Who's Max, Hermione?' But Annie already knew it was the man in the photograph.

Hermione was neither fully awake nor asleep but sliding along the boundary between the two. 'Max?' The pause that ensued was painful, expectant. 'He promised to come back.'

Annie was taken aback by this revelation. She placed a hand on Hermione's shoulder. 'Hermione, you're with us, Tom and Annie, in your bedroom in our house.'

The older woman rested her gaze on the younger – and Annie fancied that she could see Hermione's yearning and lovely dreams dissolve into the dark-hued present. 'Of course,' answered a now fully awake Hermione, with her customary hauteur.

'Shall I make you some tea?'

'What makes you think I want tea? It's the middle of the night.'

'Are you uncomfortable?'

'Wouldn't you be if you were me?' she flashed back.

The words cut into Annie. To be old. *To be old?* In that moment Annie understood better the struggle to keep positive and cheerful when your life was dwindling. She sat down on the edge of the bed. 'Who's Max? Is he the man in the photograph?'

Hermione pulled herself up on to the pillows. 'Who's talking about Max?'

'You were.'

'He's no one.'

Annie picked up one of Hermione's brittle-looking hands. 'We've known each other a long time. And don't look like that, Hermione. We're stuck with each other.' She rubbed the fingers that once had been pliable and surging with blood. 'You were waiting for Max. You said he never came.'

Hermione's narrowed eyes sheltered her secrets. 'I don't know what you're talking about.'

'OK,' conceded Annie. 'Go back to sleep now.'

Shuddering with cold and fatigue, Annie slid back into bed. Feeling was slow to creep back into her feet, and she craved warmth as the addict craved the fix. She wrapped her hands across her body. Suddenly nothing was as important as to be in the sun, limbs spread out to catch every last ray. To be dizzy with heat – swimming in heat.

Tom edged his leg over to Annie. 'Warm up on that.'

His leg was alien, his body for so long unexplored – but it was the surprise of his gesture that sparked the ember to warm her cold flesh.

'Annie,' Tom whispered. 'Thanks.'

She closed her eyes and Tom removed his leg. They lay without touching, the cold air between them.

'Annie.' Again Tom's whisper: 'Am I . . . have I been . . . such a bad father?'

How did we end up like this? she asked herself, while painful feelings of regret and pity raged through her for both of them. Whatever Tom had done, whatever she blamed on him, and whatever the many things she had *not* done, she could not bear that he was suffering as result. 'Oh, Tom, you did your best. You did.'

The following morning, Chuck summoned Annie into the big meeting room for a five-minute strategy overview. They faced each across the specially commissioned table (why hadn't Jake made it?) on which reposed folders stamped with St Brigid's crest.

'How's it going?' Then he threw in the rider, 'God, you look tired, Annie.'

Feeling dreadful was bad enough, but to be told you looked it was definitely not helpful. 'Mother-in-law,' she admitted. 'Acclimatizing.'

Chuck assumed his managerial face designed (she and Sarah agreed) to be magisterially annoying. 'Annie, are you up to this at the moment? You would say if you weren't, wouldn't you? I can't emphasize enough how important it is we get this up and going.' He stabled his pen on the crested folder and his voice deepened into the health-and-safety variety of caring. 'If things are too much . . .'

During her working life, it had become habitual to ignore the veiled threats of senior management, so much so that they weren't an insult any longer. 'Chuck,' she favoured him with her top reassuring smile, 'there's no need to worry. Shall we start? Samuel Smith. A and E have submitted their report, and the lawyer has responded. I've also read . . . the parents' account.' She glanced at her right hand, naked of her mother's ring, and thought, *A mother has lost her son.* 'It's not good, Chuck. By any measure, he should not have died. He could have been saved.'

Samuel's mother had choked out: 'No one should lose a child unnecessarily. No one should go through what we're going through.'

'Negligence?'

'I'm sure of it.'

Chuck leaned back in the chair and digested the implications. 'No one is to say anything. Understood?'

Samuel's mother was in hell. *I know a little of it*, Annie thought. *Desperation and misery, they are good companions.* Surprised by how deeply the case was affecting her, she slid the folder that contained the facts and preliminary conclusions about Samuel Smith's death to Chuck. 'I didn't want to email this, just in case. We should discuss it privately before you respond.'

'I'll read it.'

Annie crossed to the coffee machine and poured two cups into Admin's expensive china. 'OK. We also have to talk superbugs. Thinking about the infection rate and how we present it . . . It's true that the rate has gone up but I'm convinced that if we're draconian in approach we can change that very quickly.' Cups in hand, she turned. 'Schedule a meeting with the cleaning companies and the unions. Look again at the procedures for pre-assessment of incoming patients.' She placed the coffee in front of him, expertly orchestrating her boss into quiescence. 'We've got another five minutes. I'll run through some options.'

Tom rang her in the lunch hour, which was a first for many a month. 'Bad news. Telly's on the blink.'

Phone tucked into one shoulder, Annie kicked the filing cabinet shut and sat down. 'No surprise. We'll get a new one.'

'We can do without it for a couple of months. Then, you never know, things might have changed.'

Annie grew suspicious. 'What are you up to?' He didn't reply and she continued, 'We can afford a new television.'

'I think we should wait and see.'

Annie looked up and into the corridor along which a couple of orthopaedic cases were shuffling. An all too vivid vision of being forced to talk to Hermione of an evening danced a merry jig. 'I could swing a discount with the hospital suppliers.'

'No.'

'No,' she conceded. 'Not good.'

He sounded very close. 'Not good.'

Passing through the hospital corridors, Annie found herself thinking about Tom in a way she had not done for years and it struck her that she hadn't really *looked* at him properly either. Exactly when had the joint on his left forefinger become swollen, or the line between his nose and mouth deepened? She couldn't have said. Of course she knew he ate toast and marmalade for breakfast but she didn't really *know* if it was force of habit or if he actually enjoyed them.

Mia's departure had killed many things, among them curiosity about her husband, which had come to a slap-bang stop. True, before Mia left they had grown apart but until that cataclysm Annie had always wanted to *know* about Tom: if his tastes were changing, or his knees hurt, or what he felt about the book he was reading.

Five years later, Mia's words still burned: 'You and Dad are so selfish, so *inward-looking*, so *self-absorbed*.' Maybe that was right and she and Tom had been guilty as accused. Whatever the truth, Mia's words had finally smashed up the already damaged icon still cherished by Annie of the happy family.

She turned into 'Yellow Street', then right into 'Blue Street'. At the entrances to the wards, notices admonished visitors to use the handwash and offered in bold type some rather lurid statistics on *C. diff* and MRSA. She inspected them carefully and was satisfied. And that was *another* thing. Once upon a time, a hospital was considered a place of safety, a place in which you could lodge absolute trust. Where you would be tended, defended and healed. Samuel Smith had asked for those things – and he had been denied them.

Nobody believed in the place of safety any longer.

She passed the map of the hospital (which, she was proud to own, she had insisted should be posted at regular intervals in every corridor). Honeycombed as it was with departments and offices, people got lost looking for wards, theatres, labs. Often anxious and fearful, they found themselves doubling back, adrift in an alien setting. 'If you're frightened,' she had argued the case with Chuck, 'you lose your bearings quicker.'

G2 and G3 were the senior assessment wards. Obedient to the dictate, Annie paused to squirt the alcohol rub on her hands. The double doors to the ward swung open and a flock of physios and therapists surged through, their pleasure at being released registering in their chatter and easy lope.

She made her way to the nurses' station, asked for her beautiful sister-informant, and found her in a side office deep in paperwork. They exchanged greetings, Annie put her request to her and the sister agreed she would be willing to address the board on the subject of superbugs.

The sister pointed through the door to a side ward across the corridor. 'There's a statistic for you.' She indicated the group of relatives huddled around a bed. 'He got infected, beat it, but it's left him too weak to survive.'

As Annie retraced her path, the bodies and faces in the beds, and the visitors who sat beside them, impressed themselves on her as never before. The patients were old, some very, and the immediate effect was of shrunken bodies on the edge – a murmur of souls about to be set loose in goodness knew what infinities. Yet if Annie was to make a huge effort, climb out of her mental straitjacket, peel away the scales from her eyes, she would see that this was not true. Wrapped up carefully in the hospital beds, the bodies of the old did not represent the whole story. That would be to deny the gleam of interior life, the flashes of humour – 'nice to see you, dear' – and the love between patients and visitors, which was present, one way or another, in these wards.

With a bit of luck, Leonardo's angel had them all in his sights. And, with a bit more luck, he'd spotted the Nicholsons too.

The doors swung shut behind her.

Chapter Sixteen

Hermione did not settle into the family easily. The night wakings were frequent and she quickly developed a habit of ringing the hand-bell and demanding of whoever answered it a cup of coffee, a book, help with some task or other.

Added to which the weather remained cool and resolutely unsunny, and the days slid towards July without respite from the dullness. Annie wore a jacket to work and there had been several pleas at number twenty-two for the central heating to be switched on in the evenings. 'No,' said budget-conscious Annie. Tom had looked at her quizzically but said nothing.

He didn't appear to understand the panic, approaching desperation, that had crept into Annie's almost daily tallying of the accounts. Of course, they were not destitute – like so many – but they were stretched. One day, it might be to breaking point. She would have liked to talk over her worries with Tom and for him to say, 'You're overreacting,' but their habit of reserve was too entrenched.

It was raining determinedly when a dripping Annie returned from work one evening. 'What an awful June it's been.' She dumped her briefcase on a kitchen chair, peeled off her damp outer things and brushed down her plain cotton skirt.

Untidy it might be, but the kitchen was warm, the table laid – albeit in a manner that suggested haste rather than thought – and something was cooking. Annie brightened.

Tom wheeled round from the stove. 'Surprise,' he said. He moved over to the counter and began to chop cabbage with enthusiastic slashes.

Still in her office clothes, a cheerful-looking Emily searched in the cupboard by the back door, which served as a general dumping ground. 'Aha.' She extracted a carrier bag filled with old toys and games. 'Got it.'

Jake lounged against the dresser, the tell-tale anguish in his eye that indicated a bad day. Annie averted her gaze. If only she could help his suffering and take it on herself. But the time when it was possible to mend a child's broken heart with a cupcake, a hug, or a well-aimed swipe of her mother tiger's paw at an enemy had gone.

She shook out her hair and sprayed raindrops. 'What surprise?'

Whipping open the smaller of the two ovens, Tom produced a maiolica plate (much loved and bought in Siena) piled high with mash into which he had stuck sausages.

'Wonderful.' Annie instructed herself to concentrate on the surprise, and not on the treasured maiolica that might, at any second, crack from the heat of the oven.

Instead she kissed Jake, relishing the faintest whiff of the cedars of Lebanon, apple wood, olive wood, all the poetry and romance of wood that she fancied hung over him. 'Maisie OK?'

Jake pressed down affectionately on her shoulders. 'Sleeping like . . . well, she's sleeping like a baby.'

Smiling, Annie turned to Emily and kissed her. 'What *are* you doing with all that stuff?'

Emily submitted to the embrace. 'Wait and see.' Then she said, 'Mum, are you going to leave your hair like that?'

'Oh, God.' Annie ran a hand over the damp untamed mess. 'Better?'

Having heard Annie's arrival, Hermione came slowly down the stairs.

'Do you need help, Gran?' Emily called up from the kitchen doorway.

'Gran's getting a bit lame, isn't she?' Jake muttered to Annie as Hermione appeared in the doorway.

'How lovely to see you all.' Hermione was her usual orderly self. She eased herself into Annie's chair. 'Supper ready?'

'Is your back giving you trouble?' asked Tom.

'It's fine, dear. I'm just a bit stiff. It happens at my age.' She switched into Cassandra mode. 'As you will discover.'

'Are you sure, Gran? You hate admitting if anything's wrong.' Emily was concerned.

'Hermione, would you mind shifting up one?' Annie ran water into a jug and set it on the table.

'Why, dear?'

'That's my place.'

'I didn't know there were *always* set places. Are there? How very formal.'

Annie said politely, 'I wouldn't say that.'

Hermione considered. Then she appealed to her son: 'Tom, dear, would you mind if I sat here? Otherwise I'm in the draught. I'm sure Annie will see the point.'

Several pairs of eyes were trained on Tom, including those of his exasperated wife.

Annie *would* mind, she reflected tartly, and resents his lack of support.

Tom wore the despairing look of a man cornered by

241

harpies. 'Hermione . . .' He threw Annie a look. *Sorry.* He tried again. 'Hermione, it is Annie's place . . .'

The woman who was outsmarting her at her own table, Annie thought, was also the restless, troubled woman of the nights. Where Annie sat at the table was a small issue, and Hermione knew perfectly well that she was unlikely to stir up too much trouble over it. 'Oh, for goodness' sake. Hermione, sit there for today and we'll talk about it later.' The smile flickering at the corners of Hermione's pink-lipsticked mouth implied that talking about it would be over her dead body. Despite this, Annie gently refastened the rickety brooch on Hermione's blouse. 'You must get this mended or you'll lose it. I expect you're hungry. I am.'

She sat down in her unaccustomed seat with its new sightline. The kitchen was bursting at the seams. The family were like the bees coming home after searching for increasingly sparse clover banks and poppy fields, and the household had changed. How things have changed, she thought – and, after a moment, for the better?

'It's been a long time since lunch.' Hermione was on a roll, 'and I've been alone in my room all that time. No one has come near me.'

Tom said, 'Rubbish. I brought you a cup of tea.'

'But you didn't really talk to me, Tom.'

'At least you have a telly, Gran.' Jake was ranging about the kitchen like an under-exercised dog. 'I'd better have a go at mending ours.'

Emily rolled her eyes and Tom said, 'Don't be silly.'

'Dad,' said Jake, 'you've no idea what I'm capable of.'

Annie could have sworn she heard Tom mutter, 'Too right,' but since he was stooped over the oven she could not be sure. She jumped up, seized the empty water jug, jabbed Tom in the ribs and issued a *sotto voce* warning: 'Don't.'

'Don't what?' he muttered.

'You know what. What do think you're doing?'

The mash was lumpy, and that was to throw a kindly gloss over it, and the sausages required a touch more cooking. Nobody much cared, though, and to the accompaniment of companionably clacking cutlery, they ate the lot while a dismal day deepened into dusk and rain pattered against the windows.

Annie was tired and ate mostly in silence until she put herself back on duty. 'Emily, how was work?'

Emily had indulged her disgusting habit of squirting tomato ketchup into her mash. She surveyed the bloody battlefield on her plate. 'I'm getting used to it.'

'Not too unhappy, then?'

'Could be worse.' Emily poked Jake in the arm. 'It's a job.'

But the Jake who would normally have laughed at the tease did not respond. Instead he flushed and his mouth set in a tense line.

Oh, Jake, thought Annie, aching for him.

Hermione laid down her knife and fork with an elegant precision. 'I miss Mia. She always used to come and visit me.'

There was a tiny pregnant silence.

Emily turned to her grandmother. 'Do you feel more settled, Gran?'

'How do I feel? If you really want to know, I feel pointless. No, don't look like that, Tom. I am pointless, no two ways about it.'

'Oh, Gran,' said Emily. 'You mustn't feel like that.'

Hermione embarked on further mischief. 'Tom, dear

'. . . this is very good.' She hooked a final wedge of sausage on to her fork. 'Do you have to cook often?' She gestured in Annie's direction. 'I know how busy Annie is.'

The rapidity – to be precise, the beat of an eyelid – with which the determination to take in and care for her mother-in-law could turn to truly murderous rage left Annie almost breathless. 'Hermione, that's *unfair* . . .'

Having failed her once, her repentant knight-errant now whipped in. 'Actually, Annie does the lion's share of the cooking, as you will have noticed.' One eyebrow raised a fraction and sent a private signal. *Calm, Annie.* He returned his attention to his mother and deployed a diversionary tactic: 'I used to love your steak and kidney pies. Do you remember the butcher when we lived in Deadforde who used to put a calf's eyes on the newspaper and make me read through them?'

Anne breathed in deeply.

Emily gathered up the plates and stacked them in the dishwasher. Tom and Hermione were reminiscing, and Jake was helping Emily to clear the table.

Annie surveyed this activity. How was she going to cope with all this coming and going, negotiation and renegotiation? Craving peace and solitude, she let herself out into the dripping garden and squelched down the lawn.

The garden smelt drenched, and the night sky was obscured by cloud. Music floated out from the house on the right and someone in a house further down the terrace was shouting to someone else in a good-natured way.

However you dressed it up, growing older was no fun. It was a subject she and Sadie had discussed at length, the loss of looks, health, energy, and even the irrepressible

Sadie had agreed she couldn't fight it on all fronts. 'Just the face-lift one.' There was nothing for it but to accept a future scaled back to more modest lines – but she had certainly not anticipated this invasion of number twenty-two. Was it so bad? The alternative – silence and isolation – was said to be worse by those who endured it.

'Pah, to growing older,' she murmured and, because the explosive constant was pleasurable on her tongue, repeated it: '*Pah!*'

The light appeared reluctant to vanish entirely. After all, high summer was (technically) just round the corner. Weighed down under its slick of water – she smiled at the fancifulness – the garden appeared to be frustrated by its inability to get on with it. Weren't they all? Wandering down to the shed, she was surprised to see paving stones had been laid leading up to it and the grass cleared. She also spotted a new catch on the door, plus a light rigged up inside.

She turned it on and stepped inside.

Tom has been here. The interior had been cleared and swept, the window painted. Tools were arranged on the shelves and hung on wall nails. A small, battered armchair had been inserted into one corner on top of a garish red-and-white rug, which had, clearly, been brought in from a charity shop.

Exuding Essence of Masculine Refuge, it was all that the male stereotype was often described to be, and Annie liked it very much. How nice it would be to skulk in this peaceful, rooted place. How clever it had been of Tom to create a refuge. And unexpected, too, for Shed-man Tom was not the person with whom she was acquainted.

Balanced across the chair was a garden fork with a roll of duct tape slotted on to a tine. Setting them aside, she dropped down into the chair, closed her eyes and relished a little high of creosote and fresh paint.

Subject: Hermione. Question: how do I cope?

. . . An immaculately groomed Hermione had not said much when Annie, on first being brought to meet her by Tom, had turned up in jeans, T-shirt and clumpy cowboy boots. She had merely looked and thought plenty.

'How do you do?' she had said. 'I'm always delighted to meet Tom's friends. But, and you will have to forgive me, I can never remember their names. He has so many, you know.'

She had been polite, attentive and coolly well-mannered, but the look in her eye had suggested more violent feelings. Those Annie did fathom. She had served a Sunday lunch of roast beef with trimmings in a dining room furnished as if it was a miniature stately home, which was a little ridiculous for a tiny cottage. Annie had been struck by the neatness of the rooms and, despite the ancestral furniture crammed into them, their lack of personality. Save for a couple of invitations displayed on the mantelpiece, not one stray object or piece of paper had been permitted to roost on a surface. Did Tom's mother knit? Or cook using recipe books? Appreciate flowers? To Annie, she appeared a woman without form or vanity or hinterland.

They drank coffee in the garden, and the shadows thrown by the *leylandii* hedge fell across disciplined flowerbeds and a manicured lawn. Hermione worked away at her charm-school questions – where did Annie live, what did her parents do, what did she hope to do? Tom sent her lustfully loving looks and Annie felt both guilty and disloyal to him. Hermione, and her set-up, was all that she disliked.

Eventually Tom had cleared his throat. 'Mother, we want to tell you something. Annie and I are going to get married.'

In a trice, Hermione's stream of polite inquiries had dried up, and the mask was peeled back to reveal a snarl: *no one is worthy of my son*. After several painful seconds, she managed, 'That's ridiculous.'

Tom's eyes had narrowed. 'Why?'

Hermione recovered herself, but only just. 'Because you hardly know each other.'

It was only when Annie had produced her own children that she began to divine the measure of the other woman's desire to keep her son close for ever. She had had no way of knowing how instinctive, how powerful that reaction was and had been deeply hurt and offended. Neither had she understood that time would be on her side. If Annie grew older, Hermione went from older to *old*. If Annie discarded the jeans and boots in favour of the office skirt and blouse, Hermione was forced by varicose veins to give up wearing sheer stockings in favour of support tights, grew fatter at the waist and thinner in the bosom. 'Oh, how lumpen I am,' she once confessed in a rare moment to Annie, 'how desexed' . . .

'Annie, what are you doing here?'

Annie awoke from her doze with a start. The smells of creosote and paint had become almost unpleasant, and her head buzzed. She ran her hand over her face and pulled back her hair. 'Dozing,' she confessed. 'When did you do all this?'

He reached down and retrieved the discarded fork and duct tape from the floor. 'Now and then. During the day.'

'It's nice.'

247

'Yup. It is. Listen, you're wanted indoors.'

'Can't we stay out here?'

'Not really.'

He was short to the point of curtness and, with a slight shock, Annie understood she was unwelcome in *his* shed. 'I didn't mean to pry.'

'It's a bolt-hole, if you like.'

She swallowed. 'I understand.'

The disturbed moths and flies enacted their own dramas as backdrop to their conversation. Tom shrugged. 'You have your *work* . . . I have the shed.'

As if that explained everything, she thought sadly.

Tom took up a pair of scissors that had been stowed in a flowerpot, wrestled with the duct tape and cut a length. *He was waiting for her to move.* Wrestling with it, he managed to wrap it around the fork handle. 'I've been meaning to do this for some time. I'm pretty sure this fork belonged to my father.' He looked up at Annie. 'I was going to throw it out.'

Annie tried again: 'I mean it, Tom. I do understand.'

'Thanks.' He splayed a second length of tape and, with the fork in one hand, groped for the scissors.

Annie forestalled him and hacked off a length of tape. It clung stickily to her fingers and she had a bit of a tussle before she managed to disengage herself. Watching him patch over the split wood, she thought, If Jake could see his father . . . 'It was a wonderful, never-to-be repeated job but, Tom, it couldn't, wouldn't, have gone on for ever. Even if you had managed to cling on until they had to push you off the gravy train –'

'Gravy train?' he cut in. 'Is that what you think?'

She cursed silently. 'No, of course not. But, in the end,

you would have had to face being without it. Think, Tom, you're still young enough to be able to do something else.' Had she caught his attention? 'Tom . . . you're not powerless. I know you feel it, but why not use this time to think again? Re-evaluate. Think about what you find important. Do something different.' She paused. 'I'll back you.'

She spoke softly, passionately – and the words with which she was urging him had long been unused between them. He lifted his eyes briefly to hers. 'The tape may not do the trick. I suppose I should consult Jake.'

'Are you listening to me?'

'Sure.'

He turned his back on her to put away the scissors and tape. The message was clear. Tom didn't want Annie in his domain. He was closed off – and Annie discovered that she minded very much. She wanted to be welcome, she wanted to help him. And she wanted him to listen so that he could get on with the rest of his life.

'It's all right, Tom. I'm going in.'

He kept up the deaf act. 'Yup, that's what I'll do. I'll ask Jake,' he said. The indignant moths and spiders fluttered between their two figures. 'We should go in. Your presence is requested for a game of Monopoly.'

Emily looked up as Annie and Tom re-entered the kitchen. 'Listen up, everyone, we're going to have some fun.' She indicated the Monopoly board on the table. 'Mike tells me lots of people play it.'

'Oh, Mike-at-work,' said Jake. 'If *he* says so . . .'

'Leave the door open, dear,' said Hermione. 'It's nice to have a bit of fresh air.'

Annie sat down reluctantly and Emily's hands descended to her shoulders. She bent over and whispered into Annie's ear, 'I know you hate games, Mum, but I insist.'

Annie abandoned an after-supper plan of rereading the lawyer's report on Samuel Smith, which was not strictly necessary for she was aware that she had taken the case too much to heart. 'Why this particular torture?'

'Because . . .' Emily set out the cards and doled out the money.

Jake finished the sentence: 'Because she's never grown up.'

'And you have?' Emily turned to Tom. 'You remember the fun we had, Dad?'

'I have a vague memory.' Tom took the seat beside Hermione.

'You could never concentrate.' Jake pointed at his sister.

Emily ignored him and continued with her task. Annie discovered she approved of the new Emily: more settled, less wispy and very pretty in her office clothing.

Emily decided she would be banker. 'Choose what you want to play with.'

'I'll have the boot,' said Hermione.

'You always have the boot, Gran,' said Emily. 'Why not the top hat?'

Hermione tapped a fingernail on the table. 'Because, as you well know, you think of me as an old boot.'

Emily snorted, '*Gran!*' and plumped for the Scottie dog, Jake took the top hat and Tom went for the car. This left Annie with a choice between the iron and the battleship.

Mia had always chosen the iron. As a little girl, she had

liked what it represented. 'Lovely clean clothes, Mummy.' As the politicized undergraduate, however, she had laughed, tossing it from one hand to the other. 'I'm not afraid to play with an instrument of feminine repression.'

How she missed her daughter. Raising her eyes, she encountered Tom's steady gaze. *Don't go there, Annie*, he was telling her.

She chose the battleship.

Emily had got up a head of steam. 'We'll throw for playing order.'

'No,' said Hermione. 'I go first. I'm an old woman and I refuse to wait in a queue.'

'But that gives you an advantage,' Tom pointed out.

'Precisely.'

'You're not stupid, Gran, are you?' said Jake.

Hermione threw the dice and made seven. 'There are not many advantages left at my stage of life.'

Jake murmured, 'The probability of rolling a tally of seven is one in six. Whereas two and twelve are the least probable.'

'Shut up, Jake,' said Emily.

Hermione landed on 'Chance' and the card she turned up said she was drunk in charge and fined twenty pounds.

Again, Annie met Tom's amused gaze. *So, there is some justice.*

Next up was Tom. He landed on the Angel, Islington, and bought it. 'Good one. Building costs low, hotel rents high.'

'This is the man,' Jake teased, 'who argues that property is theft. Give it to me instead, Dad.'

'That was Mia, stupid,' said Emily.

Oh, Mia, thought Annie. *Where are you?*

Tom kept his eyes on the board. 'But I agree we should guard against being too acquisitive.'

'Dad . . . pompous or what?' Emily poked his arm.

Tom grinned. 'Games are useful in this way. The government should demand everyone plays Monopoly once week in order to allow our rotten impulses full rein and to purge the system. Wouldn't you say, Annie?'

Was this his way of making up for being so unresponsive earlier? Once, he had used this easy good humour to woo Annie and she had loved it. She hadn't thought back to that time very much in recent years but when she did so her heart took on a life of its own.

She got up, ran water into a glass and drank it thirstily.

Jake threw a six for the second time running and edged into the lead. Emily stared at him suspiciously. 'Are you cheating, Jake?'

'How could you ask such a thing?'

'*Very* easily.'

This is good, this is pleasant, Annie thought. Jake looked better, Emily was enjoying herself, Shed man was happier, Hermione was (relatively) silent.

In this companionable way they played for half an hour or so. Then Tom took a look at Jake's hotels and properties – and competitiveness kicked in. 'You *are* cheating.'

The edge to his voice was unmistakable. *Testosterone. Rivalry.* Annie knew them well. 'Tom . . .' she warned.

Jake flushed, and took his time to move his top hat forward. 'Actually, Dad, that's a bit insulting.'

Tom leaned over the board and counted up Jake's properties, then did the same for his own, lower, tally. 'That can't be right.'

Jake held his father's gaze. 'Dad, I have not cheated. Do you understand?' The hazel eyes were steady – and just a trifle contemptuous.

A second ticked by. Two seconds. Three. It was touch and go. Tom backed off. 'Sorry, Jake. Of course you haven't.'

Jake dickered over whether he should buy King's Cross. Emily rolled a couple of duffs and remained in jail. Hermione's nails clicked on the table. The game stumbled on, punctuated by the occasional exclamation and counter-accusation.

Later, Hermione bought Pentonville Road. Tom said, 'You sell me Pentonville, and I'll cut you a deal on Fleet Street.'

At that, Emily protested, 'No, you don't, Gran. Give up the blue and you'll give away the game.' She picked up the unused iron token from its slot in the box and tossed it from hand to hand.

Don't, thought Annie. Mia's absence was draining the strength out of her – a discordant, unresolved loss of the large-eyed, naughty, teasing and, yet, utterly contained child, who had been replaced by the crop-haired, dungaree-clad vegan, with a cold, critical gaze.

'Dear Mother,' ran the letter hidden in the ex-chocolate-now-memory box. 'I won't be forgiving you and Dad any time soon.' Annie pictured Mia writing it, sitting gracefully upright, using one of the graphology pens she favoured. 'Nor, if I know you, will you be forgiving me.' Was Annie an unforgiving person? She puzzled over and over the point and it hurt her immeasurably that Mia should see her in that way. 'I've turned out different from the rest of the family, and you refuse to understand what those differences are, or what I believe and what I feel . . . You are worse than

Dad for you say that you love me and, yet, you can't accept what I am . . .' Was this true? Annie asked herself. Could I not accept that, despite having made her from my body, Mia was not in my mould? 'PS I'm told that you have been up looking for me. Don't. I am no longer part of your life, or you of mine. We are finished.'

Funnily enough, it was the last line that managed to penetrate Annie's grief. It showed how little Mia knew – how profoundly she misunderstood the interleaved connections between parent and child. These were impossible to kill and Mia had no idea that Annie would no more give up on her daughter than breathing. Mia might have, and had, covered her tracks thoroughly and finally, yet Annie would spend the rest of her life waiting to glimpse the face in the crowd, to hear a voice in the hubbub, to watch without resting.

That was all she could do. It was nothing. It was everything.

It had begun to rain again and the kitchen was turning chilly. Annie got up to close the door. 'Sorry, Hermione.'

'Don't mind me, dear.'

Emily's mobile buzzed and played 'Scotland the Brave' and practically danced over the table. She threw herself at it. 'That would be *great*.' She glanced at her watch. 'In an hour? Yup. The café . . .'

Jake finessed a hotel on Coventry Street. He did not look up. 'Mike-from-work, at a guess.'

Emily shook the dice and trotted her Scottie five places forward. 'Let's get a move on.'

'Poor Tod.' Jake took revenge on his sister for the cheating jibe. 'Poor cast-away Tod.'

'Shut up.'

'Got you.' Tom snaffled a wodge of cash from Jake, who had landed on his hotel-infested site. 'One more push, and I'm there.'

'Tom, dear, I want you to have this.' Hermione held out the Pentonville Road card.

'No,' protested Annie. 'You'll give the game to him. Sell it to me.'

'I want Tom to have it.'

'Of *course* you do.' She heard her voice rise. 'How stupid of me.'

'Mum . . .' Jake laid a hand on hers.

'Right, that's it.' Emily slithered to her feet. 'Well done, Gran. You've decided the day. I'm just going to put my face on.'

'A word of advice,' said Jake. 'Don't be too eager.'

'Shut up.'

'Never does. Take it from me.'

'Back off, Jake.'

Jake turned to his mother and managed a flicker of a smile. 'Joking. Well, a little. I'll check on Maisie.'

After everything had been stowed away and Hermione had gone upstairs, Tom and Annie sat opposite each other at the table and drank tea.

'Almost like old times,' he said.

Dear Mother, I won't be forgiving you and Dad any time soon . . .

'Tom,' she said urgently. 'Go and talk to Jake. Tell him you really didn't mean it about the cheating.'

Tom frowned. 'He knows I didn't.'

'No, he doesn't. That's the point. He doesn't believe you, however often you say sorry after a row.'

'He'll have to learn to take a bit of teasing.'

'Sometimes,' she said bitterly, 'I think you're utterly with-out wits. And cruel.'

That got to him as she'd meant it too. 'You've been just as critical at times.'

'I know,' she admitted. 'We've made mistakes with our children and we shouldn't make them in the future.'

'He's a grown man with a child.'

'Believe it or not, grown men cry.' She moved around the table towards him and pulled him to his feet. 'You do. I've seen you, many times. Remember? You hurt and bleed just like Jake. *Especially* now.'

'Do I?' he ventured at last, and smiled down at her. Then he hooked a finger under her chin and made her look up.

'Tell him you're sorry,' she murmured, scrutinizing the face that, these days, smiled so rarely at her. 'That's all it takes.'

Rain trickled down Emily's neck as she dashed along the street, and lodged in the collar of her blouse. Her heart was beating a little too fast for comfort, and she told herself that it was because she was hurrying and not because of Mike's phone call. He knew it was a bit late and spur-of-the-moment, but he just wanted to check over a few things with her about work, he'd said. And, anyway, wasn't it a good idea for them to get to know each other better?

Emily could hardly disagree, could she? In fact, she considered it a sensible plan. If she was to work in an office, it would only be prudent to get a handle on her immediate superior. This was not, she realized, a view that laid-back counter-culture Tod would share.

'Emily.'

She whipped around. 'Jake?'

He tucked his hand under her elbow. 'Had to get out. Now and long term. But I just can't see my way at the moment.'

Emily was sympathetic, of course she was, but also preoccupied about the meeting with Mike. 'Get Jocasta to pay off the mortgage and give you the house. She must be earning millions by now.'

More often than she admitted, Emily found herself uttering not so much stupid as ill-considered remarks to Jake, which she usually regretted. It was partly that, these days, she was always in a hurry or distracted by things outside the family.

But it was also partly – and it was distressing to have to come to this conclusion – that some of the sillier things she said were the result of her ignorance.

Jake peered at her in the street light. 'I wish it hadn't happened,' he admitted haltingly. 'Almost, I wouldn't have minded if Jocasta had stayed and we lived like Mum and Dad do.'

'They're estranged,' offered Emily, tartly.

'They tolerate each other. Maybe that's all that can be hoped for. Maybe there's more going on between them than we know.'

'What planet are you on, Jake? The last few years have been awful. And they don't exactly tolerate each other, as you put it. Mum and Dad are cold, icy, at times unforgiving.' She recollected Tom's secret on-line playing with the stock market and how uneasy it made her feel. Should she tell Jake about it? Should she tell her *mother*? 'Dad never talks to Mum, and Mum is taken up with the hospital. God knows why they haven't divorced. It's far better that you and Jocasta make a clean break.'

He was silent for a moment. 'You can say that because you've never loved someone.' He gestured sadly. 'It's very simple. I loved her and it's bloody painful.'

Emily was silenced. Love, she thought, had nothing to do with reason and everything to do with mayhem, which left you sad and damaged.

'But perhaps you're right.' He dropped a kiss on her cheek.

'About what?'

'I don't know,' he said. 'I don't know.'

Conscious that she had failed him but unsure in which way, Emily hurried on to the bus stop, lured by the prospect of Mike and his flipcharts, the whole new world of office hierarchies, alliances and procedures.

Tom went to bed and, late as it was, Annie worked on the neglected report. Eventually, stupid with fatigue and having undressed, she went to check on her mother-in-law before going to bed.

The night light threw its subdued gleam over a sleeping Hermione. *Her thorn in the flesh? The cuckoo in the nest of number twenty-two?* There's no greater intrusion, thought Annie, than to watch someone sleeping without their permission. Hermione's light, puffing breaths betrayed the state of her lungs, and her wrinkled arm her age. But, elderly as this adversary might be, Annie understood that Hermione had her secrets and she had no right to divulge them to Tom.

She bent over to straighten the duvet and became aware that Hermione had woken and was regarding her with the direct stare so often a characteristic of the very young.

'That's a pretty nightdress.' Her mouth creased in what was – and Annie never imagined she would see on Hermione – a naughty smile.

Annie's hand crept up to her neckline. Trimmed with Brussels lace and of fine muslin, it was an indulgence she had bought in a Parisian flea market.

Hermione's eyebrows lifted. 'Tom is fortunate,' she murmured, and closed her eyes.

Back in her bedroom, she regarded Tom's unconscious figure, shrouded in his duvet like the elderly patients in the hospital ward. Shaken by terror that either he or she might be alone when they, too, reached the end of the line, she leaned over and gently, oh, so gently, touched his cheek.

She got into bed, and the customary gap remained open between her and him. The soft folds of the antique nightdress settled over her – the brush of a spider's web, or unripe barley, or warm white sand.

She turned her head to look at the dark wedge beside her. Outside, the world was broken. Along with millions of others, she longed for things to be whole in her house, her head and her heart.

Tom, she thought, with a catch in her throat.

Tom?

Where are you?

Chapter Seventeen

The sulky summer had thrown yet another chilly and blustery day.

Tom was cold and regretted he hadn't fished out his overcoat but it was not smart enough. The joke was he could have afforded several coats on his previous salary, but he had deliberately cultivated the statement shabby look. Deluded? Absolutely. Originally a method of indicating his membership of the BBC's priestly caste, it had become second nature. Now that he felt he could not justify the outlay on a new one, he discovered that a tatty coat worked differently, conveying the message that he had fallen to the bottom of the ladder.

The offices of Hidebrande & Ephron, Headhunters, were in Piccadilly and he was heading towards them.

'Tell you what,' offered James, when he had rung Tom after a considerable period of not ringing Tom, 'I'll put in a word with my mate John Ephron. He runs the agency. They might be able to do something.'

Aware that even his walk was different – less certain and slower than in the days when he had carried all before him – Tom paid attention to how he placed his feet on the pavement. Despite James's intervention, it had been necessary to cajole John Ephron into granting Tom an interview and he was apprehensive.

A few months ago, in the fat and fertile days, people had

begged to see *him*. In that triumphant past, James had even begged Tom, for God's sake, to help him out. 'I owe you big-time, mate.' Tom recollected James's expression of deferential gratitude, the glow of doling out patronage – and had thought nothing of it.

Shown into Reception, he was asked to wait five minutes. Five minutes stretched to ten, ten to fifteen, then twenty.

The set-up in the basement of what used to be a smart townhouse, now parcelled up into offices, sported well-tended pot plants, leather furniture, an espresso machine and serious financial magazines. Tom stared at the state-of-the-art machine and the early German Futurist painting on the wall, which he coveted instantly. That bothered him. Since when had he turned into the envious sort who minded that others enjoyed bigger houses, better paintings? Since when had he measured himself against the nimbler, the more successful, the better-loved? To be jobless pitchforked one into a new psychological landscape. To say that he was reluctant to travel over it was to put it mildly.

At last he was shown into an office where he was greeted by a (much) younger man, with a mass of brushed-back fair hair, in a three-piece suit that exuded Savile Row. 'I'm Joe Hidebrande.' He exuded a tutored politesse. 'John asked me to give you the heads-up and sends his apologies but he's a bit tied up.' He leaned back in his leather chair. 'What did you wish to discuss?'

Tom stared at him. How old was Joe Hidebrande? Twenty-five, possibly twenty-seven – and light years away in sensibility? 'I was hoping . . .' Oh, God, why had he said 'hoping'? It was always a sign of weakness. He began again.

'I wanted to talk over the situation and to sort out where you could fit me in.'

Joe Hidebrande cleared his throat. It was not a reassuring noise. 'As you will know, our business tends to operate the other way around. We come to you when we're franchised to fill a position . . .'

Franchised to fill a position . . . The terms had certainly changed.

'But . . .' The word carried a burden of favours having been called in, of charity, even. 'Why don't we go over your CV?'

Between the two men stretched an expanding reservoir of non-comprehension. Tom swallowed, and an image of Annie hurrying out of the house, weighed down by a briefcase stuffed with documents to do with on-going work concerns, passed through his mind. At that, the competitive gene asserted itself and he swore he would sit it out.

The clock on the building opposite was registering noon when Tom emerged from the expensive offices. He took a few steps in the direction of the Underground, changed his mind, reversed in the opposite direction past the scene of his recent humiliation and came to a halt.

I don't know what to do, he thought. Until now, he had refused to allow himself to consider that he might fail to get another job – but the near-certainty had come home to roost. Had he really been the man who had thrown a credit card on to the salver on which reposed a staggering bill for dinner with colleagues? *I'll see to it.* In that once-upon-a-time, he had been careless, heedless, expansive and more than a little flown with drink. He remembered tapping his crocodile wallet against the edge of the table and the puck-puck sound it made, then collecting his shabby overcoat from the cloakroom.

'You like all that too much,' Annie had once accused him, which had brought him up short. 'Be careful.'

He speed-dialled her.

'Hallo.' She was guarded, which usually meant someone was in the office with her – in her world of lino corridors, surgical gloves and statistical juggling about which he knew little.

'It's me.'

'I know it's you.'

Tom turned on his heel and walked towards the park.

'Is something the matter?' Annie clipped out the question.

He wanted to shout, *Everything*. Instead he said, 'I just wanted to hear your voice.'

It was as if he had waved Prospero's wand, for now Annie's voice swooped tenderly: 'That's nice.'

He enjoyed the pause that followed – a pleasurable, almost-forgotten moment of anticipation after which anything might happen. It was the moment when you listened to the unspoken words of the other. In the early days they would have been: *I love you*.

'How did it go, Tom?'

'Badly. I was fobbed off. Not their fault, but they couldn't have been less interested, and I can't blame them.' He prayed that Annie would not respond with platitudes about short-sightedness and ageism.

She did not let him down. 'There's no question you're up against it. We're just going to have to think round the problem more cleverly.'

'I made mistakes, didn't I?'

'Surely not.' Annie barely missed a beat. 'The god of the radio.' She turned serious. 'You're not alone, Tom. I, too, thought I could do good. Instead I just hold up a wall of paper and try to limit damage when patients die who shouldn't.'

'Why didn't you say anything?'

'I don't know,' she said. 'Not talking, I suppose.'

Tom dodged an oncoming car and crossed the street. 'If I was a god you were a goddess.'

He heard her snort of amusement.

He raised his eyes to the blustery skies. At least Annie appeared to be with him. 'Annie . . .' he struggled with a lump that had sprung – shamingly – into his throat. 'The other night . . . I mean . . . you can come into my shed any time.'

At that she laughed properly, and it was a very nice sound.

He continued: 'In the meantime, while we think round the problem, as you say, more cleverly, I can look after Maisie for a bit, which would help out Jake.'

'Tom, now I've heard everything.'

The trouble with having troubles was how stupid they made him feel. Where had his confidence gone – the bright underpinning that had powered him into Jocasta's bed and into his workshop to produce his creations? Having lost it, he was semi-paralysed and diminished. So habituated to achieving things without effort, Jake was nonplussed by the effort it required to function halfway decently.

He unlocked the workshop door and manoeuvred the pushchair inside. One way or another, he hadn't been there for a week and the air was noticeably stale. The dust made Maisie sneeze.

Jake opened a window, shrugged off his jacket and bent

over to tuck the rug over the baby. After the buffeting from the wind outside, she was sleepy. Parking her in a patch of sunlight under the window, he left her to it.

He yawned, stretched and bent over to push a pot of varnish back on to a bottom shelf. When he stood upright, Ruth was in the doorway, toting a large canvas holdall.

Since they had last met some weeks ago, her hair had grown. She wore a high-waisted fifties pencil skirt, which was just a shade too tight – it didn't matter because the effect was fabulous. But she did look a little strained. 'Here, can you take this?'

Obediently, he wrested it from her grip and set it down on the bench. 'What on earth . . . ?'

'Your next lunch . . . so to speak. If you want it.' Hauling out a couple of toasters and a wooden box with a broken lid, she presented them to him like votive offerings. 'Word's got around.'

'What?'

She stuck her hands on her hips. 'I didn't take you for stupid. They need mending. Interested or not?'

'Of course,' he replied uncertainly.

Ruth tiptoed over to inspect the sleeping Maisie. 'She's got one red cheek.'

'It happens with babies.'

Her eyes travelled around the room. 'I'd love to see some of the things you've made.'

'The furniture's gone to the people who commissioned it.'

'Big pieces?'

'Some of them. But any size, and . . .' he grinned wryly '. . . hopefully handed down to the next generations. That's their point. To be used and passed on.'

'I can take the stuff back, you know.' Her eyes were wary, almost goading him to rebuff her yet hoping he wouldn't. 'Easy.'

He glanced down at the jumble. Already he was assessing and sorting, anxious to make them whole again. 'Leave them with me.'

Ruth seemed to relax. 'You should put a notice up at the entrance to the workshop. Then people will know.' She cocked her head as if she was explaining a basic fact to Year One, which made Jake laugh.

'You're a very practical person.'

'I have to be,' she said simply.

'I'm practical but not businesslike,' he confessed. 'It drove – it drove my wife mad.' He paused. 'But it's a good idea. The notice.' He laid out the stuff on the bench. 'Do you need receipts?' She shook her head. 'OK. If you can wait, I'll do the easy job now.'

Maisie stirred from her all-too-brief nap and uttered a hungry noise. Jake pointed to his bag. 'There's juice and a biscuit in there. Would you . . . ?'

Ruth did not appear that willing, but obliged. She hunkered down beside Maisie and gingerly offered her the bottle. 'I don't have much practice.'

'It's not rocket science.'

She observed Maisie attack the teat. 'Perhaps not.'

Now that Jake had grown used to, and took for granted, the umbilical cord that stretched between him and his daughter (however smelly or grubby), it always gave him a prod when others were lukewarm about the baby package. 'If you talk to her, she'll get to know you.'

'Get to know me? That's nice,' she murmured.

266

The order book had happened to fall open at Jake's last substantial order. *Dining table. Seating up to 16. 2 Leaves. Claw legs. Inlay. Walnut.* It was like looking at an object behind the glass at a museum that belonged to a different era. He shut it. He applied himself to the task at hand. The jewellery box was made of cherry and inlaid. Its owner had taken care of it but the inlay required a tweak, the lid a new hinge and the lining replacing.

He checked the drawer, which contained a selection of silk, velvet and cured leather. 'Red or green for the lining?'

She did not look up. 'Green. Suits the wood better.' She guided Maisie's hand around a biscuit. 'I know you're used to doing bigger, classier projects. You probably consider a jewellery box beneath you.'

'I'll take what comes,' he said, after a pause. 'Easy come, easy go.'

At that, Ruth did look up. 'Really?'

'No,' he admitted. 'It isn't. I mind very much.'

Maisie had made a good job of mutilating the biscuit and a dollop dropped to the floor. Bending down, Ruth mopped it up – and her spine curved in a delicious movement that reminded him of the swoop of a banister on a Palladian staircase. He grinned as she straightened.

'What's so funny?'

'Do you really want to know?'

'I asked,' she pointed out reasonably.

'Your back reminded me of a banister . . . one of those beautiful sinuous staircases where the daylight and sun drifts down from the fanlight in the roof . . .'

'Steady on,' she said.

'You've been very nice to me, Ruth. Helpful.'

'And you thank me by comparing me to a banister?'

'You've no idea what a compliment that is.'

'You're right. I don't.' She scrubbed Maisie's mouth with a tissue.

'I *am* grateful.'

She smiled and dropped the tissue into the bin.

It seemed warmer and the sky outside looked more promising. There might even be a chance of some sun. Even so, as Jake stretched the green silk into the box's interior, the tiny frisson of attraction stirred up by Ruth withered, leaving him longing to be alone.

'Knock, knock,' said a voice.

Jake glanced up. Tom, looking smarter than he had seen him for a long while, was framed in the doorway. 'Dad.'

'Thought I'd come and see if I could help with Maisie.' He paused at the sight of Ruth. 'Am I interrupting?'

Jake introduced them. Ruth smiled radiantly at Tom, and Jake was astonished. Night had turned into glorious day. 'What Jake means is that I've been bombarding him with stuff,' she said.

Jake noted that his father was transfixed.

'It's not exactly what he's been used to but, round here, people need things mended and someone like Jake is difficult to find.'

'A good thing,' said Tom, and Jake understood that a seal of approval had been bestowed on Ruth. 'Adapting . . . If we don't we won't survive.'

Bastard, thought Jake. Sounding like David Attenborough and wearing that stupid corduroy jacket too.

'Shouldn't just be the economy that makes us change our behaviour.' Ruth continued to glow. 'We should do it anyway.'

'True, and that's what my elder daughter might say. But when have humans ever really got ahead of the game? They're too busy making hay with the present.'

Tom was being very, very nice. A tiny flush crept into Ruth's face. 'Maybe.'

Tom's gaze rested on Ruth a fraction longer than Jake reckoned it needed to. 'What do you think?'

'Any progress is better than nothing.' Ruth tucked her hair behind her ear. 'We have to be realistic, and any result is the best result because that's all we have.'

'You're very wise very young,' replied Tom. 'It's taken me years to get to that point.'

You old dog, thought Jake. Seizing a screwdriver, he set about replacing the faulty hinge while Tom and Ruth (the ultra-receptive audience) talked away, his father waxing eloquent and animated in a manner Jake had not seen in him for some time, a small relief that Jake could hardly begrudge him.

'Do you work?' Ruth asked, in such a careful manner that Jake realized she probably came from a situation where work was not a given.

There was a short pause. 'I lost my job, but I'm looking for another.' Tom glanced at Jake. 'I'm afraid it's made me rather short-tempered, as Jake could tell you.'

Jake slotted the final screw into place and closed the lid of the box. He slid it over to Ruth. 'First job done. The rest will take a few days.'

'Here, let me.' Tom inserted the box carefully into the holdall and zipped it up.

Again Ruth's features melted into a smile. 'Thank you.'

He could see his father reflected in Ruth's eyes, *a charming, interesting man*. And perhaps he was.

Interposing himself between Tom and Ruth, he took possession of the holdall. 'Dad, if you could look after a Maisie for a moment, I'll carry this over for you, Ruth.'

'No need.'

'All the same.'

She sidestepped to face Tom and the fall of her hair lodged against her neck. 'Very nice to meet you.'

Together, Jake and Ruth picked their way over the cobbles and headed for the block of flats. 'Is business OK for you?' he asked.

'OK-ish. I'm hoping to find a bigger space – the flat's tiny – so I can hire someone to help with the orders and run the website. But . . .' She shrugged. 'Meanwhile I help keep an eye on the elderly in the flats. As I said, lots of lonely old ladies.'

At the entrance, which looked in need of some robust upkeep, she held out her hand for the holdall. 'Thanks.'

'Sorry about my father.'

Ruth looked puzzled. 'What for? He's nice. You're lucky to have a father.'

That gave Jake pause. *A charming, interesting man.* 'And you don't?'

'I have a father but he's not particularly nice.'

Clearly the subject was not one she wished to pursue, which made both of them a little uncomfortable.

Ruth seemed sweet, and her sweetness was balm to his fractious feelings. He decided to take the bull by the horns. 'Do you share the flat with someone?'

'I did.' The answer arrived reluctantly. 'Matt. But he's gone now.' Her eyes reflected pain and distress. 'We'd been together a little while, but . . .'

'Sorry.' Jake hated to see the distress. 'If it's of any comfort . . .' thinking, *Of course it's no comfort* '. . . my wife's just left me.' They were the hardest words to say and not that brilliantly put. If being cut off at the knees by Jocasta had left him so inept and fatuous, he would have to do something fast.

Her eyes widened at the information. '*Not* good.'

Thank God. There was no false sympathy. And, even if he had evolved into a fatuous, witless idiot, he might as well continue this conversation because it brought relief of sorts. 'It's a bit like having a brain fever and waking up feeling a different person.'

'Yes,' she said. 'I do know.'

Jake scuffed his boot on the kerb. 'I'd better be going.'

She smiled her light-bulb smile. 'If you like I'll make the notice and put it up for you. What sort of hours do you think you'll be here?'

He looked into the beautiful eyes, containing their hint of anguish. 'You mustn't bother.'

She blinked. 'I must bother. That's the point. I'm telling myself that if I take control of some things, others will fall into place. Making a notice is easy.'

Struck by this point of view, Jake promised to get in touch with the wording.

On returning to the workshop, he discovered Tom walking up and down with Maisie in his arms, pointing out objects – 'Window, Maisie . . . chair' – in a manner Jake found mildly irritating. At his entrance, Tom turned round. 'This is a good place to be.' He yielded Maisie up to Jake. 'I hadn't appreciated how much so.' He wandered over to the stack of wood and laid a hand on it, a priest bestowing a blessing. 'It's the basic stuff in the best sense. The stuff of life.' He seemed a little bemused by his own conclusions. 'It smells good. It smells *truthful*. Solid.' He turned and smiled at Jake. 'I hadn't appreciated this before. I didn't know.'

'Nice as it is to see you, Dad,' Jake was puzzled, 'why are you here?'

'Thought I might take Maisie off your hands, which would allow you to get on. If it would help I could do it on a regular basis. While I can.'

He meant: *Until I get a new job*. Suddenly anxious for his father, Jake kissed the top of Maisie's head. 'You love Maisie, don't you?'

'Yes . . . Actually, I adore her. But that isn't the sole reason I'm here.' Tom was extra gruff. 'I wanted to say . . . sorry.'

Jake settled a protesting Maisie in her pushchair. He did not look at Tom. 'Do I know for what exactly?'

'You do. Playing Monopoly. Other times, too. You feel I get at you . . . and I want to say I'm sorry about that.' Jake was gathering up his tools and deliberately didn't look at Tom. 'Of course you make things. I'm afraid I've been very angry and impatient with the way things have turned out.' He sounded deeply chastened. 'But you will understand what it feels like. The shock, I mean.'

Jake checked the blade on his Stanley knife before retracting it into the handle. The wounds inflicted by Tom still smarted sufficiently to tempt him to tell his father not to worry because Jake never paid much attention to what he said in the first place. But that would be a lie. Also, it had cost his father to apologize. 'Both of us could do with a break.'

'I know. I'm sorry.' Picking up a length of beading lying on the bench, Tom admitted, 'I'm pretty useless at the moment.' He twisted it this way and that and forced it into a curve.

The beading threatened to snap. 'Give it here, Dad.' Jake wrested it away.

The sun had moved round from one window to the other. Empty-handed, head bent, his father was encased in a patch of shadow, a man with the stuffing knocked out of him. Pity, plus a slightly shameful satisfaction in this apparent power shift between father and son, went through Jake.

'Dad, it would be great if you could look after Maisie.'

Tom lifted his head and a spark of animation lit his dulled eyes. 'Then I will.'

Jake rolled up his sleeves. 'Since you're here could you help me move the wood? I need to clear a space. It's looks as though I'm going to turn into a repair shop.'

Mia had maintained that it happened overnight. 'One day you're sewn into the family. The next you're cut off and quite separate.'

She couldn't have known how prescient her words were. They had been sitting together in her pink and white bedroom – Mia on the bed with her laptop on her knee, tapping into a chatroom, and Emily sort of crouched on the stool in the corner as though she didn't quite dare sit next to her sister.

She was fifteen and still inclined to the literal, and Mia was eighteen and busy with thoughts on climate change and her plans to save the animal kingdom. The separation bit set off alarm bells in Emily. Would this include her, or only Mia? Was everyone ejected on to the streets, whether they liked it or not?

She gazed at the carpet, an attractive oatmeal-beige that

Mia had made a fuss over choosing and which no one else was allowed as it was impractical. But Mia was because she could be trusted to look after it. Emily had had a *big* fight with her mother over the unfairness. Out of the corner of her eye, she spotted a sultana that must have dropped out of Mia's lunch box. Under the pretext of doing up her lace, she placed her foot on it and squashed it down hard into the carpet.

'The unsewing? Is it painful?'

'Not particularly. Most children can't wait for the off.' She snapped the laptop shut. 'I've been reading about it. Young children experience a series of disconnections that prepare them for later. Going to school . . . well, you know.'

'You want to leave home?'

Mia threw her the look she reserved for the perpetrators of cruelty to animals. 'I do. As soon as A levels are over, I'm off.'

In reality, Mia had done no such thing and Emily had noted that she had stuck around long enough for the parents to fund her through university. It was only after she'd met Pete at the end of her second year that the real change took place. Before Pete, Mia's crusading fervour exhibited a lovely frothy quality. After Pete, she turned serious and her expressive features no longer invited anyone to laugh.

From the start, Pete had hated everything about the Nicholsons and made his feelings clear. Emily used to watch him sniffing around the house as if it was built on a plague pit, picking on bits of furniture as bourgeois hate objects. Dark and bulky, he had held the slender coppery Mia in thrall. Be careful, Emily wanted to warn her sister. He's an enemy.

One of the first signs had been when Mia cut her hair

very short and joined the Marxist Society. Or was it the other way around? Then, at the end of the second year at Manchester, she had arrived home and cleared out her wardrobe. She threw out skirts, coloured sweaters and high heels but kept jeans, black sweaters, flat shoes and lace-up boots. From then on, she had made a point of dressing exclusively in them.

'Do you like Pete?' Mia asked Emily, in a rare instance of eliciting Emily's opinion.

That was really tricky. Emily knew enough to grasp that it would be unwise to be truthful. On the other hand, she did not know enough to understand how to dodge difficult questions. She fell back on her arsenal of references.

'He's a bit like Heathcliff,' she hazarded.

'Meaning?'

'He likes to be rude to people who don't agree with him.' She couldn't quite bring herself to say that Pete was a bully and Mia was making herself ridiculous the way she trailed around after him, and pretended she was as bold and free-thinking as Pete told everyone he was.

Mia's eyes narrowed. 'How stupid is that?'

After the big bust-up and Mia's departure, Emily had stolen into Mia's now empty room, searched the carpet for the sultana stain and found a brownish shadow that definitely marred the sweep of oatmeal. She had regarded it thoughtfully and with a sheepish pleasure. It was complicated. All her childhood, she had loved Mia and longed to be part of the inner circle. Now she didn't, and she felt nothing but guilty relief that Mia had gone, leaving Emily free to focus on other things.

Chapter Eighteen

Annie packed up the clothes she had selected for the second-hand shop. Bought in the glory days, the silk evening dress, the designer trouser suit and several (hardly worn) cashmere sweaters would fetch – if not a reasonable sum as everyone was now in the same boat – something that would help. Wrapping them in tissue paper, she felt a pang at their going.

She refused to think about her mother's ring.

'I'm off for a walk,' Hermione called, from across the corridor.

Annie poked her head out of the door. 'Will you be all right? You know the way to the park now?'

'Would anyone like to come with me?'

Oh dear. Annie quashed any misgivings and ducked that one. 'I think everyone's busy. Tom is trying to get the lawn-mower to work, Emily is going out and Jake's at the workshop.'

From out of the window, she could see Tom wrestling with the machine. The interview with the headhunter had depressed him, and the last few days had seen him polite, but subdued. But if the marital atmospheric pressure was not exactly sunny, it was more or less calm.

Hermione emerged into the passage. 'No one, then?' She made a play of twisting her favourite and much worn Jaeger scarf around her neck and buttoned her jacket. Her uncharacteristically wistful expression smote Annie as, of course, Hermione had calculated it would do.

'Let me tie that scarf properly. You might lose it.' Annie knew that Hermione didn't like to be touched, but she tucked the scarf ends into the jacket. 'You won't be too warm in all this?'

'I've been feeling a bit chilly lately, dear.'

Sub-text: the house was cold.

Downstairs, Tom lumbered into the hall. 'I need some oil for the mower. See you later.'

'Wait!' cried Hermione, her face lighting up. 'I'm coming with you.'

Thankfully, Annie returned to her task.

She could never accuse her mother-in-law of being *that* difficult. Hermione kept herself to herself in the mornings and watched a tactful amount of television (still the only set functioning in the house) in her room after supper. Yet her shadow fell across them. It was akin to peering over a neighbour's fence with a telescope and spying on private routines and habits. 'She drinks coffee for breakfast and a cup of tea at half past eleven, regular as clockwork,' she told Sadie. 'She won't have anything else but sixty-denier tights in a ghastly tan colour, uses talcum powder and insists on a night light.'

'At least she doesn't have a drug habit,' said Sadie. 'When my friend Laura Desmond sent her son over from Boston she forgot to mention he was half crazed by skunk. He smashed a few glasses, I can tell you. And I won't go into the state of the bedroom.'

Information, however mundane, about people you didn't love could often be distasteful, even repugnant. So were their things. With people whom you loved, everything was precious, even a dirty sock. Annie paused in the act of folding the trouser-suit jacket. She would give almost anything to know if Mia still wore a vest, if her shoes fitted properly and whether or not she still suffered from the occasional chilblain.

'Oh, Mum, you're so nosy,' Mia had often said. But what was wrong with wanting to know even the tiny details? Surely you couldn't give up on your blood and bone just because they had inconveniently grown up. Or even if they swore they wanted nothing more to do with you.

A scorched-soup smell drifted upstairs. Annie arranged the final layer of tissue, shut the suitcase and descended into the kitchen.

Emily was scrubbing a pan. 'I'm not sure I've got the hang of this damn cooker.' She ran clean water into the sink. 'Don't think it likes me.'

'Well, you'd better be nice to it.' She searched in her bag for the latest invoices and sorted them before pinning them up on the noticeboard. From his pole position, Leonardo's angel watched her from under heavy lids with the tender, steady grace she coveted for herself. Absorbed in her task, she did not register the doorbell.

Emily abandoned the saucepan. 'I'll go.'

'My God.' She heard Emily's angry exclamation and rose to her feet.

Emily edged into the kitchen. 'Look who's turned up, Mum.'

'Yes, look who's turned up,' echoed a familiar voice.

Jocasta. Whippet thin, armed with bronzed confidence, a laptop, from which dangled an American Airlines label, plus a designer bag weighed down with chains and locks. Judging her entrance precisely, she remained framed in the doorway, importing into the quiet kitchen a flavour of the Big Apple's optimism, its heat and traffic.

('Didn't you beg her to stay for Maisie's sake?' Annie had asked Jake, and was silenced by the finality of the answer: 'She doesn't want either of us.')

Annie slumped back against the dresser, which rattled the precious blue-and-whites. 'Oh, no.'

On the surface, Jocasta was calm, even amused, at the effect of her arrival. 'Are you going to ask me what I'm doing here?'

Emily cut across her: 'Do you want some tea?'

Jocasta glanced at her watch. 'Coffee. Got used to drinking it a lot more, you know.' She glanced around. 'Is Jake here?'

Annie shook her head. 'You should have rung.'

'Perhaps.' Jocasta helped herself to a chair and accepted the mug of coffee Emily stuck in front of her. 'It would have made things complicated. I was over and I thought I should see Maisie.'

Annie sprang to the championship of her granddaughter. 'You *thought* you should see Maisie?'

'No need to be angry, Annie.' Jocasta examined the coffee before hazarding a mouthful. 'Just my way of putting it.'

'Shouldn't you be coming over *expressly* to see your daughter?'

Jocasta looked enigmatic. She gazed down at the mug. 'Actually, that's what I meant.'

The back of Annie's neck prickled. Jocasta never, as far as she knew, did anything without an intention. However,

Jake would not forgive her if she antagonized Jocasta and she moderated her tone. 'Of course you've come to see Maisie.'

'Nice cooker.' Jocasta gestured towards it. 'Credit crunch isn't having too bad an effect, then?'

Emily grabbed a chair. 'You have a nerve, Jocasta, coming back with no warning. Do you know what you've done to Jake?'

'Of course I do.' Jocasta retained her customary cool. 'But you might spare a thought for my side of the argument.'

Annie stiffened.

Jocasta examined the residue of coffee in the mug. 'I was unwise and unfair but I'm fully aware of it. So was Jake . . . but he doesn't own to it.'

'Stop there,' said Annie. 'OK?'

A trace of coffee winked at the corner of the red mouth and Jocasta wiped it off, smearing her chin with red.

'Your lipstick's smudged,' Emily pointed out, with obvious satisfaction. 'And on your teeth.'

Jocasta dabbed it away and winched her professional smile back into place. She picked up the mug. She put it down again. She paused. Then she spoke: 'I've come for Maisie.'

It was Emily who cottoned on first what Jocasta was really about and got in, way before Annie: 'But you didn't want her. You left her with Jake.'

'You may be surprised . . . but I've changed my mind, and Noah has agreed. I found . . . I *find* that I miss her. I never thought I would . . . but things have a way of surprising one. We're all set up. Big house in upstate New York. Good jobs.' Jocasta looked directly at Annie – and Annie

280

caught a hint of the confusions that lay behind the glossy patina. 'After all, I am her mother.'

Annie searched her memory for similar eventualities that she might have come across and found nothing remotely approaching this situation. 'I'm not sure . . .'

'Not sure that I'm her mother?'

'You know what I mean,' said Annie. 'Don't play games.'

'Careful, Annie.' Jocasta bent down and searched in her bag, and Annie seized the opportunity to mouth at Emily. *Go phone Jake.* Emily leaped to her feet and disappeared upstairs.

Jocasta produced a sheaf of documents. 'There's quite a bit to straighten out. Obviously, there's the divorce and the house . . .'

'I thought you were going to hand that over to Jake?'

'Here's the thing,' said Jocasta. 'My lawyer has advised me that I was far too upset at the time to think straight. I agree with him. So, I intend to pay off the tenants and repossess the house, and we can go from there. Meanwhile, I'm applying for Leave to Remove Maisie.'

'You can't do that,' said Annie.

When Jake had first produced Jocasta with a proud flourish, Annie had understood exactly what he saw in her: beauty, the astute practical operator, the alpha-ness, and she had told herself that Jake had been clever in choosing a partner whose qualities complemented his very different ones.

The front door opened and shut, and Jake called out, 'Anyone in?'

Emily leaned over the banisters. 'Jake, I've been trying to call you.' She clattered downstairs but not quickly enough.

Seconds later, he walked into the kitchen, accompanied by a tall, curvy girl in a full skirt and impractical satin ballet shoes carrying Maisie. 'Mum, this is Ruth.' Then he saw Jocasta. 'What on earth . . . ?'

This should only happen in films, thought Annie, unsure whether to laugh or cry. Normal, run-of-the-mill families are jogging along in the boondocks, or at least getting by, until, without warning, Jack Nicholson or Angelina Jolie arrives and a landmine is detonated.

'Hallo, Jake.' Jocasta kissed him on the cheek. 'I'm sorry I didn't warn you. I've come straight from the airport.'

Jake submitted to the kiss but his fists clenched, and he did not reciprocate.

Ruth shifted Maisie to the other hip. 'Jake,' she said. 'I think . . .'

The baby in her arms twisted round towards its mother, observed her gravely, but did not react in any way.

'She doesn't recognize me.' Jocasta stated the obvious. 'But that's not so surprising.'

'Are you her mother?' asked Ruth.

'I am. I'd like to take her, please.'

Ruth glanced at Jake. Jocasta frowned. 'I *am* her mother.' She stepped forward, and detached Maisie from Ruth. 'Hallo, honey. It's Mummy.'

Annie winced at 'honey'.

Little Maisie searched her mother's face and Annie found herself holding her breath. What did she see? The one for whom, in her baby way, she longed? But Maisie was thrown. Her bottom lip wobbled, her eyes did the welling-fountain trick and she reared back. A clearly disconcerted Jocasta kissed the top of her head and said, 'Never mind, she'll get used to me again.'

Ruth touched Jake's arm. 'Another time,' she murmured. 'I'll go now.'

Victim transfixed by the executioner or, reflected Annie grimly, a man still in love, Jake did not take his eyes off his wife. 'I'll phone you, Ruth.'

Maisie began to sob in earnest. Ruth swivelled on her ballet-pumped feet and her skirt swayed like a bell. She held out a hand to Annie. 'Mrs Nicholson.'

'Ruth.' Annie stepped into the breach and ushered her out of the front door, following her on to the step. 'I'm sorry about this.'

In the daylight, the colours Ruth wore were almost dazzling. She smiled gravely at Annie. 'That's all right.'

'I hope another time I get to meet you properly.'

Ruth said quickly, 'So do I . . . You have . . . you seem such a lovely family.'

To which Annie had no reply and retreated indoors with a heightened pulse.

Back in the kitchen, Maisie was wailing and Jake demanded of Jocasta in an unfamiliar authoritarian voice, 'Give Maisie to me.' A nonplussed Jocasta obeyed. Maisie buried her face in Jake's neck, and he soothed and cosseted her until she quietened.

Jocasta said, 'You've certainly got the hang of it.'

'I don't imagine that you've come all this way to praise my parenting skills.'

'Jake, I can't disappear totally out of your life. But you're right. I want to talk to you about Maisie.'

Emily slid over to Jake, flanking him like the loyal foot

soldier she was. 'Let me take her. I think it would be best.'

'Thanks, Em.'

'The thing is,' Jocasta positioned the coffee mug on the table, 'I miss her. I didn't think I would, but I do.' Her eyes rested on her daughter. 'You haven't got any work at the moment, right?'

'I'm mending and making-do,' said Jake. 'It's work.'

Jocasta frowned. Maisie slotted on her hip, Emily rocked back and forth. Annie looked from Jake to Jocasta and her knees felt peculiar with fright. 'Jake, why don't you take Jocasta into the sitting room and you can talk in there?'

The door shut behind them. Annie and Emily exchanged glances and Annie sat down with a thump at the table.

A murmur of raised voices issued from behind the sitting-room door, mostly Jocasta's . . . *big house . . . Noah willing . . . best for baby.*

Annie said, without much conviction, 'We mustn't listen.'

Emily caressed Maisie's hair and observed her mother. 'She doesn't really mean it.'

'She does.'

Emily's pretty mouth set in a hard line. 'Look. She does. Here.' She posted Maisie on to Annie's knee. 'I'll do the washing-up.'

For what appeared an unconscionable time, the sounds of swishing water and clattering cutlery were all that could be heard in the kitchen.

Behind the closed door, the voices rose harshly and fell. 'Who's the girl?' asked Emily.

'I don't know. He hasn't mentioned her.' Annie had forgotten about Ruth.

Eventually the door snapped open and Jocasta's voice

floated across the passage. 'I can provide her with a better life.'

When they emerged from the sitting room, Annie perceived with a shock that the old sweet Jake had been replaced by a grim, white-lipped stranger she barely recognized. 'If you imagine that by dropping in on the off-chance everything will be sorted, then . . .' He checked himself, and Annie applauded the last-ditch prudence. 'If you want to discuss things, arrange a meeting. I should warn you, I'm not going to let Maisie go.'

'Goodness,' Jocasta murmured, almost with approval. 'I've never seen you so masterful.'

Emily made to intervene but Annie shook her head. *No.*

'Right now,' continued Jake, 'Maisie needs her lunch. I suggest you go, and contact me later.'

The front door opened and banged shut. 'Let me, Hermione.' Tom sounded exasperated.

'You mustn't be cross with me,' countered Hermione. 'What was I to do?'

A dog's bark cut through this exchange.

'Am I hearing things?' Emily whirled round and Maisie cried out with excitement.

Annie shot into the hall. 'What on earth . . . ?'

A can of oil had been dumped on the hall table. Tom was on the front step, kicking mud from his shoes. Inside, Hermione was struggling to divest herself of her jacket. The helmet hairdo had been severely ruffled and she was minus the treasured Jaeger scarf. This was because, as Annie saw with incipient hysteria, it had been deployed to tether a small, unkempt dog of uncertain lineage.

An uncharacteristically hesitant Hermione confronted

Annie. 'He's lost. I couldn't stop him following me home. He just wouldn't go away.'

Minor chaos was unleashed. Dog and baby gave vent together while Annie and Hermione were engaged in a frank, almost no-holds-barred conversation about Hermione's decision to act as a one-woman lost-dogs' home.

Jake took the opportunity to hustle Jocasta outside on to the pavement.

Here, the summer light was less forgiving and revealed Jocasta's eyes and skin to be dull and jetlagged. Her lipstick had backed up into a rim around her lips, exposing a naked pink area, and one of her nails had broken off – the vulnerabilities that Jocasta always tried to cover up.

Jake clocked all this relatively dispassionately. The smart, seemingly armour-plated, recently deplaned businesswoman was also the woman with whom he had shared a bed and a bathroom. He knew that she liked to sleep on her side. He knew that, as a result of a childhood injury, she found it harder to raise her left leg when putting on her tights than her right. He knew she liked her showers dangerously hot and, however cold the weather, never wore a vest. Those tiny details had been the markers of a former intimacy: secret and precious. Yet, with a slight shock, he understood they no longer possessed the power to move him as once they had.

'And?' Jocasta searched in her expensive bag and produced her sunglasses. Naturally, they were expensive but, he noted unworthily, pretty vulgar with the monogram.

'I beg you to think of Maisie.'

She tapped a high heel down on the pavement. 'I *am* thinking of Maisie,' she explained, as if to an imbecile.

'That's the point. Have *you* thought about Maisie and what's best for her rather than for you? I don't think so.'

Since the break-up of his marriage, Jake had explored the depths and complexity of anger. Before then, cushioned by his family and an easy cruise through life, he hadn't understood that anger came in so many guises. He had known about the red-hot variety (he had done that with parents and sisters), but bitter, choking, murderous, acid and contemptuous? This was emotional new-found land. Yet, for the sake of his daughter, he was required to be calm. If that was what would secure him an advantage in the war Jocasta had declared, then he would make damn sure that the flat, glassy Sargasso Sea appeared turbulent beside him.

'Jocasta, why the sudden change of heart?'

'I don't know. It's muddled.' She surprised Jake by shedding her usual fluency and stumbling over sentences. 'I missed Maisie. But I think you understand what I'm saying, even if you pretend not to.'

A hint that the feelings he had for his daughter might be shared by Jocasta? Behind her, a sorbus tree had had one of its lower branches torn off by vandals. The ragged scar appeared to sprout out of the top of Jocasta's head. The effect was a touch ridiculous and made him feel a lot better.

He shrugged. 'I haven't understood you since the day you walked out. One day, maybe . . .'

'I see.' Jocasta pulled back from a threatened display of emotion. 'Just to reiterate. America is a great place for kids. And our house, the pool, the school . . .'

Maisie might have been a missing piece of household décor. 'You mean you need a child to complete this cosy set-up.'

Clapboard house, swing in the garden fringed by maples, turquoise pool, white towels on a lounger.

'Don't you and Noah plan a family? Or is Noah only a stepping stone?'

'For God's sake, Jake.'

The vivid mental scenario was now augmented by a male figure moving around the edge of the pool – but Jake couldn't make up his mind if the Noah in question was a WASP showcase or a foxy, pallid banker on the run from banking scandals. Either way, the picture proved to be too painful. 'Actually, I don't wish to know what you and Noah are getting up to.'

Jocasta dropped her eyes. 'It's none of your business.'

'Right.' He smiled thinly. 'But Maisie is. I won't allow you to take her away from all that she knows.'

Jocasta shrugged. 'Children forget.' She settled the strap of her handbag more securely. 'You're being sentimental again. The old Jake still rules.' Jake made no move and she peered at him. 'Then again, perhaps not. You're definitely older, sterner and less compliant.' The notion pleased her, or amused her, and she smiled and touched him fleetingly on the cheek. 'More interesting?'

To his relief, the display left him quite cold. During their marriage, Jocasta had called the shots – and he, submerged in lust and sweet love, had freely admitted it. Jocasta's mistake was to imagine that she still held that whip in her hand.

'You've done me a favour coming back, Jocasta.'

She looked mystified – but Jake was not going to enlighten her. 'I'll be in touch, then,' she said, after a moment, and moved away down the street. Already she was talking into the mobile. Ordering a taxi? Jocasta rarely operated without a taxi waiting for her, which meant she must have been very unsure of her reception – and its outcome.

The front door opened and Tom, Annie, with Maisie in her arms, and Emily filed out and gathered on the pavement. Together they observed Jocasta's graceful retreat.

'She's not having Maisie,' announced Jake. 'I'll fight tooth and nail.'

His father clapped a hand on his shoulder. 'Don't panic, Jake.'

As she neared the crossroads, Jocasta glanced around and her step faltered. For a long time to come, Jake would derive satisfaction that her final snapshot of her husband and daughter would have been of them surrounded by a bunch of Nicholsons.

The chaos of the day subsided – but not that much.

Maisie was unsure how to react to the dog and alternated between shrieks of pleasure and wails of fear so Jake bore her away upstairs.

Hermione sat in the kitchen while Emily sponged out a stain on the precious scarf. 'I hope it's not what I think it is.' She hung it over the drying-rack.

Small, thin, rough-coated and an indeterminate shade of dun-beige, the dog shivered with nerves and apprehension. 'Its owner is probably going mad looking for it,' said Annie, examining the matted coat for wounds.

'Have you looked at it, Mum?' Emily said. 'It hasn't been near an owner for weeks. I bet they abandoned it because they couldn't afford it any more.'

'What is it, do you think?

Emily hazarded, 'Dachshund crossed with haystack?'

Reluctantly, Annie poured it some milk and hacked a gobbet of chicken off the carcass in the fridge. The dog flung itself on this bounty and devoured it, proving Emily correct.

'I don't know why it attached itself to me,' said Hermione.

'As if we don't have enough on our plates,' said Annie.

At that the dog bolted out of the kitchen and up the stairs and took refuge, *of course*, in Hermione's room. She had set off in pursuit when Tom and Jake, who had been conferring outside, came back in. She leaned over the banister. 'Your mother,' she hissed. 'We can't have a dog. We just *can't.*'

Tom glanced up. 'Calm down.'

There was no sign of the dog in Hermione's bedroom. Annie dropped on to her hands and knees by the bed. Lifting up the bedspread, she peered underneath. 'There you are.' The little body was pressed hard against the wall. Its flanks heaved and a pair of terrified eyes met hers.

Human and animal exchanged glances – one beaten, the other about to be. Neither quite understood – yet – what was required of them. The little dog's weary eyes closed for a second – and Annie felt the weight of its unjust world transfer itself to her: all the cruelties and betrayals that it had encountered and did not deserve. 'Not you as well,' she said.

'Where's Tom?' she demanded, on returning to the kitchen.

No one bothered to answer but Hermione asked, 'Where's the dog?'

Annie stuck a hand on her hip. 'In your room, Hermione, as it happens. It won't come out from under the bed.'

'Leave it to me,' she said grandly. 'I'm good with dogs.'

'Since when, Hermione?' Annie strained to remember the last possible time Hermione might have had an opportunity to be good with dogs.

'Rollo, dear,' Hermione reproved her.

'Oh, him.' Rollo, the fat and gentle Labrador with whom Hermione had shared the cottage when Annie had first met Tom.

Hermione helped herself to a bowl and a packet of HobNobs from the cupboard, then made for the door.

'Hermione, where are you going with those?'

'Bait, Annie.'

'Over my dead body.'

'In all the years I've known you, I had no idea you were so harsh.'

'Hermione, you can't keep him. The house is full.' Hermione paid no attention. 'Hermione, did you hear me?'

HobNobs in one hand, bowl in the other, Hermione halted in her flight path. 'I wish Mia was here. She was my ally.' Within seconds, she could be heard stiffly ascending the stairs to her room.

Annie gazed after her. It was true. Mia could always be relied on to champion her grandmother. Favouritism, protested Jake and Emily, who resented the way in which Hermione dished out presents to Mia and not to them. Defending herself after it had come to a head and there had been a really big argument, Mia had declared that some animals did better than others and there would always be jealousy. (That was one way of explaining it, reflected an enraged Annie, who had had to deal with the fallout from Hermione's mischief.) Subsequently, in a touching scene,

Mia had confessed that she hadn't realized how resentful the other two felt and, from then on, she would share out her presents with them. She had been quite distressed about it, and her small, thin hands had trembled as she owned up to her short-sightedness.

The familiar fist squeezed Annie's insides. *Don't* think about Mia. She sat down with a thump. What more was there? 'Where's your father?' she demanded of Jake – he had returned downstairs with Maisie, who was dressed for an outing.

'Garden? He said he needed some air.'

Emily said, ''Bye, everyone. I've got to go. Office stuff . . . good luck.'

'It's Saturday,' Annie pointed out.

'Rats and sinking ships,' Jake addressed Emily. 'Mean anything to you?'

'Can't think what you're talking about.'

'But forgiveness for scarpering at the first whiff of a family crisis is yours because you're a Good Sister.'

Emily smiled happily at him.

Hand still anchored on hip, Annie said, 'So, it'll be me ringing the vet? Or the dogs' home?' She visualized the bleak procedure. Lure dog into car. Drive to dogs' home. Leave dog in cage while she trudged back along the concrete aisles between other cages that contained howling or hopeless canines.

''Bye,' said Emily again.

Maisie under one arm, Jake hoicked the pushchair into the hall with the other hand. ''Bye.'

Tom was in the shed. Of course. Annie wrenched open the door and found him cleaning the clippers with a rag.

'You come back inside this minute, and help me sort this out.'

He knew of old that Annie in this mood was inexorable and he found himself marched smartly into the sitting room.

The computer was on. The shoal of brightly coloured fish swam across it and the light from the window exposed with particular clarity a level of deep litter on the desk, which he knew would distress Annie.

'Maisie and the dog. What are we going to do?'

Tom paced the carpet. 'I don't care about the dog. Let my mother keep it, if it makes her happy. We've got Maisie to sort out.'

Annie picked up the magazines and banged a cushion into shape. 'Tom, this house is bulging.' As she talked, her indignation swelled. *Bang.* 'It's becoming impossible.' *Bang.* 'Claustrophobic.' She tossed the cushion on to the sofa. 'I can't do it all. The dog has to go.'

Actually, to Tom's fine-tuned ear, she didn't sound *that* decided. Every so often Annie had episodes of cushion-bashing or saucepan-clattering, which served as an outlet for her feelings. Afterwards, she was – usually – perfectly reasonable.

'It's an animal in trouble, and my mother could look after it.'

She practically bared her teeth at him. 'Your *mother*? What planet are you on? It wouldn't be your mother taking it for walks at all hours of the day and night.'

They were like pumice, rubbing away at each other's skin, which struck him as amusing.

Annie halted in her frenzy. 'What's so funny?'

'The cushion-bashing. Haven't seen you do that for some time. I quite like it.'

'No dog,' she reiterated, and sat down on the sofa.

He sighed nostalgically. 'You never listen to me.'

She had in the early days, when she'd walked alongside him. Then they had shared the same outlook. Each morning, she had watched him set off for the office in his shabby overcoat or jacket and radiated love. He was, she confided to him, doing the right thing as he and his colleagues wrestled to expose discrimination and political turmoil – and her whispered approval had been music to his ears.

'The *dog*, Tom –' She checked herself. 'Why am I going on about the dog? Maisie is much more important.'

Tom resumed his pacing. 'It can't happen,' he declared passionately. 'I won't let it.'

At that, Annie unravelled herself from the sofa and blocked his exit. 'No, Tom. Listen. *Listen*. We've got to be very careful. It's Jake and Jocasta's business, not ours. We have to understand that.' She placed her hands on his shoulders. 'She's Maisie's *mother*. We are going to have to be very clever . . . and realistic.' She searched his face. '*Are* you listening? Whatever we may feel, Jocasta has a right to her daughter as well as Jake. We must be sure that we're fair, otherwise we'll make problems for the future. And mothers count for a lot in court.'

He said stubbornly, 'Maisie belongs here.' She dropped her hands and turned away. 'Annie, look at me. I'm not going to stand by and allow that – witch to take Jake's daughter.'

Because we let Mia go. *The unspoken words.*

'Tom. If you cause trouble . . .' Annie pulled frantically at a curl. 'Don't you understand? You can't.'

'What?'

She squared up to him. 'You can't do it again.'

At a stroke, the air grew thick and poisoned. Words that had never been uttered trembled on the tips of their tongues. '*Meaning?*' He couldn't quite control his voice. '*Say* it.' He ran his fingers through his hair. 'Say what we never say.'

Annie broke the long, long, destructive silence. 'Mia.'

'Mia went because she was infatuated with a man who didn't want anything to do with us. He told her we were smug and useless and bourgeois and she believed him.' Pete's lowering features flashed through Tom's memory. 'He was a sponger.'

'Maybe.'

Tom struggled for control. 'Not maybe. He was.'

'You didn't like him because he challenged you.' She added quietly, which Tom found more devastating than hot temper, 'You preached tolerance, Tom, but when it came to your daughter it was another matter. That's what I couldn't swallow. You disliked Pete for being different.'

'Then why didn't *you* make her stay? Why didn't you speak up, Annie? Why didn't you say I was a hypocrite?'

'I've asked myself that a million times.'

They stared at each other, each blaming the other – as they had done for years.

'Why didn't you go after her, Tom?'

'Because . . .'

Why? Why?

That night in the kitchen. Mia blazing. Pete hostile. Annie a long,

295

long way from him in every respect. And he, Tom, exhausted and played out after hours in the office.

Annie had gone chalk white and she looked deathly tired. 'We should have talked about this long ago. I tried . . .' She shrugged. 'I know, I know, it sounds so simple and obvious but it's none of those things. I did try but I was too angry with you. Then it all got set in stone.'

Second chances did not come very often. 'If you must know . . .' he began but, almost overpowered by the blackness and bleakness of the past, stuttered to a halt. *Second chance.* 'How can I put this, how can I say this? I didn't go after Mia because I was so . . . ashamed.'

There was a long pause. 'Why didn't you say?'

. . . Mia confronting him: hair roughly cropped, a contemptuous smile wrenching her mouth awry. 'Basically, Dad, I hate everything you stand for . . .'

'After all we've done for you?'

'You've done me no favours, Dad. None at all.'

He relived the blow to his stomach, the sick feeling and the hurt . . .

'I tried. But you weren't listening, Annie.'

'That's true,' she admitted.

'Well, it certainly buggered up our . . . faltering marriage. And if I'd known . . .' Tom sidestepped a felled magazine, cursed and threw it on to the pile. 'If I'd known how things would go from bad to worse . . . But I always sort of hoped . . .' He raised an eyebrow and quizzed her: 'So why did you stay?'

'We were married. There were the children. Emily was at a tricky stage.' She recited the reasons like a school lesson.

Tom could not help wishing . . . Well, what, precisely?

That Annie could imply, even with the lightest of hints, that she had stayed because, despite everything, she loved him.

. . . 'How can you say this, Mia?'

'Easily. Listen again, Dad.'

'No.' Annie had tried to head him off. She had even interposed herself between him and Mia. 'Tom, be careful what you say. Don't, Tom . . . Don't, Tom.'

Don't, Tom . . .

He hadn't listened.

He remembered as yesterday the anger that had smashed through him, and the hurt inflicted by his daughter, whom he loved, which was a knife in his guts.

'Then get out, Mia. Get out and never come back.'

She had taken him at his word, leaving the remaining occupants in the house to pick up the pieces. Separately, they had gone about their lives. They talked to each other. Of course. From time to time, they ate meals together, did things together, but the heart had gone out of the family. The heart had also stopped beating in their marriage . . .

Annie got up, crossed to the window and fiddled with the curtain tie-backs. 'Mia will always haunt us.' She sounded desolate. 'Always. It's what we are now. What we will be.'

'Annie . . .' Tom searched for the right way – for this was a moment to seize. He stood behind her. 'Annie, I *know* it was my fault. I should never have said what I said.'

She didn't reply immediately, but her hand clenched on the curtain. *Please*, he prayed. *Let the past go. Let something else take its place.* She turned round. 'You've never admitted that before.' With that, she pressed her forehead against his shoulder – and he experienced a cathartic sense of relief. 'Never.'

He did not dare touch her back – for the moment was

too fragile to call it one way or the other. 'Would you believe me if I told you I think of Mia every day?'

'I wish I'd known.'

'This sounds stupid . . . but I thought if you loved me you would know.' Annie gave a tiny shrug but he pressed on: 'It's precisely because I made the mistake over Mia that we must act over Maisie.'

She looked up with grey eyes that already seemed to him lighter and clearer, and corrected him. '*We*' – he noted the pronoun – 'made the mistakes, Tom, OK? We can't intervene between Maisie's parents, and there's the law to consider. We'll back Jake to the hilt, but we mustn't let him do anything he'll regret.'

'I like the "we".'

'Do you?' The suggestion of a smile trembled on her lips. She looked around at the untidy, dusty room. 'This place is a mess, Tom. Just like us.'

When he took her hand, she made to pull it away. 'Annie, let me. Are we such a mess?' Slowly, slowly, her hand relaxed into his.

'Perhaps we can do something, Tom. We could look for her.'

'We could.' He lifted her hand and held it to his cheek.

'Or . . .' the grey eyes reflected years of distress '. . . maybe we have to accept Mia's choice.'

There were two aspects to proximity. The one to which both had grown used – brushing up against the other most days but maintaining an icy separateness. Then there was this, thought Tom, when a touch on someone's hand began to build a pathway into a heart and mind. 'The one doesn't exclude the other.'

'You think so?' There was a catch in her voice.

'I do.' He dropped her hand and began to gather up the newspapers. These he stacked in a pile and shovelled other papers into the bin.

She folded her hands across her chest. 'Well, this *is* new.'

The exchange that had just taken place between them had been so momentous, so charged – too much to take in at once – and the atmosphere had changed to almost light-hearted. He could sense her astonishment: *Tom clearing up?*

Annie pointed to an unharvested bit of paper on the floor and her eyes shone. 'Actually, Tom, you've missed a bit.'

'You wretch,' he said – but he picked it up and dropped it into the bin. 'About the dog . . .' He took his revenge. 'I vote it stays. It will keep Hermione amused and I know you won't mind the late-night walks.'

'Tom!'

'Or the early-morning ones. You can fit it in before work. Easy.'

'You utter devil,' and, with that, Annie aimed a punch at his chest.

It was a hard one. Her fist pounded jarringly into his breastbone and sent a tingle through his flesh. But Tom didn't mind in the least for it was the first time she had touched him with anything approaching passion in years.

Chapter Nineteen

First thing on Monday Jake hit the phone to Robin Tyler, his solicitor.

Having assumed that he had a reasonably straightforward divorce to handle, Robin registered concern on being told of Jocasta's change of heart. 'No need to panic,' he cautioned, 'but we will have to think this through carefully. As a matter of interest, does your wife have a work permit for the US? Are we sure that she'll be allowed to remain?'

'The bank's sorted it.' He tried not to sound angry and bitter and, because he was angry and bitter, didn't succeed.

'At least she hasn't gone to Australia or the Far East,' said Robin. 'New York isn't so far . . .'

'Far enough.'

'And things like term times roughly coincide with the UK for future visits et cetera.'

Jake blinked rapidly. 'Isn't that getting a little ahead of ourselves?'

'You have to think about it,' said Robin, 'and I suggest you do. You are now entering a legal process and you have to be clear in your mind about your objectives. You wish to keep Maisie, but Jocasta will have to be granted her rights too. Obviously.'

'Why's she changed her mind?' cried Jake.

'That's irrelevant,' replied Robin, calmly. 'Her initial actions of assigning you your daughter and handing over the house were almost certainly motivated by guilt. Not uncommon but the law regards the guilt motive as suspect. It is not the best way to decide a child's future. Almost certainly, there are going to be some adjustments.'

Jake finished the call with his head reeling and, having handed Maisie over to his father, went jogging. Sweat pouring, he pounded the flat, unforgiving pavements and tried to master his rage and lust for revenge. Their colonization of him felt like a sickness – intense and unignorable – which left him as winded as the run.

Back at number twenty-two, he deployed himself by checking up on Maisie's clothes and nappies. Her cot sheet required changing so he fetched a clean one from the airing cupboard and eased it over the mattress.

How ignorant he had been – and still was. Adversity fouled up and poisoned the system, and he was the one who had put a premium on politeness, went to great lengths not to hurt other people, and tried always to empathize. Yet, at the first blast of difficulty, he found he no longer cared.

He longed to phone Mia and say: *Help me*. And she would respond in that breathy way of hers: *Tell me*.

Looking out over the London garden where the foxes and squirrels fought territorial battles among the hollyhocks and lavender bushes, he imagined relating the story to Mia and her saying something like *You must steel yourself. You're up against the structures of capitalist society and she's the one with money.*

But Mia had gone, deliberately wielding an axe to the ties that bound her to her twin – because, as she'd told him, with tears running down her face, ' You would pull me back, Jake.' Never before had they lived separately – even if they had been physically apart – and he felt the lack in every cell of his body. She had warned him: 'Don't get in touch. It won't do any good.' At first he had rebelled and tried to contact her but Mia, deep in love with her new political beliefs and with Pete, had determinedly, bloody-mindedly, concealed all traces of her whereabouts.

Returning downstairs, Jake ran a hand along the banister and over the newel post. *That* never failed. Sure enough, the smooth, polished feel under his touch helped to ground him. 'Where's Maisie?' he called.

'I put her in the garden for a nap,' Tom answered from the sitting room, where Jake discovered him. Surrounded by the latest Appointments sections of various papers, his father was at the makeshift desk with his head in his hands. The computer screen illuminated financial graphs with arrows in red and black.

Jake said. 'Is everything OK, Dad?'

Tom started. A flash that could have been fear went across his features. 'Sure.' He avoided Jake's eye.

Jake glanced at the Appointments. A couple of the boxes had black crosses scrawled at the corner. Another had been outlined with red slashes and he sniffed out the negative vibe. 'Don't worry.' He prepared to retreat. 'I can see you're busy.'

Again the suggestion of fear and – even – panic. 'Do you want something, Jake?' He sounded clipped, almost antagonistic, and it was obvious he did not want Jake in the room.

And Jake thought: *Here we go again. Nothing's changed.* He could almost taste his disappointment and, illogically, a sense of betrayal. 'You look as though you've seen a ghost, Dad.'

Tom's expression darkened. 'Markets aren't so good. That's all.'

Silence.

'I'll leave you,' said Jake, and headed for the door.

'Jake. Stop. Sorry. What was it?'

'I was going to ask for some advice.'

Tom's tensed shoulders relaxed visibly. 'My help?'

'Yup.'

'Oh, well, sure. What's going on?' Gesturing to the screen, Tom said, and he sounded strained, 'Job-hunting. CV. I'm getting quite proficient in this game. But so far, no good.'

'And the graphs, Dad?'

Tom glanced at the computer screen where a couple of indices had turned red. His jaw tightened. 'Oh, those. Nothing much.'

'Dad, are you up to something?'

Tom switched the screen off pretty smartish. 'As I say, job-hunting. I'm yours, Tom. What can I do?'

Jake explained that some research was required, and could Tom help him?

Tom listened carefully to Jake's précis of Robin Tyler's advice. 'I want you to know,' he said, at the finish, 'that I and your mother will do everything in our power to help you. I . . . we feel that you should always be fair, Jake, which is difficult, given the circumstances. I'm not sure what we may be up against. It may be a horrible battle – in fact, I'm pretty sure it will be – but I'll be there.' He was working himself up to a powerful manifesto and Jake began to feel marginally better. 'We must find out everything we can.'

'So I'm not alone,' said Jake. 'You're on my side.'

'What made you think I wouldn't be?' That was a loaded question. Tom had not been on Mia's side but Jake wasn't going to go into that now. He had Maisie to think about and he would need the new, fragile relationship with his father.

'There's a payback, though.'

Once upon a time Jake would have grinned. Now, weighed by heaviness and foreboding, he merely growled, 'What?'

To Jake's surprise, Tom got up and put an arm around him. 'It's OK. Nothing too terrible. Could you do a repair on the garden fork? I've tried, but it needs your expert eye. I'm going to dig up the bed at the end of the garden and grow vegetables.'

Jake entertained an unpleasant vision of turnips and swedes, of battling slugs and foxes. 'Not like you, Dad.'

Tom dropped his arm and Jake sensed embarrassment. 'Helps the exchequer.'

'Mum won't like the shrubs being dug up.'

'That's half the fun,' confessed Tom.

'I'll look at the fork later,' said Jake, heading out to check on Maisie.

Tom called after him. 'You're not to torture yourself. OK?'

Despite its frailties, the dog was a shrewd and cunning survivalist. Annie marvelled at the instinct that told him with whom to throw in his lot. A couple of forays in the park where he had been (almost certainly) abandoned, and he had sniffed out a weak point in Hermione (which the majority would never have spotted) and followed her with the doggedness of the superdog.

But on arrival at number twenty-two, his courage and resourcefulness had taken a rain-check. Hermione having extracted him from her room, he was relegated by Annie to the downstairs cloakroom, where he sat and shivered. But maybe that was strategy too.

With the family gathered for supper, Annie coaxed him out. Flanks pumping, he advanced warily into the kitchen. 'Come on,' she said.

Like a trusting child, he looked up at her – innocent, at bay, uncertain of his life. The little body seemed brittle and starved, and his coat was badly in need of attention. Annie swooped down and picked him up. At first he remained rigid. Then, responding to the whispered, 'It's OK', he relaxed. Annie cradled him and he settled his head on her arm. Too late, she realized this was a mistake: she would struggle to consign him to the cages and concrete floors of the dog pound.

She carried him into the kitchen and placed him on a cushion. 'I want you all to know that this is not a good idea.'

'See what I've got.' Emily rummaged in her bag and produced a tin of upmarket dog food. 'The best.' She doled out a portion on to a plate.

Jake glanced at the label. 'That costs more than rump steak.'

It was demolished in seconds. Observing this, Annie asked, 'Has *anyone* rung the vet to check if someone has been looking for him? Answer: I have. And the local police. And, no, no one has reported him missing.'

Hermione regarded the dog with imperfectly concealed pride of ownership. 'I'd like to call him Rollo in memory of dear Rollo.'

Oh, God, thought Annie. This *is* happening.

The new Rollo was not a pushover. Tempered by experience – abandonment, cruelty (there were suspicious scars on his flanks)? – he made it clear in the days that followed that he guarded his affections and was careful to bestow his trust only on Hermione and Annie. Prudently, he maintained a distance from Maisie, who had decided it was uproarious to throw objects at him, and made little effort with Tom. Jake he ignored. 'You shouldn't make remarks about the cost of dog food,' said Emily.

Hermione, however, was a marked woman. Furthermore, she succumbed to her fate with the fervour of one newly in love and sent the family mad with her fussing.

Coming home from work, Annie was not surprised to find Rollo ensconced in Hermione's room. Nose tucked on his matted and calloused front paws, he had positioned himself at Hermione's feet with all the authority of Cerberus guarding the gates of Hell.

Hermione was on the phone to Sheila at the Manor House Home. 'That girl was always a nasty one. Remember when I caught her going through my things?' At Annie's entrance, she looked round and continued, without missing a beat. 'Did I tell you, Sheila? I've been given a dog. Pedigree. Very sweet. But I have to go now . . .'

Annie intercepted a look that Rollo cast Hermione: the wide-eyed, I-was-ill-treated-but-you-have-saved-me look. 'Hermione, what do you mean you've been *given* a pedigree dog?'

'Did I say that, dear?'

'You must remember what you just said.'

'We were talking about that awful girl who used to go through our drawers. Still does, according to Sheila. I'm sure she took money. Are you tired, Annie? You must be if you walked back.'

At the word 'walk', Rollo's ragged tail stirred.

'It's all very peculiar,' she reported back to Tom, as they

got ready for bed later. 'I definitely overheard her telling Sheila Reade that she had been given a pedigree dog. But she denied it when I asked her about it. Why Sheila would care one way or another if it's a pedigree I don't know. Maybe it's Hermione's way of making sure we can't get rid of him.'

'His name's Rollo,' said Tom.

Annie stared at him, incredulous. 'He's got to you.'

Tom was propped up on the pillows reading the *Guardian*. 'You should know by now that dealing with my mother is like nailing jelly to the wall.'

Annie paused in brushing her hair. 'Seriously, Tom, it was odd she felt she had to big up Rollo for Sheila. It is as if she had to prove to Sheila that she mattered to us.'

'Aha, *you*'ve just said "Rollo".'

'On second thoughts,' Annie concluded grimly, 'Hermione knew exactly what she was doing.'

For all its normality, the conversation was curiously stilted. Tom and she appeared to have slipped into a guarded phase. They were considerate to each other in the manner that strangers were with fellow strangers. After their recent conversations, when a tiny aperture had opened on to each other's private thoughts, Annie had imagined that relations between them would be easier.

Tom turned to the financial pages. 'Oh, God,' he exclaimed, under his breath.

'What?'

'Nothing. Just a rumble about the state of the banks.'

There was a polite pause, during which Annie bent to pick up a discarded sock. 'How's the job-hunting?'

'So-so.'

307

'Tom, has something else happened?'

He retreated behind the paper. '*Nothing.*'

She trod carefully. 'Tom, are you going about it in the right way? I mean . . .'

'Annie, I'm doing my best.'

'Yes,' she said, with a rush of contrition, 'I know you are. But if you want to bandy some ideas around . . .' She faltered to a halt. Tom had thrown the paper aside and, if she wasn't mistaken, he was staring at the neckline of her nightdress. She coloured. He pursed his lips and whistled – and she heard an echo of being young together. Of the passion that had turned out not to be eternal, but humiliatingly mortal.

'You're blushing,' Tom said.

'I've just cleaned my face. It does that.'

'No, it doesn't.'

'Stop it,' she said, but she didn't mean it.

Annie resumed the hair ritual. It was very strange, but she had become re-sensitized to Tom's presence. When he entered the room, she registered it in a significant manner. When he left it, she registered that too. With each stroke of the hairbrush, the tiny hairs on the back of her neck sent a prickle through her flesh.

These inner shifts and adjustments were not reflected outwardly. Neither did they impinge on her routines, which, apart from agonized conversations with Jake about Maisie, were normal. Morning and evening, Annie creamed her face and thought, Oh, Lord, what's happening to my jaw-line? She got dressed in her office uniform and went out to do battle in the hospital. *Samuel Smith, you should not have died.* There were the odd variations – dropping her shoes at the cobbler's, dithering over whether macaroni cheese or stew would go further to feed the family, a frantic hunt for a mislaid twenty-pound note. *How is Zosia? Must get in contact and tell her how much I miss her.* At work, she walked through the hospital corridors on the trail of the cleaners, expertly dodging porters, stretchers, wheelchairs and patients. (It was curious: even if they knew exactly where they were going, patients and visitors always exuded the anxiety of the refugee.) In the evening she came home, went over the accounts and, occasionally, packed up more of her possessions to sell. Just in case.

Had she been good with people? Her track record suggested yes. But it was easier to be clever with people who weren't close to you. She had chosen her work because she had wanted to help make things better and easier for the sick. Only today she had spent several hours with the manager of the new crack cleaning teams and they had understood each other fine.

She sneaked a look at Tom. Their relationship was another matter. With that, the image of Mia sprang into her head and, so strong, so vivid, so living was it, her heart almost stopped. The coppery hair, the thin little hands, the breathy 'Mum'. Annie held the image suspended in the silvery spaces of memory, gazed on it, endured the pain it provoked. Then, with a huge effort, she banished it.

She dropped the brush on to the dressing-table and sat on the edge of the bed. 'Tom, I'm here if you want to talk things over.'

'Thank you.'

He didn't move. In fact, he remained quite still but it felt to Annie as though he had reached out a hand and drawn her close.

Chapter Twenty

The decision to push Mia to the back of her mind worked. It was a breakthrough and proved to Annie that she had wrested back some control. And if the Jocasta affair threatened to turn the family inside out, extraordinarily she breathed easier because of it.

Frantically busy, Jake divided his time between childcare and the workshop. He asked if he might bring Ruth home for a meal and she turned up for a Sunday lunch, which they ate in the garden. Jake and Ruth took turns to sit Maisie on their knees and they ate roast chicken and minted peas. Ruth had brought with her a bottle of Sancerre – 'Sweet of you,' said Tom – and they drank it with the meal. A tardy summer sun shone down on them so Tom and Jake fetched the big umbrella from the shed and there was general hilarity as they tried to avoid the dead spiders and cobwebs that threatened to festoon them. The conversation meandered this way and that. For that moment, and for the first time in years, Annie felt entirely peaceful.

Maisie succeeded in squashing a pea into the skirt of Ruth's bright red halter-neck sundress. 'Couldn't matter less,' she said, as Jake made a fuss about scraping it off. 'It's vegetable.'

Tom asked her about her parents and what her father did. Ruth flushed. 'My father . . . he started out on the printing presses but he hasn't worked for years.' Maisie demanded her attention and Ruth stood her up on her knee and bounced her up and down. 'Unemployment did things to him,' she said. 'My mum says it changed him. *He* says he isn't a proper person without a job.' She glanced at Tom and her flush deepened to dark red. 'What I mean is . . . I didn't mean . . .'

'No, but he's right,' said Tom. 'That's exactly what it feels like.'

Jake leaped up. 'I'll make some coffee.' He bent over and whispered something into Ruth's ear and she gave him her radiant smile. While Jake was indoors, she said to Tom, 'Are you sure I wasn't speaking out of turn?'

'No,' said Tom. 'I agree with your father. It should be said.'

In early September, Jake sought out Annie and asked for a loan so that he could pay the solicitor's bill. He was pale, his nails were bitten and he looked as though smiling was an outlawed activity. Without hesitation, she gave him what she had to spare. 'Don't worry,' he promised, 'I will pay it back. I'm going to sell my wood stockpile.' When Annie protested that it was his insurance for the future, he replied, 'That's what Ruth thinks. But it has to be.'

A few days later, Annie discovered Tom's notes on the hall table: 'Jocasta served court petition. Jocasta applied for Leave to Remove. Family court decides Residence Orders. Best result? Split Residence Order. Would this be practical? Judge will request Family Court Advisers (Cafcass) to make report. Courts almost always pay attention to contents of report.'

Wandering into the kitchen, she discovered Hermione with Rollo ensconced cosily on her knee. On the table, a cup of tea steamed beside an open packet of HobNobs. Hermione was murmuring to Rollo who, ears pricked, was paying careful attention. She snapped a biscuit in two and gave half to him.

Annie stuffed Tom's notes into her pocket. 'You shouldn't give dogs chocolate biscuits.'

'He was crying,' said Hermione, as if that explained everything. 'I couldn't bear it.'

Annie glanced at her sharply. 'Are you feeling all right?'

'Fine. Rollo needed some comfort, that's all.'

Annie surveyed the touching tableau. 'He certainly got it.'

Hermione shifted in her seat. 'We are definitely, definitely keeping him, aren't we? You're not going to whisk him away?'

Annie was shocked that, after so many weeks, Hermione would consider that she could do such a thing. 'What do you think?'

Hermione clutched Rollo. 'That means you don't want to keep him.'

Annie began to see that working in Administration in a huge National Health hospital was mere child's play, and fell gamely into the trap. 'Of course I want to keep him.'

'He's got used to us now. It would be wicked to disrupt him again.' Hermione administered more comfort to Rollo in the shape of the second half of the HobNob. 'She's not really cruel,' she informed him.

Annie winced. 'We're bulging at the seams and money is a bit tight.'

'I pay my share of the bills. I'll pay for Rollo.'

'Yes, you do. And we must keep something back. Just in case . . .'

'In case I need to be carted off, you mean.'

Annie was accustomed to dealing with tricky conversations

but this one was close to the bone. She reached over and ran a gentle finger down Rollo's muzzle.

'I'll say this, Annie. I sincerely hope you're never in my shoes. I'm on the slide and it's getting faster and I can't stop it, and I'm . . .' Hermione was both enjoying and frightening herself with the dramatic scenario she was painting. 'I worry where I'll end up.'

Annie hunkered down beside her. 'You don't sound quite yourself.'

Hermione's tone was desolate. 'When you're old, you're not yourself.' She sighed heavily, then gave Annie a look so on-the-ball, and so cunning, that Annie should have known she was being wound up. 'Still, it helps if you have someone to look after. Someone and something to think of other than your aches and pains.' She glanced at her watch. 'I'll go and watch *Countdown*.'

Annie did her own check on the kitchen clock. 'You know it's changed times?'

'I record it, dear, so I can watch it at its usual time. I'm too old to change my routine because of some thoughtless programmer. They never think, do they?'

Last thing before she went to bed, Annie looked in on the sleeping Hermione. 'OK, Rollo will stay.' She had laid down the house rules, knowing that she had little chance of being heeded. 'But he's not to go on the bed. *Any* bed.'

Wasted breath. Rollo was settled beside his new mistress who had backed up awkwardly against the wall, one arm encircling him like a lover. The little dog opened an eye, observed her calmly and went back to sleep.

At two a.m., Annie was ram-raided from unconsciousness into full alert in approximately five seconds flat. Who had made the noise? Baby? Mother-in-law? Or now, for God's sake, the dog?

She sat up. Tom was sleeping quietly and efficiently, a hand tucked under his chin. Again the noise came to her through the hush. Now it sounded like 'Help'. Annie wasted no more time and shot across the landing to Hermione's room.

Hermione lay on the floor with Rollo beside her. One arm was crumpled under her body, her left ankle was heavily bruised and swelling and she was groaning with pain.

'I'm here, Hermione. Tell me where it hurts.'

Hermione's face was white. She opened her eyes with difficulty. 'Hurts,' she whispered. 'It hurts.' Then she said, 'Max?'

'Hermione, it's Annie. Can you move at all?'

Hermione didn't respond.

Annie bent over and said very clearly, 'I'm going to get help.'

In a trice, she was on her feet, in her room and shaking Tom awake. 'Your mother has had an accident. Ring for the ambulance.'

Returning to Hermione, she snatched up a rug and tucked it round her. 'What happened? Can you tell me?'

Hermione replied, with difficulty, 'I tripped over Rollo. Leg. Arm. Hurt.'

'You tripped over the dog?'

Hermione's colour was now alarming. 'Not Rollo's fault.'

'I know. Tom's getting help. We'll just wait quietly here.'

A fully dressed Tom stuck his head through the door but he didn't come in, which didn't surprise Annie. Tom was squeamish.

'Ambulance on way,' he said. 'I'll go and let them in.'

The commotion had woken Jake, who ran down from

his bedroom. 'Oh, Lord,' he said, sizing up the situation. 'Poor Gran.' He knelt beside her. 'It's all right, Gran. We'll sort you out.'

Annie smiled at Jake gratefully. 'You'd better alert Emily.'

Jake ducked his head. 'Not sure she's here, Mum.' He shifted upright. 'Why don't I pack up some water and stuff? You'll need it. You might be in for a long wait.'

He smiled reassuringly, and Annie felt a surge of love for her son. 'Thanks, Jake,' she called after him.

Hermione's teeth had begun to chatter. She looked up into Annie's face and Annie thought she knew what she was thinking. Was this only a small accident? Or was this a big moment of death? 'You'll be more comfortable very soon.'

'Photo,' Hermione managed. 'Drawer.'

Which drawer? Annie finally lighted on the bedside table. On opening, it contained a prayer book, a Glacier mint, a pair of gloves and an envelope containing the photograph that Annie now knew was of the mysterious Max. 'Do you want me to bring this with me?'

Hermione did not answer. She had shut her eyes and retreated into pain and shock.

Annie replaced the photo in the bedside drawer. She would deal with it another time.

The ambulance men arrived. Very soon, as Annie had promised, Hermione was lifted on to a stretcher and taken away.

At five past six in the morning, Annie let herself back into the house. She placed her keys in the bowl on the hall table and went into the kitchen. Sinking down on to a chair, she closed her eyes. Hermione's left arm was broken and required pinning and her ankle was also horribly wrenched. They were keeping her in hospital. 'But there's a hitch . . .' The staff nurse in charge, who had recognized Annie, was a little embarrassed. 'The orthopaedic wards are full and there won't be a bed until morning.'

Tom elected to stay with Hermione in A and E. He pushed Annie gently towards the exit. 'Go. You need some rest before work.'

How strange Annie felt. As if her heart was growing extra space. Various sensations – agreeable and disagreeable, admissible and inadmissible – were making themselves at home in it. Again, she heard Tom say, 'Go home, Annie,' and, then, she understood that, far from being static, her inner world was changing.

Bath, breakfast, change of clothes. Work.

There was a clatter of claws on the kitchen floor. Rollo. *Rollo?* Annie opened her eyes wearily. 'I knew there was something I was forgetting,' she said to the anxious dog. 'I'll have to take you out.'

In the park, summer had dried up swathes of the grass and cracked the soil under the shrubs. Annie wandered here and there while Rollo, who had no apparent wish to be independent, pottered ahead for five yards or so before halting and waiting for her to catch up.

It was so long since she had been out early. Remember coming home with Tom – before the children arrived – in hot summer dawns? Footsore from dancing. A little drunk, perhaps. So played out they couldn't speak.

Despite her fatigue, Annie knew she would cope. She would have to cope with whatever was thrown at Tom and her. *We* will have to cope. Meanwhile the sun warmed her, the comparative peace of the park had a beneficent effect and, unless she was dreaming, it looked very much as though Emily was heading along the path towards her.

As she might have predicted, her mother looked mighty disapproving. As if Annie wouldn't have tales of her own. From time to time, Emily speculated about her parents before they had become parents and were still individuals. But not that often any more. It wasn't that she was uninterested or unconcerned, but events in her own life were happening too fast and taking up too much time and energy.

A pigeon cooed in the tree, and was answered. It was a nice sound. Emily paused to observe a middle-aged woman on a bench, hands clutching a paperback, apparently, transfixed by its contents.

She hadn't thought about her writing for weeks now, an omission that troubled her. There were shelves of novels about painfully thin clerks or teachers who had sacrificed their health and, sometimes, their lives to write. That was the point about writing. Like the Minotaur in his cave, hungry for the bull dancers, writing demanded sacrifice, the bloodier the better. Not so long ago, Emily would have willingly knelt down and bowed her head.

What the novels on the shelves failed to portray was the awkward (and complicated) position of the would-be writer who had been seduced . . . not exactly by prosperity but at least the prospect of earning a good living. And, if Emily was to be more precise, it wasn't so much the *good* living but the *predictable* living. She was deeply mindful that she had a job and many others did not, and the solid clink of wages dropping into the bank account each month possessed an

317

affirmation she would not have believed possible. She had only to consider the lure of the black taffeta skirt with the bow on one hip (located on a Topshop pedi-conference with Katya), the blinis and sour cream lunch at Finzi's, the weekend trip to Paris mooted by Dido and Carole at work – in fact, quite a few of life's baubles (which had turned out to be doable on her wages) – to realize that the alternative had lost its allure.

In the distance, Rollo skirled around her mother. He was uttering half-baked barks designed to draw attention, to which Annie was not responding. She watched him dance around Annie's legs, and her mother's clumsy efforts to get out of his way.

All of a sudden, Emily felt very tired. She had been counting on sneaking back home unobserved, and she had also been counting on a little space to reflect, which was why she was walking across the park instead of taking the direct route from the bus stop.

She thought back.

'You're doing fine.' Mike's late-afternoon email pinged into Emily's in-box. 'See me before leaving.'

He was – she trusted – referring to the press release she had sent him in which, as instructed, she had striven to suggest the company's overriding concern with climate issues without committing it to doing anything about them.

Anything in particular? She hoped that the winged-back reply did not betray nervousness.

Who was it who got their fingers burned for being nosy?

No idea.

Ping.

Thought you were the literary one. Tell me something I should know.

Her cheeks burned and recklessness gripped her.

Poets are put on this earth to startle us out of our trance into an awareness of life . . . I can't remember which poet said it or the exact words but I love the idea of the poet as Prince Charming, kissing us awake.

Oh, God, oh, God, she thought, after she had pressed the 'send' button. That was idiotic. And pretentious. *Cubed*.

There was an appreciable interval before the in-box pinged back.

Eh?

'See me before leaving' turned into a bottle of Pinot Grigio at the Rat and Fiddle where Mike praised her grasp on literature, which made Emily feel he viewed her as a creature from another element – a fish in an aquarium, say. It was a curious feeling. Over a second bottle, the seared salmon and sugar snaps, they discussed the firm, the office and their work. He was very much at ease and, in contrast to Tod's comfortable shabbiness, immaculately clean and shiny.

Naturally, they talked about themselves a little.

'Is there anyone special at the moment?' Mike divided the remaining wine between their two glasses, apparently fascinated by the lace edging of her powder-blue camisole.

'Yes and no.'

'More yes than no? Or more no than yes?'

'Does it matter?'

His shrewd, slightly hard gaze measured her. 'Only you can decide.'

She dismissed any residual loyalty to Tod. Mike's indifference to the latter's existence suggested a thrilling liberty to which she could help herself.

And she did.

The episode had been thoroughly satisfactory . . . almost dusted with magic, and funny too. She thought how sweet it was that Mike's bed was a single and they had been crammed together for the remainder of the night. 'It does its job,' he said, when she mentioned it.

Then she had spotted her mother in the park and a cloud whisked across her sunny recollections.

They met at the intersection of two paths where a big and ugly laurel partially obscured the path. She decided to be perfectly matter-of-fact. 'Hi, Mum,' she said. 'You look exhausted. Why so early?'

Annie explained about the night's events and that Hermione would be having an operation to pin her arm that morning. 'It was small mayhem.' She paused. 'You were missed.'

Never apologize, never explain. 'Oh, how awful. But she'll be OK?'

'Hopefully.' Annie allowed a small sigh to escape. 'She'll need to be looked after when she gets home.' She pointed at Rollo. 'Wretched, wretched dog.'

Emily leaped to the defence. 'You mustn't blame him.'

A preoccupied Annie pulled back a lock of wavy hair. 'No, of course not. But it's going to be a bit of problem when your grandmother comes home.'

Entertaining a vague idea of ferrying meals upstairs on a tray and running an errand or two, Emily was taken aback when her mother continued, 'Depending on the situation, I'll look into nursing care, which will be expensive.'

'Mum, you make it sound serious.'

Annie regarded her daughter thoughtfully. 'It probably is.'

They fell into step, with Rollo busy sniffing about at their heels, and skirted the pond, which was of the London variety – greenish, dingy and scummy with additional detritus thrown into it. The water undulated with light and the day appeared to be a nice one.

'Emily . . .' her mother was looking the other way '. . . you are careful, aren't you?'

The question was so loaded that it almost tipped over. The sun nipped behind a cloud and Emily lost some of her sang-froid, a blush creeping over her face. 'Mum, none of your business.' She lost the advantage by adding, 'How do you know I wasn't staying with a girlfriend?'

'You could have been,' said Annie, lightly, 'but I'm guessing not.'

Emily neither confirmed nor denied.

Her mother went on, in a bright tone that set Emily's teeth on edge, 'It seems to me that we've been persuaded to spend more time choosing a pair of shoes than who we sleep with.'

'Mum, you should listen to yourself.'

' Don't you – I mean, doesn't anyone wish to give themselves the chance to . . . get to know someone first?'

'How do you know I don't know him?'

Annie's lips twitched. 'Well, do you?'

Before Emily could answer, Annie's mobile shrilled and her hand dived into her pocket. 'Tom . . . OK . . . She's sleeping . . . G3 ward? Yes, I know it. Fine . . . 'Bye.' She dropped the phone back into her pocket.

Emily felt the first faint throb of a headache. She was trying to remember if Mike had actually said they should meet again out of the office. And what would happen in the office if it all went wrong?

Her mother smiled. 'I'm not trying to interfere.'

Again the mobile interrupted them. This time it was Jake. 'Thank you, Jake . . . No, Gran will not be coming home today so no need to get anything. Sweet of you to think about it. Thank you, Jake . . . Big kiss.'

Annie signed off tenderly and, because she was battling a combination of fatigue and headache, jealousy wrapped its knotty fingers around Emily. *Aha. Got you*, it hissed into her ear. Always, always, the twins were ahead of her, whatever she did, however tough she was on herself and however much she told herself that she didn't mind. In fact, when she compared herself with the golden, gifted Jake and Mia, it was logical that her mother preferred them.

'I only sail a wilder sea/A darker wave . . .' but, as was increasingly the case, Emily B was no help at all. She had spent most of her life ignoring her body and its surroundings and turning inward. How else could she have written *Wuthering Heights*? Smarting, jealous, ashamed and, at the same time, stirred by her stolen night, this Emily knew she was unlikely to produce a *Wuthering Heights*. Or, for that matter, to reject the body as comprehensively as her namesake had done.

'Jake rang up to see if he could do anything. So thoughtful of him.' Annie swapped Rollo's lead from one hand to the other and they continued walking in a silence that had turned slightly ominous.

Emily returned to the original topic of conversation. 'Sex is different, these days. It's not so revered. It's lost the moral element. Your generation started it.'

'I'm just concerned you don't run into trouble, Em. Or spoil your chances of developing a relationship. That's all.'

Definitely quaint, thought Emily, and shrugged off the faint question mark as to why Mike hadn't rung to check she had got home safely. (She had planned to describe the tantalizing early light thrown over the park et cetera, et cetera, designed to convey her empathy with the natural world.)

Her mother rubbed at her empty finger in the absent-minded way she had developed and, recollecting with some pain the ring and its five-stone sparkle, Emily said, 'I'm sorry about your ring, Mum. At least you won't have to choose which daughter to leave it to.'

They had moved into a patch of sunlight in which the distress on her mother's tired features was all too evident. 'Oh, Emily . . .' She turned away, bent down and clipped on Rollo's lead. 'I wish you hadn't said that.'

Emily backtracked. 'Sorry, Mum, it was tactless.'

To her horror, Annie grabbed her by the shoulders. A vein beat at her temple and her eyes were dark with fatigue. 'Don't you understand that if you lose a child, they haunt you? Pray that you will never know. They are far more with you, more present, I mean, than if they were there. They're stamped on your consciousness and there's nothing you can do about it.'

'It was a joke, Mum.'

'Bad one.'

Partly because she was feeling sensitive over the non-call from Mike, partly because the jealousy fingers had not done squeezing, Emily lost it. 'Don't *you* understand?' she blazed at her mother. 'You have another daughter. Isn't she good enough for you?'

Chapter Twenty-one

Tom was at the computer. The front door slammed. Moments later, it slammed a second time. The noise oscillated through the house. No doubt someone was angry but Tom paid no attention. Even the most basic acquaintance with the law of averages would suggest that, in a full house, someone in it was bound to be indignant, irritated or fed-up. 'Sometimes I think we'll suffer colony collapse, like bees,' Annie had remarked.

'Sometimes I think I'll kill everyone,' Tom bit back. 'We're like rats in a sack.'

Formerly so contained, well-mannered and often silent, the house had metamorphosed into the crammed old woman's shoe of the nursery rhyme. Or, alternatively, the witch's gingerbread house with bulging walls and sugar partitions. It featured in his dreams, with lights flickering in the windows, surrounded by darkness where the wild animals roamed.

He reapplied himself to the screen and scrutinized it with mounting anxiety. It definitely looked choppy and the City was awash with rumours. Curious how one's attitudes could change. In common with many of his former colleagues, Tom was sceptical of the money men. He had always regarded bankers like laxatives, unpleasant but necessary. But now? As Tom fought to make the kind of smart, rapid decisions that they made all day and every day (even with the small amounts he was using) he was, to his astonishment, developing a grudging respect.

Some people could not pay their gas and water bills. (At least, he and Annie could still do that.) Some went down and lived half-lives on the pond bottom. Some threw themselves off bridges. He wasn't at that stage.

But he was running with risk. He knew that and wrestled with it – but it was difficult to shuck it off. The queasiness of the market sucked him in. Its promise and lure of rewards were one thing – its dark side almost as addictive. Mixing with it made him feel alive.

Above the computer on the bookshelves, and immediately accessible to anyone entering the room, were ranged the books he had bought in a former life. There were fat volumes of political memoirs ... *Confessions of an Economic Hit-Man* and *The Frock-Coated Communist*, that sort of thing, allied with respectable poetry (invariably edited by an intellectual well known to the BBC), with Richard Dawkins thrown in.

They were perfectly displayed to impress. He pulled out the one closest to him, a biography of Orwell. Its spine creaked in the way those of hardback books often did – and Tom crazily imagined that he had released a sound wave from his past that he almost couldn't recognize. He shoved it back into place. Everyone should read about George Orwell. One day he would too. He really, really would.

The more he thought about the job he used to have, the more Tom was astonished that he had pulled it off for so long. In those days, he had worn competence and confidence like a second skin. These days, he doubted he would ever be competent or confident again.

He reapplied himself to the screen. Share prices were yo-yoing. *Get out*, said a voice in his head.

Get out.

Later on that day he went to visit his mother in St Brigid's.

Hermione's bed was at the end of G3 ward, under a window that looked out over a concrete strip in which dozens of refuse bins were lined up like skittles.

Bearing a bedpan, a nurse drew the curtains around the bed next door. From it issued her cheerful 'How are we today, Mrs Siddons?' and the fretful, murmured reply, 'I was sleeping.' A couple of physios flanked the bed of a bottle blonde in full makeup – seventy-five if she was a day, Tom reckoned – and discussed whether or not the bathroom in her flat had a handrail. All three were thoroughly absorbed in the subject. A staff nurse inspected a couple of clipboards at the ends of bed, moving in a magisterial manner that belied her youth.

Lapped in hospital sheets, Hermione was tucked in tightly and, encased in plaster, her pinned arm resembled a piece of plumbing. A drip fed into her uninjured arm, and a catheter was draped modestly under the blanket. Her eyes were closed and, from time to time, she emitted a shuddering breath.

Tom sat on the plastic chair by the bed and, avoiding the tubes, took possession of her undamaged hand. It was the most affectionate gesture he could ever remember making towards his mother and he felt out of practice.

Bill, his father, had been given to bear hugs and Tom had loved him with all the capacity of his boyish heart. Could he remember being cuddled by Hermione as a child? Not really. There *must* have been times because Tom never doubted that Hermione loved him – even if she hadn't been the easiest of mothers.

Hermione's eyes opened and fixed on Tom. 'What are you doing here?'

'Visiting you.'

She closed them again and appeared to fall asleep. Tom got up and collared the staff nurse tapping a keyboard at the desk. She informed him that Hermione was fine but a little out of it post-op. 'The elderly take a while to settle down after an anaesthetic,' she pointed out. 'It's a big deal for them.' Her fingers never ceased their tarantella. 'Oh, and by the way, Physio will want to talk to you about her return. They need to know if there are safeguards in place.'

Going back to his vigil, Tom almost collided with Annie, who had descended from Admin. 'I've been warned we'll have to put in safeguards when Hermione comes home,' he said. 'Handrails and things, I imagine.'

The news must have been unwelcome but by not so much as a flicker did she reveal it. 'Handrails are only the beginning. She'll need extra care, Tom. We'll have to think about that.'

'Oh, Lord,' said Tom. 'I don't really have the time.'

'Don't say that.'

Old sins.

'What?' He knew perfectly well 'what'.

'You never have time.'

They exchanged a look. Both knew what the other was thinking. Both understood. 'Correction,' he said. 'I'll make time.'

Annie poked his arm in a friendly way. 'The last thing on earth you want to do is to look after an elderly lady, even if she is your mother, but you'll look after a baby.'

Old flesh versus new unblemished flesh. 'Wouldn't you?'

'Oh, my God . . .' Annie was struck by a problem. 'How are we going to bath Hermione? She hates showers.'

They had reached Hermione's bed. 'You mustn't talk about me behind my back.' Hermione had woken up and was observing their approach.

She looked cross and uncomfortable. A tear rolled out of the corner of one eye and Annie dabbed it away with a tissue. 'Of course we're talking about you. What do you expect? Does this eye hurt?'

'A bit.'

'And the arm?'

'It's had a pin put into it,' Hermione explained, to her seven-year-old daughter-in-law. 'It's going to hurt.'

'Hermione!'

She lifted her good hand and beckoned to Annie. 'Have you got it?'

'Got what?' asked Tom.

'Never you mind.' Annie interposed herself between Tom and his mother, bent over and whispered something to Hermione.

'Is there a mystery?' inquired Tom, as they left the ward.

'I'm not sure, to be honest,' said Annie, 'but I can't tell you unless I have her permission.'

That night as he undressed, Tom felt peculiarly conscious of Hermione's absence. He eased off his shirt to reveal a ribcage under which beat a fragile heart. Mortality had pointed half a finger at his mother and, by extension, at himself. Then there were the practical problems to sort out. He stared out of the window.

'Are you all right, Tom?'

Annie had crept up behind him.

'I'm fine.'

She placed a hand on his bare back. 'No, you're not.'

The weight of her hand was comforting. He wanted to turn around and face her – but was nervous that her comfort might prove an illusion.

'Tom,' said Annie. 'Losing your job is a form of bereavement, and it's not surprising you feel so dreadful.'

'Thanks,' he said, after a moment.

'You're trying not to mind that I still have one and you think I don't understand?'

He swallowed. 'Something like that.'

She left her hand where it was, and her fingers splayed around the curve of his ribs. 'You can't make me feel sorry or guilty that I have a job,' she pointed out entirely fairly, 'but I can try to put myself in your place.'

'I know.'

'Once upon a time . . .'

'Once upon a time?'

'We understood what each other was thinking.'

'Did we? Nice to think so.'

She sighed. 'You weren't always so cynical.'

Some of her hair had worked free from the combs she wore to the office, lending her a charming dishevelment. There was a tiny scratch on her chin – a badge donated by Maisie's sharp little nails – and her red lipstick had worn off, leaving a penumbra of colour at the edge of her lips, the kind of effect seen after a long night out. He would not draw attention to these imperfections. Actually, 'imperfections' was the wrong word: they seemed to him to enhance Annie. Even odder, Tom felt the nightclub lipstick and rogue curls *belonged* to him.

'What are you looking at?'

'You.'

She breathed in sharply. 'Any particular reason?'

He shook his head. 'No.'

She observed his slippers on the floor. 'It's late and I have to do some work before going to bed.' But she remained where she was. 'Tom . . .' She lifted her eyes to his. 'I've quarrelled with Emily and I feel dreadful.'

'What about?'

'The usual,' she responded miserably. 'Mia.' She rubbed her finger. 'Something's gone between me and Emily. Perhaps it wasn't ever there, but I've been too busy to notice.' He watched regret . . . disappointment . . . bewilderment . . . cross her features. 'Tom, why have I failed my daughters? Children grow up and you can't speak to them any more. They go away. They don't *want* you.'

Tom moved closer to her. She was warm, and scented with a fragrance he recognized: he had given it to her long ago.

'What are you doing?' she murmured. She turned her head towards him, the movement exposing the long neck, and smiled at him shyly. It struck him as extraordinary that, after all these years, she should be shy with him.

He pulled her to him. 'This.' She was half resisting, half surrendering. She was both familiar and unknown. To his astonishment, he was embarking on a crash course about what the woman he had lived with for so long felt like, moved like, smelt like.

Tom kissed the nape of Annie's neck where he knew it pleased her. She murmured, cupping the back of his head with a hand. He moved his mouth up to her jaw and, then, with increasing intensity, kissed the corner of her mouth.

Her body surrendered in the old way. He tightened his grip and edged them both towards the bed. Annie breathed fast. Anticipation and pleasure swept away other considerations. There was a place behind her ear where he had loved to put his mouth and to breathe in the scent of her skin and hair. It was his private act of possession and no one else owned the right of trespass. 'I'm no beauty,' she had said to him once. But, ignorant of the effect of her creamy skin and fine bones, she was.

Giggling a little, Annie fell backwards on to the bed, and he levered himself on top of her. Raising his head, he gazed into her face. 'I don't believe this.'

She smiled up at him and, for once, there was no hesitation or distrust.

'Annie . . .'

There was a knock on the door. 'Hey, Dad, are you in there? Can I come in?'

Before either of them could answer, Jake thrust his way into the room and came to a dead halt. 'Oh. My. God. *Sorry.*'

'Get out,' said Tom, not unpleasantly.

'I thought Mum was working downstairs . . . otherwise . . .' Jake grinned offensively in a way only children could do. 'Parents snogging, eh? Need any advice?'

Annie rolled over and slid her feet to the floor. 'Spare us, Jake.' She glanced at her watch. 'Oh, Lord, I must go and get a report I *have* to read before I go to bed.'

An unfazed Jake hooked his thumbs into his (Oxfam) waistcoat pockets. Annie reckoned it was a gesture adopted to give himself back some of the swagger Jocasta had stolen from him. 'When you're ready, Dad, could we have a quick word about Maisie?'

Annie was patting her hair back into order in front of the mirror.

'Jake,' Tom shrugged on his dressing-gown, 'does the word "tact" figure at all in your vocabulary?'

'Sorry.' Jake was clearly not sorry and highly amused. 'But I have to book Dad in for babysitting.' His levity died. 'I've been summoned by Jocasta to a meeting and I won't be taking Maisie.'

Annie turned round. 'Jake, Jocasta has a right to see her.'

His shoulders sagged. 'This is with a mediator. To soften me up for the real proceedings. I expect she thinks she can win concessions right from the start.'

'Oh, Jake.' Annie gave him a hug. 'I'm so sorry. Please don't lose your temper or anything.' She cupped his cheeks tenderly in her hands. 'I mean it, darling, it'll matter if you do.'

Jake topped Annie by a head but, to Tom, he appeared very lost and he hastened to say, 'Don't worry – I can look after Maisie, so take your time.'

Jake disappeared. Tom and Annie exchanged glances. All thoughts of sex were replaced by anxiety for their son. All the same, Tom held Annie close and dropped a light kiss on her mouth. 'There.'

She halted in her exit from the room and touched her mouth with a finger. 'That was nice.' Then she hurried away.

In the old days at times of potential disaster, like the one facing him, Mia and he would have holed up somewhere and thrashed out the problem.

What do you think? Tell me what to do. How can I kill Jocasta?

As teenagers, they had formed a solid front against the world. United, they faced teachers, school bullies, rival gangs from the neighbouring school and the tennis club, which they both loathed with a passion. And when Emily was being a pain it had got them through loathing *her*.

Mia's sparkle and lightness had enchanted family and friends. It had also hoodwinked them for there was a blacker, astringent side to her, which only Jake knew because . . . well, simply because they were an extension of each other.

. . . 'It's no one's business what I really feel, or what you feel,' she had confided. They were smoking illicit roll-ups behind a lump of granite where they had taken shelter from the wind. 'It's no one's business except ours, of course.'

Jake had laughed and squeezed her hand.

All around them fields were marked out by dry-stone walls that ran up the fells like fish spines. The wind blew about and over them. Their roll-ups spluttered. Mia shivered. 'How does anyone survive up here?'

'It's Yorkshire, not the Arctic.'

Those were the days of plenty when the family had taken two holidays a year but their father had decreed that the second should be UK-based. It was good for his children to know something about their own country, he argued. 'Purely,' Mia pointed out, 'so he could rabbit on to his work about his green credentials.' This year they were staying near Haworth because Emily (and they were hating her on this holiday) wanted to visit the Brontës' house. But the truth was, they yearned to be at home, or anywhere where they were not being urged into healthy activities by their father, who harried them from one end of the week to the other.

Mia had cast around the big horizon and moorland. In the distance, a kestrel swooped down over heather whose purple shades varied from vivid to pastel. Further in the distance, the blades in a forest of wind turbines ground relentlessly. The contrast between ancient and modern was, to put it mildly, incongruous. 'We're here under false pretences,' she remarked. 'We don't understand about this bit of England, any more than it understands about us.' She had stubbed out the rollie, taking care to extinguish every spark. 'Dad's a pill . . .'

For his sake, the old Mia would have been quick to instigate a hate session for Jocasta. The old Mia would have spluttered with unholy joy at the notion that Jake had walked in on their parents at the wrong moment. How the new Mia would respond, he could not guess.

Instead, seeking solace before he went to bed, he knocked on Emily's bedroom door. She was in her dressing-gown typing into her laptop. As ever her room was neat and smelt delicious.

He asked miserably, 'How am I going to cope with the fight ahead?'

Emily jumped to her feet. 'Jake . . . sit down.'

Keeping half an ear open for Maisie, Jake sat on the extreme edge of the bed. 'I don't know why I'm bothering you,' he said. 'Sorry.'

'I'm here to listen,' offered Emily eagerly. 'And you will cope.'

'I feel terrible,' he heard himself confessing. 'The ground has been cut away from under my feet.'

'It has.'

Her apparent wish to hang on Jake's every word was very soothing. 'I was unprepared, Em. For real life, I suppose. When Mia went it took me a while to learn to cope. Then I met Jocasta and I couldn't believe my luck . . . Mia or no

Mia, she was everything I wanted.' He glanced down at his lap. 'I really loved her. She was the moon and the stars, and that was the trouble. I had my head in the clouds.'

She clicked her tongue sympathetically. 'Falling in love is such a *big* thing and one hopes for so much from it. One longs . . .' she faltered. 'One longs . . .'

'Speaking from experience?'

Emily shook her head. 'Not . . .'

'Right. Remind me to remind you of this conversation.'

She sat down beside him and slid her arm around his shoulders. 'I think we're all unprepared until the bad things happen.' She pulled him over to her and kissed him on the cheek. Rather sweetly and with authority. 'If you keep your nerve, Jake, it will come good.'

He turned his head to look at this rather surprising Emily. 'I hope you're right.'

They talked over what was likely to happen, and how Jake was going to pay for the lawyers, and how Ruth had helped to bring him in quite a bit of work. 'Ruth is lovely, Jake.'

'Yes, she is.' At the thought of Ruth, he felt more hopeful, better braced to face everything.

Emily returned to the subject of Mia. 'Are you quite sure you don't know where she is?'

'No, I don't.'

She looked at him steadily. 'I find that so difficult to believe when you were such . . . *twins*.'

Jake shrugged. 'When someone doesn't *want* to be part of you any longer, it kills all that.' He thought for a second. 'I can't tap into her any more. Nor she into me.' He turned and looked at his other sister. 'That left both of us free to make mistakes.'

Chapter Twenty-two

After she had stormed out of number twenty-two with Pete trailing behind, Mia had written to Jake: 'Dad shocked me, Jake. He has shown how uncompromising he can be . . .' which was precisely as Jake feared Jocasta would be when he faced her in the mediator's office.

Robin Tyler's advice had been: 'Go and negotiate and see what you can get out of it while we work on the case.' Jake had listened and acted on that advice. Not so long afterwards, he found himself sitting side by side with Jocasta in a carefully bland, neutral meeting room.

Jocasta had flown into London the previous evening and Jake marvelled at her composure. She was lithe and buffed, with no trace of jetlag, wearing a composed and, ominously, expectant expression. Jake searched her face for a hint of the past that they shared, some clue that would indicate that, once, they had been together. But there was nothing.

Pat Anderton, the mediator, was a lanky man with thinning brown hair who looked as though he could not tie up his own shoelaces. Careful. Jake issued himself the warning. It would be unwise to assume that this was the case. Jocasta would have made sure she hired the mediator equivalent of the Raptor.

Anderton launched in: 'I am here as a completely neutral and non-directive presence.' He indicated the paper in front of Jake. 'In a while, I'll be asking you to consider what's on the paper but first I wish to discuss the reasons why you are here today. Are you both ready?'

Jake glanced at Jocasta. She was staring with a fixed expression at Anderton. At his question, she nodded and pulled her skirt a little further over her knees.

'First of all, let me establish that you are both anxious to have matters run smoothly.' He looked from one to the other. 'Good. Together you got married. Together you had your daughter. There is no reason why together you cannot manage a divorce amicably and reasonably. That is my first point. The second is that matters will only run smoothly if you consider carefully the areas of contention now and resolve how best to deal with them.'

Jake decided that he disliked Anderton more than anyone he could think of.

'My third point. What most people don't understand is that marriage is a legal process and so, too, is divorce. Divorce always has to go through the courts in one way or another, and there are procedures over which the parties involved have little influence. Once the procedure is under way, you will have limited control. In this case, Jake, your wife, the petitioner, has cited incompatibility and no common interests.'

The new dark Jake said, 'I noticed there was no mention of adultery.'

Jocasta swallowed but her composure remained intact. 'The adultery was irrelevant.'

'My God,' said Jake.

Anderton extracted a pair of glasses from his pocket. 'I reiterate that it is best to try to discover now the areas on which you do agree, which you will then report back to your respective solicitors.'

337

Jocasta shot Jake a look as if to say: See how reasonable I'm being in consulting this man.

'I understand,' said Jake.

Anderton regarded him thoughtfully and Jake suddenly perceived the Raptor strolling into view. 'Your wife, the petitioner, has given me the background, but I would like to hear your version of events as the respondent. When she left, she agreed at first to sign over the house and its contents to you. Since then, the position has changed and the courts will take note of your separate resources. It is noted that you always maintained separate finances and held nothing else in common.'

Jocasta nipped in: 'Correct.'

'The main considerations, however, are your daughter and her maintenance.'

Here Jake interjected: 'My wife left Maisie to my care. She was quite clear that she did not wish to take her. I, on the other hand, want her.'

Anderton observed the notes in front of him. 'I have to ask you both to think carefully. Is it possible that you could reach an agreement over this?'

Jocasta stared at the floor. Then she lifted her eyes to Jake's. They contained an unmistakable light of battle, with no trace of shame or guilt.

'Once you go through the door of a court, you will be at the mercy of what the judge decides.' Anderton paused to allow this to sink in. Was he daunted? Was he haunted? If not he ought to be. What sort of person was it anyway who wished to dig around in other people's marital traumas? Sniffing up the rankness. Measuring the poison. Lapping up the details. *Not adultery. Incompatibility and no common interests*. How inept language was. All the same, Pat Anderton knew what he was talking about. 'You have no idea how devastating this can be for the party who feels they have lost out . . .'

Jake could not bear to look at him. Outside a horn blared and he focused on its discordance, and tried to still the judders of his heart. Even the merest hint of losing Maisie induced agony and almost murderous anger.

'. . . I can't tell you what to do, or advise a particular route. All I can do is encourage you to talk and to guide you gently towards a solution.'

Jocasta got to her feet. 'OK. Back to the beginning. I'll give you the house, Jake, if you let me have Maisie.'

'A house in return for my daughter?'

Anderton's intervention was practised and measured. 'You should be aware that the term "custody" has been abolished in favour of "residence" orders, and emphasis is laid on the idea that each parent is equally responsible whichever the child may be residing with.'

'Could you stop right there?' said Jake.

'I understand you are angry,' said Anderton.

'Shut up,' said Jake.

He knew – he certainly knew now – that he had the fight of his life on his hands. The death of his passionate mistaken love had left him with a vacuum at his centre. Nature being what it was, the vacuum was quickly filled with other feelings, bitterness, hatred, anger being only fractions of the complexity of the emotions currently buffeting him. As much as anything, he would have to come to terms with the recently discovered vengeful aspects of his own nature.

Jocasta said, 'Jake, be reasonable.'

'You *left* her,' he said, with such ferocity that it startled even him.

'Jake.' Jocasta had assumed her business voice. 'You don't have a job and, God knows, you hadn't much of an income when you did. How are you going to look after Maisie?'

'I'll manage as I am managing.'

She looked so glossy, so organized, so – if it was possible – American. In the short time she had been away, Jocasta had sloughed her old identity and slid into a new one.

'Jocasta?'

She flushed and, her composure slipping a trifle, she fiddled with the big bracelet cuff on her right arm.

'It was the deal.' Jake also rose to his feet and faced Jocasta. 'You went and you left Maisie to me. You freed yourself up for what you wanted to be and to go . . . with Noah.'

'I didn't know . . . I hadn't thought . . .' She frowned. 'I was trapped by you, Jake . . . so *needy*.' She averted her face. 'It drove me crazy at times. And I couldn't bear all that sanctimonious stuff about how awful commerce was, and how you hated to conform like everyone else. How else did you think you were going to live?'

'You never said.'

'It should have been obvious.'

'Whenever we talked about my feelings, you seemed happy enough to be in the driving seat. You liked all that. You *wanted* to do it. That's what made us special. We worked things a different way.'

'That's just it,' she said. 'You never grew up. Our life was fantasy.'

'Look at me, Jocasta . . .' It was extraordinary but it

seemed to Jake that this exchange, raw and painful as it was, cut to the heart in a way they should have done months ago.

But she refused to meet his gaze and addressed Anderton: 'My husband's business has more or less collapsed.'

'For the moment. There's a recession on. Things will get better.'

'And he's been forced to move in with his parents.'

Anderton did not miss a beat. 'I'm not here to pass judgement.'

Jocasta readdressed herself to Jake. 'I offer stability.'

Jake said, 'Stability? I don't think so.'

'A good home, plenty of space, an education. Everything that you could wish for your daughter.'

'And a boyfriend who might, or might not, be permanent.'

She shrugged. 'I've said I'll marry Noah if that's what is required.'

'And you reckon you will give Maisie a better home than I will?'

He recollected the times Jocasta arrived home late – 'sorry, sorry, meeting' – which meant she had been networking in a bar. Or, as she had neglected to mention, networking with Noah. He thought of her spiky, restless energy, which infected anyone who came into contact with it – a force field that had drawn him to her – and her impatience with domesticity and carelessness with promises.

'Yes, I do.'

He turned his back on Anderton, and willed Jocasta to remember what had been between them – moments of mental and physical intimacy that she could never deny because they had happened. The memories would shame her and maybe, he thought, in his new murderous guise, hurt her.

It was *High Noon* and they were emerging from cover into cruel, blaring daylight to shoot at one another.

'Here I should reiterate . . .' Anderton reasserted his authority '. . . that a child will benefit ultimately from the knowledge that its parents have decided on its fate together.'

In a gun battle, no doubt, nerves screamed and bodies flooded with adrenalin, which triggered the fight-or-flight reflex. Jake was aware that he should not allow anything so crude or overwhelming to master him. The situation called for cleverness, subtlety and strategy, with a softly twitching long tail, and those he would give it.

He considered what had grown in him since the arrival of Maisie – a heart palpitating with love, the acceptance of a finer, unselfish commitment and the commanding imperative to guard his daughter.

'Come on,' Jocasta said. 'Give in.'

She was taunting him. The blackest feelings swirled in Jake but also the determination to control the situation. He glanced at Jocasta. Lips pressed together, chin tense, her features were as stiff and implacable as those of a marble bust.

He said. 'I won't agree to you taking Maisie out of the country. If you wish for custody, residence or whatever it is called . . .' however hopeless, however pointless, he was going to take the gamble '. . . you'll have to live in the UK.' He gestured at his soon-to-be-ex wife. *Take it or leave it.* 'It's as simple as that.'

Hurrying across the patch of ground edged by flowerbeds (hubristically named the Millennium Square), which served as a short-cut between the Middleton and Chambers wings, Annie stooped to pinch a salvia leaf between her fingers. She couldn't remember the last time she had stopped to relish a flower or plant and, because it was a moment of pleasure, she lingered. Satisfied, she straightened up and the Sea Island cotton T-shirt under her jacket pressed against her skin. Spotted on-line, it was new, expensive and luxurious – and she had ordered five.

Tom had been standing behind her as she did so. 'I can't afford it,' she had said.

He had dropped a hand on to her shoulder and squeezed the muscle that ran from neck to shoulder. 'Go on. To hell with it.' She had dickered further. 'They would be a change from the blouses,' he pointed out, 'your uniform.' That did it. Decades earlier as the new widow, Hermione had picked on the tweed skirt, cashmere sweater and leather lace-up shoes as her uniform and it hadn't changed. Annie wasn't going to do the same.

Hoping to find a trace of the old Buccaneer Tom, she had searched his face and found only a sea-change in the dark eyes. 'Smile, Annie,' he said, as pity, powerful and erotic, surged through her. She had reached up, pulled down his head and kissed his mouth.

The first autumn leaves were falling. A few had drifted into the square and lay, mustardy splodges, on the ground. The spicy salvia aroma clinging to her fingers, she moved on.

Chuck sent her one of his 'now-now' looks as, a trifle late, she let herself into the meeting room. Annie settled herself into her chair and greeted the board members.

Top of the agenda was the Samuel Smith case. 'The board needs to be reassured,' said the chairman, on opening the discussion, 'that this is not a negligence case.' The non-executives nodded vigorously.

Chuck referred them to the report, which broke events down minute by minute. 'All the guidelines were observed,' he pointed out. *And they had been – guidelines drafted to create the best of all possible worlds.*

Annie looked around the table. She was aware that all of them were thinking much the same thing: how could they have gone so wrong?

The non-exec Lady Carter – sharp, successful, power-suited – said, 'I've been through this report very carefully. Of course, I'm not a medic but it seems to me that these systems don't do their job. Tell me,' she addressed Chuck, 'when the guidelines were agreed was everyone consulted?'

'So what are we doing?' Annie asked Chuck, as they walked together back to their offices. 'Did we make the mess?'

He surprised her. 'I don't know.' Normally Chuck didn't tolerate woolliness – he was in too much of a hurry – but, today, he acted chastened. He halted by the castor-oil plant in the trendy glassed-in atrium that the hospital was currently struggling to pay off: 'When rationing comes in this will be the least of our worries.' He was not given to introspection either but, on this occasion, he gave in to it. 'And come it will, Annie. The money will run out. The money *is* running out. Think of the rows as we try and sort out who merits which treatments and who doesn't,' he said darkly.

'But Samuel Smith died on our watch,' she reminded him painfully. 'We should never lose sight of that.'

Before leaving at the end of the day, Annie stopped to check on Hermione.

It was not official visiting time and the ward sister huffed and puffed a little before allowing her in. This was partly to underline that Admin might think it had the upper hand on most things but when it came to *some* things the medical staff were in charge.

Sheathed in sheets and tubes, her pinned arm at an awkward angle, Hermione had her head turned towards the window and was gazing out of it at the vista of dustbins and concrete flanked by overgrown sycamores. At Annie's approach she asked, 'When can I go home?' She looked flushed and seemed uncomfortable.

'Are you feeling worse, Hermione?'

'I want to go home. Take me home.'

Annie wondered which home she meant. 'I promise we'll get you home as soon as you're better.'

Hermione clung to Annie's hand. The white hair was streaked with sweat and straggled over the pillow. 'Please, *home.*'

Annie arranged the black grapes on the plastic plate alongside an apple and an orange. 'As soon as we can.' She poured a little elderflower cordial into a mug. 'I thought you might enjoy this. I got it from the deli near us. The one you said you liked.'

She helped Hermione to drink a couple of mouthfuls and searched in the locker for a flannel with which to bath her face and hands. 'Here, let me do this. You might feel better.'

Hermione's skin felt dry, and burned with fever. Annie settled her back on the pillow and said, 'I just want to have a word with Sister.'

At the nurses' station, she waited for the sister to terminate a long conversation with the discharge sister about an elderly man who required transport. Finally, she turned her attention to Annie and assured her that Hermione was under observation.

Annie abandoned her plans to do an evening shop and returned to Hermione's bedside. She took Hermione's hand and held it in silence. Figures came and went. The girl with the hot drinks trolley stopped to tell Annie that the new equipment had arrived, and a porter bringing in a new patient said, 'Nice to see you, Mrs Nicholson.'

Hermione's over-bright eyes fixed on Annie. 'You're someone here, aren't you?' She only just managed to get out the words.

'Yes,' said Annie. To divert Hermione she asked: 'Do you miss Bill much?'

It was clear that Hermione had to think who Bill was and Annie prompted her. 'Your husband?'

'Bill . . . yes. Of course. But he died.'

Annie asked carefully. 'And Max? Do you miss him?'

'Max . . .' Hermione's good hand crept up to her neck and covered it as if to shield Annie from its reptilian folds. 'What do you know about him?'

'You told me about him one night.'

'Ah.' Blotched with age, Hermione's hand now rested on her chest and her frown imperfectly masked an old longing. 'You shouldn't be asking.'

Annie considered. 'But I am.'

Hermione moved her head restlessly. 'Things were different then. I told myself . . . I told myself that I didn't really want him. Only the idea of him. But it's in the past. It's gone.' Her voice drifted away.

Annie continued to mount vigil beside the bed. Did one

346

manage at the end of life to make sense of it? Or was it as slippery to master as ever? 'Rollo sits in your room, waiting for you,' she said.

Hermione frowned. 'Rollo? Rollo?'

'The dog you found in the park.'

'The dog I found in the park . . .' She repeated the words as if they should be learned by rote. They seemed to exhaust her and that was the end of their conversation.

On arriving home, number twenty-two echoed to the sound of Maisie's evening wails. Annie put her head around the kitchen door. Tom was seated in front of a furious baby, endeavouring to feed her puréed broccoli and cheese. Jake was on his phone, a hand over his free ear, and Emily was consulting Nigella Lawson while an ever-hopeful Rollo paraded up and down under the table.

Go, Team Nicholson, she thought. And then, *Team Nicholson?* Sounded good.

Tom looked up, smiled at her and wiped spatter off his hand.

Emily said, 'Do you think Mirin Salmon would do? I'm cooking at Mike's.' She looked up. 'Oh, hi, Mum.' The greeting wasn't particularly friendly. 'Do we have any mirin? We used to.'

'What do you think? And don't say it.'

Emily mouthed, *False economy.*

Annie put down her briefcase and shook her unruly hair loose. 'We need to have a talk about Hermione.'

Jake snapped his phone off. 'She's OK?'

'I'm not sure. Bit confused, if I'm honest, but that might be the effect of the anaesthetic. But she probably won't be able to cope quite as she has been doing.'

Tom fetched one of the remaining bottles of his good wine, then poured it. Jake sat down first and grabbed gratefully at a glass. 'You look tired.' Annie tipped her glass with his.

Tom and Emily drifted about the kitchen.

'Sit down, please,' said Annie. 'I can't concentrate otherwise.'

Emily perched on a corner of the table and swung a leg.

Tom wheeled a chair round and straddled it. 'Mum can't do it all,' he pointed out to Jake and Emily. 'Her job is getting bigger all the time.'

There was only a tinge of regret in his tone and Annie admired him for it.

He continued: 'I think we were over-optimistic when we offered your grandmother a home. We didn't fully understand what it entailed. We didn't foresee the problems when someone gets older and their health isn't so good. We're going to have to look after her more than we have been. Especially when she gets out of hospital.'

A voice in Annie cried: *There goes my freedom.*

'Bit like looking after a baby?' said Jake, which didn't go down well with any of them and he backed off. 'Only joking. But I do have my hands full.'

'I'll do what I can.' Emily levered herself upright and took a chair in a businesslike way. 'I know I must and I want to. But, cards on table, I'm thinking of moving out. If things continue to go well. I've been meaning to talk to you about it.'

Jake leaned over to his sister. 'You haven't listened to me. Treat 'em mean, keep 'em keen.' He pulled his vicar's face. 'He won't respect you, Em.'

She grinned and swatted him on the arm. 'Not with Mike,' she said. 'Katya.' She added affectionately, 'As if you're the expert.'

'You're really thinking of leaving?' She sounded calm, but Annie's inner voice was at full throat: *Please don't. Not my last daughter.* At least, not with their differences unresolved and their relations still (as the weathermen might say) cool with storms threatening.

'I can't stay here for ever,' said Emily, tactfully.

Annie took refuge in her wine and kept up the normal voice. 'Of course not.' There was no need to take this *personally*, she told herself. Emily's moving out was the logical result of an evolving process throughout human history. *The young left.* It would leave space for her and Tom to mend fences . . . properly. A programme of banging in rickety posts and rehanging the picket gate. Would they? Could they? Was it worth it? Perhaps a better phrase was the one favoured by the self-help guru: with no children around, it would leave time for Annie and Tom to mend their souls.

She cast a look at Tom and thought, *Yes, maybe there is life after children.* 'You'll never guess what,' she said. 'I wanted the builder to come and put in a handrail for Gran. Bear in mind he's six foot two and burly. He's busy until the thirty-first of October but he said he wouldn't come on Hallowe'en because of the churchyard down the road. He's frightened of the spirits.'

'As well to be careful,' said Tom, catching her eye.

They talked over the various options, and routines to be put in place for Hermione's return, but Annie knew, as she suspected Tom knew, their children's hearts were not engaged in the process. Whether they wished it or not, they were being drawn to wider horizons and towards a future that did not contain the needy elderly – and that, concluded Annie, with a wry grimace, would in time include her and Tom.

'I'm sorry.' Emily glanced at her watch. 'I'll do what I can. Of course I will. But, right now, I've got to go.'

'Sorry,' said Jake, indicating his sleepy baby. 'I don't think Maisie can stay awake a moment longer.'

He carried Maisie up to bed and Emily rushed around, gathering up the salmon recipe ingredients. 'Dad, would it be possible for you to give me a lift to the bus stop?'

The phone rang and Annie answered it. It was the hospital. She listened intently and put down the phone. 'Tom,' she said. 'That was the ward sister. They're worried about Hermione. They're doing some tests.'

Chapter Twenty-three

The woman in a shiny PVC mac and matching boots cut in front of Emily at the entrance to St Brigid's and almost tripped her.

It took Emily a good ten seconds to dismiss her annoyance and then to register who it was. She raced after the woman and tapped her on the arm. 'Kate? Kate Sinclair, isn't it?'

'Oh, my God, it's little Emily. How are you?' Kate Sinclair had been a stalwart of the Mia set at school, and something of a bully. The PVC crackled as she dropped a kiss on Emily's cheek. 'Not ill, I hope?'

'My grandmother is. And you?'

A shadow crossed Kate Sinclair's now pleasant, settled expression, which made her look older than Emily knew she was. 'My mother. Chemo.' She glanced at her watch. 'Actually, the train from Northampton was late. Whenever is it not? I don't like to keep her waiting.'

Emily stepped aside for a woman who was pushing, with some difficulty, a trolley stacked with a library books. She heard herself say, 'You haven't heard from Mia at all, have you?'

'Mia! The wonderful Mia. Not for ages.' The penny dropped. 'Of course, you had a family falling out. She told me all about it. Like the rest of the world, I was training at the time to be a counsellor and I think she was desperate for a sympathetic ear . . . How many counsellors must there be in this country?' She laughed. 'That didn't work out. I got married instead. But, no, I haven't heard from her – not since she was teaching at the . . . Oh, where was it? That place near Hammersmith . . . The William Davies. That must have been four or so years ago. We seem to have lost touch. Pity. But what can you do?' Again, she glanced at her watch. 'Must go. But we should catch up. Yes? Facebook me.'

'Sure.'

Serendipity. How extraordinary it could be. The casualness with which a momentous and burning piece of information had been dropped into her lap whistled the breath out of Emily's lungs. She watched Kate Sinclair's shinily clad figure shoot into the lift with all the astonishment that she might have experienced while looking at Niagara Falls or the Grand Canyon. And what would she do with this knowledge?

Her grandmother was not good. Even the medically ignorant, and Emily was profoundly so, could have told that at one glance. Propped up on her pillows, she was shrunken, motionless and, if Emily could describe her this way, removed.

It was a scene that – once – she might have tried to write. The ritual of the handwash at the ward entrance, the reverent procession along the corridor lined with machinery and stretchers, the silence, the urgency and the waiting.

The ward was stuffy and smelt of age and other unmentionable things that they had endeavoured to mask with disinfectant. There was no getting away from it and she tried not to mind. No one else seemed to, which made Emily ashamed of her squeamishness. As surreptitiously as possible, she lifted her wrist to her nose and sniffed the scent she had sprayed over it before leaving the office.

Her parents were already there, talking to the staff, and Emily elected to sit awhile by the bed. A woman shouted from across the corridor. No one paid any attention. Someone else coughed horribly and wetly. A nurse came into sight carrying a covered bedpan.

Sitting by a bed was a tiny thing to do and yet it wasn't. Emily couldn't help feeling that she had been put to a test that it was important to pass. Neither must she flinch. *The writer should be able to stare death and the bedpan in the face.* This was followed by: *So should a sentient human being who cares about others.* A calm, matter-of-fact acceptance would be, she imagined, a state of mind that one grew into. Watching her parents confer with the staff nurse, she hoped that this *was* true. In fact, it was vital that it was. If most people felt as she did, and were overcome with a craven desire to run, then the world would, indeed, be a charnel house.

'Hallo, Gran,' she said.

There was no reply. Her mother had warned her that her grandmother would probably be doped up.

'You could brush her hair,' her mother had suggested. 'It usually helps.' Helps whom? wondered Emily. She opened the locker and extracted Hermione's hairbrush. A few grey hairs and some fluff were trapped in the bristles. She swallowed, her stomach twitched queasily, and she almost shoved it back. She made herself think about the sick and the suffering in Africa. She made herself think of cities in the poorest parts of the world with sewage flowing down their streets. She made herself think of those whose illnesses had condemned them to a living hell or death.

Consider those, she admonished herself. Of course she could bring herself to brush her grandmother's hair.

Gingerly, she made a pass over Hermione's now tangled locks, which needed a wash. Hermione did not move but, as she continued to brush, Emily was sure that she relaxed a little. 'There now, Gran,' she said. 'Hope that feels better.' Hermione sighed and murmured and Emily was sure she'd said, 'Nice.'

That made it more palatable. It really did.

After a while, she replaced the hairbrush in the locker. Hermione lay quiet and motionless so she joined her parents in the corridor.

'It can't be . . .' Annie was clearly distressed. 'We've done everything, *everything* we can . . .'

Emily looked from one parent to the other for elucidation. 'They're doing tests for MRSA,' her father murmured in her ear. 'I'm going to get some coffee.'

The staff nurse did not trouble to hide a suggestion of *Schadenfreude*. So much for Administration's statistics and targets, was the message her body language conveyed. Now you'll understand that it's quite different when it happens to you. 'I'm sure we've all done what we can, Mrs Nicholson, but until there is more space between the beds, and more time is allocated for cleaning . . .'

It was educative to observe her mother in her work capacity. Emily watched as Annie pulled herself together. 'No, of course not. What I mean is that we're all in the fight together.'

The staff nurse softened. 'Let's not jump to conclusions. There are other things. It could be just an infection.'

Annie looked exhausted, and Emily's conscience and pity pricked in equal measure. The grudges she had nurtured against her mother, the so-called lack of mutual comprehension, plus her impatience with Annie's tendency to meddle, did not exactly vanish but were relegated to a minor, insignificant slot. All she could think of was that Annie had suffered, and continued to suffer. She slipped a hand through her mother's elbow. 'Don't worry.'

It was as anodyne a gesture as you get, but the effect was almost miraculous. Annie turned to Emily and said, her voice quivering with gratitude, 'Thanks, Em.'

Such a fervent reaction could not fail to touch the newly activated deeps in Emily. *Oh, Mum*, she thought. Directing a smile at Annie that was far more adult and confident than she felt, she said, '*Don't* worry.'

The test results came. As it turned out, Hermione was not suffering from any of the feared hospital infections. Shock, the anaesthetic and a reaction to her medication had probably triggered the fever and left her very weak. She would be in hospital for at least a fortnight.

Tom visited most afternoons. He took in grapes and soft drinks and fed them to her. In the morning, he searched the paper for articles he thought might amuse her and read them to her. He even took Rollo in the car and held him up among the dustbins so that Hermione could see him out of the window. Once Hermione's memory had been jogged, she begged Tom to bring Rollo in more often. Tom couldn't make up his mind whether Rollo or Hermione was affected more.

Occasionally Annie swept in for a quick visit and they conducted a halting, three-way conversation because Hermione's concentration was not at its peak and the subject had a habit of slipping between the floorboards.

The hospital visit became routine and, however hard Tom tried, other things fell by the wayside. The level of job applications dropped and the vegetable plot never did get under way. Nor was he as free to babysit Maisie as he had expected – which meant Jake did not get as much done at the workshop as he had planned.

Returning home one day in the late afternoon, he discovered Jake and Maisie holed up in the kitchen, with Rollo on ever hopeful patrol under Maisie's chair. When she saw her grandfather, Maisie laughed and held out her hands. Tom swept her up and settled her into his lap, as always poleaxed by feelings of love and protectiveness triggered by a pair of blue eyes and a fairy body.

How could he have permitted himself to miss this with his own children? All those times when he hadn't read a story, played the game, comforted a childish sorrow, or shouted himself hoarse at the finishing tape in the egg-and-spoon race. Had failed to hug Jake. These were memories that weren't there – because they hadn't happened – and he regretted them.

Extremely pleased by her perch on his lap, Maisie tried out one of her new noises on him: 'Ga.'

'Am I Ga?'

'Sounds like it.'

He kissed the top of her head. 'Ga I am, then.'

Jake asked, 'Cup of tea, Dad?'

It was a simple offer, but Tom felt inordinately pleased that Jake was making it. 'Love one,' he said, which was a white lie as he had already drunk two cups of brown liquid at St Brigid's, sufficient to put one off tea for life.

He watched Jake boil the kettle and dunk two teabags

into mugs, and decided closer proximity to him was good. Tom was acquainting himself with the physical reality of his son. How he walked. How he gestured. The sound of his voice. These were all pieces of information to store in the memory bank that Tom would have known when Jake had been the small, trudging twin but had lost sight of in the adult.

But he knew enough now to see that the spring had gone out of Jake's step and, for a young man, he was weary. 'Jake?'

Kettle in hand, he looked around. 'Yes?'

'Do you want to brief me on what's happening about Maisie and Jocasta?'

Jake grabbed the milk bottle. 'I've declared war.' He described what had taken place in Pat Anderton's office. 'And don't think that my decision is just a desire for revenge, because it isn't.'

'Jake, listen. No, really listen to me. This is vitally important. It would be extraordinary if you didn't feel badly towards Jocasta, but you must never let it get the better of you. What you have to do is to prove Maisie will flourish better here.'

Jake stirred his coffee. 'Point taken.'

'Have you got a stack of paperwork from the lawyers?' Jake nodded. 'Can I ask if you've done it?'

Jake screwed up his face. 'Not quite.'

'Would you like me to go through it with you?'

Jake was startled by this unusual offer. 'Do you mean that?'

Tom could have taken umbrage at Jake's scepticism. *The sins of the negligent father.* 'What have I just said?'

Jake fetched the relevant papers and Tom his calculator.

With Maisie relegated to the baby-walker, they sat down and worked their way through the financial calculations.

Jake consulted his order books and totted up his outgoings. 'Forty per cent down on the previous year,' he said, and Tom added the figure to the list.

A little later, Tom asked, 'Our wedding present to you, does that have to be included?' He was referring to the money given to Jocasta and Jake when they married. 'And, Jake, you will have to think seriously about the house.'

Jake gestured at the papers. 'I don't mind what she gets, as long as Maisie stays.'

Tom chose his words carefully. 'You will need every penny to bring up Maisie.'

Jake's eyes narrowed. 'Dad, *nothing* is more important than Maisie. The rest can follow.'

Tom revised tactics. 'OK, Jake, it can be done.' As he spoke, his former resolution sneaked back. 'I'm going to ring up one or two contacts who know about this sort of thing and see what they think.'

Jake dropped his head into his hands and muttered, 'Old-boy network.'

'Yup,' said Tom. 'That.'

Which was the reason he found himself waiting three days later (evening paper turned down at the Cassandra-warning of economic forecasters) for Roger Gard in L'Estimet on the South Bank.

Not having seen Roger since they had sat on a broadcasting committee several years back, he was lucky to have made contact so easily. Such were the riches that Roger had accrued in his successful legal practice that he devoted most of August and September to the historic and beautiful

French *manoir* on which he had lavished them. 'Tom,' he said silkily, down the phone, 'it's good to hear you and I happen to be flying over for a visit.'

Never mind any qualms Tom might have had at exposing himself as the-man-who-had-lost-his-job or appearing the washed-up loser: this had to be endured for Jake, and for Maisie.

Roger swept in: tanned, in control, expensively dressed. *Once upon a time, Tom had been up there with him in the confidence and expense-account stakes.* The two men enacted the hearty greeting rituals, ordered a good bottle of wine – 'On me, Tom, for old times' sake. Really, it's nothing' – and discussed the cricket scores until the bottle was three-quarters empty. This was a familiar game, and Tom fell back into the moves without too much trouble.

Eventually, he opened the batting. 'I need a bit of advice. My son . . . divorce . . . custody.' He explained the position. 'How should one play it?'

Roger tapped his nose with a forefinger. 'We'd better have a second bottle.'

An hour later, Roger got to his feet and shook Tom's hand. 'Did I say I was really sorry about the job? Have you anything else lined up?'

Even a few weeks previously, the question would have caused Tom acute pain. Now, he answered matter-of-factly, 'No.'

'You should have. Man like you.' Roger sent him a shrewd look. 'Got to you, did it?'

'It did,' Tom admitted. 'But that has passed.'

He observed Roger's manicured, emollient figure make its way out of the bar and hail a taxi. If someone admitted to weakness, however transient, then that someone was perceived as weak, ran his old way of thinking. *Never, ever expose the flank.* But that, too, had changed and the lift in his spirits confirmed it. He had been weak. He had been anguished. But he had survived. End of story.

When he got up the next morning, Annie had already left and Tom was surprised to find a text from Roger Gard waiting on his mobile. Ring Ian Watt at Carbon Trust.

Jake pinioned his wriggling daughter on the orange and white flowered mat and changed her nappy. Neither of them was paying much attention to the operation, which resulted in it taking longer than necessary, and, more than once, he checked the time on the Donald Duck clock. Nappy anchored, he aimed a damp flannel at Maisie's face, ran the baby brush over her head, and carried her downstairs.

Tom was waiting to take over in the sitting room where he had rigged up a play area with cushions and toys – thus absolutely guaranteeing that any elegance the room might have clung to was relegated to distant memory. Jake's mother had not been pleased. 'I'm going to go crazy with the mess,' she said.

'All in a good cause, Mum.'

'Do you know what I dream of?' His mother hadn't waited for an answer. 'Uncluttered white rooms.'

'You've been looking at the mags again, Mum. Don't do it. You'll end up incurably anal, like Emily.'

'Do you know how patronizing you are?'

'Never,' he had said, and they had laughed.

Jake wasn't as unsympathetic as he sounded. Everyone should have an aesthetic vision. It was important. Jocasta had agreed with him on that – one of their rare moments of accord.

The sick feeling that always accompanied any thought of Jocasta took its customary bow. They hadn't spoken since the mediation failure but she sent regular emails asking for details of Maisie's size, her food preferences and sleeping habits, which he considered tactless in the extreme. Yet Jake imagined that he detected a touch of desperation behind the requests – a hint that Jocasta's achieving persona was being buffeted by normal emotions of loss, regret and, possibly, guilt.

His father prised Maisie from him, settled her down in the makeshift play area and gave her the tokens to push into the plastic box. 'Ready?'

'As ready as I'll ever be.'

'It's a risk, Jake, taking this route. But it may be a justified one.'

Tom seemed tense and Jake hastened to reassure him. 'I understand, Dad.'

United by their mutual adoration of a small child, father and son watched Maisie who, having discovered the joys of feeding different shapes through their corresponding slots, was noisy with her stupendous achievements.

Jake let himself out of number twenty-two and headed for the first of two buses that would take him to Hampstead. It being no longer rush-hour, the passengers were the normal payload of shoppers, students, mums and babies and unemployed, some of whom were so shabby and depressed-looking he couldn't bear it.

Menton Street was situated in an area of tranquil, well-tended but unflashy affluence. It was a street that acknowledged its exclusivity but didn't make a fuss about it and number five's front door had been recently repainted in the lime-based green much favoured by the heritage organizations.

He knew he had been living in Cloud Cuckoo Land for far too long and was neither confident nor optimistic but black-spirited and heavy with anticipated disaster. This was a last-ditch gamble – and the odds were against him. His being here meant he had surrendered the powers of decision to others and there was a strong probability the ground would be cut from beneath his feet. He assessed the green paint, the garden with its good-taste shrubs and flowers and the expensive curtains in the windows, ratification if he needed it that, even with help from his parents (which he hated accepting), the fees would be hefty.

Recommended by Roger Gard, whose network spanned far and wide, Reginald Brown, FRCPsych, fiftyish and big, with the bulky mien of a regular gym user, was younger than Jake had expected and seemed pleasant enough. Which, to put it more precisely, meant visceral dislike did not smack him in the face as it had with Pat Anderton. Jake was even a little surprised: he had been expecting a more obvious intellectual – a cross between Einstein and Freud.

Reginald Brown wasted no time in preliminaries. 'This is a difficult situation. You are the father of Maisie, and in order to fast-track proceedings you have agreed with your wife not to wait for the Cafcass expert because there is a waiting list of nine months. Instead, you have agreed to hire me in a private capacity because you wish for a quicker hearing. This is something I do frequently. Just to be clear, I will interview you and your wife separately and at length, and I will prepare a report and submit it to the judge. You have also put in an application for an emergency hearing.'

'Very often a psychiatrist doesn't see the child,' Roger Gard had told Tom, who had passed it on to Jake. 'And they see spouses separately. Cafcass insist on home visits where all manner of evils can be winkled out by them. Or they think they see all manner of ills.'

The questions began.

'You and your wife have tried mediation, but agreement was impossible because of the situation with your daughter.'

'Correct.'

'I see.' Reginald Brown smiled neutrally. 'Can you tell me why you want this dealt with so quickly?'

'Anyone would wish it resolved . . . for Maisie's sake.'

'Ah. So we agree the interests of your daughter come first?'

'Yes.'

Reginald Brown made a few notes. 'We have a starting point. The interests of your daughter come first. It's a regrettable situation and you do not wish your wife to have the main custody. Why?'

'Isn't it obvious?'

'Because she isn't a fit parent?'

Jake hesitated for a tiny fraction. 'Because she would be taking Maisie out of the country.'

'I see. And you don't feel your wife has a right to look after Maisie as well?'

If he says 'I see' again, thought Jake, I'm leaving. 'Look,' he said, in a reasonable voice, 'it's hardly likely I'm going to escape from the breakdown of a marriage without negative feelings. But they're totally under control and it doesn't mean I'm not fit to look after my daughter.'

363

'Was I suggesting you weren't? It's natural that you will feel hostile towards your wife.'

The session continued for a couple of hours. There were moments when Jake thought anger would overpower him, others when he felt utterly at bay as they fought each other to establish who and what Jake was. Reginald Brown ferreted and dug and harried – and gave no quarter. Again and again, Jake slammed up against his terror of losing Maisie – and up against the implacable professionalism of his interlocutor.

'Everyone has blotted their copybook, one way or another. You mustn't be afraid of me,' said Brown, at one point.

I'd be a fool not to be, thought Jake.

'How deep do you rate Maisie's attachment to her mother?' Trick question? Jake had a vague recollection of Mia, in the days before she became political, describing a psychoanalytic theory of attachment and loss. But it was no good, he couldn't remember the hypothesis.

Brown observed him calmly and said, 'I'm not trying to catch you out, Jake. I'm trying to sort out the situation.'

'Yes. Maisie *was* attached.'

'If you're awarded custody of Maisie, you'll face upheaval. Have you thought of this?'

'The balance will shift,' replied Jake. 'Sometimes fathers feel part-timers in the business. But that won't be an option any more.'

'Do you think your wife was a good mother?' Jake shrugged. Then he nodded. 'And do you think you can be a mother?'

Jake was ready with the answer to that one. 'What is the

main requirement for my daughter? The answer is absolute unconditional love, consistent attention, and to keep her warm and fed. Those things I can give her.'

Brown was expertly drilling down into the reservoir of bitterness that Jake knew, in order to keep sane, he had ignored. Now the point-counterpoint of speculation and blame gathered like hornets. How long had Jocasta deceived him with Noah? Had she done so right from the beginning? Surely not when she was pregnant? (The idea made him feel nauseous.) How could he possibly not have known? How, in God's name, given all this, had he persuaded Jocasta to marry him in the first place?

'Let me ask you again. How do you feel about your wife?'

'She left Maisie,' he said. 'Doesn't that speak for itself?'

He had been a love-struck fool. Worse, Jocasta had seen him entirely for what he was and, for whatever reason, had ridden on the back of his deepest feelings. He thought of the times in the large soft bed when, curled up with her, he had murmured to her of his love. He thought of the moment when, in the worst part of labour, she had fixed wet eyes on him and implored, 'Help me.' He thought of the trust he had placed in Jocasta.

'Actually . . .' A surge of bitter anger smashed up against him. 'There are times when I hate her.' To his surprise, the relief of voicing it was total. Saying it was like plunging into bright, clear water. 'Yes . . . yes, I hate her.'

'I see,' said Brown.

Limp and wrung out, he left Reginald Brown, took himself off to the main street and into the nearest coffee bar.

There were two messages on his mobile from his mother

and father, each requesting to know how it had gone. He ignored them. The barista rearranged individual panettones on a tray, and ground more coffee. Its unmistakable fragrance drifted across the steamy café.

Jocasta had gone. And he was facing it. 'You were so . . . *needy* . . .' Her words would retain their sting for years . . . decades, even. He would think about them at fifty and seventy, turn them over and see what he had made of them. He had never explained properly to Jocasta that being a twin had its advantages and disadvantages and that, overall, it was inescapable. He might have turned to her and said, 'Sharing the first flutter in the womb, the first spurt of blood through the veins, the first kick of the limbs, was to be roped and bound for life.' But he never did.

He drank a mouthful of the over-sweetened coffee and almost gagged.

Water under the bridge. (His mother would appreciate the cliché.) The plain fact was that even if he longed for Mia like you might long for a phantom limb she wasn't there and she hadn't been *there* for more than five years. Mia had chosen Pete over him . . . and the family.

He twirled his mobile between his fingers. Lying on the corpse-strewn marital battlefield was some useful plunder: never expect happiness and, in the end, everyone was on their own, were the most obvious of conclusions to this affair. Above all: never give up – which was where Maisie came in, of course.

As he drank his coffee and energy crept back, his distress and worry subsided a little. He called Ruth. 'That was gruelling. But I got a few things straight.'

'I'm glad you rang,' she said simply. 'I wanted to put an

idea to you. Are you coming up to the workshop any time soon?'

'Actually, I've got some repairs to do. Could you look after Maisie?'

'I'd like to.'

Something of Ruth's quietness . . . no, it would be more precise to say her centredness . . . flowed down the phone and over Jake. 'Thanks,' he said.

She hesitated. 'Jake, you sound good.'

The previous night he had dreamed of carved devil and witch gargoyles grinning at him from their wooden vantages. Lolling tongues . . . hollow sockets . . . screaming skulls. In this black dream, the witch had had a stake driven through her heart.

He had loved Jocasta. Now she was the enemy.

Chapter Twenty-four

Since the computer was half in sun, the light blotted out the figures and graphs. Tom adjusted the curtain at the window, and settled down to a session. The clock in the upper left-hand corner of the screen read 14:00 and the date 15 September.

Out of habit he switched into the BBC website and watched as the ticker-tape headline dived from left to right: *Lehman Brothers files for bankruptcy.*

Lehman Brothers files for bankruptcy.

Tom's lips were dry, his throat a dustbowl.

Already the stock market was falling off a cliff.

He was going to lose money. He had lost money.

'Annie . . .'

She had come home a little earlier and he had listened to her moving around the kitchen – the rattle of saucepans, the thud of the fridge door, music from the radio. He had remained frozen at his desk. After a while, she let herself out into the garden and he followed her.

'Hey . . .' She was hunkered down over a clump of thyme with a pair of scissors. She looked up at him, smiling, light-hearted. 'Tom, what's wrong? You look as though the weight of the world is on your shoulders.'

The thyme smelt sharp and sweet – just like it had that

time they holidayed in France and they had walked in the *maquis* and she had bought him the cufflinks. Except it wasn't. 'It's not good.' Pause. 'It's difficult . . .'

'How difficult?'

'Excruciatingly difficult . . . Annie . . . I want you to know . . .'

Suddenly serious, she got to her feet. 'What is it? The children? Your mother?'

'Nothing like that. I've come to tell you that I've . . . lost money.'

She said stupidly, 'Do you mean you've lost your wallet? Why didn't you say?'

'No, I've lost money.'

'Don't look like that. I'm sure we'll live. Cashpoint fraud or something.' She took another look at his face. 'How much?'

'At least four thousand. Possibly a bit more.'

She swallowed. 'But how?'

'That's it, Annie. That's the point. On the stock market. I made a wrong decision and now I owe it.'

The bunch of cropped thyme sifted down from her grasp and fell to the ground. 'My God,' she said. He watched her anger mount. 'My God.'

'Sorry,' he said miserably. 'I took matters into my own hands and did a bit of spread-betting on the market. I bet on recovery.'

'You did *what?*' She struggled for mastery. 'When we had been so careful.'

He couldn't tell her the whole truth but his explanation was as frank as he could manage and he finished by adding: 'I wanted to make some money. Not much but enough to

369

pay some of our bills.' He scuffed at the stones on the path. 'That was important to me.'

Annie groped her way towards the garden bench and sank down. 'So you risked our money? But I don't understand why you'd do so when we were coping.'

'Actually, Annie, I wanted to make enough to buy you a ring.'

'A ring!'

'I wanted to make up for your mother's. I thought it would please you.'

'A *ring* would please me?'

'You always said how much it meant to you.'

'Yes,' she admitted. 'It would have done once upon a time. But it isn't once upon a time. If you wanted to *please* me you could have taken me out to lunch, taken me walking, anything . . . like we used to . . . and that would have done, Tom. Perfectly.'

To his shame, tears ran down her cheeks and he rammed his hands into his pockets.

'OK . . . OK . . .' Annie scrubbed at them. 'I'm trying to see this your way. You were doing a nice thing but you also knew things were getting difficult in the financial markets. You said so many times. Why didn't you stop?' She grabbed his arm. 'Why?'

'Because . . .' He faced her. 'I'm not sure you'd understand.'

'Try me.'

'All right. It made me feel better. I needed to know I was bringing in some money. I needed to do something.'

'Tom, I was selling my clothes, sacking Zosia, selling . . . whatever I could lay hands on. We were doing our best to economize.'

'I'm sorry.'

'And you didn't think how addictive these things are? How many people lose their shirts?'

'No, of course not.' Inside the pockets, his fingers clenched. 'Yes.'

I am addicted to its unpredictable nature . . . to my desire for mastery.

I was . . .

At that Annie whirled to her feet. Blazingly, spittingly angry, tear-stained and beside herself. 'I never want to set eyes on you again.'

Leaving him on the bench, she disappeared back into the house. He noted the white rose had put forth a second phase of blooms . . . a squirrel chatting in the sycamore . . . the scattering of shredded thyme on the path.

A few minutes later, the front door slammed.

Sadie took one look at the shaking, incandescent Annie and drew her into the flat. 'I guess you need a brandy,' she said.

Very shortly, they were seated on Sadie and Andrew's tiny balcony at their Westminster flat, sipping brandy and eating nuts. The traffic roared, the sirens sounded, and car fumes floated through the air.

'You'll stay here tonight,' Sadie said. 'I'll lend you what you need. Andrew won't be back till late, and we can eat pasta and get pleasantly pie-eyed.'

The brandy made Annie gag. 'I hope Tom looks in on his mother.'

'Not your problem, sweetie. *His*. Now, tell me all about it.'

At one point, Sadie interrupted her. With that little shake

of her blonde head, she said, 'You do have an option, sweetie, and at risk of repeating myself, you *can* dump the guy.'

Late that night, in Sadie's tiny spare bedroom, Annie tossed and turned on the single divan, which was all that could be fitted into the space.

'Four thousand . . .' she said aloud. 'I should have known Tom was up to something.' She dragged the hair back from her face so savagely that it hurt and she stuffed a fist into her mouth.

She thought of all the lists she had made. Lists to manage and contain their life. Stretching back to . . . oh, she wasn't sure when. When first she tumbled to the fact that her job was not going to change the world? When she realized that Tom showed signs of loving his job more than his family? When Mia told her parents she hated them and left. Shopping lists. Lists for the children's uniform. For the perfect Christmas. For a holiday . . . No one else could match Annie for her forward thinking. *Annie the commissariat.* In her kit, every possible medical eventuality was catered for, every instance of sunburn, every sleepless night. There were jelly shoes for stony beaches, tin-openers, spare sunglasses. She thought, too, of her meticulous keeping of the accounts . . . all those occasions she had applied herself to these activities in order – and this was frightening – to make the time pass and not to notice too much what was going on around her.

Those past years felt smothering – a new and peculiar sensation. And, if that wasn't bad enough, Annie knew that she no longer had a 'stop' button to press to bring herself to order.

She had never seen Tom looking quite so at bay as when he had approached her in the garden. She had run through the options: was he ill? Drunk? No, Tom wasn't drunk. *Divorce finally because, despite all the strides they had made, they had not quite made it?* One had to be realistic about human behaviour and about expectation. But why, *why*, now (she had thought), just as things were better and more equable? There was an argument for saying that unhappiness was akin to depression in the way it played with its victims. In its grip it was impossible to do anything. It was only when it backed off a bit that action could be taken. Maybe that was where Tom was at.

In the small, stuffy room, she clutched the sides of the narrow bed and tears rolled down her neck on to the sheets.

The next day Sadie gave her breakfast, kissed her tenderly and ordered her to report back. Annie struggled to work, put in a skimpy day and left early.

To her surprise, Tom was lurking in the kitchen. Even more surprising, he was dressed in his walking shorts and T-shirt. Beside him, on the table, were his rucksack and – unused for longer than Annie could remember – the canvas bag had carried their boots.

'You've come back.'

She didn't want to look at him. 'As you see. Children? Hermione?' She stuck her handbag on the table and ran a glass of water from the tap.

'All sorted. I told them you and Sadie were having one of your evenings.'

'Tom –'

He cut her off. 'Go and get changed, Annie. Walking things. Now.'

She considered saying no. But, to be honest, she was astonished that Tom had taken an initiative. So she didn't.

373

An hour later, Tom drove into a car park on the edge of the North Downs and jerked on the brake.

'Hey,' said Annie, as she emerged into the warm evening. 'Mind the brake.' She spoke mechanically. The journey had been accomplished in silence, and she had concentrated on the early-autumn landscape, which was so much more colourful than those of the previous dismal months. The summer's colours had been so pallid and unsure of themselves – neurasthenic whites, pale, pale yellows, disappointingly cool pinks. Now the riots of ochre, orange and brown, the fat red hips and the untidy, non-conformist sprawl of Old Man's Beard extended a generous invitation to experience the sensations of a season on the turn.

'Sorry.' Tom flung open the boot and pulled out his stuff.

'Did you bring socks?' Annie sat down on the lip of the boot to change her shoes. Tom tossed her a pair. She flexed them and put them on. Bending down to fasten the laces, she felt the now slanting sun target her arms and head. Straightening up, she slotted a bottle of water into the day sack – *old habits* – and handed it to Tom to carry. 'OK.'

Howell Wood nestled at the bottom of the ridge leading up into the downs and Tom headed at a fast lick along its main ride to the centre. Annie knew better than to try to match him at this stage and concentrated on loosening and warming up her muscles. The walk was one they both knew and, once in the swing, she would catch up and probably pass him.

Under the trees, which were mostly deciduous – beech, ash and hornbeam, so much more attractive than depressing, airless pine – the going underfoot was dry and tussocky. Wood pigeons were busy calling and grey squirrels scurried about. Otherwise, whatever other animals there were remained hidden and silent: no doubt, a watchful silence.

Tom slowed and Annie drew abreast. 'Are you ready to talk?' he asked.

She quickened her pace and threw over her shoulder, 'No.'

Tom was forced to pound along beside her and they neared the edge of the wood. Ahead, the path led up the turf escarpment to the ridge.

Tom stopped.

A leaf fluttered above them. Within her boot, Annie's toe cramped and she hopped up and down while it passed.

'Can we talk, Annie?'

'I don't want to talk to you.'

'You must talk to me.'

'There's no must about it.' Abandoning the disconsolate figure of Tom, she whirled around and headed at a lope towards the path up the ridge. Behind her, Tom called out, 'Annie,' and she responded by quickening her pace.

Scrambling and sometimes slipping, she forced herself up the path as fast as she could manage. Cramp threatened in her right calf and her breath came in gasps. Close to the rise, she stumbled over a heap of flints and grabbed the turf, plus a handful of sheep droppings. Dirt lodged under her fingernails. Cursing, she scrubbed at her fingers with a tissue until they reddened. An Adonis Blue butterfly fluttered past, and a second.

Once at the top, she was forced to draw breath. 'Annie . . .' Tom had caught up. He bent over to catch his breath but he managed to grab her by the arm. 'We are going to discuss this. Now.'

'It's not the money,' she said, and bit her lip. 'That's bad enough. It's you keeping it secret. You didn't trust me.'

'I wanted to surprise you with the ring.'

'Don't give me that.' She looked directly into his eyes. 'Please.'

They were high enough for the wind to catch at her hair, which blew back in a wild tangle and he smoothed it behind her ears.

'You never gave me any reason to think you would trust me, Annie.' He placed his hands on either side of her head and anchored her hair. 'It could have gone either way. If I'd closed down my position a couple of weeks ago we would be holding a different conversation. I misjudged.'

'That's what they all say.' She stepped away from him.

'Don't make it worse, Annie.'

'How can it be any worse?'

'Didn't you ever ask yourself why I spent so much time on the computer?'

'Job applications,' she bit out at him. 'Which any normal person would have been doing. I didn't realize it was attention-seeking.'

'I wish you'd asked me what I was doing.' Tom checked himself. 'Not that I blame you.'

Annie began to run.

This time Tom made no move to follow her. Soon she was loping along the ridge, her feet slapping down on the path. A tiny spray of chalk marked her passing, and she wove and dodged around the flints. Up here on the ridge, the wind strengthened, buffeting her face, and any tears of grief were replaced by wind ones. Her lungs threatened to burst but she persisted and, quite quickly, found her level.

An observer, seeing her silhouetted against the big sky, might think her a mad woman. She didn't care. The exhilaration of the run had caught her up. In this semi-wild area she felt free, elementally connected with the air, weightless and stripped back to the essentials. A creature of light and sun.

She continued running until her legs gave out. Dropping down on to the grass, she lay on her back, knees bent, and waited for her breathing to slow to normal. *Patience.* The grass was softish and a convenient indentation cradled her body. High up, a skylark emitted its thin, sweet sound. She needed to wipe her eyes and blow her nose, and scrabbled for a tissue but, remembering the sheep droppings, shoved it back into her pocket. The edge of the T-shirt had to do. The day was ending with a burst of glowing light and she allowed it to stream through her. She thought of how tired she was from everything – but of how, actually, in the long run, it didn't matter. She thought how tiredness could be overcome if you laughed, and that was more important.

She remembered Tom in the garden, his face heavy with despair and sadness – and, in the micro-second before he opened his mouth and confessed, how she had thought, *I don't care what he says, I don't want a divorce.*

It was almost seven o'clock by the time she retraced her steps back down the path to Howell Wood. Leaning against a stack of wood, Tom was waiting. At her approach, he levered himself upright. 'I want you to listen to something.' He handed her the bottle of water, drew her towards the log pile and made her sit down. 'Wait.'

She was too weary to ask what, but sat where Tom indicated. Balancing on the wood, she tucked up her knees and crossed her arms. A minute passed, then several. It was growing cooler, and she shivered. Tom put his arm experimentally around her and left it there when she didn't shake him off.

Then Annie heard it. *Hoo, hoo. Who cooks for you?* The call of the owl. As the bird swooped from one roost to another, it floated under the tree canopy, its sound as ancient as the woods and the land.

Tom extracted a handkerchief from his pocket, leaned over and wiped Annie's face. 'I remembered.' He dabbed at her chin. 'There,' he said, and flicked her jaw with his finger. 'Because you're worth it.'

Annie hoped for a repeat, but the owl had fallen silent. She held out dirty hands to Tom. 'Sheep droppings.'

Tom grasped the water bottle, poured it over her fingers and wiped away the stains. 'I'm happy to say that you're now less disgusting.'

'Thanks,' she said. She lifted her eyes to his. 'Four thousand?'

'At least.' The skin round his eyes puckered with distress.

She stirred, sighed. 'Oh, well, then.'

He placed his hands on her shoulders. 'I'm so very sorry. About so much.'

She touched his hand. 'So am I, Tom.'

They returned to the car, shrugged on jerseys and Tom remembered he had packed granola bars and orange juice. Leaning against the side of the car, they ate and drank and watched the sunset.

They didn't talk much on the return journey, but the silence was different: easier, less charged. Annie concentrated on easing her calf, and her toe, which was, again, threatening cramp, and relished the feel of a body that had taken vigorous exercise.

She flicked on the radio – and they caught mid-way Tom's programme on HIV in India.

He was inordinately pleased. 'It's a repeat.'

As they approached the house, he asked, 'You're not going away tonight, are you?'

'No. I'm at home.' Annie squeezed her eyes shut and summoned up the golden light, the wind in her hair and the *hoo, hoo* in the silent wood. 'Who cooks for you?' she whispered to herself.

Chapter Twenty-five

Fetching Hermione home from hospital occupied an afternoon – an afternoon that Annie could ill spare from work but Tom had announced he wouldn't be around.

'What do you mean you won't be around? Whose mother is she? I'll have to take a half-day holiday.'

'I'm sorry.' He took one of her hands. 'I wouldn't do this to you if it wasn't important.'

'It's like the old days,' she accused him.

'No, no, Annie.' His grip on her hand tightened. 'I promise. It's not.'

'What are you doing?'

'I will tell you, but not now.'

'You mean you won't.'

'Just trust me?'

She searched his face. 'Now, why would I do that?'

Hermione was restless, fretful and weak. The discharge procedure took for ever and they waited even longer for her medication to arrive from the pharmacy. By the time Annie manhandled her up the stairs to her bedroom, which she and Emily had cleaned within an inch of its life, Hermione was white and sweaty.

Settled in bed, she lay back and closed her eyes. Concerned by her apparent weakness and lack of interest in her homecoming, Annie moved around the room unpacking and stowing clothes, magazines and pills. 'You see that Sheila's sent you a get-well plant?' It was a particularly uninspiring pink miniature rose in, of all things, a hat box. But because it was awful and Sheila had tried so hard, Annie felt it deserved special care. She tried again. 'There's someone waiting to see you.'

Hermione murmured from between white lips, 'Not now.'

'I think you'll want to see him.'

Running downstairs, she liberated Rollo from the back room where he had been shut up, carried him into Hermione's room and placed him (breaking your own rules – satisfactory or not?) on the bed.

Contrary to what Annie expected, Rollo did not bark or wag his tail. He was silent and had adopted his most mournful expression. Annie had spent some time grooming him but the mismatch between his shaggy, wiry coat and the small body underneath it seemed particularly marked.

'You know, "Rollo" doesn't really suit him,' she said. 'He needs a smaller name.'

Hermione opened her eyes. Rollo dropped his muzzle and closed his eyes.

'I think he's cross with you for leaving him, Hermione.'

Rollo remained motionless but was now staring at Hermione. She looked down at him. He emitted a noise, half snuffle, half whine, and cocked his ears. A tear slid out the corner of one of Hermione's eyes. 'Rollo?'

He raised his head and Hermione took the full brunt of his tragic, liquid gaze. Very slowly, she raised her hand and touched his paw. Rollo quivered.

'Oh, Rollo,' said Hermione, and her hand shook. 'I've missed you.'

'Here,' said Annie, and wiped Hermione's eyes with a tissue. 'I'll get you some tea.'

When she arrived back upstairs with a tray, it was to find that Rollo had whisked up closer to Hermione and was tucked into the crook of her good arm, his nose on her torso. At Annie's approach, he kept his eyes firmly closed. *You do not exist.*

'You won't take him away?' Hermione held Rollo closer.

Annie surveyed the pair of them. 'No.'

Hermione was a rotten patient. Why would Annie have expected different? Jake did his best to run up and down stairs with her many requests, but he was preoccupied and had his hands full with Maisie. Emily could only help out in the evenings. Tom did a lot but on a couple of occasions he did his mysterious vanishing act. More than once, Annie arrived back in the evenings to the sound of Hermione's bell.

It was at full peal when, at the end of a long week, she let herself in and discovered Jake (ignoring it) at the kitchen table with a glass of wine.

'Something up?' Anxiety struck. 'The report? Is it unfavourable?'

'Don't know. But Jocasta has flown over to be grilled by Reginald Brown. She's asked to see me afterwards and I'm thinking about it.'

'Right,' said Annie. She glanced up at the ceiling. 'I'd better see to your grandmother before we go mad.'

Hermione was angry and restless. She was sitting in her chair by the window and Rollo was in the basket that Annie had triumphantly bid for on eBay. The television was on, but the sound had been turned down. As it was now well into autumn, the sun slanted into the window at a lower angle, revealing that the room, once so fresh and sparkling, had disintegrated into unkemptness. Several weeks on from Hermione's arrival back from hospital, the rose in the hat box looked miserable and was shedding petals like spoor on the savannah.

Hermione announced, 'I haven't seen anyone all day.'

'I'm sorry.' Annie straightened the bedcover and picked up a cushion from the floor. She fetched a dustpan from the cupboard and crouched to sweep up the petals.

'I find it hard not seeing anyone.' Hermione addressed the space over Annie's head.

'Didn't the physio turn up? She should have done.'

'She cancelled.'

Annie grabbed the side of the chair and hauled herself upright. 'You never minded when you were living on your own.'

'Ah.' With her good hand, Hermione bent over to pick up a stray petal. 'Then I was in charge of my life. It makes a difference.'

'I must get Tom to see if there are any spaces in the bridge group in the street,' said Annie. 'I forgot to remind him.' She slotted the brush back into the dustpan. 'There's Mrs Connor in the basement next door. She lives alone and might like to come over for a cup of tea.'

'She wears white shoes,' said Hermione, as if that clinched the matter.

Annie bit her lip.

Hermione read her thoughts. 'You think I'm an old woman and out of touch. You're also thinking that you have enough to do without having to worry about me.'

Oh, God, not now, thought Annie, wearily.

'I wish.' Hermione's eyes misted over. 'I wish . . . oh, I don't know what I wish. Except that I wish it wasn't now.'

Supper. Laundry. Change the sheets. Annie threw away her inner list and sat down in the chair opposite Hermione. She looked across to the portrait of sweet, filmy, supple young Hermione, dreaming in her yellow dress. Wasn't everyone, even the most trying and demanding of us, entitled to the comfort of others? To be soothed by music and food, to have the peace of living among your own people and your own things acquired over a lifetime and to die among them?

She reached over, grabbed the remote and snapped off the television. 'In hospital you were telling me about Max.'

'Do you really want to know?'

'Yes, I do.'

Hermione focused on the portrait of her young self and frowned. 'I'd never seen a man's bare chest before,' she said, as if that explained everything.

But then, Annie reflected, it probably did.

'Max was the gardener's eldest son. The family lived in a cottage not so far from my father's house. In fact, if I craned out of my bedroom window, I could see their front door. I think I must have been about eighteen.' She cradled her bad arm with her good hand. 'I was too happy, and silly with it.' Her voice sank very low. 'We didn't have much time, as it turned out, before he went to Korea and the war there.'

'And?' Annie was very gentle.

'I can only remember bits and pieces. I try to pull them together but they won't do it. I would like to remember *everything* but . . . I sometimes wonder if not remembering everything is my punishment.'

'No, Hermione. It's not.'

'Max was set to clearing the riverbank . . . the river ran through the bottom of the garden. It had rained all winter but the spring was hot. At least, I think it was. I was walking there one day, and there he was. He hadn't seen me, otherwise he wouldn't have taken off his shirt, but he did . . . and that was that.' There was a long pause. She added, 'Bill was very suitable, you know.'

'But what happened to Max?'

'I was very young. Younger than my years – girls tended to be then. And I didn't understand the problems, though he did.'

'What problems?' Annie felt she was watching a performance on a stage so badly lit that the drama was lost.

Hermione frowned. 'As I said, he was the gardener's son. Now do you see?'

'But did he come back from Korea?'

Hermione's eyes were bright with tears – or it might have been a trick of the light. 'No, he didn't.'

'But if he had it might have been different.'

Hermione relapsed into irritation. 'You *don't* understand.'

Annie refused to rise to the bait. The women exchanged glances and Annie could have sworn that Hermione was begging her to look beyond the wrinkled face and crossness to the girl who had yearned and wept and lost.

'I'll get supper,' she said.

She felt sad thinking about it as she got ready for bed. She had seen contemporary photos of the period Hermione had been talking about and the contrast between the well-fed bodies of today and the pitiful, half-starved men of the post-war period would strike anybody with an ounce of sensibility. (What must they have felt, those innocent boys, who, having grown up during the Second World War, and having congratulated themselves at missing the fighting, suddenly found themselves packed off to eastern jungles to die in droves?)

She fought with a tangle in her hair, wielding the brush with such ruthlessness that it made her wince. It was extraordinary the obstacles that men and women put in the way of their happiness. It was almost as if they didn't *wish* to be happy. A gardener's son and the daughter of the big house: it was ridiculous they considered themselves irrevocably divided. But if you did, you did.

The bathroom was now full of Tom's paraphernalia. Extra tins of shaving foam. Plastic razors. A telephone soap-on-a-rope that Maddie had given him on leaving and which he had unearthed a few days ago. In the old days it would have been put into the charity box. No longer. Tom lurched in as Annie was stroking night cream into her neck.

She looked round. 'Do I deduce you finished the bottle? Or is it just high spirits?'

Having returned from his mysterious outing, Tom was in a peculiar mood. He had insisted on opening a bottle of wine to go with the oxtail stew and remained in the kitchen after Annie had gone upstairs to settle Hermione for the night.

'Yes.' Unrepentant. 'Nice.'

She regarded him with some suspicion. 'Tom, what's going on?'

'Wait and see.' He was owlish and, she realized, really quite drunk. He leaned experimentally against the shower. 'How about a holiday, Annie? Like we used to do? Yes?

No? Very cheap. Shanks's pony.' He paused. 'Remember walking in Umbria?'

'Hm,' said Annie. 'That was a *huge* success. You refused to talk to the group during the day. And after a day on my feet I didn't want to talk to anyone in the evening.'

Tom grinned. 'Pointless to chat up people you were never going to see again.'

She retired to the bedroom and, after some crashing and splashing, he reappeared. The soap-on-a-rope dangled from his neck, a detail he had apparently forgotten – he made no move to take it off as he tried to get into bed.

'Tom. Come here.' Annie removed the soap. He looked up at her, rueful and shadowed by the events of the past year. 'Last time you were like this was just before you lost your job.'

He put a hand up to his eyes. 'My job.' And there was a world of grief in the words.

'Here.' Annie pushed him down on the pillows, covered him up and switched off the light. 'Sleep.'

Obediently he closed his eyes. 'World going round.' He smiled schoolboyishly. 'It's been some time.'

She had no idea what he meant. She regarded the prone figure. Why had Tom chosen now to get drunk? Suspicion rose. He couldn't, he *couldn't*, have gone betting on the stock market again? It was financial mayhem out there . . . and now he would almost certainly never get a job. Yet of late he had been more cheerful and the rapprochement between him and Jake almost made her cry. Tom hunched over. A snore escaped. The outline of his body plumped out by the duvet, he was substantial and solid – not like those poor vitamin-deprived boys who had gone to Korea to be picked off in the jungle.

Snaffling the soap, she returned it to the dish in the bathroom – cheap, but still white – that had replaced the one Tom had broken. Catching sight of herself in the mirror, she sat down on the edge of the bath.

Very soon, the year would have gone, slipping away like a ripple in the water – and the jaws of economic uncertainty snapped even harder for everyone. What good would she have done, or achieved? What sense would she have made of events? She and Tom had been lovers once, proper lovers with all the pleasure and sweetness of being so, and she had hoped it would last. But time and wear and tear – terrible wear and tear – had altered that. They had changed, become parents. The people they had once been had disappeared and she had allowed that important strand of her life to be swamped by grief and anger.

There was nothing so sad and wasteful as stupidity, or to be taken prisoner by your own worst side. And there was nothing so noble as to stand up against the menace of passing years and final oblivion when all would be silent and done.

The edge of the bath was uncomfortable to sit on and she got up and turned off the light.

Mike did not like the fact that sometimes she did not ring him back. It was not that she didn't wish to, but there were reasons. Emily found it awkward to marry the Mike who directed operations in the office with the Mike who (very generously) carried her off to dinner and the theatre, made her laugh and took her to bed.

It was complicated and possibly rocky – and this from the girl who yearned for passionate engagement and for the story of her life to begin. 'I'll lead where my own nature might be leading.' The truth was – and Emily submitted her feelings to painful scrutiny – that mixed into her exhilaration were notes of doubt and apprehension. Would she be up to dealing with this? With Mike?

'Are you playing games?' Mike asked, when he finally got through to her.

'No. But I've been sorting some things out.'

'Like what?'

'I'm moving out of my parents' house. I'm going to live in Hoxton with a friend. We've just signed the lease. It's nice. Two bedrooms, tiny kitchen, but reasonable sitting area. Quite near the square. We're lucky to have got it.'

'I'm interested, you know.'

'I wasn't sure.'

Mike was in a taxi on the way back from the airport because he had been away on a conference – Management Strategies for a Green Future. A team had flown to Barcelona and stayed in a very nice hotel, thank you. 'Next time, I'll see that you get on it, too,' he said.

Emily's immediate response was that things were either moving too fast or closing down in a way she had not quite got her head around. She rearranged a couple of biros on her desk and steadied herself. 'I thought the point of green was not to fly. Plus I also thought we now had to tighten our belts.'

'Even Greens have to confer in person. Shall we meet up tonight? I've got you some *turrón*.'

'What's that?'

'Very sweet. Very nutty and punishing on the teeth.'

'Sweet is good. Nutty is excellent, but not tonight. There's something I have to do.'

'What?' He sounded gentle, almost tender, and her stomach performed a somersault.

Emily had not been sure about her plan until the day before. For several weeks now she had lain sleepless and uncertain as to how to handle the knowledge that had tumbled into her lap. This was unexpected. She had imagined that to possess knowledge others did not would be empowering. Instead it was agonizing and erected a barrier between her and the rest of the family. What to do? How to think through its implications and possibilities? When eventually a course of action had presented itself, she had felt shaky. On consideration, her plan cohered, crystal clear and imperative, and she would follow it through. Thus she told Mike, 'I'm going to see my sister.'

'But you could see your sister any time. Can't you postpone?'

Emily reprised the long years during which Annie, and by extension all of them, had suffered from Mia's absence, plus the painful, dislocating alienation and the gnawing sense that the Nicholsons were badly askew.

'I don't *have* to see my sister,' she told Mike, 'but I want to. This is a big thing, and it needs to be done.'

'That important?' He was a little huffy, but also disappointed.

Mike minded. *That was nice.* 'That important.' And she hung up.

Mia lived in Hackney in a street where the housing stock hailed from a century earlier than it did south of river. In general, it was smartly maintained but as Emily had headed further east in her pursuit a contagious decrepitude was evident in damaged sash windows, the peeling paint and stone of the façades.

Overflowing dustbins flanked the house where Mia and Pete lived. Emily skirted them: they smelt bad and she wondered what changes in the fastidious Mia – lack of energy? Uncaring? – had permitted this to happen. Still, the geraniums in a pot by the door were managing a last bloom, which offered some encouragement. Their bright red burned into her vision while she collected her courage before ringing the bell.

Emily's heart thumped. Everyone yearned for happy endings, especially her – it was hard-wired into the soul and fiction was littered with them. Yet in real life, on which she was embarking, no insurer on earth would underwrite one.

The bell had barely fallen silent when the door, swollen from damp, was dragged open and Mia was poised on the step. She gasped and clung to the door handle. 'Emily . . . *Emily* – What are you doing here?'

'I've come to see you. Can I come in?'

Mia looked bewildered, then resigned. 'It had to happen one day . . . How on earth did you find me?'

'I found out from Kate Sinclair where you worked. The school wouldn't give any details so I hung about outside like some grim flasher until you came out and I followed you here. Easy.' Emily grinned. 'Actually, it wasn't that easy. I've lost my childhood tracking skills, plus I thought you'd spotted me on the bus.'

How much less technicolour and less threatening Mia close up appeared than the Mia of her imagination. The ethereal, beautiful girl floating through her dreams and memories turned out to be no bigger, bolder, flashier or prettier than most. Furthermore, this Mia's eyes were sad and haunted where once they had been all sparkle and beauty. Emily swallowed. Despite everything, Mia and she were connected in a profound, indissoluble way and she couldn't bear to see that her sister was unhappy.

Mia said, 'Oh, my God,' stepped forward and kissed Emily on the cheek. She smelt of cheap detergent with a fleeting whiff of turmeric – so alien to what Emily remembered.

'*Can* I come in?'

A hesitation. Then Mia beckoned Emily in with a thin, ringless hand.

The house was divided into two flats and Mia led her up an uncarpeted staircase dotted with piles of old post and flyers. 'Flock wallpaper,' Mia pointed to it. 'Very jolly and hides the sins. I like it.' At the entrance to flat two, she turned to face Emily. 'I can't believe you're here.'

The bones of the flat were good and Emily looked around with interest. Big windows and original wood floors . . . reasonable dimensions . . . but the furnishings were cheap and kept to the absolute minimum – one easy chair, one sofa, which had seen better days, no pictures and, to Emily's surprise, not that many books.

Mia gestured to the sofa. 'I'll get us a drink.' She re-appeared with a tray on which sat a bottle of lime cordial, a jug of water and two cheap glass tumblers.

Emily viewed the lack of alcohol with some dismay. She needed a slug of wine. Then she transferred her scrutiny to her sister, whom she had spent far too much of her life envying and longing to be. Mia was thinner than ever, hair still cropped, and dressed in grunge, which did not suit her.

A glass of lime cordial was pressed into Emily's unwilling hand. Oily textured and acid-sweet, it puckered the lining of her cheeks.

Mia drank hers with relish, hopping from sofa arm to chair. Ultra-restless and on the defensive. 'Needed that. Haven't had time to drink,' she said. 'Too busy. Lessons one after the other.'

'Or to eat, by the look of you,' remarked Emily.

'Tell me how everyone is.'

Emily précised the family news and Mia listened – greedily, Emily thought. 'So, that's it,' she finished. 'All under one roof.'

Mia fiddled with her glass. 'Why are you here?'

Emily did not answer that one immediately. 'Where's Pete?'

'Pete.' Mia's expression was unreadable.

Emily looked round the room for signs of another person and couldn't find any.

'He isn't living here any more.' Mia lifted a hand in warning and her eyes were huge with despair and self-loathing. 'Don't say anything, Em. I forbid it. It's the usual story. He found someone else. I wasn't prepared for him to run two women. He chose. I stayed here. The teaching goes on. I can manage. End of story.'

'I'm sorry.' Emily was. 'But you didn't think to tell us? After everything that happened?'

'You see?' Mia flashed. 'You're still judging me.'

'Sorry,' Emily backpedalled. 'Sorry, sorry. But you should have said. Then it wouldn't have been so long.'

Mia smiled, and something of the old lightness and wickedness flashed over her features. 'To confess Pete's buggered off when I'd invested so much in this relationship being right? Anyway, not having a family becomes a habit. You'll see.' She poured herself another glass of cordial. 'I made such a point of hating them, didn't I? Or, rather, what they *were*.'

'Do you still think they're spawn of the devil?'

Mia was quick to pick up Emily's disapproval. 'Dad so set himself up.' She looked down at her hands. 'He talked and talked about enlightenment but couldn't stand my political beliefs. Mum wasn't that much better.'

'Dad was trying to protect you.'

'Oh, well.' She shrugged. 'Perhaps. You and I never did see other's point of view. I felt I had to make a stand – I felt I had to dig deep into what I had got myself into, but I didn't mean it to be a long-term estrangement. But that's how it turned out. I wish . . . ' The corners of her mouth clamped down but Emily couldn't make out if it was regret or fatalism. 'It doesn't matter what I wish.' She made a visible effort and subjected Emily to the full force of the Mia gaze, which hadn't changed. 'So, what have you come to say?'

'I'm sure you've guessed.'

'Well, it can't be life and death, and I trust the parents aren't secretly ill or anything. I'm sorry about Dad's job, and Gran's illness. I'd been meaning to go and see her at the home. But I didn't.'

The casualness with which this tripped off Mia's tongue took Emily's breath away. Was Mia so airy and careless with people because she relied on the fact that they loved her? 'I've to come to say that it's time we sorted the situation out.' Emily felt angrier than she wanted to be, and checked herself. 'Do we want to continue with this estrangement?' Was this really her talking – so much older-sounding than she felt? She met her sister's headlamp gaze full on. 'Mum suffers – and this might be the moment. Yes?'

Hands clasped in her lap, Mia digested the implications of Emily's olive branch. 'Dad told me to get out. Remember?'

'That's in the past. It's what people say to each other. You lose your temper and what you say is like breathing. You don't think about it until it's done.'

Mia's fingers twisted together. 'But he should have thought about it. That's his job as a parent. He was older and bigger than us. He couldn't accept that I thought differently, had different politics . . .'

Greatly daring, Emily said, 'Or was it just Pete?'

Mia's eyes widened. 'Unkind, Em.' The old childhood nickname slipped out. Mia sighed and Emily knew she had scored a point. 'The world is rotten, corrupt and unfair, and I had to believe in *something* that might make a difference. In some parts of the world if you speak out you end up as prison fodder or pig fodder, depending. I had to hold my own against Dad, and Pete was part of that.'

'And Mum?'

There was a long, painful pause. 'Guilty by association. She never replied to a letter I wrote her. I thought, maybe, she might say or do something . . .'

'The point is, Mia, you don't know if she did or didn't. You didn't stick around to find out. You have no idea what she's been through.' Emily inspected her practically untouched cordial. 'You don't have any wine, do you?'

'God, no. Far too expensive.' Mia jumped to her feet and, paced around the room like a cat, picking up a biro and putting it down, nudging a newspaper towards the waste-paper basket. 'How's the twin?'

'Jake? Struggling with the divorce. Jocasta wants to take the baby to the US and Jake is fighting it. She's over at the moment for the psychiatrist's interview and getting re-acquainted with her daughter. Naturally, while Jocasta is here she wants to see Maisie, and he hates handing her over.'

Mia fiddled and paced. 'What's she like, this Jocasta?'

'Jocasta aims to rule the world. Chillingly efficient. Funny, though, I grew to quite admire her. She abandoned Maisie, which was dreadful, but she's regretting it and fighting like a tiger to get her back. It isn't fair on us but proves she isn't a monster.'

'She's Maisie's mother.' Mia shut the window with a snap and returned to her perch on the arm of the sofa. 'And we know that mothers cherish their daughters.' She twisted her finger. 'Not.'

'Stop it, Mia.' Mia's restlessness felt like the wash from a fast boat.

Mia turned her head away. 'Sorry.'

'Didn't you find it difficult not being in touch with Jake?

'No . . .' The word was pulled from Mia. Aha! Her sister was more torn and equivocal than she was going to let on. 'No. Yes. I was so used to us being bigger together than apart. You know what I mean? The sum of our parts . . . I don't think it was very healthy, actually, because you came to believe that you were extra powerful and invincible. Pete didn't like it much. Jake made him feel sidelined and I understood. When you're in a relationship, you make sacrifices. Jake was one of them.'

Emily said, 'I always thought he fell so heavily for Jocasta because you'd gone. There was a hole in his life.'

'Maybe.'

'Mia, you could put an end to this.'

There was a long silence.

'It's too late,' burst from Mia. 'I can't find my way back. How can I? Oh, what the hell!'

Emily put her arm around Mia. 'Try.'

Mia submitted to the embrace. Her fingers interlaced with Emily's. 'It's too late.'

Emily tightened her grip. 'Mia,' she said, fired up by the spirit of her enterprise. If she could pull this off, she could lay claim to having *done* something, rather than written it. '*Think* about it. Come and see the baby.' She glanced up to see if there was anything, anything, of Pete in the flat. And, as far as she could see, there was nothing. 'Is Pete in contact at all?'

'No, and it's better that way. I don't moon over him. I don't regret him, but I certainly don't want him back,' Her eyes blazed with defiance – and bitterness. 'Life's on hold in that department.'

'So,' Emily concluded, 'you're free to do something.'

For a long time Mia remained silent. Then she stirred and said, in a flat voice, 'What's done is done.'

The last few days had helped to restore Tom's faith – the notion of a new strategic and executive strand in his life had set his blood humming. He could put it this way: finally, he had exhumed the repair kit and was embarking on essential repairs to himself.

Part of it was that he had been dealt a simple act of

kindness by Roger Gard. True, it was an old-boy network and not open to everyone. *That* he would have to think about later but it certainly wasn't going to stop him acting on it. The gesture – a text – had been out of proportion to the extent that it had helped him. Incalculable.

Part of it had been Annie's tears. They had run through him too, cleansing and sweeping away things that were best lost.

Fallen leaves swished about his feet as he made his way along the street to number twenty-two and he kicked up one or two as he went. The old responses were surging back to life. One of the many things that had frightened him in the jobless state was the fear that that side of him had died – which did happen: he had only to think of Richard 'Goldenballs' Gilbert further down the street, one day lording it in the bank, the next a shuffling has-been. Balls cut off.

He was aware that Annie was perpetually worried and overworked – and still hated the mess in the house (mostly Maisie's stuff). 'But it's OK,' she had said to him when he mentioned it. 'I'm training myself not to mind.'

Most especially, he was looking forward to seeing her face and watching her reactions.

He let himself into the house, picked up the post and called up to his mother, 'Hermione – hallo. I'll bring you up some tea.'

The post included two hefty bills for electricity and the phone and a back-dated tax demand.

Hermione rang her bell.

For God's sake, he thought, staring at the figures, and some of his exhilaration drained away. The job at Carbon

Trust was not quite in the bag – he was waiting for the phone call – and the bills were a reminder of his financial mess. *His stupidity.* How long ago and far away the days were when Tom, nourished and plumped on an overblown BBC salary, expenses and staff back-up, had cast his credit card on to a restaurant table and thought nothing of it. *Listen, you fool. Understand this: the Nicholsons are never, ever going to be affluent again.*

But they had a roof over their heads. Good.

Tom laid a tray, made the tea and carried it up the stairs. 'Sorry, Hermione.'

At his entrance, Rollo lifted his head. Tom placed the tray on the table, and rubbed the smeared surface with his handkerchief. 'How are you feeling?' Hermione sighed and murmured that she was fine, considering. He poured a cup and handed it over. 'I'll take Rollo out before Jocasta brings Maisie back.' He glanced at his watch. 'I'll join you in a minute. There's something I've got to do.'

He ran up the stairs to the top storey and clicked the mechanism that released the retractable ladder allowing access from the landing into the attic. It was some time since he had hauled himself up it and he was stiffer than he had imagined. Not so good.

He flicked on the light and, summoned from dark relegation, the silent, dusty objects, some shrouded, some stowed any old how – a chair, a mirror with a broken frame – sprang to view. As he picked his way through myriad boxes, tea chests and superannuated suitcases, taking care his foot should not slip between the laths, he could hear Annie saying, 'Tom, we must clear it out.' And how many times had he replied, 'Don't fuss'? But, she was right. No one should have all this stuff. They should clear it out and start out again, clean and unencumbered.

Aware that Hermione was waiting, he did not linger but made for the corner where the children's discarded toys were stacked and exhumed a shape wrapped in a dirty piece of sheeting. He sneezed twice as he unwrapped it to reveal a half-finished doll's crib, patchily painted in a tooth-wrenching saccharine pink.

He held it up and, ridiculously, felt a lump come into his throat. Incomplete and rather ugly, it represented some-thing beyond taste and aesthetics. Actually, beyond price. 'If you cut that bit there, Jake . . . If you glue the join here . . .' And: 'What do I do next, Dad?' Echoes from the past, the child's treble chiming with his adult tones, stirring up nostalgia and regret. They had been close then, father and son, and he had neglected to see how that closeness could be carried on into Jake's adolescence and beyond.

But not too late? He brushed off the dust and reflected: there was so much one did in life without truly understand-ing – until one looked back.

Once upon a time and long ago. Intended for Mia, the crib had never been finished because . . . well, because Tom had never been there and Mia had grown up.

'Tom, are you coming?' Hermione's querulous demand floated up to the attic.

'Coming.' Clutching the crib, he made his way down the ladder and slotted it back into place.

Five minutes later, he was pouring a second cup of tea for Hermione and one for himself. She accepted it more or less gracefully. 'The phone went several times while you were out. I managed to get to it.'

'You should let it ring,' said Tom. 'They'll leave a message.'

Hermione examined her bad arm and said, in a low voice, 'I need to be of some use, Tom.'

'OK. What was the message?'

'It was Jocasta to say that she planned to keep Maisie overnight. And not to worry.'

'Oh.' Tom drank his tea.

Hermione talked at him. *Jocasta and Jake were never really suited. She's a smart girl. Such a pity they went ahead with a family* . . . The occasional nugget of common sense and insight broke through. *But one can't order one's emotions. Jake does his best* –

He interrupted her. 'What time did Jocasta say she would bring back Maisie tomorrow?'

Hermione wrinkled her brow. 'She said she would let us know, and repeated we were not to worry.'

But, ran the logical part of Tom's brain, Maisie didn't have her clothes or her Blanky and the things she needed. What was Jocasta playing at? With a sickening clunk, Tom realized exactly what Jocasta was doing and leaped to his feet. 'I've got to ring Jake.'

Chapter Twenty-six

Earlier, Jake had picked his way over the cobbles under the arches and made for the workshop. It had rained, but he knew the puddles were shallower than they looked and the water that filled them tended to be oily. The archways were busy this afternoon, and the sound of garage music and power drills echoed through the area. At the door, he searched for the keys in his bomber jacket and was displeased to notice that his hand shook.

Jocasta.

He tried to insert the key and missed. *Shit.* He brushed an arm across his face and steadied himself. Eventually he got the door open. A piece of paper had been shoved under it and he picked it up. 'Phone me. R.' He put it down on the bench and shrugged off his jacket.

A trapped fly buzzed despairingly at the window. Jake raised his hand to deliver the *coup de grâce* but, stayed by the thought of even a tiny murder on his conscience, opened the window and bundled it out. The air streamed in, importing the duller scent of dead, wet leaves.

Last night the dreams had been particularly bad. More malicious grinning gargoyles. He ran a finger along the shelf of reference books, plucked one out and exposed the pictures from those dreams – devils, serpents and all manner of mythical beasts.

'I didn't think you'd ever show up,' said a voice behind him.

Jake swung round to see Ruth in a pair of sailor trousers and a striped jersey, holding a mug of coffee. She was tousled and a little breathless.

'Hey.' He grinned bleakly at her. 'I was going to phone you.'

Her smile was guarded. 'You're not looking so good.'

His anger fired – which, since Jocasta had left him, it often did for no reason, which was worrying. 'Don't you start.'

Ruth's lips twitched. 'Wouldn't waste my breath.'

Jake pulled himself together. 'Sorry. I'm a bit twitchy, these days. But you look OK. Lovely, in fact.' Now that he looked closely, she did too – all fresh and glowing.

'I happened to be passing and saw you were here so I got you some coffee.' She held out the polystyrene mug.

He took it, flipped off the lid and drank a mouthful. 'Brilliant.' He had another. 'I'm really sorry for snapping at you.' He smiled wryly. 'I don't know what's got into me lately.'

After a moment, she asked, 'How's Maisie?'

'With her mother.' He wiped the bench with a cloth and gestured to Ruth to sit down. 'That's it, really. I'm worried sick about what's going to happen.'

She eased herself up and raised her face to his and he caught a suggestion of fresh young scent – wallflower? Rose? 'Tell me again.'

Jake went over the story of Pat Anderton's mediation – 'spectacularly unsuccessful' – and Reginald Brown's analysis – 'like being dunked in paint stripper'.

Ruth swung her feet as she listened. At the end, she said, 'Don't think about losing Maisie. Just think about what you can *do*.' She paused and pointed out delicately, 'I'm sure this will cost money. Would you like me to bring the books up to date?'

'No,' he said. 'No. I can manage.'

She must have sensed his withdrawal. 'Just a thought.'

'It was really nice of you, but I can manage.' Was she encroaching on him? Curiously, Jake was more or less indifferent if she was. There was a lack of urgency about Ruth, a willingness to allow events to run quietly along, which he found soothing.

Then she reached out and took Jake's hand. 'Don't babies sense when their parents are anguished?'

'Probably.'

'Well, then. No anguish.'

The face looking up into his glowed with sympathy and what he could only describe as simplicity and practicality of the best kind, and he asked himself what piece of luck had thrown Ruth across his path.

Without thinking, he bent over, placed a hand on her shoulder and kissed her. Light at first, inconsequential even, then deeper and more serious. Her flower smell enchanted Jake and her freshness acted as a balm. Spring stole across the winter in his heart, bringing relief and succour.

To his dismay, Jocasta came into his head – how different, how very different this experience was, she seemed to be saying. Jake's lips froze.

Ruth murmured, 'Don't,' and he drew back.

'Why not?'

'Because . . .' The lids dropped down over her eyes but not before he had spotted an unexpected wariness and vulnerability. 'It's not the time. You're thinking of your wife.'

'Sorry.'

'Don't be.' She jumped down from the bench and picked up a piece of discarded rosewood. 'Do you want to talk about it?' she said. 'I'm available for listening.'

What was there to say? 'I met Jocasta at a party given by a friend. There was something about her apart from her looks, a certainty that attracted me. I pursued her. We had an affair. We went to Positano for a long weekend, Jocasta got pregnant and I persuaded her to marry me. When Maisie was a year old, Jocasta left me for an American banker.'

'Would you have her back?'

He searched for the truth . . . He hated Jocasta. He loved her. He hated her. He thought of the red mouth and her cruel words. And he admitted that he was glad that Jocasta had gone. Impossible – and unproductive – to dwell on the seismic feelings and . . . the earthquake of falling for someone who didn't reciprocate, and he so frantic to make it work. Or to wish back the sick feelings when Jocasta had made it clear she was bored and indignant at having been made to marry and produce a child.

He looked at Ruth, shining in the autumn light. 'No.'

'Truly?'

'Truly.'

They were interrupted by a thundering at the door and the surprise appearance of Tom.

'Dad?'

Car keys in hand, he swept into the office. 'Jake. Ruth. Sorry about this, but what time was Jocasta's plane back to the US today?'

'Seven-ish, I think.'

'She rang to say that she was keeping Maisie overnight. Hermione took the message so she didn't understand.'

Within a micro-second Jake had mapped out the whole scenario. *Jocasta in a taxi with Maisie. Waiting in the departure lounge. Carrying her on board.* The implications sank in and anger rose in him, so implacable that he could not speak. Lose Maisie? The world did a fading trick – and Tom and Ruth turned into shapes buzzing around him.

'Dad. Give me the car.'

'That's what I'm here for. I'm driving you. It's only four, and it's possible we'll catch her at check-in.'

Snatching up his jacket, Jake turned to Ruth. 'I'll ring you.'

Visibly distressed, she shook her head. 'In good time, Jake.'

On the nightmare drive across London, Jake phoned Jocasta's hotel and confirmed that she had checked out. He phoned her New York flat and was told by the house-keeper she was expected back late that night. Then he phoned Jocasta and, as he had expected, she did not pick up.

He had searched in his and Jocasta's history to find something, besides Maisie, to which to cling – some strand of optimism that would make the sorry episode mean something, some tiny ratification of his love for her. He had recollected the occasional moments – the time she had turned to him in bed and said, 'Thank you, Jake.' The moment when she had first held Maisie and all had seemed so well and happy with the world.

At one point he touched his father's shoulder. 'Thanks, Dad. *Thanks.*'

Tom drove faster. 'We're not letting Maisie go unless the law says we have to.' He paused. 'OK?'

'Need you say it?'

Terminal 4 was knee-deep in passengers and luggage, and the general hum was high. American Airlines check-in was cordoned off and patrolled by employees wielding walkie-talkies. A queue had formed. Jake sprinted down it and returned. 'Not there. I'll check Business.'

She wasn't there either and, on inquiry, the smart-as-paint blonde at the first-class check-in desk refused to confirm or deny if a Mrs Jocasta Nicholson had checked in for the seven-fifteen flight.

'She's taken my daughter,' Jake explained.

The girl's expression registered alarm and a weary acceptance that, yet again, she probably had a difficult scenario on her hands. 'Is she the mother?' And when Jake confirmed this, she said, 'We never interfere between parents and children.'

'This time you can.'

The girl eyed Jake and, as he turned away, she picked up the phone and hissed urgently into it.

His brain was on fire. 'She'll have to be here by five thirty at the latest and, if she has Maisie, she'll leave it to the last minute. But if by six there's no sign, I'll demand to go through to Departures. I'll get the police if I have to.'

His father touched him on the arm. 'Jake, she's here.'

Jake swung around.

Threading expertly through the sea of passengers, Jocasta was talking into her phone. Following closely and wheeling the buggy, in which sat a contented-looking Maisie, was Lin, the former nanny.

Despite everything, Jake's lips twitched. How like Jocasta. How typical of her. If there was any chance of getting other people to do the hands-on work, she would take it.

Occupied with manipulating phone, luggage, laptop and tickets, and with issuing orders to Lin, she failed to notice Jake and Tom until they stepped up to her. *Oh, God*, went across her face.

'Check,' she said.

'Checkmate,' he pointed out.

'And?'

'And you're in trouble.'

'I don't think so,' she said coolly.

Maisie saw Tom and shrieked, and he bent down to kiss her. 'Hallo, Bird.'

'Did you think you'd get away with this?'

'As far as I'm aware, the word "mother" still features in the language.'

'Didn't feature when you left.'

Jocasta stepped aside to allow a flotilla of luggage trolleys to ease past. 'One of us had to go, Jake, so there's no need to stand on your high horse.'

Sweat ran coldly down Jake's back. 'Dad, why don't you take Lin and Maisie and have a coffee over there?' He turned back to Jocasta. 'When the judge hears about this, it won't look good,' he said.

A pretty crude threat, as threats went, but it would have to do.

She fiddled with her phone.

'I loved you.' He didn't bother to lower his voice, and the passengers flowed around the two of them like a river around an island. *'Many people don't get any love . . .* he stared at Jocasta *and they spend their lives aching for just a bit.*

I had enough for us both, he told her silently. If you could have accepted that it was enough then none of this – mess would have happened.'

She took a pace towards him and he had a close-up of the strand of hair behind her ear, the gold stud thrust into the lobe and the smudged lipstick line that haunted him. 'I'm sorry I hurt you. I really am.' She tucked her hair behind her ears. 'Do you believe that?'

Curiously, he knew she meant it. 'Maybe. But you can't take Maisie.'

At that, her eyebrows snapped together. 'Stop me.'

'I'll call the police.'

Her eyes were contemptuous. 'I don't think so.'

The fires roared in Jake, welding his anger from molten to set-in-stone. 'Watch me, Jocasta.'

As he pulled his phone out of his pocket, she put up her hands in surrender. 'Save your histrionics. OK?' Her gaze fixed on the group in the café. 'As a matter of interest, why is it right for you to have her and not me?'

'That's for the courts to decide,' he said. 'That's the point. We have to accept their ruling.'

'Even if it goes against you?'

'Yes.' His voice lashed: 'If you do this, Jocasta, I promise I'll pursue you until you beg for no more.'

Her face drained of colour and she whispered a confession he thought he would never hear. 'In the end, I couldn't give her up, Jake. Do you understand?'

Of course Jake understood. He could not, would not, give up his daughter either.

'There is something else.' She sighed. 'Do I always have to explain everything?'

'Yes, you do.'

'If I lose the legal battle to take Maisie to the US, she needs to know that I did not leave her willingly.'

'But you did.'

'But to know will hurt her, Jake. Even I can see that. Consider. Your daughter, whom you love, knowing that her mother abandoned her.'

The music of the airport – Tannoys, conversations, the whoosh of passenger conveyances, the hiss of coffee machines – swelled and rose.

Jocasta stepped closer and he smelt her perfume – so different from Ruth's. Her eyes had grown large and dark – and were filled with a foreign emotion. 'I won't hesitate to tell her that I tried to take her and was prevented.' She wrapped an arm across her stomach. 'I could even tell her that it was you who prevented me.'

There was no further Jocasta could go. Nothing more she could do to Jake. 'Try it,' he invited, through rigid lips. 'I will tell her the truth.'

Jocasta's eyebrows flew up. 'And you're so sure she'll believe you?'

Jocasta had a point. Children were told one thing and believed another. He glanced to where Lin was moodily contemplating her coffee, and Tom was feeding a giggling Maisie bits of bun. He had a vision of his entire life being directed by his failed marriage and rejected love. He could see it darkening all he said and thought and, worse, darkening his daughter's happiness and equilibrium. He could feel himself being swept up in its grip – until it ground away everything else in him. He could see himself in years to come: hollow and self-centred as only the truly damaged were.

'Listen to me,' he said. 'This is not going to happen.'

'I'm her mother, Jake.' Jocasta's lips trembled and her eyes filled with tears – no doubt ultra-painful because they were so rare.

A man and a woman dragging suitcases the size of fridges peered at them curiously.

Jocasta sobbed audibly.

Once upon a time, Jake would have done anything, gone anywhere, to prevent those tears but this final encounter sealed the change in him. Now he was driven by an emotion far more urgent and imperative than his love for Jocasta. It drove him to strike the bargain: 'Give up your claim to take Maisie permanently to the States and I will agree never, ever to tell to her that you left her. That will be the pact between us.'

'And the divorce and settlement?'

'That's out of our hands. But if you take her now, the judge will almost certainly rule against you.'

'But I'd have her,' she pointed out, scrabbling at her wet cheeks. 'The judge could rule away till kingdom come but he couldn't do anything.'

'Jocasta. Look at me.' Reluctantly, she did as he asked. He turned the full force of a new-minted authority on her. 'Don't.' She shrank back, glanced over to Maisie, and her bottom lip trembled. A tiny seedling of pity lodged itself in Jake and he softened his tone. 'Do we have an agreement? You tell the courts that you will abandon your claim to have main custody, and I will never tell her.'

Again, her mobile trilled and she snapped it off. 'I can't think in this place,' she said, and her voice shook. 'It's like Hell.'

'Jocasta?'

Jocasta searched in her bag and produced a pristine passport and envelope. She thrust them at Jake. 'Here. Maisie's passport and her birth certificate. You win.'

Jake's relief was so profound that his legs threatened to give way.

'Oh, don't look like that,' she said, 'all conciliatory now that you've got your way. I'll be glad not to see you again, Jake.' They walked towards the group at the coffee bar.

'You never loved me, did you?'

She halted so abruptly that he almost knocked into her. Again, there was a suggestion of painful tears. 'I see you in Maisie,' she admitted, after a long, long pause. 'And I love her . . .'

The Tannoy called all passengers for Flight AA 287.

Jocasta shrugged sadly. 'It's all too late.'

Annie was puzzled by the number of text messages Tom had left on her phone. Ring; Ring soonest; and the last, In airport. Will explain.

The day had been one long meeting – with the trustees and senior managers taking soundings from the results of a public consultation before they discussed business and financial models and board-to-board practice. Chuck was snapping the joints of his forefinger, which meant he was pleased with the way things had gone. 'Plenty of opportunities for cock-ups, though,' he had warned before the meeting.

Airport?

Before she could ring Tom back, he rang her.

He sounded odd and as if he was surrounded by fifty

thousand other people. 'I'm at Heathrow,' he said, and explained what had happened.

Annie's heart pounded. 'Poor Jocasta.'

'Poor Jocasta?' Tom growled. 'What do you mean?' Then, he said, 'You're right. It's not an easy situation.'

'But all is well?'

'As well as it can be, I suppose. We'll be bringing Maisie back in a minute.'

'And Jake?' She squeezed her eyes shut at the thought of what he must be feeling.

'He's fine,' he said. 'He's absolutely fine.'

Later, as she was going through a list of hearings for the Samuel Smith case, she shivered suddenly and felt cold.

Jocasta had tried to take Maisie away from them.

'Anything the matter?' Chuck was passing and bent over her desk.

'No. I'm fine.'

'You looked as though a goose had stamped on your grave.'

Maisie could have been in a plane flying away from them, knocking a final nail into Jake's unhappiness. To have a child taken away – to have a child go away and stay away – was almost unendurable. Except that one did endure it. One had to put up with the pain second by second, day by day and year by year. She did, Tom did, and the price it exacted was incalculable.

Again she shivered. Poor Jocasta. Terrible Jocasta.

Chapter Twenty-seven

Mike had been surprisingly sympathetic and shocked when Emily related the story of the kidnap, beefing it up a trifle – just a trifle – for maximum drama.

'My parents were divorced,' he said. 'I hated it. I used to dread the swap-over each week. They did their best but . . .' He shrugged – a little defensively, she decided. 'What's the phrase? "The kindness of strangers." I couldn't help feeling I was a perpetual stranger.'

He had his hand on Emily's cheek. Yet again she was enchanted by the difference between the inscrutable, contained Mike of the office and the man who, in their private meetings, revealed a vulnerable side. The contrast triggered in Emily a deep-rooted excitement and, to be quite frank, desire.

'Poor little Maisie,' he said. 'A football.'

'No.' Emily didn't like that idea. 'Not a football.'

'She is.' He was firm. 'But if she isn't now . . .' his eyebrow did its climbing trick '. . . she will be in the future. I know all about not-being-a-football but actually being one. They're the ones who get kicked around the most.'

Emily took a risk. 'Would you like to come home and have a meal? They'd love to meet you.'

'Is that you offering amends for my upbringing?'

'Not really,' she said, a little offended and also worried that she had gone too far too quickly. 'But sort of.'

'I've a better idea. I'll take you for pasta in Polygon's and we could go back to mine.'

Family could, and would, wait. 'OK,' she said, hotly anticipating squeezing into the single bed and the opportunities it offered to demonstrate her sympathy in other ways.

A couple of days later, Emily was still dreaming over various private recollections of the evening (and the night, during which they hadn't slept that much). Humming under her breath, she ran up the stairs at number twenty-two to her bedroom. Maisie's bath noises filtered from the bathroom, and she put her head around the door. Sponge in hand, Jake was dripping water over his chirruping daughter.

'Come on in, Emily.' He smiled at her.

Like a pair of stone and bronze figures in a church, they knelt up against the bath and diverted Maisie – all pink skin and chubby legs – until she was almost choking with laughter.

'Bad move to excite her,' said Jake. 'But, hey.' He lifted his daughter out of the water.

'Dada . . .'

'Hey,' said a delighted Jake. 'Listen to that.'

Emily gave him the towel and observed Jake deftly controlling Maisie's flailings. 'Jocasta wasn't all bad.'

'No.'

'I don't like to think of her longing for her daughter.'

Jake wrapped the towel around Maisie and looked up at Emily. 'Neither do I,' he said. 'In fact, I can't think about it.' He bent over and kissed one of Maisie's tiny fingers. 'It's muddled, isn't it?'

She nodded. 'What happens next?'

'We have to wait for the court hearing. It's in a couple of weeks.'

'Worried?'

'Yes and no.' He draped Maisie over his shoulder and carried her into the bedroom. Emily followed. 'How's work going?' he asked.

Emily hesitated. 'Don't laugh.'

'Would I?'

'You would.' She paused. 'I enjoy it.'

'That's no laughing matter. That's serious.' Jake inserted Maisie into her nightclothes and, when done, sat her tenderly on his lap for a final bottle.

Emily watched. 'It comes as a bit of a shock. Liking work, I mean.'

'And the writing?'

The writing? Where was the urge to wrestle the passionate, unhappy forces warring in her head on to the page? 'Condor Oil is committed to reducing the level of carbon emissions . . . etc., etc.' did not come under the heading of passionate forces.

'Oil got to you, Em?'

'Tamed me.' She blushed. 'For the time being.'

Jake settled Maisie more comfortably in the crook of his arm. Her eyelids were drooping and the milk intake had slowed. She had the glazed, spaced-out look of a very sleepy child. 'Most of us are tamed in the end.' His smile admitted Emily to his inner, complicit circle.

A little while later, she was following instructions left by Annie to put a chicken casserole into the oven – actually, her mother had written 'Moloch' – when Jake joined her.

'What does Mum mean by "Moloch", do you suppose?'

'God knows.'

Jake said, 'Good Lord, what's that doing here?' He was pointing to the sickly pink doll's crib askew on top of a pile of ironed sheets on the table.

Emily glanced at it. 'No idea.'

'How funny.' Jake ran a hand over it. 'Dad must have found it somewhere. We made this together.' He smiled. 'Never finished it, though.' He removed it to a safer perch. 'Might have another go at it.'

Upstairs, Rollo was barking, which probably meant their grandmother was on the way down, and Emily stuck her head out of the kitchen door. 'Can you manage, Gran?'

'Wish Rollo would shut up – he'll wake Maisie.' Jake dabbed at a sodden patch of milk on his sleeve.

Emily busied herself with plates and cutlery but, actually, she wanted to take a deep breath and confess, *I've seen Mia*, and watch his reaction. In the old days she might have rushed in (and written up the results in her notebook) but now she was cautious. So much still lay in the balance, so much feeling, so much anguish, and the past year had taught her to respect prudence.

'You know, Em, you shouldn't worry if you've given up your ambitions temporarily.'

'No,' she said. 'Nor you.'

Jake dabbed away ineffectually at his sleeve and, regarding him fondly, Emily felt a lump rise into her throat. She decided that she loved him more than she had ever done and Mia's removal from the family had opened up a space into which she could step without any worry at all.

'Here. Let me.' Seizing a clean dishcloth, she set about sponging Maisie's milk out of her brother's sleeve.

Hermione appeared in the doorway, Rollo at her ankles.

'Is it supper yet?' Since she had lost the plaster cast, she had taken to hugging her injured arm close to her chest.

'Hallo, Gran.' Jake ushered Hermione into a chair. 'Do you think you could stop Rollo barking at nights?'

Rollo's claws clicked over the kitchen floor. 'I don't think so, dear, it's his way of talking to me. Is supper on its way?'

Emily and Jake exchanged glances. 'Not so long, Gran,' said Emily.

Much later in bed, her clothes neatly folded away and her bag ready for the next day, Emily reflected on the hungers in life. Hunger for love . . . perhaps for power, certainly power to control your existence as much as possible . . . for fame . . . for fulfilment. And, yes, she wanted her life to be crowded with as much as she could fit into it.

The writing . . . the writing . . . it would wait. It would keep.

Then she thought of Mike . . . a bubble as light and joyous as a dandelion puff shimmered inside her and burst into a luminous shower.

'There's something I want to ask you,' said Ruth.

'Ask away.' Jake was reading a note that had been shoved under the door of the workshop. 'Give us a bell,' it read in an unfamiliar hand, followed by a number. He threw it down on the bench and heaved up a box of the latest objects to arrive for repair. These included an electric lamp in the guise of a globe. If you twirled it, the continents glowed in turn. The non-continents didn't seem to get a look-in.

'You know you're not here so much, these days . . .' Ruth turned in a swirl of red ballerina skirt, which she had teamed with a black satin blouse that had puff sleeves and huge buttons. She looked both striking and soft and, Jake concluded, shone with an inner purpose.

'Aren't I?' Jake was startled and Ruth flushed bright red. 'I certainly intend to be.'

The very idea of not having the workshop engendered powerful feelings of dislocation and was not to be thought of.

'Oh.'

'Well?' He smiled encouragingly. 'Go ahead.'

'My dressmaking business. I told you my flat's too small and I wondered if I could share this with you. I'd pay my way. I can't afford much but I imagine it would help.'

Was he being doled out charity – which would be a new and embarrassing position to be in? 'No need.'

'That's a yes?'

He had been meaning to say that he would like to think about it. 'You're welcome to a bit of space.'

Ruth sent him a straight look – and now there *was* a discernible hint of her charity. 'Mustn't confuse business with other things. So, shall we agree a figure?'

They haggled pleasurably. Stop being gallant, she admonished. You have to live. We're friends, he argued. Friends don't exploit other friends.

At that, she blushed again.

Jake asked her what her turnover was – he had never inquired before – and she named a sum that brought him up short. Ruth was making money. Not much, but more than him.

He made coffee for the two of them and asked her to tell him a bit more about the business. He leaned against the bench and she swung up on to it, and they discussed design, materials and her perpetual hunt for old dress patterns.

'I scale up the old patterns,' she explained, in a business-like manner that Jake found touching. 'Women are bigger, these days, and I make sure I cater for the biggest. You lose half the market otherwise, and why should bigger women be made to feel like pariahs? It's a waste of good curves.'

His gaze lingered on her waist. 'If you say so.'

'You can make fun . . .' but she was smiling.

'No,' he said gently. 'I won't make fun. Although I wouldn't mind a good laugh.'

She turned her face away. 'The other day . . .' she said. 'You don't have to . . .'

Jake moved closer. 'Don't have to what?'

'Think that kissing me is a problem. Or that it meant anything.'

He frowned. 'Didn't it?'

Ruth searched Jake's face. 'Well, it did, actually.'

'Ruth, I was kissing *you*.'

Any memories of Jocasta were knots in a rope belt pulled ever tighter round the waist, each jerk a reminder of failure and humiliation. He had got to know memory's tricks. It lay in wait and sprang on him when he was at his most vulnerable or least wary. But getting wise to the tricks meant he could deal with them and, as he grew stronger and bolder, he planned to bury them as deep as he could dig. With Maisie or – *perish the thought* – without her, he would move on, toting the weight of experience and a new real-ism. That was the way it worked. Meeting Ruth's searching gaze, he had the feeling that, despite her defensiveness, she understood.

He smiled wryly. 'That's it. Jocasta is finished.'

'She didn't have to marry,' Ruth pointed out very gently. 'Or have Maisie. Some of it she agreed to.'

'True.' Jake's eyes narrowed.

'One can brood too much. Nostalgia can fuzz things up.'

Jake's interest sharpened. 'You mean nostalgia is short-sighted? Or even blind?'

'If you like. Something like that.' She jumped down to the floor. 'If we're agreed, I'll go and get some of my stuff and bring it over.'

'I'll help you.'

She considered the offer, then said, 'OK.'

It didn't take very long. While they relayed a sewing-machine, plastic storage boxes filled with thread and sewing accessories, a couple of wheeled racks with made-up stock and her precious pattern archive, Jake was set to wondering how Ruth, despite a certain vulnerability and her own grief, managed to be so grounded.

'I've never asked about you,' he said, guilty that he had been so self-obsessed over the past months. 'You talked about your parents when you came to lunch that day.'

'You know about me.' Ruth smiled. 'Matt's gone. My parents live in Finchley and I hate the place. I set up my business a year ago. It was a struggle, but an optimistic one. The figures haven't been bad either. The website is gathering traffic. If I get any bigger, I really will have to find an assistant.'

'But *you* . . .' Jake kidnapped a box from Ruth and set it down.

She turned on her heel, and the red skirt swirled. 'This is me.'

They stood the machine as close to the window as possible without there being a danger of the sun damaging the materials. Jake liberated a couple of drawers and, while Ruth put her stuff in them, he phoned the number on the note.

'Oh, hi, mate,' said a strange voice. 'I'm Warren. Word is that you're a chippie and looking for work.'

'That's right.'

Warren explained that he had bought a block of flats around the corner that had been due for demolition and redevelopment as luxury apartments. 'Credit crunch done for that, mate. So, all change on tactics. I've downgraded the operation and will do them up for renting. I need someone to supervise the carpentry and all that. It's got to be cheap but look good, if you see what I mean.'

Jake did see what Warren meant. He saw it absolutely – as clear as day – and it was as far removed from his original ambition to create pieces with substance and inner life as it was possible to be.

'Hard times,' said Warren. 'Can't be choosy.'

Jake agreed to turn up for a site meeting the following morning.

'All being well, I'll need you on and off for around a year,' said Warren, before the phone went down.

Can't be choosy. Mustn't be choosy. He had work. Right. *Grateful.* Would be able to pay legal fees, keep Maisie. *Right.*

Ruth moved around her allotted area, shutting and opening drawers, stacking industrial-sized reels of cotton on the shelves, building a mosaic of colour. With a frou-frou of material, she unleashed a waterfall of bright blue cotton, inspected it, folded it away and ticked it off in her notebook. Absorbed in her tasks, she took no notice of Jake.

Reapplying himself to the figures jotted down during his conversation with Warren, Jake began to flesh out rough costings for kitchen units and bathroom fittings.

He peered at Ruth. Settled at her stretch of the bench, she was occupied in threading the machine. He watched as she brushed back a strand of hair and tsked with her tongue as the thread failed to slot through the eyelets. Her movements were purposeful, but curiously peaceful, too, and contented.

He must have moved for Ruth looked up. Their eyes met in an extended question mark but also in the beginning of a conversation that would continue – and she was the first to look away and return to the task in hand.

The peacefulness and contentment had percolated through to Jake, and he went back to the costings.

Tom chucked the evening paper and the biography of Lincoln on to the desk by his computer. Nowadays he could truffle through the contents of the charity shop with the best of them. Even if the stuff smelt of dust and relegation, he was proud of his new-found skills.

The room was a mess that would send Annie up to Planet Despair. He couldn't have that, so he plumped up cushions and whisked away piles of newspapers and several mugs. Then he fetched a duster and shimmied about around the lamps and the few ornaments Annie permitted in the room. She hated clutter – and he now understood why.

Next, he attacked the sofa, which displayed a suspicious-looking set of rough hairs at one end – he'd kill Rollo and stick him in a dog pie if he didn't obey the rules.

It was only by chance that he discovered Annie's account

books half shovelled under one end of the sofa. He picked them up and sat down to take a look.

Shopping and Expenses were all entered up and the numbers spent on them reasonably consistent. Travel varied, depending on what Annie was doing. But it was the 'Me' column that stopped him dead in his tracks. At the beginning of the year, the accounts registered some pretty hefty sums for hair, holidays and makeup. That was Annie. But as his finger moved down the months, it traced a story of abnegation as 'Me' dwindled into practically nothing.

The roll-call of thrift made Tom frown. What did her hair look like when he'd lost the job? If he was honest, he hadn't registered what *she* looked like. After living a long time with someone, the outer appearance became not exactly unimportant but irrelevant. One only took note of it from time to time. Annie's hair now? Tom frowned. It *seemed* longer, even less tamed. More to the point, he didn't like to think of her without her hair appointments as he knew how much they mattered to her.

He rechecked the Input column. Annie had noted her salary to the last pence. The remainder of the column was blank. Output? The sale of her mother's ring was recorded and, more recently, not huge but significant additional sums of money that helped to balance the books for the month. Puzzled, he searched further among the figures and realized that Annie, in the last month, had sold what remained of her jewellery. Items: garnet cross, pearl-drop earrings, a sapphire brooch, which (as if it helped the case) she had never liked.

Tom's cheeks burned. Annie was selling her possessions, not to keep the household but to help him pay his losses.

424

His debt. The poles between her husbandry and his reckless-ness had never appeared greater or more black and shameful.

Dustpan in hand, he got down on his knees and brushed away at more of Rollo's hair. Exuding a faint whiff of dog, they adhered to the carpet nap with the obstinacy of their owner.

His marriage was never meant to be like this – the estrangement of a child, the end of a job, the coldness and misunderstanding. *Debt.* Neither was a self-imposed ban on trips to the hairdresser part of the master plan.

He had started out so convinced that things would fall into place, so sure that, in love and work, it took only good-will, good communication and a strong overview to achieve success. Annie's accounts, their secret revelations, and his joblessness indicated a different pattern.

A little later, he sought out Hermione. *You must talk to your mother more*, Annie had instructed before leaving for work.

'Is there an agenda?' he had asked.

'No. But I think she's struggling a bit. She hasn't really settled since coming back from hospital. Haven't you noticed she's not eating much?'

Hermione's eating habits had always been sparing. 'She's a one-biscuit person, yes.'

Annie grimaced. 'Give me strength.'

Hermione had taken to sitting in the kitchen with whoever was making supper and he discovered her there with Jake and Emily. As he shoved a macaroni cheese into Moloch to heat up, he asked her, 'Would you like me to take you to church this Sunday? You haven't been for some time.'

'Church?' Since the accident, Hermione was noticeably more confused about some things.

'You used to go regularly.'

'That was at my church. This one is among . . . alien thorns.'

Emily piped up. 'Alien corn, I think you mean.'

Tom threw her the watch-how-you-go look. 'Corn or thorns, isn't God there?'

'I'm not sure that was the point, Dad,' Emily murmured.

'Alien porn or corn,' Jake muttered audibly into Emily's ear, and she smothered a giggle. He looked at his father, raised a hand of surrender. 'Sorry, Dad.'

'Shut up, you two,' Tom said, with a grin.

Emily got up to turn down the gas. Jake fiddled with the baby alarm and glottal noises filtered into the kitchen.

'If you wanted to take me anywhere, Tom, you could take me to visit my friend Sheila at the home.' Also since her illness, Hermione's voice had developed a waver. 'She said she'd love to see me.'

Emily nudged Tom and he rolled his eyes. 'OK, Hermione, I'll take you down there. We'll look at the diaries.'

There was a tiny pause and Tom knew what everyone was thinking: what does he *have* in his diary? But that didn't matter any more. He was way past that.

'By the way . . .' Jake jabbed a finger at the corner where the pink doll's cradle had now migrated. 'Where did you find it?'

'In the attic. I knew I'd put it up there,' Tom replied. 'I thought if you, we, finished it, Maisie could have it.'

'Grief,' exclaimed Jake. 'That old thing? I suppose so.'

But Tom could tell that Jake was really, really pleased – and that pleased him more than he could say.

A little later, Annie arrived home and drifted into the kitchen. Chin in hands, she sat with drooping eyelids at the table, her skin transparent with fatigue. 'Thanks, Tom,' she said gratefully, as he chopped and cooked vegetables and served up the macaroni.

He had just sat down when Hermione said, 'Tom, I would love a little tomato ketchup.' As he heaved himself to his feet, she added, 'Do you know? I don't think I've seen anyone all day.'

This was becoming quite a theme.

'Not quite fair, is it, Hermione?' he replied, in his most reasonable manner. 'I gave you lunch before I went out.'

'No need to look like that, dear,' she said.

Annie reached out a hand. 'Hermione, are you very unhappy here?'

Rollo snuffled about under the table, and Emily said, 'This dog is a dustbin.'

Hermione grabbed Annie's hand like a drowning woman. 'I hope you don't ever have to be in my position.'

Tom's composure cracked. 'You're given the best we can manage, Hermione. I even moved out of my bloody bedroom to accommodate you.'

A sudden dense embarrassment seized everyone, and Tom cursed silently. Hermione dropped a piece of bread down to Rollo, Annie turned away and Jake and Emily looked everywhere but at their father.

Jake jumped to his feet and created a kerfuffle in clearing the plates. 'Coffee, anyone?'

Tom observed Annie make a huge effort. 'We love having

427

you here, Hermione, and you must tell us if there's anything we can do to make you more comfortable,' she said, and stroked Hermione's hand.

In penance, Tom made the coffee and offered a cup to his mother. 'If you had the choice, Hermione, would you like to go back to the home?'

Several expressions chased across his mother's face, and he couldn't make sense of any of them, except for an angry despair – and that did not augur well or solve the problem.

She thrust the coffee cup towards Annie. 'Dear, I think this coffee is a little bit cold,' she said.

'I'm going upstairs to pack,' said Emily. 'Thanks for supper.'

'Just a moment, Emily,' Tom said. 'I'd like to say something to you all. I have an announcement.'

Obligingly, Emily hovered by the door. Jake leaned against the sink. Annie sat up upright. Hermione cupped a hand around her coffee. 'Well,' she asked, 'what is it, dear?'

He savoured the moment, allowing his pleasure and pride to spill out. 'I've got a job,' he said. 'Carbon Trust. Two days a week, which means there will be plenty of time for other things, important things, if you like, but it's a good job.' He paused. 'Two days a week is what I wanted.'

The hubbub that ensued was worth a lot. In fact, almost everything.

'Hermione didn't answer the question,' Tom said to Annie, as they lay in bed. 'About whether she wanted to stay here or not.'

'We're going to have to think about her.' Annie was drowsy. 'I'm not sure she's settling long-term. I'll have to try to introduce her to some people. But who?'

'I'll help,' said Tom. 'She's my mother. By the way, have you seen Zosia lately?'

'We had coffee last week and caught up with each other's news.'

'Still friends?'

'Sure.'

'Annie,' he said, 'I found your accounts book.' Beside him, he felt her stiffen. 'You've sold your jewellery because of my debts? You shouldn't have done.'

She turned her head to look at him and her hair spilled across the pillow. 'Who's to say what I do or don't do?'

Tom propped himself up on an elbow and looked down at her. 'It's almost the worst thing. You did it because of me and I feel so guilty.'

She smiled sleepily. 'Tom. All of us are guilty of a lot of things. Go to sleep.'

He reached over and snapped off his bedside light. *All of us are guilty* 'Annie . . .'

There was no answer. She had neither condemned nor forgiven him – a fluid state of affairs that, he supposed, was true of most situations. He would have liked Annie to stretch out a hand to him and tell him she didn't care a toss about her jewellery. But that would not have been quite the truth. He would have liked some kind of physical contact where he could have made absolutely clear the depth of his regret.

But he would content himself with a warm bed, the slight suggestion of scented fabric conditioner emanating from her nightdress, the tangled skeins of her hair on the pillow.

Annie gave a soft snuffle as she slipped into sleep and Tom grinned up into the dark.

There had been Annie in the beginning: thin, perpetually surprised that anyone should take notice of her, curious, tentative. Annie post-partum: taking command, busy, whippet thin, twenty-four-hour mother. The Annie of the last few years: grieving, holding down her job, remote. Hating him. Blaming him.

But wasn't hate good? It indicated strong feelings had survived.

Another snuffle, and Annie rolled over, reached for the light and snapped it back on.

He sat up. 'What are you doing?'

She blinked up at him. 'I wanted to check out your face.'

'For God's sake, you see it all the time.'

She caught her bottom lip between her teeth, hauled herself up the pillows, folded her arms across her breasts — and laughed. 'Tom, you've got a job. It's the best thing . . . and I wanted to take a second look at that very smug expression.'

It was one of the sweetest things she had ever said. Tom gazed at the white neck and the tangled hair, the slope of shoulder and outline of breast under the white cotton. She was so far away, yet closer than anyone. Closer than anyone would ever be. Tenderness gushed through him. 'Go to sleep. You've got a big meeting tomorrow.'

She touched his chin with a finger. 'Never so peacefully.'

Chapter Twenty-eight

Curious how it was possible to live more than one life at the same time. While Annie went through the motions – job, house, accounts, rejoicing at Tom's job with the Carbon Trust (part-time, mind you, but strategic and managerial), she reprised the past and rehearsed a future. House emptying? Could they afford to put Hermione back in the home? Where would Jake fetch up? He was making noises about moving out in the not-so-distant future.

Annie's life had been unremarkable, ordinary – she would never argue otherwise and its ordinariness was precious. But the past months had triggered reminders of the time when she had lived closer to the emotional bone – the time when she had expected *so much*, and yearned to touch the heights.

It was as if a huge wooden spoon had dipped into her head and was stirring it up. She rubbed the place on her finger where her mother's ring used to sit. *Sufficient unto the day . . . Seize the day . . .* She remembered the old truisms and helpful clichés her mother had trotted out. She had had a great capacity for living in the present, which her daughter decided she must emulate.

As a young woman, Annie had believed there had to be some sort of explanation for existence, some significance attached to it. There had to be a force pulling the strands together. These days, she didn't consider the subject much at all, and perhaps it was time she did.

The wooden spoon was doing its work pretty thoroughly. It mixed up many recollections. Tom in the beginning: raven-haired, outrageous, strong. Tom after the children arrived: very busy being the BBC stalwart, increasingly preoccupied, a touch smug, not at ease with his son and daughters, mainly because he didn't know them very well. Switch to Tom of the past few months: wounded, bitter, trying not to be. Almost broken.

But not.

A Midlands landscape rushed past the train window and the mutter of voices, phone calls and movement ebbed and flowed inside.

Sarah looked up from the armful of papers spread out across the table. In one of his periodic managerial fits, Chuck had packed them off to a one-day Department of Health course in Birmingham and they were on their way back.

'Useless, wasn't it?' Annie concluded. 'Except for the last speaker who was good.'

Sarah shrugged. 'Do I care? Yes, I do. I do, Annie. Promise.'

'Do you think we contribute at all? Are we any help to society?'

Coming at the end of a long day, it was not the first question that Sarah wished to address. 'If you mean does our work, which is basically a series of hand-to-hand combats with medical staff, mean anything more than hand-to-hand combat, no.'

Annie laughed. 'Go back to your newspaper.'

Large bureaucracies were designed to kill clear,

unconstrained thinking stone dead and, guess what, Annie had devoted her working life to one.

. . . 'Pessimist,' Tom had accused her.

'Have you ever worked in a large bureaucracy?'

He had frowned. 'As it happens, yes.'

'Chicken feed,' she had teased. 'The BBC isn't even a footnote on the NHS . . .'

From now on, she was going to refuse, absolutely refuse, to get bogged down in the metaphysics of her work life. Life was complicated enough. It was best to leave it to beings like the angel on the kitchen noticeboard – a heavenly post-boy emerging out of Leonardo's shadows bearing with him all sorts of invitations and promises, which you could take note of or not.

The train drew into the station. Stepping out, Annie inhaled the familiar coffee-cum-overheated-pastry smell of a British station. Sarah hopped out behind her and they threaded their way on to the concourse. Annie turned to say goodbye and jumped as the Tannoy boomed: "'Let's start at the very beginning . . .'" and the unmistakable voice of Julie Andrews soared above the hubbub.

'Good grief!' For once that was all Sarah could manage.

In the middle of the concourse a man in chinos and trainers threw out his hands and turned in time to the music. A girl with blue hair mimicked him. Two others in footless tights and plimsolls were sucked like atoms to the nucleus. They, too, threw up their arms and fell into step. Within half a minute, sixty or so were dancing. They were serious in their movements, intent but also smiling.

'That's rehearsed,' said Sarah, fingers clenching and unclenching on her shoulder strap.

433

The man beside Annie hoisted his small boy on to his shoulders and the crowd that had gathered behind them swept the two women towards the dancers.

"'Doh . . .'" sang Julie.

The notes ricocheted around Annie's head and, deep in her bones, she felt something shift.

Julie's voice soared higher.

The dancers swirled round as one and, as they did so, a youth with Rasta hair and leathers grabbed Annie. 'Look after my bags,' she shrieked at an open-mouthed Sarah.

"'Ray . . .'"

She was singing of sun . . . warm, bright sun

Round Annie went. Hands up, arms windmilling, feet clicking and sliding over the concourse, pushed and willingly pulled by a leathered Prince Charming. *What am I doing?* She whirled past an elderly couple doing a brisk waltz and past a girl with her school satchel on her back kicking her legs up as if there would be no tomorrow.

"'Me . . .'"

What name did one call oneself?

My name is Annie.

And as the song progressed, the music prised up the claws of the succubus of bitterness and regret so long dug into her back. It grew to be less and less burdensome, *weightless*, until it rolled off and away, to leave her leaf-light and cleansed.

Reborn?

Once again, she was the Annie who had danced with Tom and stolen home in a white and violet dawn. Once again she was dancing in the alpine meadows above Salzburg and at the beginning of the journey.

Remade?

Not quite. She was breathless and the protest from her pelvic floor reminded her that she had given birth to three babies. But, in that last moment of free-fall, she had shaken free of the shackles that bound her to float on a thermal of excitement and hope.

'And *what* was all that about?' Sarah handed back her bags when, as quickly as it had cohered, the dance and the dancers melted back into the crowd of commuters and passengers.

Between pants, Annie managed a grin. 'I don't know,' she said. 'But it was marvellous.'

It was dark as she emerged from the Tube station. As she headed home, lights were switched on, looping a necklace of brilliance along the streets like Christmas lights. Each one sheltered a melting, radiant centre that pierced her vision. Piles of leaves in the gutter shuffled and whispered in draughts created by traffic. The cold on her cheeks felt as crisp as baked salt and yet the warmth from her body was lazily languorous. Now she felt hungry – and crazily expectant.

She phoned Tom but his mobile was switched off. Instead, she flipped down the speed dial and rang Sadie. 'You'll never guess what I've just done.'

'Let me see. What choices do I have? I could waste the equivalent of six months in guessing or you could tell me.'

'Flash danced in a station.'

Sadie hooted. 'There's hope . . . there's hope.'

'Well, actually, I think there is,' said Annie.

She wondered what Jake and Emily were up to. Had Emily finished packing – and what was the latest on the divorce? Life Lesson 110. Children discard their parents, and she must get used to being ... not exactly last but fourth or fifth in the line when they had news to tell.

What was Mia doing?

A little stiff from the dancing, she paused on the front step to find her key. The door opened.

'Thought it was you,' said Tom. He drew her inside and kissed her. 'You're late. What have you been doing?'

'Flash dancing, as it happens.' She enjoyed the expression on his face. 'Actually, I need to change. Got a bit hot.'

'Hot,' he murmured, following her up the stairs. 'We like hot.'

He banged the bedroom shut behind him. 'Are you going to take off your clothes, Mrs Nicholson?'

'Guess.' Annie dangled her skirt from a finger in a manner that would have done credit to a world-class stripper. 'Will that do?'

'I can't tell until you've taken more off.'

Annie shrugged off the incredibly expensive T-shirt. 'You look pleased with yourself.'

'Signed the contract.'

He *was* pleased and happy. How like him. Now that he was back in harness, Tom could allow himself to be himself and she was delighted for him.

'I need to get closer to inspect the situation.'

She shot a look at him from under her lashes. 'I need a shower.'

'I definitely agree.'

She headed into the bathroom and Tom followed her.

'What are you doing?'

'What do you think?'

'On reflection, I think you're nuzzling my neck.'

'Good guess. Next question.'

'What are you planning to do after that?'

'This.' His hand snaked around her back and undid her bra. 'Now what?'

'I was going to run the water until it was hot.'

'Can't afford it,' he said flatly and, pushing her up against the tiles, kissed her throat. 'Micro-economy. Are you wearing the same perfume I gave you – oh, years ago?'

'I am.'

'Good. Cost a king's ransom.'

Annie turned her head and found his ear and bit it. He yelped – but with approval.

With a hand, she grasped his hair and forced his face up so that he was looking into her eyes. 'I have to learn you all over again,' she said. 'And I might as well do it properly.'

'The world has changed. It's all changed. It'll be difficult.' He smiled, and his transformation from the man whom she had once loved, then hated and now discovered she loved again was complete.

'Are we going to stay in here?' she asked – not unreasonably.

Reason? What was reason?

'One thing, Tom.'

'Stop talking, Annie.'

'Tom . . .'

'*What?*'

'We'll look for Mia?'

Pause. 'Yes. Yes, we will.'

Half an hour later, Annie struggled into a pair of jeans and a sweater and ran downstairs. Hermione was sitting in the kitchen talking to Jake, who was describing Maisie's first sentence. Annie reminded herself that she must cut up

Hermione's supper before giving it to her. She had also promised to wash her mother-in-law's hair after supper.

Annie bent down and kissed Hermione. It seemed the thing to do when one's heart had been, for a transcendental second, fresh minted. Then she reached down and kissed Rollo too.

'Hallo, Mum.' Jake sent her one of his heartbreaking smiles.

'You look . . . happy?' Nowadays, Annie was sparing in how she used the word.

'Not happy, exactly,' said the careful Jake. 'But there is news.'

The baby alarm chose to broadcast Maisie's sneeze.

'And?'

'Much of it was Dad's doing,' said Jake. 'He found out about it. By using a psychiatrist like Reginald Brown, we gave ourselves an advantage. He's known to favour fathers. He's sent in a report to the court recommending that Jocasta should not be allowed to take Maisie out of the country, but she should come over regularly and that a visiting schedule is worked out. Apparently, he was of the opinion that Jocasta's lot ran a very unattractive case . . . falling over themselves to cite how many houses and material advantages they could give Maisie. And, apparently, this particular judge always listens to the psychiatrist's report.'

Annie sat down. 'So, we'll see.'

'No. There's more. Jocasta has formerly notified the court that she's given up her claim to take Maisie permanently. She's prepared to accept Reginald Brown's recommendations.'

Annie looked deep into her son's face. 'I'm so glad,' she said. 'So very glad for you.'

Emily clattered in her clogs down the stairs and into the kitchen. 'If I paid you,' said Jake, 'would you get rid of them?'

'I'll consider it when you've paid me.'

'Do you think I'm a complete idiot?'

'I do.'

'Packed?' asked Annie.

'Sort of.' Emily smiled at her mother – and, suddenly, Annie saw the woman Emily would become. 'Here.' She unpinned Leonardo's angel from the noticeboard and closed her daughter's hands over it. 'You must take this. He'll guard you.' She paused. 'He'll keep tight my other daughter.'

'Oh, Mum.'

The doorbell rang. Rollo gave tongue. Holding the angel, Emily twirled around and said she would get it. She disappeared into the hall. There was a silence, a muffled shriek – and Emily called out, 'Mum, Dad, I think you should come.'

Annie stepped into the hall just as Tom emerged from their bedroom. For ever after, she remembered the sound of the door banging shut behind him. At that crucial moment she glanced up – and noted that she and Tom were frozen in roughly similar poses.

He looked down at Annie. She looked up at him. A little while earlier, he had cupped her head in his hands. *Hallo, Annie.*

She turned back to the front door and Rollo danced underfoot like a dervish.

A small, thin figure stood on the step, clasping a canvas shoulder bag.

Mia.

Acknowledgements

As always, I owe to many much gratitude. To my editors, Louise Moore, and her Penguin team in the UK, and Kendra Harpster, and the Viking team in the US, thank you. Brilliant and patient, they are the best. My agent, Mark Lucas, is my veritable rock. Many thanks are also owed to Peta Nightingale, Kate Burke, Clare Ledingham and, for her expert help, Frances Hughes. Any mistakes are mine. As always, I rely totally on the incomparable Hazel Orme. Life would not be worth living and novels not worth writing without the support of friends and they certainly did not fail me. Thank you, Fanny Blake, Margot Chaundler, Marika Cobbold, Natasha Cooper, Shirley Eskapa, Belle Grey, William Gill, Alastair Lack, Vanessa Hannam and Pamela Norris and everyone else who has been forced to listen to the groans. My sisters Alison Souter and Rosie Hobhouse did sterling work, too, on the support front. But, as always, Benjie, Adam and Eleanor bore the brunt. Without them, nothing would be possible.

Elizabeth Buchan

talks exclusively about her life
as a writer, and answers
questions on *Separate Beds*

Author photo by Ian Philpott

BECOMING A WRITER

Looking back, I think I always wanted to be a writer without knowing it. A rather solitary child, I read voraciously for solace and to escape. I scribbled down notes about what I had read and what it had meant to me. As a small child, I loved stories of wild animals, and very often ended up sobbing when something terrible happened to them (which it usually did). I can also remember the Famous Five and the sense of galloping excitement I got as I was precipitated into their adventures. Luckily, as a teenager, I was much more ambitious, and made myself read history and biography as well as fiction. It did not take long to learn from my reading of biography that I was incurably nosy about other people's lives. My responses – being enraptured, sometimes puzzled or shocked, or just plain swept away – to the treasure chest in the local library that I plundered on a daily basis were, I am sure, a subconscious preparation for a writing life.

In my late twenties, I began to realize that there was something niggling at the back of my mind, a desire that I could not quite pin down. At the time I was working at Penguin Books as a blurb writer, which turned out to be just the right nursery slope for the apprentice novelist. Part of my job was to read through the Penguin list – from classics to cookery books, and political polemics to poetry. It was a free education for which they paid me. All the same, I sensed I was marking the time, but I also had small children and it was difficult enough to pack everything into a day. However, it was the stuffed-day conundrum that provided the answer because I finally realized there was never going to be a right time to write. Thus the only thing to do was to get on with it.

In general, I wanted to write the books I loved to read. I wanted to be educated and provoked, I wanted to be made to think and to be entertained in the wildest possible sense and I wanted to laugh and, sometimes, to cry. If I could achieve some of those things in my own writing, I would be happy. Between that ambition and the blank page which now faced me, there was a considerable mountain to climb. Not least was the task of developing the writer's muscles – technical skill, confidence, stubbornness and the ability to concentrate. The learning curve was steep. Writing, in my case at least, proved hard work, but the process was full of surprises and never-ending interest.

MY LIFE AS A WRITER

The early days of my writing career were exacting. I got up very early in the morning to write one page before the children woke up and I went off to work. In the evenings, after the children were in bed, I wrote one more page. Eleven novels later, my working life is less penitential, and I look back and wonder how I did it, but at the time it seemed the only way. I calculated that if I wrote one page it would turn into two, and two would turn into four, and so on. That tiny, daily progression was an optimistic and thrilling one, and made the difficult schedule worthwhile.

Where I write is very important to me. I have a little eyrie at the top of my house that once used to be a baby's room. Up there, I'm surrounded by a haphazard pile of books and papers. I usually have about thirty to fifty reference books in easy reach for any one book that I'm writing and every so often I'll pick one out to check a fact or a date. From the window, I look down on to my terraced London garden and every twenty minutes or so (the limit of my concentration span) I look up and out at a motley garden theatre below – squirrels, foxes and jays all competing for territory – and I am constantly haring downstairs to rescue frogs from the jaws of my two cats.

Routine is very important to me too. Most days, I get up early, feed the cats, make breakfast and take it to the spare room so I don't wake my husband. Breakfast in bed is my great luxury. The cats come up and settle either side of me and I read the newspaper. I'm usually in my office by about 8.30 a.m. where I work until lunchtime. Often I get tempted out to lunch but if I'm in the last stages of a book I work through the day. To limber up for the day's writing, I will read through my most recently written chapter, tweaking sentences and correcting words or phrases. This gets me back into the flow of the book before I start the proper writing.

I always write three drafts of each novel. I use the first to work out its structure or scaffolding – theme, plot and narrative. The second is for constructing the muscles, by which I mean the characters' motivations and psychology. By the time I reach the third draft, I really know the novel and I am writing from a position of strength which allows me to work in all sorts of subtleties, resonances and ironies that were not there in my first draft. Instead of adding or amending the previous draft, I usually write from scratch so in total I rewrite a novel three times.

Separate Beds

1) Where did the idea for *Separate Beds* come from?

Recently, there has been a lot of discussion about the family –
what is happening to it? Is it changing? Do people still think of
the family as important? Coinciding with this ongoing debate
was a financial crisis that has – literally – shaken the world.
It seemed obvious that what was happening in the financial
markets was, as night follows day, going to affect ordinary
men and women and, by extension, their families. In a flash,
Separate Beds arrived in my head.

2) You often write about contemporary life. What are the themes that will strike a chord with readers of *Separate Beds* as it is published in the current economic climate?

The loss of a loved job must be one. It is well known that
unemployment can often have devastating effects on the psyche
and on physical health. Not only that, it has an enormous
impact on those who live with someone who is literally in a
state of bereavement, mourning the loss of their job. Another
theme explores the relationships between parents and their
now adult children and, yet another, the deep pleasures and
tendernesses of love reborn and renegotiated.

3) In *Separate Beds,* four generations of the Nicholson family come together to live in the same house, a situation which is becoming increasingly common as people have

children later and the elderly live longer. How does this new set-up affect the bonds between the family in the book?

Historically, families have often had to exist hugger-mugger. For our generation, it is a new idea – a real shift which involves re-thinking notions of independence and, on an emotional level, tackling the claustrophobia and irritations of close-knit living. In *Separate Beds*, the baby is always waking somebody up at night. Tom's mother levies a series of demands on the already hard-pressed Annie. Tom has nowhere to hide his humiliation and despair. Emily longs to get out. Yet, despite all these individual anguishes, something begins to happen. The family is a crucible, and new and unexpected chemistry between its members is triggered.

4) Tom is devastated when he loses his job, and struggles with redundancy, whilst Jake is desperately looking for ways to revive his ailing business. Did you make a conscious decision for this to affect the men rather than the women in the family? What impact does it have on them as individuals and the family as a whole?

I didn't start out to make it a male–female division but, after thinking about it, I felt that making Annie (already quite senior at her workplace) the main breadwinner would put her on a new trajectory, and in Emily's case having to face the work treadmill was also important. (I also couldn't resist poking a little fun at the writer, which was really poking a little fun at myself!) But, actually, I was not making any comments about work patterns with regard to the sexes – I think as a society we have established that women work too – but I was interested to explore how a proud man like Tom would deal with his situation and how a gentle dreamer like Jake would face up to the new reality.

5) The loss or disappearance of a child is every parent's worst nightmare. In *Separate Beds,* Annie and Tom's daughter Mia makes a conscious decision to walk out of her family's life. Why did you decide to have her leave in this way and what impact does it have on the family?

In one sense, families are extremely complex. In another, they are quite primitive and tribal. There has been some fascinating work on the ways families can hide, and tolerate, bad behaviour and of how they (unconsciously) assign roles to members. What they are less successful at doing is accommodating members of the family who turn out to be quite different – and I don't mean learning to flamenco dance while the others stick to a soft-shoe shuffle. Mia decides to be different both politically and in the manner of how she chooses to live. In doing so, she not only clashes bitterly with her father in particular but also exposes his double-thinking. Fictionally speaking, this is a gold mine.

6) As the title suggests, when the novel begins Annie and Tom are sleeping in separate bedrooms. Some couples claim they have a happier, healthier relationship if they sleep or even live separately. Do you think this can ever be true?

I suppose it must be! Personally, I would hate to be in a separate room or bed from my partner. Think of never being able to say, 'I think I heard a noise' to the other half and expecting them to deal with it.

7) Reviewers often comment that you write very perceptively about marriage and relationships. What draws you to revisit this subject?

Simple. All human life is there and that is the novelist's business.

8) You used to be a copywriter and an editor – what prompted you to make the switch to the other side of the fence and become an author?

It was a cunning plan. One of the tricks in life is to decide whether you are an early flowerer or a late bloomer. I was emphatically the latter so I knew I had to wait before I put pen to paper. While I was waiting I decided to sit at the feet of the throne, so to speak, and what better than to work in publishing where I would learn the business of producing a book? Anyway, there is enormous fun and pleasure to be derived from being both a poacher and a gamekeeper. (I would say that, I suppose, because I'm a Gemini.) I have never regretted my years in publishing. I look on them as the antechamber.

Discover Elizabeth's fabulous new website ...

Dig deeper into the life of Elizabeth Buchan at **www.elizabethbuchan.com**. Read her blog, short stories, extracts from her books and much more. Elizabeth loves to hear from her fans, so you can also contact her with your questions and comments.

For even more up-to-the-minute news, follow Elizabeth on Twitter (@elizabethbuchan) or join her fan page on Facebook!

ELIZABETH BUCHAN

THE GOOD WIFE

Fanny Savage has always been the dutiful wife. Married to Will, a politician with big ambitions, her life is a whirlwind of public engagements. Bound by loyalty to the party, she is required to look good and remain silent. But Fanny is no fool. She's well aware that the world outside her privileged home is one that seethes with despair, danger, division and lack of faith. She knows how fragile happiness can be. After twenty years of marriage and self-sacrifice, she begins to question her own concepts of fulfilment. Was being the Good Wife worth it, after all?

'Enthralling, sophisticated storytelling' *Woman and Home*

'Buchan writes beautifully. Depicting Fanny's dilemma with wit and warmth
. . . neatly anatomizing the compromises and complexities of both domestic and parliamentary life' *Daily Mail*

ELIZABETH BUCHAN

THAT CERTAIN AGE

Barbara and Siena – two women living fifty years apart. Both constrained by choice; one has too little and one has too much.

Siena, a 21st century woman, has so far managed to avoid the tick of the biological clock – her high-powered career as a stylist, making over a succession of tired, fraught housewives, has given her a horror of the toll family can take on a woman. Without children she can control her own wonderful, ordered life. Only thing is, her husband Charlie longs for a baby . . .

In 1959, Barbara is married to Ryder, an airline pilot, for twenty-four years. Her life revolves around her house and family and she is happy that it is that way. Then, she meets the young and brilliant Alexander who tells her that she has a mind and a life of her own. And, to her astonishment, Barbara is seduced into a different way of thinking.

The intimate, inner lives of two women are woven together as they struggle to find resolution – between the families they love and their own desires.

'Wise, melancholy, funny and sophisticated . . . more satisfying than a romance'
The Times

ELIZABETH BUCHAN

REVENGE OF THE MIDDLE-AGED WOMAN

Rose Lloyd was the last to suspect that Nathan, her husband of over twenty years, was having an affair, and that he was planning to leave her. But the greatest shock was yet to come; for his mistress was Rose's colleague and friend, Minty.

So Rose was left alone in their once-happy family home, where she and Nathan had brought up their children. Then she started thinking – about the man she'd married, and how well she really knew him. Twenty years ago Rose had to make the choice between two very different lives. Could she recapture what she nearly chose back then, and bring new meaning to her life now?

'This perceptive, beautifully written book brings a fresh perspective to an age-old situation . . . For women of all ages, a poignant, unforgettable novel'
Mail on Sunday

ELIZABETH BUCHAN

THE SECOND WIFE

What if The Other Woman accidently gets her man?

That's what happened to Minty. She stole her best friend Rose's husband Nathan and made him her own. But now she's got what she wanted – marriage, kids, a happy home – she's discovering a few things she didn't bargain on: like the cold shoulder from Nathan's *other* family; her husband's middle-age and growing distance; and the fact that first wives don't just go away.

Age also brings one or two other problems for Minty. Problems that will lead her back to the one person she really doesn't want to have to face …

The Second Wife is a tale of growing older, of making difficult choices – and of finding hope where you least expect to come across it.

'An irresistible story of love, loss and renewal' *Woman's Own*

ELIZABETH BUCHAN

If you enjoyed this book, there are several ways you can read more by the same author and make sure you get the inside track on all Penguin books.

Order any of the following titles direct:

9780141009797 THE GOOD WIFE		£7.99
9780141009803 THAT CERTAIN AGE		£6.99
9780140290080 REVENGE OF THE MIDDLE-AGED WOMAN		£7.99
9780141019888 THE SECOND WIFE		£6.99

Simply call Penguin c/o Bookpost on **01624 677237** and have your credit/debit card ready. Alternatively e-mail your order to **bookshop@enterprise.net**. Postage and package is free in mainland UK. Overseas customers must add £2 per book. Prices and availability subject to change without notice.

Visit www.penguin.com and find out first about forthcoming titles, read exclusive material and author interviews, and enter exciting competitions. You can also browse through thousands of Penguin books and buy online.

IT'S NEVER BEEN EASIER TO READ MORE WITH PENGUIN

Frustrated by the quality of books available at Exeter station for his journey back to London one day in 1935, Allen Lane decided to do something about it. The Penguin paperback was born that day, and with it first-class writing became available to a mass audience for the very first time. This book is a direct descendant of those original Penguins and Lane's momentous vision. What will you read next?